SHEM CREEK

SHEM CREEK

A Lowcountry Tale

DOROTHEA BENTON FRANK

BERKLEY BOOKS, NEW YORK

B

A Berkley Book
Published by The Berkley Publishing Group
A division of Penguin Group (USA) Inc.
375 Hudson Street
New York, New York 10014

PRINTING HISTORY
Berkley hardcover edition / August 2004

Library of Congress Cataloging-in-Publication Data

Frank, Dorothea Benton.
    Shem Creek : a Lowcountry tale / Dorothea Benton Frank
        p. cm.
    ISBN 0-425-19608-9
    1. Mothers and daughters—Fiction. 2. Single mothers—Fiction. 3.South Carolina—
Fiction. 4. Divorced men—Fiction. I. Title.

PS3556.R3338S47 2004
813'.6—dc22

                                                                            2004049877

Printed in the United States of America

        10   9   8   7   6   5   4   3   2

For
my great friend
Debra Pietromonaco Zammit

SHEM CREEK

The ripe earth swells,
splitting its skin
into waterways
scattered and winding
in every direction,
releasing winds
that carve the land
to shreds. Where
sun filled clumps
of spartina, smoothed
into supplicating rows
of bent heads, crowd
the edges of Shem Creek;
marsh wrens build
their tiny nests.
Porpoises appear
then disappear
below the water
as if they are playing
hide and seek.
Fish birds litter the sky:
egrets, herons, and leaf terns,
oyster catchers, pelicans,
gulls diving and turning
through the thick air.

As the creek weaves
through treeless subdivisions,
strip malls, and parking lots;
it gathers everything.
from oil, soap, and gasoline
to tires and old refrigerators.
Run-off fills the oyster beds
with unpronounceable toxins.
Arsenic and mercury
drift through the water
in invisible clouds.

Beyond the clutter of traffic,
seafood restaurants,
hotels, bars, and parking lots;
docked shrimp boats,
bobbing up and down
beside the docks
wait where the creek
opens into the endless sea.

—MARJORY HEATH
WENTWORTH
South Carolina Poet Laureate

ACKNOWLEDGMENTS

In the making of a book there are many hands besides those of the author. I would like to thank the following people who gladly picked up the phone, sent information and answered my questions and gave me their support: Tim Mink of Poe's Tavern on Sullivan's Island; Dana Beach, Nancy Vinson, and Jane Lareau of the South Carolina Coastal Conservation League; Fred Holland, Ph.D.; Nancy Rhyne of Pawleys Island; Vickie Crafton and Tom Warner of Litchfield Books; Tom Schaefer of Atlanta; Michael F. Nickell and Trisha Boorman of Cypress restaurant in Charleston; Dr. Ian Smith of New York; Nathalie Dupree of Charleston, South Carolina; and Mark Hiebel of the Renaissance Grand Beach Hotel in St. Thomas. Huge thanks to Diane Razzano and Bella Kovtun of Atlantic Express, Staten Island, New York, especially for the cookies!

Special thanks to Mary Allen of Montclair, New Jersey, for resurrecting my computer from its many crashes and to George Zur for his technical expertise on numerous occasions in all areas pertaining to my Web site.

To Marjory Wentworth, South Carolina Poet Laureate, for the creation and use of her exquisite poem "Shem Creek," I am always and forever in awe of your enormous talent and grateful to the skies for your friendship.

To Debbie Zammit of New York, whom I found after an absence of decades, without you, this book could never have come to pass. I am thrilled to have you back in my life and I thank you with my whole heart.

To the following folks whose names appear as characters: Robert and Susan Rosen, Louise Waring, Patti Elliott, Gretchen and Sandy Prater, Louie and Cherry Provost, Bill Thompson, Mimi Bagnal, Mike "the Zone Man" Evans, Barbara and Lowell Epstein, and Philip Ragone, M.D., many thanks and I hope y'all get a kick out of seeing your names in this crazy story. If your *namesakes* do something you would never do, which I think almost all of them do, remember, they could not help themselves, I could not stop them, and it's all meant in good humor anyway, just to make this more fun for you to read.

The Honorable Joseph P. Riley Jr., Mayor of the City of Charleston, is one of my heroes in many areas, not the least of which is his advocacy and leadership in all areas aimed at preserving and maintaining the great beauty and quality of the landscape, water, and wildlife of the Lowcountry. The reference in this text to the ease with which someone can secure his company at their dinner table is meant to be humorous.

To Scott Bagnal (husband of Mimi, who in real life *is* the queen of pound cake in addition to a thousand other things), the Birdman of Edisto Beach, and my brother-in-law for almost all my life, who is a prince, I thank him for his wisdom and good humor, neither of which is ever in short supply.

To my brother and his wife, Michael and Jennifer Benton of Irving, Texas; Vicki Oliver of Savannah, Georgia; to Dr. and Mrs. Michael Hay of Orangeburg, South Carolina; Tom Houck and Patsy Thomas of Atlanta, Georgia; Margot Sage-El; Val Fisher of Montclair, New Jersey; Mary Jo McInerny of Greenville, South Carolina; and most especially to Robert and Susan Rosen of Charleston, who collectively feted over one thousand people in the name of celebrating the publication of my last book, during the hottest and most humid weather of our lives, and did so in grand style, I love y'all forever and thank you over and over.

Huge bowing and scraping starts with Norman Lidofsky and the whole sales team at Berkley, especially Ernie Petrillo, Sharon Gamboa, Don Rieck, Patrick Nolan, Trish Weyenberg, Don Redpath, Rich Adamonis, Joe Crockford and Ken Kaye—I love y'all forever. To Rick Pascocello and the whole promotion team who dream up all the wonderful ideas that add the sparkle to sales, huge thanks for your generous support. As always, thanks to Joni Friedman and Rich Hasselberger for their extraordinary vision and efforts for my covers. And huge love to the publicity wizards, Liz Perl and Heather Connor. Wow! I don't know how you do all you do and you know, I am going nowhere without y'all. Ever!

Obviously, I am still kissing the footprints of Leslie Gelbman, who is still my magnificent and fearless publisher. Leslie, what can I say? I get this big lump in my throat when I think about your faith in my work and how generous and wonderful you have been to me. Seriously, I send you endless thanks and love. And right behind Leslie is my editor, Gail Fortune, who knows I hold her judgment in the highest esteem and that I treasure her friendship and always will. Someday, we are all going to the Lowcountry and I am going to show you what the magic is all about.

To my agent, Amy Berkower, what can I say? You'll make a woman of me yet! Thanks for all your great advice, your friendship and for being my best advocate. And even though we are just warming up, many thanks in advance to Sandy Mendelson for your warmth, excellent humor and expertise.

Okay, Buzzy, you're next. Insiders know that the wondrous Buzzy Porter left South Carolina to work for B&N in New York and Southern writers are weeping. Don't weep. Patty Morrison is still holding the fort, the fort will endure, and who knows? Maybe our New York numbers will rise? Love you, Patty and Buzzy, and thanks for everything! Especially for the plantation gig . . . people who give poor directions should be shot.

Special thanks to Kevin Sherry for going over all the recipes with us and making sure they were usable. To booksellers everywhere, I curtsy deeply to you and thank you profoundly for each time you have recommended me to a new reader. I mean that with all my heart. I loved being in your stores last summer and thank you again for your gracious hospitality and generous support.

And, last but most assuredly not least, to Peter, Victoria and William. My, oh my! I love you all so much and with all I've got. Thank you for your patience, your love and faith and your endless understanding. My door might be closed half the time but my heart is always open wide for you. At the end of the day, it's just us.

CONTENTS

SHEM CREEK

A POSTCARD FROM LINDA

CAN I just tell you why I am so deliriously happy to drive all through the night from New Jersey to South Carolina? Here we are, boxed in between this wall of eighteen-wheelers on our left and right, in front and behind, in this little pocket of flying road, racing down I-95 at seventy-six miles an hour. My daughters are asleep beside me and in the backseat. I don't care that it's pouring rain. I don't care that it's dark. On another night, I would be terrified out of my skin by the blasting of horns. But not tonight. Let me tell you something. These trucks are like huge guardian angels rushing us to safety and the rain is washing us clean. Life has been a little rough around the edges and it was time to break out. Yeah. A *little rough* would be one way of understating it.

Oh, eventually you'll hear the whole story, because this is a long ride and there ain't much to do besides tell secrets and think about life. Thinking about life is what I had been doing for one *very* long time. I finally decided to quit the thinking nonsense and *do* something. I mean, I was even driving *myself* crazy from my own whining. Then I came to this conclusion. You don't like your life? Go get another one and shut the heck up already, right?

Look, I know I'm not the only single parent in the world. And I know I'm not the only one who's tight for money all the time, okay? And,

I might not be the biggest gambler you ever met, but I know when it's time to change the scenery and if you don't do it when you feel the urge, you might be blowing off the last life raft that ever floats your way. It's probably worth noting that I waited to change the scenery until I went digging for my mascara in Gracie's makeup bag (my fifteen-year-old daughter, thank you), and I found birth control pills, some other unidentifiable pills and a baggie of pot. Then, I hemmed and hawed around until I found Lindsey weeping over her weight—she's five feet five inches tall and weighs one hundred and twenty pounds, the same as Gracie. She doesn't even have a freckle. Her date for the prom told her he couldn't go with her, that she was too fat. She was standing naked in front of the full-length mirror, sobbing and reading Sylvia Plath aloud—remember her? She's the poet who stuck her head in the oven and killed herself. The final straw was the romantic dinner I had with Louie Provost at Epernay when his wife, Cherry, showed up to introduce herself. Um, didn't know there was a wife? Thanks, Louie. Can't have dinner there anymore.

I said to myself, Linda? You can definitely do better than this. All of a sudden it was clear to me that I had a stupid job and we had a very stupid life. So I called my sister and she said, *Honey chile? You put yourself and your girls in your car and come on down to me!*

So, that's what I'm doing out here in the middle of the night in Virginia, traveling under the wing of all these trucks. But can you keep a secret? I quit my job. We're *moving* to Mount Pleasant and no one knows it except you and me. I know it seems slightly sneaky and a little impetuous but you know what? It's not. Look, if New Jersey had wanted us, it would have given us a reason to stay. It didn't.

I told the girls it was a vacation. I told the girls I told my employer I would be back in four weeks. They knew I had vacation time piled up like laundry. Maybe they know, maybe they don't.

I have to find a job. And that, my friend, should be the easiest part. I could get hired as a grave digger and make myself believe that I was working at Mardi Gras. But hey, brighter days and better days are coming. I can feel it in my bones! I really can. I am absolutely going to make this work.

PROLOGUE

M Y mother always used to say that if a man could count his real friends on just one hand that he was a wealthy man indeed. My mother was right. I'm going to tell you a story about heaven and hell and how I got out of one and found the other both with the help of a true-blue friend. *Hell* was being married to Loretta and working for her father. *Heaven* is our restaurant on Shem Creek, which we would never have had, except for the generosity and ingenuity of my best friend and partner, Robert. We call it Jackson Hole because my last name is Jackson and I guess you could say it is a hole in the wall. Yeah, it's definitely a hole in the wall. And, Robert likes to ski *guess where*. I know. It's a less than nimble play on words, but let's get this on the record right now—when the whole world conspires against you, a healthy sense of humor can be a very valuable tool. And, up until eight months ago, the world conspired. Worse, I was thrashing around in my quagmire of self-deception watching it happen and didn't do a thing about it.

I used to come down here all the time, in between deals, and I guess I've been fishing the waters around Charleston for fifteen years. There isn't a creek in this whole area that hasn't seen the bottom of my boat, but that said, every time I dropped a hook in the salty creeks and rivers, it always seemed like the first time. The landscape and the light—well, it was always a little different. Quiet but vibrant. You could have made yourself believe that the good Lord Himself was somewhere in the thicket, waiting patiently for you to remember that He was still there. It finally got to the point where I just left my boat in South Carolina. And my heart? Well, looking back, it seems now that the only time I ever thought about it was when I was floating on the Lowcountry waters.

We should discuss this heaven and hell thing, which all begins with my newly-acquired-at-great-personal-loss philosophy. Here it is in a nutshell. When you choose the wrong partner at the dance (whether it's marriage or profession), you will surely bust your ass.

Women seem to know this by instinct. Men don't. Men are conditioned from birth to be providers and basically, our success is measured by how well we do that job. This somehow neatly translates to how much we earn and how many trophies we can accumulate over a lifetime. Cars, second houses, antiques, jewelry for the wife . . . the list goes on and on. We have to graduate from the right schools, become a partner in the right firm, marry the right girl, be invited to join the right club and develop a decent game of golf and tennis.

Right? Wrong! That entire unholy plan, my friends, is a truckload of manure.

Isn't it? I swear, I laugh now when I think about the years I spent chasing the almighty buck. Money, money, money. And, chasing the almighty buck with my wife, Loretta, who always was and continues to be a misery. Well, I can laugh now, but a few months ago, it was not funny at all.

Overall, daughters are so much luckier than sons. Their mothers tell them to follow their hearts, right? They say, *Darlin'? If you want to go study history, you go right ahead. Honey? If you want to be a chemist, go right ahead!* Sure enough, women will graduate and can usually earn a decent living with their degree, doing something they love. Of course, women get screwed right and left because they don't earn the same money that their male colleagues do for performing the same jobs and for a whole variety of other reasons, but for the most part, I think women are happier in their professional lives. And yes, I guess you could say that I am kind of a male feminist.

But, sons are another matter entirely. When I look at the number of kids coming out of graduate school with business degrees, I am absolutely astonished. I mean, where are they all going to find the fortunes that they think are waiting for them? The ones they think they are entitled to? And law school? Don't get me started! Do we really need more lawyers?

What has happened to humanity is this. The world has become vicious, because the devil's real name is greed. Our ability to justify our greed is staggering. If you believe what you read, see and hear around you, our children's future will be all about heeding the call and joining the detestable clamor for money and power. It breaks your heart.

When I think about how I used to run my life, I am sure I must have been completely out of my mind. Besides working seventy-hour weeks, I used to read three newspapers every day—*The Wall Street Journal, The New York Times* and *The Atlanta Journal-Constitution*. No more. Now I read the front page of the *Post & Courier* and guess what? It's as much as I want to know about what's going on "out there." And, I check the weather and the tide tables.

Let me ask you something. Have you ever been to Italy? Did you know that Italy has the sixth largest economy in the world? But when you go there, you see shops closed for hours in the middle of the day, everyone seems to be drinking wine and espresso, smoking Marlboro Reds, and it looks like no one's working! What is going on in Italy? Ahem. They are *really* living. And, guess what? Their lives last just as long as ours do. But! They're *enjoying* their lives one helluva lot more than we are. So, I said to myself, Brad? One day, you're gonna be dead and buried. That's when I decided to become Italian.

I want to have a romance with life! I want to love women and children and savor all the beauty and good to be found in the world. I was missing everything! So hitting rock bottom was a good thing. Otherwise, I'd still be a hamster, running on a worthless, pointless wheel, racing to the grave.

"Mr. Brad? Your appointment is here."

"Okay, I'll be right there! Thanks!"

That was Louise Waring. Who's she? Well, Louise is the greatest woman in the world, that's all. She runs the kitchen, everybody and everything. She's the chef when Duane takes days off, and the assistant chef when he's here. She is capable of almost anything, thank God. Shoot, just last week she stopped a knife fight in the kitchen between a busboy and a dishwasher. Seems one guy made a slanderous remark about the dubious nature of the other's birth, which was followed by a reference to the other fellow's lewd preference for his mother. Well, after that, the conversation switched to Spanish and could have escalated to a life-threatening situation but Louise stepped in and threatened to call the police. It's a good thing our customers don't know what goes on in the kitchen. It's bad enough what goes on in the dining room!

Rock bottom? It's almost embarrassing to tell you how I got there, but I've been thinking about it a lot. I figure that if I can save some other poor son of a gun from the hell I went through then it's worth it to put my pride aside. No, I've come to some very new conclusions and it all began with becoming separated from Loretta and going broke. I was forty-two, a smart fellow (or so I thought) with a platinum resume and suddenly I didn't have a pot to pee in or a window to throw it out of, like my grand-father used to say. It was the best thing that ever happened to me.

Look, you'll have to excuse me for just a few minutes. This interview shouldn't take very long. And, when I get back I'll tell you why simplify-ing life is such a beautiful thing. Yep, think like an Italian and keep it simple. Just hold that thought.

FISH OUT OF WATER

———————————

I walked across the floor from the kitchen door to the bar where my appointment was waiting. She hopped down from the bar stool and took a very deep breath. Nervous enthusiasm was a good sign.

"Hey! I'm Brad Jackson. Thanks for coming."

"Hi! I'm Linda Breland."

I took the resume she offered me, we shook hands and all my knuckles cracked.

"That's a healthy grip you've got there."

"Oh, God, sorry. Comes from throwing bundles of newspapers. Not very feminine. You okay?"

"Yeah, I'm fine. Really."

She was applying for the job of manager and how feminine she was didn't matter one whit.

Louise had her hands full with the mushrooming kitchen staff—a little restaurant humor—and business was going gangbusters. Robert, Louise and I agreed it was time to hire someone with a good disposition and a head for details.

At first glance, Linda Breland seemed like a nice woman, the kind you could depend on. I would have said she was somewhere in her mid-thirties.

If her grip was any indication, she was a healthy specimen. Her brown hair was highlighted with some streaks of blonde, perhaps even done for the interview, but her hair color made no difference to me. She was dressed conservatively, not in expensive clothes, but stylish enough to say that she cared about her appearance. That was what really mattered. Looking professional was important. Having the strength of a stevedore wouldn't hurt either. You never knew what you might wind up having to do—stack cases of wine, crates of vegetables, racks of glasses—anything could happen at any moment.

"Why don't we sit over there by the windows?" I said. "Would you like something to drink? Tea?"

"Actually, if you have Diet Coke, that would be luv-ley." She lifted her jacket and pumped it lightly for airflow. "Augh! It's so hot today. I'm parched like tha Sa-HA-rah!"

"No problem. You sit and I'll be right back."

There was a Civil War going on in her accent. In one breath she was Scarlett, and in the next moment she was a flawless Edith Bunker. It was amusing. Weird, but amusing.

The dining room was almost empty as it was after lunch and before dinner. We had an abbreviated menu that we served all day long, but today was Tuesday and Tuesdays were sort of slow for some reason I had yet to figure out.

As the glass filled, I glanced at her resume and saw she had worked in New Jersey for a number of years. No surprise there—not with *that* accent. She was employed by the Newark *Star-Ledger* in distribution. How that qualified her to run a restaurant was a mystery, but what did I know?

I placed the glass in front of her, she smiled at me and then she crossed her legs. She had a nice face. There was nothing in her smile that was inappropriate—merely pleasant.

I sat opposite her and looked over the resume again. She was crossing her legs again in the other direction. Probably nervous.

"Ms. Breland, there's no restaurant experience on your resume and that concerns me a little."

"Yeah, I know but I understood you were looking for a manager, right? And, I have four years of management experience from the *Star-Ledger*, where I ran distribution."

"And, what did that entail?"

She crossed her legs for the third time and was all squirmy in her chair, which even I had to admit wasn't very bahunkus-friendly.

"Are you okay in that chair? Should I get you another one?"

"Nah, it's fine. I'm fine."

"Okay, so tell me about this job. How did your day begin? I mean, what did you actually do?"

"Oh, not much. Just get up at four-thirty in the morning, scrape ice or snow or both from my car, drive down to Jersey City in the pitch of night, make sure all the truckers showed up, make sure their trucks got loaded and then make sure the papers got delivered. Not very glamorous, I'm afraid, but it paid the bills."

Any woman who could deal with teamsters in the middle of the night in a New Jersey winter, well, she must possess some bodacious spunk. Spunk was good.

"Tell me about yourself," I said.

"Me? Oh, Lord, it's a long story. Well, first, I grew up here. I went to Carolina and then married this guy from New Jersey in my senior year, which, yeah I know, was crazy."

"He was crazy?"

"No! I was pregnant! Nice Catholic girl, right? I mean, oh Lord, it was probably crazy to quit school and run off like that. But things have a way of working out all right."

Linda Breland blushed. I guess she hadn't expected to blurt out the detail of her unexpected pregnancy. I smiled, trying to put her at ease.

"Well, these things happen."

"Right. So that's how I wound up married to the old ball and chain, Fred, and living in New Jersey for all these years. Then Fred freaked out when his hair started thinning . . ."

I patted the crown of my hair and she blushed again.

"And then we got divorced almost five years ago and I've been raising our girls ever since. Anyway, it finally occurred to me that there were plenty of ways to make the same amount of money I made and probably, they all didn't require getting up in the middle of the night! Right?"

"Right."

"I mean, I was never going to be the publisher of the paper, so why was I killing myself in that awful job? Why not do something else that would give me a better life? You know what I mean? Like, I have never had breakfast with my girls the entire time they have been in high school? I mean, my girls are the most important people in my life, like ever, and I guess I'm trying to grab the last couple of years with my youngest. I guess I think things like that are important. I guess."

Well, Linda Breland was not the most articulate woman I had ever met, but she certainly was not stupid. She had some good solid values. A woman willing to uproot her life to spend more time with her children had to be a decent human being.

"I couldn't agree with you more. How many children do you have?"

"Two. My oldest, Lindsey, is going to college this fall and Gracie will be a junior in high school."

"So, I take it you're moving back to Mount Pleasant?"

"Yeah, I mean, if I can get everything organized. My sister still lives here and we're staying with her for the moment, and I guess soon I'll be looking for a house. And, I'm looking for a job." She was silent for a moment and then added, "Obviously."

"Right. Obviously."

"And, I've done other things too. If you look down there, you'll see I have a little business called How She Does It All. I pay bills and organize home offices for women around Montclair. Um, Montclair's where we live or lived, depending on how well this is going?"

"It's going fine, Ms. Breland."

The legs changed position one more time but I ignored it.

"Uh, you can just call me Linda. I mean, everyone does."

"Okay, Linda, and you call me Brad."

"And, I sold Avon products too. Uh, Brad. Home products and makeup, that is. I mean, it was pretty funny. While I was balancing somebody's checkbook I'd look at them and say, *Lord, girlfriend, you need some color on your face!* Then, I'd reach down in my big bag, pull out some samples and give them Lopez lips!"

"Lopez?" What in the world was she talking about?

"Jennifer?"

A-ha!

"Yes, of course. Jennifer Lopez, the rock star. And they didn't get mad? I mean, you'd tell someone they looked like the dog's breakfast and . . ."

"Dog's breakfast?"

She started to laugh and the twinkling sound of it was disarming. Musical. Infectious.

"Yeah, dog's breakfast? You never heard that? It means all messy and—"

"No, I understand the general drift. Dog's breakfast. I love that."

"You can use it. No charge."

"Thanks, I will. See? That's another thing I like about living in the south. Sayings like that. Even talking is just a little more fun. Am I right about that?"

"Yes, generally, but it depends on who you're talking to. In this business you can say just about anything you want, but when I was an investment banker, the other guy was always waiting for you to make a slip they could hammer you with."

"You were an investment banker?"

"Yeah, in Atlanta. I worked for my father-in-law. It was a pretty tense way to make a living. Not as bad as being a day trader, but stressful enough."

"So, you don't come from a restaurant background either?"

"Are you kidding? Before this I lived on another planet!"

"And, so, I mean, is it okay to ask how you wound up here, doing this?"

"Sure. My wife ran off with my worst enemy and my father-in-law sold him the business I was supposed to inherit. How's that?"

There followed a very long silence and then she found her tongue.

"Holy Mother of God! Didn't you want to rip their throats out with your bare hands?"

Rip their throats out? She had a way with words. Now the legs were uncrossed, her eyes had grown large and she was leaning on her elbows, staring at me. I just loved watching the reactions of people when I told the Cliffs Notes version of the train wreck of my past life.

"The thought did cross my mind about every three seconds for a very long time."

"So, what did you do? Jeez! I thought *Fred* was bad!"

"Well, I did a lot of soul searching and a lot of fishing, and then I finally came to the conclusion that I hated, I mean *really* hated doing mergers and acquisitions day in and day out. I was sitting just up this very creek in a boat with my friend Robert, and I turned to him and said, *You know what? I could stare at this creek every day for the rest of my life and never get tired of it.* Then he said, *Well, why don't you?* That's when we knew we were going in the restaurant business."

"Well, you're sure right about the view. Like my daughter Gracie says, it's killer."

Linda leaned back in her chair and looked through the floor-to-ceiling plate-glass windows beside us. In the time it took to change her position, her face became transformed. She was strangely luminous in that afternoon's light and I knew she belonged here. For a few moments, we watched the sunlight dance on the endless ripples of the salt water, the shrimp boats pulling alongside the docks and the birds swooping in majestic arcs. She seemed like she was looking at something miraculous. For my money, it was. That was when I decided to hire Linda. I liked her and I was going to give her a shot.

But, first and only, if she could pass muster with Louise.

"There's someone I'd like you to meet," I said. "Come with me."

"Sure."

I pushed open the swinging door to the kitchen and there was Louise, giving hell to the chef.

"Doo-wayne? People don't come to Shem Creek to eat no grapefruit *coo-lee* with their flounder! They want a clean piece of fish!"

The chef, Duane, slammed his hand on the counter and said, "At Johnson and Wales, they taught us—"

"I don't give a daggum rat's behind—"

"All right, you two! We can discuss this later, please? Louise, come on with me to my office. This is Linda Breland and I'd like you to talk to her for a few minutes."

Gently, I took Louise's arm, turned her around and walked her out, giving the five-minute signal to Duane, letting him know I'd be back and we'd settle the argument.

Louise continued to mutter under her breath. *Pretty boys and cooking schools! In my day, never! I don't know what kind of fool thing goes on! Whoever heard of grapefruit and flounder? Nasty! That's what! Nasty!*

"You said it, Louise," Linda said.

"Louise is slightly opinionated," I said.

Linda giggled, Louise said *humph*, and we all stopped in our tracks. Louise turned to Linda and narrowed her eyes, her jaw set with steel cable.

"He said your name is Miss Linda, right?"

"That's me."

"You ever eat grapefruit with fish?"

"Nope. Never." Linda emphasized her opinion with a guttural noise that sounded like *Bleck!*

Louise gave her the slow *once-over* from head to toe.

"I like her, Mr. Brad. You hire her, 'eah? She's got sense in her head."

"Okay. Hey, Louise?"

"Yeah?"

"Don't kill Duane. Let him have his coulis."

"One of these days, I'm gonna *cut* his coulis! Humph!"

"Oh, Louise! You're a she-devil!"

The deal was almost cut. Louise returned to the stir-fried Armageddon in the kitchen and I opened my office door. I sat at the desk that

Linda would occupy if she came on board and she sat opposite me once again.

"Okay, here's my problem," I said.

"Shoot," she said.

"It's this restaurant experience thing."

She leaned forward once more, but this time, she smiled not in horror as she had when I told her about Loretta; this time she smiled in defiance.

"You didn't have any either," she said.

The balls! She had me there.

"How much do you want to do the job?"

"What's the job?"

We started to laugh and then she said, "I mean, you'll have to tell me what my responsibilities are, right? God knows, I don't want to get in Louise's way!"

"No, you *really* don't want to do that."

Briefly, I explained that I would like her to manage all the bills, deal with the purveyors and with the chef to keep them both honest, do payroll and oversee the front of the house.

"Front of the house being?"

"Everything that happens before you get to the kitchen. Hostesses, waitstaff, busboys—and special events—keep the customers happy. We have a pretty good crew but they could always use a sharp eye to keep them in line. Most of them are young and earning their way through college, so they rush around too much and tend to cluster and gab. And sometimes, they forget to come to work. You'll like the bartender, though. His name's Mike O'Malley. Irish guy."

"Irish? Really?"

"Sorry. That was stupid."

"It's okay. I say dumb things all the time. My grandmother was Irish and I can help bartend."

"That would be great. Look, basically, Louise and I, and now you, do anything that needs to get done."

"Okay, so, what are the hours?"

Yes, I was trying to hire a woman who would undoubtedly point out everything I said or did that was not well thought through. Oh well. We would wash the well-meaning but definitely Jersey girl out of her over time. A southern woman would *never* correct her boss, especially on an interview. But I don't mind; she'll keep me on my toes. She couldn't be worse to spend my days with than Loretta had been and God knows, she couldn't be as challenging as Louise.

"Rotating shifts of eight hours, Monday through Saturday. You have to alternate Sundays with me and Louise and just be flexible."

"Oh, so big deal. Benefits?"

"Management will have health insurance as soon as we get it set up."

"Well, that doesn't matter really. We're covered on Cobra. Vacation?"

"Standard. After one year, one week. Two years, two weeks. Up to four weeks, but not all at once."

"Okay. Done."

"Um, Linda. We didn't talk money."

"Oh, God, I hate asking for money."

"Yeah, money's ugly. Root of all evil and all that. But still . . . okay, what were you earning in New Jersey?"

"Stinking peanuts for the hell I put up with!"

Nicely put, I thought. "How many peanuts?"

"Well, I earned thirty-four thousand at the paper and about six thousand in my other jobs."

"Whew! That's forty thousand!"

"You watch television?"

"No, not much. Why?"

"Well, there's this ad for hair color and this chick says, *I'm worth it.* So there you have it. You want to buy my heart and soul? Forty thousand."

Then, Linda Breland started to laugh. She put her hand over her mouth and laughed at her own boldness.

"All right then, give me your Social Security number and nobody gets hurt," I said.

"Okay!"

I walked her to the door and watched her actually strut to her car, snapping her fingers in the air a couple of times. I could not remember when I had ever seen a woman do something so funny and theatrical, not giving a damn if the world was watching. Linda Breland's courage spread a lightheartedness over me I hadn't felt in years. I found myself remembering the reckless gambles of my youth and I smiled so wide it surprised me. Robert's relationship with our investors, the will of Louise, my determination and the mirth of Linda. We would be a culinary SWAT team.

Two

LINDA AND MIMI

I pulled the car into my sister's yard and stopped. Anyone passing along London Bridge Road would have thought that Mimi's house was a picture of what life was supposed to look like in a perfect world. Pink and green caladiums bordered her azaleas, pink and white vinca was nestled in between and her grass lawn was cut and edged. Her small but charming front porch was furnished with painted white rockers and her hanging baskets overflowed with asparagus ferns and more pink and white flowers, whose name I couldn't recall. It bothered me that I had forgotten the name of those flowers and all at once it seemed I had forgotten too many things.

There had been a time, not too long ago, that I thought I would never get over Fred's remarriage. I became seriously depressed and I think it wasn't just because Patti (his new wife) was younger than me or that she was gorgeous and successful in her own right, although that *was* enough to make me hate her guts with a white heat, even after she had proven herself to be completely reasonable and intelligent with a saint's patience to boot. No, her litany of qualities was grounds for justifiable homicide. But, part of me said, *Shit! If Fred's the best a gal like Patti can do, who's left for me? Lurch?*

The real reason for my depression was that I had fallen into this state of complete and utter despair that my life was never going to get any better

and would never be any different than it was. I would never feel like anything more than bone tired all the time. I hated my job, um, *jobs*. I hated
never quite making ends meet; I hated the winters, fall allergies, frozen
seafood, traffic jams, fear of terrorism, pollution and the fact that I was
surrounded by a million and one things I couldn't take advantage of in
New York. Lincoln Center, all the museums, restaurants, shoes I could
never afford, never mind what was in art galleries or in the breathtaking
showrooms of antique dealers and, I guess, here's the point . . . have you
ever seen a mother take a child to Toys "R" Us and then tell them they
can't have anything? They say, *Sorry, honey, we're just here to get something
for Blah Blah's birthday!* The poor child just wants to break down and wail.
I mean, if you don't want to buy that child a *little* something, *don't* put
that child in that store!

I did not have to be Albert Einstein to come to the conclusion that I
had no business surrounding myself with an Everest I would never conquer or possess.

Just for a while, I wanted to try living in an environment where the
comforts were within my reach. At least, I could try.

Maybe by moving back to Mount Pleasant, my sister would help me
reacquaint myself with all the details that would make my new life at least
appear to approach something more cheerful and hopeful. I could begin
again in a home without drafty windows and uneven floors. I'd find a house
with enough closets, a sunny kitchen and a little screened porch where I
could sit and read or talk to a friend.

You could say that appearances don't mean everything and you wouldn't
be wrong, but frequently, I have found the opposite to be true. What you
wear and how you are groomed has a lot to do with how you are treated at a
restaurant or a teacher's conference. Mimi's house and yard spoke volumes
about her life. If nothing else, she was *perceived* as satisfied and proud of
her lot.

Her home was not only regulation Americana, but regulation belle.
Thoughtfully arranged photographs in small silver frames of our long-
deceased parents and grandparents were but one small demonstration of

her regard for our heritage. Our mother's mahogany secretary in her living room had other small but precious family relics on display—our mother's miniature first Bible, our grandmother's wire-rimmed reading glasses folded neatly over its open pages and our father's silver mint julep cup filled with sprigs of dried rosemary from her yard. Next to the cup rested his baptismal cap of lace, tatted by our grandmother's own hands.

The care and thought that went into each small detail of her world was a constant amazement to me. I, the Oscar to her Felix, had been living life on a roaring freight train, almost laughing at my sister's prissiness for years. I used to think, *What good had it done her?* I ran a crazy house, she ran a show house and both of us got dumped by our husbands. The major difference was that I had two children and for a whole assortment of medical and emotional reasons, Mimi never had any.

All that said, when I came to the end of what I could endure on my own, I secretly believed that the temple to tradition she had built would be a place where we could not only heal, but change. Besides, there was the outside chance that she knew something I didn't, but I doubted it.

I couldn't get out of the car. I just kept thinking about what I had done. In less than one measly hour, I had made a decision that would alter the course of my whole life. Incredible. You would date somebody for years before you would even consider marriage or you could wrack your brains for years studying before you practiced medicine, but you could have one interview and change your world. Just like that. I had done it. I, Linda Breland, the biggest chicken on the face of the earth, had caught the boomerang that would land me back in my hometown. Somewhere along the line, I had developed some very impressive nerve.

I gathered up my purse and newspapers and got out of the car, opening the back hatch to bring in the steaks I'd bought at the Piggly Wiggly. This important day demanded an important supper. In a moment of wild abandon, I had even sprung for a bottle of champagne, deciding we needed to do something celebratory for the occasion.

I couldn't wait to tell Mimi the news—she would be thrilled—but I was dreading telling my daughters. Lindsey, who was going to college in the fall, probably wouldn't care very much but Gracie was going to explode. Well, that was just too bad for her. We'd had more than a few hair-raising experiences in New Jersey that told me Miss Gracie needed a benevolent dictator to appear in her life, blow up her nonsense and restructure her days. I was to be that benevolent dictator. Solid ground. She needed solid ground. I knew of no better place than Mount Pleasant, South Carolina, to take a wild hare like my Gracie and straighten her out. She had no choice but to move with me, and that was that.

The front door opened and Lindsey came outside, squinting.

"Need help?"

"Yeah! Thanks!" Lindsey's ponytail was halfway undone and her shorts and T-shirt were sweaty and wrinkled. "Don't tell me you just got up?"

"Yep. I'm just so tired, I went back to bed. I don't know what's the matter with me."

"Here, take these. Salt air, kiddo. Best sleeping pill in the world. But you really shouldn't stay in bed all day, you know."

"Why not?"

Classic teenage response.

I held the door open to let her pass and followed her into the kitchen. "Because decent people get up and do something with their time, that's why! Unless they're sick. You're not sick, are you?" I dropped the bags on the counter and put my hand on her forehead.

"Mom! *Stop it!* God!"

I ignored that remark. Long ago, I had become deaf to the objections of my children.

"You're fine. Where's Mimi?"

"Out getting her nails done."

"Oh." I stopped and dialed her cell phone but there was no answer. I hadn't had a manicure in a thousand years. "Where's Gracie?"

"At the beach. Where else?"

I started unpacking groceries and obsessing. *Gracie at the beach. Gracie swimming in water over her head! Sharks! Riptides! Jellyfish! My daughter's dead body, white, bloated and stone cold, crabs eating her eyes from their sockets . . .* But, I was cool. "Did she say when she'd be back?"

"Dunno. Gotta ask the guys she went with."

"Guys?"

"Yeah. We met some kids at Taco Bell and she went with them."

"I don't like it when she takes off like this, you know. She makes me nervous. What if they're related to Charles Manson?"

"Who's Charles Manson?"

"A psycho killer, *q'est-que c'est.*"

"Mom, you are so weird sometimes." Lindsey started fishing through the bags, not really pulling things out, just digging around.

"Thanks, hon. Just what are you doing?"

"Looking for a snack. How come you never buy chips? And, whoa! You bought steaks? What's up with that?"

I debated for a moment whether to tell her now or to wait until dinner as I had planned. I decided to tell her.

"Okay. Guess what?"

"What?"

"I got a fabulous job managing a restaurant on Shem Creek for more money than I make in New Jersey!"

"*What?*"

"You heard me. We're going back to Montclair as fast as we can, putting the house on the market and we are moving down here."

"Holy shit! Are you serious?"

"Language, please. I am as serious as I have ever been. I've got a thousand and one things to do because I start work in ten days."

"Gracie is gonna flip a shit."

"Language!"

"Sorry. But she will. You know that, *don't* you? I mean, I know you've been talking about it, but this is for real now. Mom, I can't believe you actually took a job here!"

"Well, I did. Let's put this stuff away and I'll tell you all about it."

Lindsey followed me around the room, not helping anything except the pharmaceutical industry that manufactures my anxiety medication.

"Momma, listen. *I'm* not moving here. *I'm* going to NYU. This isn't about me. I mean, look. Okay. Whew! Damn! I'll help you. I mean, I'll go back to Jersey with you and pack up all my stuff . . ."

"We're all going back together. I can't pack up a lifetime of your belongings without you to sort through it all. . . ."

"You're right. When do we leave?"

"Tomorrow. We're driving."

"Oh my God! Fourteen more hours in the car? Crap! We just did this. And then turn around and come back here? Just like that?"

"You always were the smart one, Lindsey! I'm thinking you can leave your winter clothes at Daddy's and maybe he can keep some other stuff for us until I find us a house here. And, I can't buy a house here until I know how much we're gonna get for the house in Montclair, right? So, either we will stay with Aunt Mimi for a little longer or we can look for something to rent. Anyway, the most important thing is to get the Montclair house looking right to go on the market. That means . . ."

"Throwing out tons of shit!"

"Language! Really, Lindsey! But, that's the general plan. We'll probably put some stuff in storage for a while."

"God, Mom! This is so depressing! I mean, I'm going to Montclair, coming back here, then going back to New York Labor Day weekend and starting school and you won't be in Montclair for me to come home to on the weekends! I don't want to spend my weekends with Daddy and Patti! She drives me crazy and he *is* crazy! You *know* that!"

Lindsey choked up and started to cry like I hadn't seen her do in ages. I knew what was upsetting her—too much change in too short a period of time. She hated change. Always had. I put my arms around her and let her cry on my shoulder.

"Baby, listen to your momma. Everything's going to be fine. This will all work out just fine. It's the best thing for all of us. Right?"

"I know," she said. Her voice was shaking with uncertainty. "I'll just be the one in Daddy's backyard, burying cash in coffee cans and counting Cipro for when the cloud of terror floats over from Manhattan!"

"Don't worry, honey. I just know this is for the best. Your momma has never done a crazy thing in her whole life."

She raised her head and looked at me, half smiling. "Well, you just did."

"Thanks a lot! And you know that extra money I'm getting from my new job?"

"Is this the part where you buy me off? I need a Coke."

"Yep! It's for airline tickets. Get me a Coke too, honey. Diet, if there's any left. Listen, Mimi says you can fly from LaGuardia to Myrtle Beach for under two hundred dollars. That's ten trips, which I have to tell you I don't think you'll even want to take! Once you get into the swing of college you'll forget about your old momma."

She filled two glasses with ice from the door of the refrigerator and poured, handing me one. "Don't say that, Mom. I know I can come here but I don't like the idea of you not being there!"

"So, you want me to sit in Montclair and wait to see if you want to come home for the weekend?"

"Pretty much sucks, right?"

"Pretty much a little-girl-with-a-potty-mouth thing to say, sweetheart."

"Ugh! I hate growing up! You want a piece of cake?"

"Sure, why not? A sliver, though."

I looked around my sister's kitchen, doing inventory. The sparkling clean white countertops and shining oak floors were beautiful. Her cabinets were white too, with paned glass doors. Old linen napkins with lace borders tipped over the edges of her shelves. Her cobalt glasses, all lined up in rows, were not chipped. Her red-and-cobalt patterned plates, all stacked, matched. Everything in the room and especially the pound cake on the footed platter sang of a happy life, an organized life. The appeal of it was becoming addictive!

The front door opened and closed and my sister had returned.

"Heeeey! What are y'all doooo-ing?" She sailed in the room singsong-ing and gave Lindsey a peck on the cheek. "Isn't that cake the best thing you ever put in your mouth? I swear, sometimes they just *turn out.*"

"It's like eating velvet!" I said with my mouth full. "Why didn't you an-swer your cell phone?"

"Honey baby! I was getting my nails done! I can't be fooling around in my purse with wet nails!"

"Aunt Mimi! Momma has some news!"

"Did you get the job?"

I nodded my head and Mimi started whooping and hugging my neck and then Lindsey's.

"This is the best, best news! I swear! Oh, y'all! I am so thrilled!"

"Me too!"

Lindsey stood on the sidelines, shaking her head.

We carried on for a few more minutes and then we heard the front door open and close—very quietly. Gracie appeared in the kitchen, sunburned and wobbling. She was reeking of beer. There was a hickey on her neck the size of a prune.

"Waddup?" she said.

I was mortified and for my sister to see her behave this way was almost unspeakable. No one said a word. We simply stared at her. She must have decided she was too trashed to pass for sober because she turned to leave the room, holding on to the door for support.

"I gotta go to ma room," she said, "I'm grounded."

"This is one reason why we're moving back here," I said to no one in particular.

"You need a hand with *this* one," Mimi said. "She's as drunk as a coot!"

In the distance, as my young hellion ascended the stairs, we heard her lilting call in the music of the debauched. "Ah maight beeee shit-faaaaced, but Ah suuuure had fuuuun!"

"I'll make a lady out of her if it's the last thing I ever do," I said.

"Good luck," said Lindsey.

"It might just *be* the last thing you ever do!" Mimi said.

"Watch me," I said with supreme confidence, seriously doubting that I could do a thing except to frustrate the hell out of myself. "The hopeless battle will begin as soon as she sobers up."

"Two are stronger than one," Mimi said, "I'll help."

Three hours passed and no word from my lovely younger daughter. No word, but plenty of snoring. Her snorts and grunts could be heard all over the hallway upstairs. Supper was ready and it was time for her to rise and join the living. Mimi and I passed each other on the steps.

"Want me to get her up?" she said. "She's been sawing logs forever!"

"Yeah, I guess we have to," I said. "Let's go in there together."

We opened the door and there was my Gracie, curled up in a ball under the sheet. Her breathing was soft and even. Part of me wanted to wake her tenderly and another part of me wanted to pull her hair out by the roots. I still had to get us all packed for tomorrow's trip and she had yet to learn about our plans.

"She looks so innocent," Mimi said, "like an angel."

"*Angel* my big fat foot," I said. "That's Fred Breland's child, not mine."

"Humph to that!" Mimi leaned over her and shook her shoulder. "Gracie? Gracie? Sugar, it's time to get up. Come on, now. Let's go."

Gracie groaned and rolled over, blinking her eyes and yawning. "Lemme sleep a little longer, 'kay? Close the door!"

"No way, honey, you've got to get up now," Mimi said. "Supper's ready."

"Not hungry," she said and rolled over again.

There was no reason for Mimi to be so nice to her. My temper zoomed to boiling. I threw back the sheet and pulled her feet to the floor. "Get up and go wash your face," I said, "we've had enough drama from you. You come home trashy drunk and with a hickey on your neck? You will not embarrass me in front of my sister for one more minute! Move it!"

It would have seemed that the theater department should have closed for the day but as soon as we were gathered around the table (that would be champagne for three, thank you), the news of my job and our move became the topic of heated conversation.

"Well, *you* can move down here if you want to," Gracie said, "but I'm not living around a bunch of rednecks."

"Thank you, Gracie," Mimi said.

"I don't mean *you*, Aunt Mimi. You *know* that. Look, I love my life in New Jersey and I can live with Daddy. He said so."

"Yo! You want to live with Patti?" Lindsey said. "Are you *nuts?*"

"Negative. No one's moving in with Daddy and his wife," I said. "The court awarded me custody and that's how it is."

"Mom? We're gonna have a *big* problem here if you try to force me to do this. I'm not kidding!"

"A big problem?" I said with surprising calm.

"Yeah! A huge one! Here's the line and here's you!" She drew a line with her fingertip and then stabbed at a point on the other side.

I was not amused.

"Are you threatening me, Gracie?"

"I wish you wouldn't use that tone with your mother," Mimi said.

Gracie was pushing her food around the plate, seething with anger. Lindsey stepped in.

"Listen to your sister here, Gracie. Big deal. You get to spend the summer at the beach. You get the tan of your lifetime. You're smarter than half the population here. You can dance with Charleston Ballet Company, which is *professional!* Let's see if they teach modern dance. Who knows? You get to perform at the Gaillard Auditorium! In two years Juilliard will be licking their lips to have you!"

"Yeah, right," Gracie said. "They left a message this afternoon."

"You know, I am really not enjoying these implications about southerners. Northerners are no smarter than—"

"God! Why is everybody *so sensitive?*" Gracie said.

"I didn't mean that the way it sounded, Aunt Mimi. I meant that Gracie is smarter *in the ways of the world.*"

"And, that's the *problem*," I said, unable to filter the sarcasm from my voice.

"Well, I am not moving here!" Gracie said, in a low voice. "And, that's final."

"You don't get to pick *final*," I said. "You're a minor."

"Never mind now," Mimi said. "Look, I have an idea. Gracie? Why don't you stay here with me while your momma and Lindsey make the trip to New Jersey? I'd like to spend some time with you and hear *your* side of things."

Gracie looked at me and I could see her mind at work. Which was worse? Two days of endless driving on I-95 and packing your life in boxes? Or, five or more days at the hands of the Taliban—make that Talibelle? Tough call.

"You can stay if you want," I said, with what I thought was a nonchalant delivery.

Gracie looked from one of us to the other and then, after what seemed like forever, she spoke.

"Okay, here's the deal. I'll stay with Aunt Mimi on one condition."

"Which is?" Mimi said.

"That if I tell you *my* side and you *agree* with me that I get to go back to New Jersey in August."

Maybe Gracie *did* have her own point of view. Maybe I *was* making the wrong decision for her life. One thing was for sure. I wouldn't miss her for the next week. No. I wouldn't miss her one damn bit.

"Nope," I said, "quit campaigning because *here's* the deal. There's no bargaining. Period. I made the decision to move us here, for very good reasons and that's it. I am sick to death of your fresh mouth and the million and one stupid things I have seen you do over the last two years. Your behavior is going to change!"

"*Mom! Stop . . .*"

Gracie pounded her fist on the table and my anger exploded. At this point my heart was pounding in my ears.

"No! You don't tell me when to stop and you listen to me, Gracie. I mean it. Do you think that I enjoyed pulling you out of the police station?

Do you think I have enjoyed all the phone calls from the faculty at Montclair High regarding your behavior in class? Your endless wisecracks? Your foul language? Your grades? No, no. Things are changed as of *right now, this minute!* Unless you want to spend your life making French fries or delivering pizza, you are going to do your homework, get good grades and behave yourself! You don't have to come to New Jersey with us because then I would just be worried about what you're doing anyway. No. You stay here with my sister and give me a few days of peace with Lindsey. And, let me warn you now, if I hear one word about you picking up thugs at Taco Bell or any other place and you coming home like you did today, I will ground you for a thousand years! Am I understood?"

There was silence at the table, followed by more silence. I was breathing rapidly and everyone knew I was within seconds of slapping Gracie to the floor if she made one objection. At that moment, she realized she had no support, and to my surprise she said nothing. In New Jersey, we would have been at a level of mother-daughter anger that would have frightened the neighbors. Lindsey would have been screaming over us to stop yelling and she might have been holding me back from hitting Gracie. Maybe it was because of Mimi's presence and because we were in Mimi's house that Gracie opted not to throw a full-scale fit of temper. Or, maybe Gracie *wanted* to be stopped. Now, there was a possibility worth exploration. And, hellfire, she had to grow up at some point, didn't she?

THREE

GRACIE SPEAKS

———————

MOMMA and Lindsey left early this morning. Personally, I thought Lindsey was crazy as hell to make the trip without a fight, but that's how she always was—the good DooBee of the family. And, I guess I was feeling a little guilty about yesterday, so I got up first and made pancakes for everyone. Aunt Mimi was right on my heels, re-setting the table, moving the forks to the left and the knives to the right. She was like a little obsessed with the table looking like a magazine layout. I mean, who was gonna see it? I said zero about it. I hoped I hadn't been left behind to get trapped for a giant lecture on alcohol and hickeys.

The morning speeches came from Mom, who rushed in the kitchen all nervous and clucking around.

"Now, Gracie? No nonsense from you while I'm gone. Is that under-stood?"

"Yeah, I understand," I said.

"I'll call from Richmond and check on you," Mom said. "Do we have gas? Oh, yes, I filled up last night. Anyway, Gracie, you behave yourself or else!"

"I already said I would, didn't I?"

I was standing by the stove, filling plates with food. When Lindsey

snickered, I gave her the finger behind everyone's back. She shot one
back to me and we giggled.

"What's so funny?" Aunt Mimi said.

"My daughters are making obscene gestures to each other," Mom said.

Mom had eyes in the back *and* the sides of her head.

"Oh, Lordy! I have my work cut out for me!" Aunt Mimi said, with a
sigh.

I knew what *that* meant—that Aunt Mimi was going to make this gargantuan effort to *Carolina-ize* me. I could deal. It was still better than a
million hours in the car, driving up and down I-95.

Anyway, by the time they took off, I was exhausted and considering
going back to bed. No such luck. Aunt Mimi, the general, was waiting
for me.

"Come on, Gracie, let's get these dishes."

I said, "At home whoever cooks doesn't have to wash."

"Well, this ain't Kansas," she said. "Here's a sponge."

Normally, I would have flat-out refused, but it was too early to bicker,
even for me. Besides, she said it smiling and it's harder to bite someone
who is smiling at you.

"So, Miss Gracie? Tell me what's going on. Why don't you want to be
down here with your aunt Mimi? What's the problem with South Carolina?"

"It's not you, Aunt Mimi. It's just that it's *weird*, you know?"

"Honey, you're gonna have to spell it out for me. I gave up mind reading a long time ago."

The hot water was running, filling the sink area with steam. She rinsed
and placed the plates in the dishwasher. I scooped crumbs from the
counter and put the milk, butter and syrup back in the refrigerator. How
was I going to explain this to her without insulting her?

"Look, I've been living in New Jersey all my life! All my friends are
there! And my friends are *very* different from what I see around here.
They're black, Hispanic, Asian, everything! I mean, there are two thousand kids in my high school in Montclair!"

"There are over two thousand kids at Wando here."

"There are?"

She nodded her head, thinking she had me, but it cut no ice.

"Yeah, two thousand *bubbas!* Look, I have kids in my bio lab with gunshot wounds and they didn't come from deer hunting, okay?"

"Gracious! Honey . . ."

"I know thugs with four-point-three GPAs that pack heat in their lockers!"

"Heat?"

"Handguns."

"What's the matter with these children? And, more importantly, why would you *want* to know them? Aren't you afraid you'll get tangled up with them and get hurt?"

"Not at all. Look, we've got the Bloods and the Crips for sure, but we've got every kind of nationality you can name. We think and talk about different things than the kids down here. . . ."

"Bloods and Crips? What in the world?"

"Gangs, Aunt Mimi. Like the Bloods and the Crips are totally famous all over the country. There's this initiation you have to go—"

"I've never heard of such a thing in all my life. . . ."

"And that's the point. Neither has anybody else down here. I mean, my term paper for world history last year was on female genital mutilation!"

"Dear heavenly mother!"

"See? People here are all the same. White kids hang out with only white kids. Black kids hang with blacks. In Montclair, we don't care about that stuff. I mean, the black kids and the white kids in my school sort of go their own ways after school and even in school but the difference is we don't look *down* on each other. You know what I mean? We live in the whole world! Not just one tiny pocket like this?"

"Well, sort of, I guess. I mean, everybody thinks that the north, in general, is more tolerant of cultural differences."

"Aunt Mimi! Listen! It's not about being *tolerant!* Cultural differences are how the whole world *is!* I think it's *interesting!* Listen, you should see the black girls in my class—it's *all* about hair and nails. And, shoes! They got some long nails and hair weaves that you wouldn't believe! And, they are *hilarious!* They love me because they know I think they are very, very cool. I don't want to *be* them; I just want to understand their world and how they think. Even the fat girls wear tight clothes and they aren't all hung up on being skinny, you know what I mean?"

"I think you'd find the same thing here, Gracie."

"Well, I don't."

"You'll never know until you take a look at it. I mean, we could sign you up for driver's ed at Wando this summer, even today, and you could see who shows up, right?"

"That's nice, but here's the problem. I don't fit in here and I never will."

Aunt Mimi turned on the dishwasher and rinsed her hands for the hundredth time. Then she sighed and turned to me. "Baby? I have to tell you something. I think I have spent my entire forty-three years just trying to figure out where I fit in. And, you might be right, but only to a point. You've got the old 'How're You Gonna Keep 'Em Down on the Farm After They've Seen Paree' Syndrome!"

"*What?* In English, please?"

"Our grandmother had this problem with Granddaddy. He went off to World War Two, but actually spent four years in Paris, going to the Moulin Rouge and the Lido and God knows, French whorehouses, for all she knew."

We both snickered at that, because who ever thinks about their great grandparents having a sex life?

"Ew!" I said.

"Precisely. Anyway, after the war so many men didn't want to go back to rural America that they wrote a song about it. My grandmother used to sing it whenever Granddaddy pulled her chain about attending covered-dish dinners at church or bingo or who knows? So, that's what *you've* got! Lindsey was right. You know a whole lot more about how the world ticks than a lot of kids around here. But, not all of them. At least one kid a year pulls a sixteen hundred on their SATs and we do have cable TV, you know. Four hundred stations?"

"The problem is that it's *dull!* I mean, in Montclair I can see Manhattan from the hill!"

"But how often do you go there?"

"Actually, more than you might think. We have this new train connection that takes you there in less than thirty minutes for under five bucks."

"No kidding."

"Yep, no kidding."

"Well, Gracie, here's what I think."

She folded the damp kitchen towel, hung it over the oven door rail and sat next to me at the table, slapping my hand for picking the sweet crust from the sides of her pound cake. I smiled at her then. My aunt Mimi was so smart and she listened really well—for a grown-up, that is.

"Shoot," I said.

"I think that if I were your mother, I'd be worried about you   even as sophisticated as you are—going off into Manhattan at your age by yourself."

"I never go alone," I said, hoping that would make her see I wasn't completely out of control or something.

"No! I'm sure you don't. But, here's the thing. If you lived here, the pace of living—which is *slower,* I'll admit—that alone would make you take your time about other things. Decisions that are more important. You can only be a kid for two more years and then you're cooked! You have college, graduate school, career, marriage, kids and that's it! Boom, boom, boom! One after another. High school is the last level playing field you'll ever have!"

"What do you mean? You don't think teachers are mean as hell to students and pigeonhole kids in high school? And, you don't think kids try to ruin your reputation because of *any* reason they think up?"

"Not at all. That's the same everywhere. What I mean is everybody has the same textbooks, the same tests, and at least on paper you have the same chance at excellence as everyone else. When you get out in the real world, other factors carry more weight. Your personality, your appearance . . ."

"Aunt Mimi? No offense, but that's a bullshit argument." She raised her eyebrows but didn't give me hell for saying *bullshit* to her. So, I continued. "Look, your personality and appearance make a huge difference to teachers. If they like you, they cut you some slack. If they don't, it can make a B turn into a C."

"Okay, that's probably true. I guess what I'm saying is that you have one cloister left, unless you become a nun, which is highly unlikely. And, high school is that cloister. Being with your mom is that cloister. In two short years, you'll be gone and on your own. If you were really as smart as I think you are, instead of kicking the fence to break out, you'd see the value in having the time to slow down, be with your mom and with me and learn something more from us. You don't *have* to be grown-up today. You can grow up *later on*. But you can *never* be a kid again. This is your last chance."

So, she had me on that. I knew she was right. I had been caught in some pretty bad stuff recently. Mimi knew all about everything that had been happening in my life and maybe that was part of why she and Mom wanted to get me out of Jersey.

"Well, I don't mind spending the summer here, but there ain't *no way* I'm moving here forever! Stinking Lindsey has all the luck! Just because she was born two years before me . . ."

"Look, Gracie, sometimes we do things for other people, right? Your mom is entitled to a life too, don't you think?"

"Yeah, I guess."

"And what kind of a life did she truly have in New Jersey?"

"Zero."

"So, you must have some opinion on this. Why do you *really* think your mom is suddenly so anxious to move back here? I mean, I'm thrilled, but I'm a little surprised."

I didn't really feel like getting into it. The whole thing was so complicated that if I got started telling my side, we might be in the kitchen all day.

"Uck. Aunt Mimi? I wouldn't even know where to begin telling you and I'm not even sure there's one answer. I think she's just *had* it."

"Fed up?"

"Yeah."

"I thought right after last Thanksgiving there was a marked change in her attitude."

"Well, it all *started* last Thanksgiving, when Daddy announced that he was marrying Patti, which, just for the record, he handled the whole thing like *fuggetaboutit*. Mom almost fainted when we told her the news."

"Less than graceful? Old Fred not quite the diplomat? Left that bit of news to you girls to deliver?"

"Yeah, *ex-aaaaactly*. It was the worst Thanksgiving of our lives, for Lindsey and me, that is. Mom was down here with you, which is probably the best thing because if she had found out about them like we did, she would've killed Daddy. I felt like killing him anyway, for the sake of Momma's pride."

"I don't know a woman alive who wants to see their husband remarry some gal with a perfect body and a successful career, do you?"

"Nope. But, it's a good thing she's got her own dough because she'll never get a dime out of Dad."

"That's the truth. Well, on Thanksgiving your momma started falling in love with the idea of coming home again. I think she knew how much it meant to me to have her around. I wish y'all had all come."

"Me too. Thanksgiving in New Jersey was reeeally, reeeally bad."

I couldn't talk about it. I started remembering . . .

Lindsey and I had decided that Mom was on a heavy-duty downer and that a trip to visit Mimi would do her some good. And she *was* depressed. Every date she had had in the last year was with a man who forgot to mention that he was married. I mean, if a man wants to take you out to dinner on Route 3 at four in the afternoon and bring you home by eight, your bullshit meter ought to be going berserk, right? Anyway, we'd heard her crying through the walls for long enough and decided she needed face time with her sister.

We had scraped up the money for her airline ticket from my babysitting and Lindsey's tutoring, which left us completely broke. Then in a shocking moment of generosity, Daddy paid us for the ticket and insisted we spend the holiday with him . . . we should have been wary, because like they say down here in the south, old Fred was tighter than a gnat's ass.

"Gracie! Quit daydreaming and tell me what happened!"

"Are you sure you want to hear this? You won't be very proud of what Lindsey and I did to Patti."

"I'll bet you a driving lesson this afternoon that I'll love it. You can drive in South Carolina at sixteen, you know."

"Really? I think I knew that."

Drive a car? Okay, besides the beaches, driving at sixteen might be the only other decent thing about South Carolina. She had found the price of my secrecy. Against my better judgment, I decided to tell her. What the hell, right? Mom was probably already out of Charleston County anyway. Still, we Brelands didn't tell on each other.

"If you tell Mom this, I'll never trust you again, okay? I mean, we gotta have an aunt-niece pact here."

"Deal," she said, and we shook hands.

"Okay, Dad picks us up early Thursday morning and drives us to his house. But first of all, you have to know that when he and Mom split, he moved into this dirtball condo in West Caldwell, and all of a sudden, he's like, moved into this giant *house*."

Aunt Mimi's eyes stretched and she turbo-inhaled. "Well, Fred always did like to fool around in the yard. And, men like to have garages so they can have tools and things."

"Right. So, he picks us up and the whole way there he's talking like Chatty Chuckie or something, which should have made us suspicious. I mean, I knew he had a girlfriend so I was thinking she was probably there."

"How did you find out he was seeing someone?"

"Lindsey told me."

"Continue. . . ."

"Okay, we walk into Daddy's new house in Essex Fells and we notice the new furniture in the living room. And there was a little dog, who was going nuts barking and barking. . . ."

It was like watching a movie run in my head. I couldn't make it stop.

Oh, look! He's adorable! Lindsey said.

He's Patti's dog, Dad said. *His name is Buster.*

"Like I said, I knew that Dad had a girlfriend and I couldn't have cared less. I was way more interested in the dog. You know, Lindsey and I could *never* have a dog because we weren't home all day. Until then, I had forgotten how cute they could be. This precious little Buster was jumping up on us and licking us like crazy and between the new furniture and the cute dog, I was very off guard.

"So I said, *What kind of a dog is he? He sort of looks like a cocker spaniel.* And Dad said, *He's a Cavalier King Charles spaniel. Well, he's a cute patoot! Come here, boy! Scratch your ears?*

"So I'm petting the dog and looking around. The only time we had seen the new house, it had been furnished with his cheap junk from Mom's basement. So Lindsey and I were like looking at each other wondering if old Ebenezer had won the lottery and lost his mind in Bloomingdale's Home Store.

"There was a tan sectional sofa with a fabric that looked like velvet, a large square coffee table with a glass top and two huge armchairs with matching footstools. On the coffee table sat a glass vase, as big as a public monument, stuffed with branches of pine and some kind of extra-long white tulips. There were monkey pillows, monkey lamps, monkey curtains and let's just say the 'monkey thing' was well beyond making its point."

"All those monkey things give me nightmares," Aunt Mimi said.

"Me too. So wait! Check this out! There was a fire burning in the fireplace—even though it wasn't that cold—and scented candles burning all around the room. I'm thinking, where am I? And, what the hell is going on?

"The dining room table had more flowers in the center and candles in little cups. I didn't recognize *anything* and then it dawned on me. *She had moved in.* My daddy was *living* with this woman. I was speechless. Lindsey and I just stared at each other in major horror.

"So then, Dad took our coats and hung them in the hall closet and put our backpacks on the bottom step to take upstairs later. That may appear to have been a normal courtesy, but let me assure you, it was anything *but*.

"For a second, I thought maybe he thought that Lindsey hadn't told me about his girlfriend. Then I thought, no, surely he knew better. Fred was acting all peculiar because he had not revealed the entire truth. And, let's be honest, he knew us well enough to worry about how we would react to his new living situation. So, as usual, because of his emotional laziness, he trapped us and hoped for the best. Not only was he a coward, and this is what really hurt the most, he hadn't cared enough about us to prepare us. I started feeling mighty angry. Yes, sir. Angry as only a teenage girl can. What's that saying? *Hell has no fury like the ice on the tongue of a vixen bitch.* Well, something like that."

"Hell hath no fury like a woman scorned, I think," Aunt Mimi said.

"Right. Well, we were standing around in the living room feeling awkward and suddenly Patti Elliott appeared. Buster abandoned us and ran to her."

"What was she wearing?"

Wasn't it like Aunt Mimi to ask that? I remembered every detail.

"Augh! She was wearing this stupid burgundy apron with pilgrims on it. But, never mind her ridiculous apron, there was diva all around her. Okay, Jersey diva, but diva all the same. This was a *very* put-together woman. She was holding a wooden spoon and a burgundy oven mitt that matched. All I could think was holy hell, Momma's gonna *die* when she hears about this. It's funny how you remember things like that spoon.

"She was way more glamour queen than I had expected. Her hair had been blown out by a salon; that much was definite. She had on tan pants, brown pumps and a tan turtleneck sweater that showed off what a plastic surgeon had probably, no, *definitely* enlarged. I remember thinking that she should've had her flat butt fixed when she bought her big boobs.

"The sparkles coming from her diamond stud earrings were like *completely blinding.* Her sweater was probably cashmere, which really made me mad. I'm thinking, *this bitch!* Do you know my mom has never owned one cashmere sweater? But, actually, she's not really a bitch and I was just wishing Mom had a thousand cashmere sweaters or something.

"Daddy went over to her and kissed her cheek and then he turned to us.

"*Girls? I want you to meet Patti Elliott. Patti? This is Lindsey and this is Gracie, my daughters.*

"*Well, look at you all!* she said with a twang that set my inner Bruce Lee immediately on notice. *Y'all are just as pretty as y'all's daddy said! And, Happy Thanksgiving.*

"I'm thinking, holy hell, she's a southern belle to boot. So then Lindsey pipes up . . .

"*Thanks, it's nice to meet you.*

"I'll admit that Lindsey was the more mature daughter, being polite but not too warm. But I was a mess. I got a huge lump in my throat, my insides got wobbly. I said *nothing* to Patti but just stared at her, wondering what in the world a woman like her would see in our dad, a guy with a loser name like Fred.

"I mean, look, Dad's balding, has gray teeth, a gut hanging over his belt and he's a total wank. Maybe he was okay-looking when Mom married him, but man, he looked old to me now. Definite geezer.

"Anyway, Daddy was talking and I hadn't heard a word. I asked him what he said.

"*I said, say something, Gracie,* Dad said.

"*Happy Thanksgiving, Patti Elliott,* I said.

"My adrenaline kicked in and I marched myself right out the front door, with this urge to spend the day in the yard kicking squirrels. I *couldn't* stay in the house with them. I could see that Patti Elliott was probably a nice woman and all, but I couldn't pretend that everything was fine. It *wasn't*. I just wanted to get away from all of them. I considered walking back to our house on Park Street. It couldn't have been more than five miles and I could make that. But I didn't do it.

"The front of the yard has a steep slope and three steps down to the sidewalk. I just sat on the steps, leaning against the wrought-iron rail. I figured I'd just stay on the steps until Mom got home on Sunday.

"I sat there wishing I had my own cell phone so I could have called someone to come rescue me. Right? I could see me with my own cell phone. How about, *not ever*? It was getting colder and damper by the second, my coat was inside and I was getting more and more bummed out. If I went back in for my coat, Dad would start yelling at me. If I stayed outside, I'd get tonsillitis for sure. I heard the door open and close and turned to see Lindsey and Buster coming toward me.

"*Thanks a lot, you sniveling Benedict Arnold,* she said. *Would you mind telling me what got into you?*

"*I can't take it, Lind,* I said and could feel my eyes filling up with tears. *He sandbagged us! And, she's just too much for me. I mean, look at her! She's filthy rich! She must be wearing a thousand dollars' worth of clothes!*

"She sat down next to me, leaning on the other rail. *What's the matter with you? Have you been thinking that maybe Dad should come home?* I said, no. I mean, there was some small part of me that wanted to have my mother and father under the same roof, even though it wouldn't be good for them or us. Naturally, Lindsey and I started talking about it and, she said, *She's not competing with Mom and she owns a clothing store, dumb ass.* I picked my cuticles for a minute and didn't say anything. I had forgotten about her store. So then Lindsey starts defending her.

"*Look, I don't like this either but I gotta tell you something. The minute you walked out of the house Dad got crazy and you know what she said?*

"I said, *like I give a crap. . . .*

"She said that Patti said, *Calm down, Fred. If I were Grace, I'd walk out of this house too!* Apparently, Patti was a little ticked off with Dad about something. *Soooo, I said I'd come to get you. Soooo, let's go back in. We're in this together, right?*

"Whatever, I said. So she's got a brain. So what? Daddy's acting like an ass.

"He's not acting, Lindsey said, he is one.

"Lindsey agreed with me that it was a little sudden for Dad to be moving in with someone. Okay, he dates a woman. Fine. But now he's living with someone? We decided she must be desperate.

"So Lindsey and I sat there for a few minutes, staring across the street and all around at Daddy and Patti's neighborhood, with its rolling lawns, clipped hedges, the population of Range Rovers, BMWs, and Benzes and it was plain as day that the money gulf between his life and ours had widened again. It was like this—Daddy owned the power company, Mom had a flashlight and we sat in the dark trying to light a match.

"It didn't matter what we thought about fairness. Money was the only reason we ever fought. He gave and he didn't give, depending on his mood and how hard we begged. It's awful. I don't understand how he can just do what he wants and never consult anyone. I mean, he bought himself a Range Rover but refused to buy . . . listen, he wouldn't even pay for Lindsey's SAT tutor! How cheap is that? And how stupid? I mean, Lindsey is the brain in the family! If she thinks she needs a tutor, why would anyone say no?"

"I don't understand your father," Aunt Mimi said.

"It's so complicated," I said. "It's just so complicated."

It was barely eight o'clock in the morning and I felt my eyes burning with tears.

"Baby, I am so sorry you had to go through that," Aunt Mimi said. "Let me fix you a glass of tea. Come on now."

She handed me a tissue and I blew my nose. I couldn't help it; I just started crying all over again. Big fat tears just came pouring out of my eyes. Aunt Mimi pulled me into her side and when I started to gulp, she just said, Oh, Lord, honey. It's gonna be all right. She hugged me so hard, I just gave in and wailed like a baby. It felt kind of good to let it all go. I had not cried that hard since Daddy walked out on us.

Maybe one of the reasons Mom wanted us to move to South Carolina was to get all of us out from under the thumb of Dad's endless insults. It wasn't only about money, really, it was about being *considered* in someone else's life. And, it was about your father loving you and wanting to take care of you.

That should not have been too much to expect.

FOUR

NO TRAVELING FOOLS

———◦—◦—◦———

THE very first thing I did when I reached the outskirts of Montclair was make a mental list of all the real estate brokers I knew, deciding at last to call Gretchen Prater. She would tell me exactly what I needed to do to put the house up for sale. I had never sold a house and I had no idea what ours was worth. I knew the train connection to Manhattan had pushed real estate values up and I was hoping we would clear enough to buy a reasonable house in South Carolina.

Because Lindsey helped me with the driving, we had made the trip to New Jersey in one day—a very long day. It would be a week before my knees would stop hurting. I had called from Richmond as I had said I would, and spoke to Mimi, who said everything was fine, that I shouldn't worry about a single solitary thing. All I could think was, what I didn't know couldn't hurt me, and I knew Mimi well enough to know that she was probably fully steeped in Gracie's baloney, thinking there was no bottom to her well of complaints.

Gracie had yet to become fully acquainted with the grace and steel of my sister's spine. Mimi would muster up her strength, Gracie would find herself put in her proper place and she would never know how it happened. Gracie would never remember a battle or the pain of a fall, only that somehow, without a single raised voice or any kind of argument, she had come to a new point of view about a few things. That was the Magic of Mimi.

I was weary and light rain was falling. A thick mist, typical of New Jersey rains, was all around the traffic. Lindsey had fallen asleep in the front seat, leaning against the window. She seemed so innocent. I saw for the millionth time that her mouth was the same shape as mine. Glancing over every now and then, I was reminded of how angelic she looked as a baby, sleeping on her stomach in her crib, cheek pressed against the sheet, breathing through her mouth. Soon, she would be leaving me and I wondered how I would adjust in the coming months without her. What a wonderful daughter she was—never a moment of trouble, but she was moody in a dark kind of way that worried me sometimes. She dreamed vividly and as a small child of seven or eight, she would wake up over and over all night, frequently having trouble separating her dreams from reality. But as she had immersed herself in school, her flute and in astronomy, she had become more withdrawn from us, except for her daily scream fests with Gracie, who usually provoked them. I was very relieved to have this time with her because for once I needed her more than she needed me.

We came into town from Route 280 and stopped at the traffic light by Pal's Cabin. It was after midnight but the roads were still busy. I never ceased to wonder what all these folks were doing up so late. But, living as close as we did to Manhattan, I knew they could be doing any number of things, going to work, coming home from work, looking for an all-night pharmacy and God knows, looking for someone to make them feel better, even if only for an hour or two. Sometimes the sheer masses of people all around me were overwhelming. I knew they all had lives, many of them had children, spouses, in-laws . . . who were they? These hordes of humanity?

Sometimes living in the New York area seemed like a great experiment in anthropology. Perhaps we had not really come so far since the cave. The only difference between high-rise apartment buildings and cave dwellings were creature comforts. (And, things like penicillin and thank

God, cosmetics.) It seemed like we still ventured out to hunt and gather, hurried home with the kill and enjoyed what we could glean from our lives.

What I had been able to glean had always been precious little. Things would be better for us in the Lowcountry if for no other reason than the difference in the cost of living. Maybe I could even save some money for once. I waited at the light at Bloomfield Avenue, thinking about what South Carolina would bring. Even though a huge task lay before me, I was energized for all of it.

I liked Brad Jackson a lot. I was looking forward to working for him, being around people again during the daytime, doing things with Mimi, and most of all having a real life for myself. Obviously, I had my cross to bear with Gracie and I wasn't too thrilled about the inevitable mental gymnastics and exhaustion that would come along with trying to get her on the right path and keep her there. How could two daughters from the same womb be so different?

Lindsey began to stir.

"Where are we?" she said.

"Almost home, baby. Probably time to sit up and look alive, huh?"

"Oh, God! I could sleep for a thousand years."

"Well, you just stay in bed in the morning and I'll get you up when I get things organized, okay?"

"Okay," she said.

She was watching our town whiz past us with melancholy eyes. This might be one of the last times we passed the Montclair Art Museum together, Whole Foods, the police station . . . each of these landmarks was part of the collage of our lives together.

In minutes, I pulled into our driveway. We got out, groaning from stiffness, and took our duffle bags from the back of the car, and walked across our yard. We were traveling light, saving room for the return trip. The house was dark, newspapers thrown all over the stoop, even though I had canceled it, and the mailbox was jammed with catalogs and circulars.

"Forget it," I said, "we can get this junk in the morning."

"Good idea."

Once I could see that robbers had not carried away the beat-up and worn-out contents of our house, sleep came easily. In the morning, the warmth of streaming light roused me like a gentle hand nudging my shoulder. I was surprised that I had slept so long. It was after eight o'clock. I smelled coffee and hurried down to the kitchen.

"Morning, Mom! Hey, here's your coffee!"

"Thanks, sweetheart. What got you up so early?"

"I don't know, I woke up around six and couldn't go back to sleep. My mind was all cranked, you know? I figured well, I couldn't do a lot of stuff around here to *really* help you, but I could gather up all the magazines and the tons of crap mail and put it in bags to throw out, right? So, that's what I've been doing."

The coffee was so weak I could see the bottom of my cup. She had filled three shopping bags. As a tribute to her thoughtfulness, I complimented her.

"Hot coffee. Stuff of the gods."

Lindsey smiled and I smiled with her.

All morning long, she cleaned closets while I worked with Gretchen, my broker friend.

"What do you think?" I said.

"I think that if you spend a thousand dollars, you'll make another twenty!"

"Really?"

"Linda. Think about it. You can walk to the train station from here. This house is a commuter's dream. There are only so many locations that are in walking distance."

"I've been here for twenty years."

"Yeah, it's a lifetime, isn't it?" She smiled at me, probably remembering when her daughters would babysit for mine. Those were sweet years. And, so long ago.

I stopped for a moment to think back to what we had paid for the house and I remembered it had seemed like a fortune at the time. One hundred eighty thousand dollars. Surely it had gone up in value. Anything in the neighborhood of three hundred thousand would thrill me right out of my mind.

"Call Tony at Metropolitan Plant Exchange," she said. "Let's stuff the flower beds with pink and white impatiens. Then let's put some bowls of potpourri around in the bathrooms and the living room. And, the front door and stoop need a coat of paint. I'll get a wreath. Pots of flowers too. Maybe a wicker love seat from Pier One . . ."

"God, Gretchen, you are so smart."

"Not really. Just experience. Think about it. If the front of the house is welcoming, people overlook other things."

"Like the worn-out wall-to-wall carpet in the living room?"

"You got it! Listen, even if you changed it, the new owner is gonna want something else. That's how it is. I had a client once who spent a fortune on her kitchen. I promise you, it looked like a rocket ship! Modern this, state-of-the-art that . . . Anyway, I find her a buyer and the buyer wants an English country kitchen so, out it all goes! Probably a hundred fifty thousand down the drain! So, listen to me, you just freshen up the place and that's it!"

"A little lipstick on the old pig?"

"Yes!"

Gretchen took pictures and notes and left saying, "As soon as we get these little jobs done, I'll have you a buyer in two weeks! No sweat!"

I just shook my head and watched her leave, clicking her heels down my bluestone walkway to where her car was parked. She was beautiful, confident and successful. I wanted to be just like her.

"Hey, Mom!"

I couldn't answer Lindsey because I had momentary brain freeze from the dream of becoming like Gretchen and the reality of selling our house, leaving Montclair forever. She came to my side and pulled on my arm.

"*Mom!*"

"Sorry, honey, I was just thinking about everything. . . ."

"I found my baby album. . . ."

"I definitely want to take that back with us. Did you find Gracie's?"

"No, it's probably in her room. God, I thought I was gonna start crying or something when I looked at some of the pictures of us."

I was having none of that. No indulging in mood swings. "Lindsey. Over the next few days, your hands and my hands are going to touch every memory we have." Then I sang a little in my fake opera voice, "*Ya gotta be strong, ya gotta be tough* . . . isn't that how the song goes?"

"Mom?"

"What? Off-key?"

"No, I'm just glad you didn't decide to become a lounge singer, that's all."

"Very funny, missy. I'll have you know I have Tina Turner's legs, okay?"

"Yeah. Sure. Um, your legs are white?"

"You know what I mean."

"Well, all I can tell you is that it's a good thing Gracie didn't come. This house would be like the war in Iraq. She *really* doesn't want to live in South Carolina, you know."

"Yeah, well, that may be true, but she *needs* to live in South Carolina! After all the nonsense she's pulled? You think your daddy would put up with that?"

"No. And, you're right. Gracie needs to bring it *down* a little. And, forget Patti. She takes shit from no one."

"*Um?*" I hated hearing vulgar slang come from the lips of my children, although I used slang myself, and for good reason too, but that was entirely another matter.

"Sorry, but really! You should have seen Patti last Thanksgiving when we were trying to stake out our territory." Lindsey giggled.

"Well, I won't miss having to deal with her all the time or Fred; that's for sure. And, while we're on the subject of Patti and your dad, you never told me exactly what happened, except that he announced over dinner about them getting married, which is proof of *her* Swiss cheese judgment about men. So, tell me what Gracie did. . . ."

"Uh, it wasn't Gracie. It was me. And, it wasn't pretty. No, it wasn't pretty at all."

I sank to the couch and put my feet on the coffee table, waiting for Lindsey to tell, hoping against hope that she had wrecked Fred's holiday to a fare-thee-well and that Patti had received an undiluted lesson on the teeth-grinding frustrations of raising teenagers. These thoughts made me feel only one-half an ounce of guilt.

"Gee, I hope you girls weren't rude to them," I lied.

Lindsey giggled again and made a two-year-old face, the kind you made when you got caught playing in your mom's makeup. "Linda? We were *baaaaad* girls."

"Don't call me Linda or I'll spank your bottom!" I patted the cushion next to me. "Sit! *Linda* doesn't have all day!"

Lindsey plopped herself on the sofa, and as usual she twisted her hair while looking out the window, gathering her thoughts, deciding where to begin.

"Okay," she said, "Gracie and I got to Dad's new house and in two seconds realized he had moved Patti in and they had redecorated like, I don't know, like some television program was going to do a big story on them. At first, we were furious—Gracie, especially. She takes one look at Patti and walks out of the house. Daddy started yelling *how dare she walk out like this* and then the next thing I know, Patti is defending Gracie because she realizes Dad didn't tell either one of us that they were living together."

"Poor Patti," I said. "She should've interviewed me before she moved in with Fred. I could have told her a thing or two. But then, like my momma used to say, one woman's trash is another woman's treasure, right?"

"Yeah, I guess," she said. "So then I went outside to talk Gracie into coming back into the house. You see, we were formulating a last-minute plan to get back at Dad for being such a creep to us but Gracie was so pissed off at the world, I couldn't get her to move.

"We saw that he was so involved with Patti that he didn't give a damn about us and so we both got pissed off in advance of him proving it.

"I remember that Gracie said, *Does Mom know about this?* And I distinctly remember that I said, *I don't think so.*"

"You're right. I mean, I suspected he was seeing someone for a number of reasons. First, he seemed, I don't know, *cheerful,* that is to the extent that your father can seem cheerful. And, when he bought my ticket to South Carolina, I knew something was up. But, I never thought in a million years that he was involved with someone at that level. It was shocking." I looked at Lindsey and realized she felt sorry for me for getting bamboozled and I hated that. To make things worse, I had given Fred a little jab, and I knew that was in poor form to speak badly of him to the girls, but now and then I couldn't help myself. Hell, I wasn't a saint, you know. But I tried to redeem myself by saying, "Look, it's okay now. I am happier and so is your father and so are we all . . . so continue!"

"Okay. Eventually, we went back inside and Operation Kill Thanksgiving continued but, with slightly less enthusiasm, because it was pretty depressing. Our next step was the silent treatment. Whatever Patti asked us, we gave her one-word answers. It was truly a beautiful thing. I loved it.

"*So, where are you going to college, Lindsey?*

"*Dunno.*

"*So, Gracie? Do you like sweet potatoes?*

"*No.*

"*Have you ever gone to the Macy's parade?*

"*No.*

"We could tell by her body language that Patti was uncomfortable because she had failed to charm us right off the bat. Daddy shot us multitudinous looks of threatening anger and we would stare back at him with innocent blank faces. I knew he thought we were torturing her, when actually we were torturing him *through* her. We didn't give a damn about her. He, however, was supposed to care about us. Eventually, in between flipping channels on the television, he finally started getting mad, which was what we had hoped for.

"Patti said something like, *Do you girls like the turkey livers fried?* To which we both replied with a loud *Ew!* Gracie made some extreme gagging noises for special effect. Anyway, Dad slammed the remote so hard on the arm of his chair that the batteries fell out. Patti left the room to baste her bird.

"*Dinner's almost ready,* she said over her shoulder in an exasperated voice.

"Rather than deal with Dad exploding, we quickly changed tactics. *Come on, Gracie,* I said, *let's go help Patti in the kitchen.*

"Daddy eyed us with suspicion. Who could blame him for that? *Sure,* Gracie said, *why not? You're right.*

"Silence for a moment from Dad. Then he sat back down and prepared to resume ignoring us as humans. But before that he hurled us a threat.

"*Finally!* Daddy said, and took a deep breath. *You had better be nice. She means a lot to me. Bring me a beer and help Patti. Your old man needs a moment of peace around here.*

"Not for nothing, but what would he do if we were *not* nice? Withhold our allowance? Um, he didn't give us one?

"Anyway, Gracie took Daddy a Budweiser and I leaned against the counter watching Patti. She was peeling carrots, letting the skins fall into the garbage disposal.

"*You'd better grind them as you go,* I said.

"*Why?* she said.

"*I dunno,* I said, and shrugged my shoulders. *It's what Mom does though.*

"That was when the nice Patti left and the real Patti looked me right in the eye and said, *Look, sweetie, I don't give a damn how your momma does things, okay?*

"I thought, *Well! Jeez! How about that?* Hmmm, Patti Elliott had a temper after all. But as a member of the Breland clan, I'd been dealing with angry adults all my life and mood swings were my specialty. I took a deep breath and rose to it. I wasn't ready yet to remind her that as far as we were concerned she was still below insignificance in our world. So I quickly said, *I'm sure you don't.* Before she could show me some more tooth, I added, *Want me to put plates on the table?*

"*Suit yourself,* she said. *Dinner's in thirty minutes.*

"Just then, Gracie came back and I said, *Hey, Gracie, grab four dinner plates from the cabinet, okay? I'll get glasses.*

"*Sure,* Gracie said.

"The silence from the sink area was deafening. She was scraping carrots with a vengeance. Gracie gave me an elbow and mouthed, *What's going on? It's all good,* I mouthed back, giving her the *okay* hand sign. I opened the cabinet where the glasses used to live and they had been replaced by vitamin pill bottles and dried spices. So I said something like, *Hey! Where are the glasses?*

"*Over there,* Patti said and pointed to the other side of the kitchen. *The plates are over there too.*

"*Why'd Dad move everything?* Gracie said.

"*He didn't,* I said, *I've got five bucks that Patti Elliott did. That's what women like her do. They move in and take over.* I was mumbling loud enough for her to hear because I was now officially furious. I mean, who did she think she was?

"Gracie stopped breathing and looked at me in surprise. Full assaults were not part of our plan. We had agreed to be just obnoxious enough to drive them crazy, but not rude enough to truly piss anybody off. Patti stopped and turned to us.

"She had her hand on her hip and there we stood, waiting for Miss Chitlins to rip us a new one. All she said was, *Your daddy doesn't cook. I cook. So, therefore, I rearranged the kitchen to suit me. Y'all got a problem with that? Let's hear it, right now.*

"*Makes sense to me,* Gracie said, and I wanted to kill her for agreeing with Patti. *No problem here.*

"Both of them waited for me to say something. *Whatever,* I said with a trace of a sneer and felt lousy for giving away a point. But, let's face it. We still had to get through Thanksgiving dinner, dishes, Friday, Saturday, and we couldn't get out of that hellhole until Sunday when you came back. That was a long time to concentrate on being obnoxious, even for us. And, stupidly, we hadn't calculated in the part about Patti Elliott having a mind of her own. Who knew?

"Anyway, I realized Gracie and I were going to need an escape strategy. Being in the house twenty-four-seven was going to be too much. So I decided I'd find the newspaper and check all the listings. Maybe we could go to the movies Friday night. I would call around and see if I could get us a ride to the football game on Saturday. Sunday, I would sleep until noon.

"I took the dishes and set the table with Gracie, whispering to her that we needed to talk. She pointed upstairs.

"*Gonna go unpack*, I said out loud to anyone who cared to listen.

"*Me too!* Gracie said.

"We passed Dad when we went through the living room. *How's it going?* he said. *Perfect*, I said, *everything's great*. Gracie said, *Yeah, everything's great*, and followed me up the steps.

"When Dad first moved into the new house, he had set up a room for us. Twin beds, one end table, one chest of drawers—no layout from *Architectural Digest*, okay? But, we had a room and a place to put our stuff. All of a sudden this Patti person moves in and she's flitting around like I don't know what, decorating everything in sight with a monkey-something. So when we opened the door to our room we should not have been surprised to see that everything was changed. But we were. Our bedroom was now an office slash storage room, with moving boxes piled up to the ceiling.

"*Maybe we're in the wrong room?* Gracie said. *Wasn't this our room?*

"*Try next door*, I said.

"She opened the door and peeked in. *Aw, God! Aw, shit! Lindsey!*

"She stepped aside for me. I took one look and said, *Oh, hell!* The bedroom had been completely redecorated for us. There were pictures of the Backstreet Boys over my bed and a poster of Christina Aguilera over Gracie's. The beds were covered in these wild geometric, primary colored, tacky comforters and pillows. I thought I was going to throw up on the lime-green carpet. So Gracie says, *What are we gonna do?* And I said, *We're gonna raise some hell, that's what. What did she do? Go through all our stuff?*

"Gracie and I were snorting around, getting madder by the minute. We opened the drawers and what do you think we found? Our underwear, pajamas, T-shirts and socks were there, newly laundered, pressed and folded. In the closet, our sneakers had been washed and our clothes hung on plastic hangers, all in one direction, hung by category. Not that we had that much stuff there, but it was as neat as a pin and mysteriously correctly divided between what I owned and what Gracie owned. However, and I mean the *big* however, we now had the ammunition we needed. But then I worried a little about starting a full-scale battle on Thanksgiving, so I said to Gracie, *Well? At least it's clean and at least we got a bigger room?*

"Gracie said I was always making lemonade out of lemons and it had to stop. *Look, Lindsey,* she said, and believe me she was in no mood to be grateful for anything, *here's my problem. She's out of control! You don't just go in somebody's drawers, rearrange everything and organize it like this! I freaking hate Christina Aguilera and you haven't listened to the Backstreet Boys in a thousand years! I mean, she might have asked us if we wanted puke-green carpet!*

"So I said, *You're right, you're right, you're right. But we gotta do something!* And she said something like, *So what should we do, genius? Burn the place down?* I mean, if she'd really study, she could make better grades, Mom. I wish she wouldn't call me names like that."

I looked at Lindsey's face, so filled with passion, and tried to imagine what it must be like to be a child of a divorce, and to be the more academic one, the more reasonable one. I didn't blame her at all for having been angry, but at the same time I knew Patti had probably had good intentions. And, well, Gracie called Lindsey names but Lindsey had a few choice ones for Gracie too.

"Lindsey, baby, your sister is just insecure, that's all. She's really proud of you, you know." I reached over and squeezed her hand. "I am too." My poor daughters! What havoc had I brought into their lives with the failure of my marriage? Growing up was hard enough when everything was in place. More and more, it seemed to be the way of the world that nothing lasted as long as it should.

Lindsey shrugged a few times, looked out the window and then continued to tell me her story.

"Anyway, Gracie was getting seriously crazy. She was ready to rip the room apart and tear the posters off the wall. *Tell her to stay out of our room!* She was screaming loud enough for everybody from Essex Fells to Newark to stop what they were doing! So I said, *No! Let me tell her. You're too angry!*

"She said okay, I could. Eventually, we had dinner, which I basically pushed around the plate, even though what made it into my mouth was delicious.

"All the while Daddy talked to us about how wonderful Patti was and to Patti about how wonderful we were. He was in selling mode, which was completely unnecessary, because we would never like this woman. Ever. Even if she could cook like I don't know who. The entire time we ate, Buster went from one of us to the next, hoping against hope that some crumb would fall his way. I was biding my time.

"Finally, at some point I said something like, *You know, Patti, we appreciate what you did to our room.* Old Patti brightened up for a second and Daddy said some inane thing about how it was nice that we had the presence of mind to say thank you. But then I dropped the small bomb, saying, *But since you don't have teenage girls, you probably don't understand how sensitive we can be about someone we don't even know for two minutes going through all our things, moving our room around, decorating without asking us what we liked and we were pretty upset when we saw it.* Then I paused and added, *But, we appreciate it.*

"Well, that was it. Daddy slammed his napkin on the table and stood up. *You girls have no idea how hard Patti has worked! Why, she agonized over every little detail. I've had just about enough of both of you. . . .*

"*We wouldn't go through her stuff, Dad,* Gracie said, in a quiet little mouse way. *It's a violation of privacy. It's like reading someone's diary.*

"So, Patti's upper lip started to quiver and I thought, *Oh, hell, here we go. We've got a weeper.* But, we had her nailed. She knew we were right. *Cry like a dog,* I thought. *Cry and go to hell.* I decided to move before the dam opened up so I said, *I'll go get the pie,* and went to the kitchen.

"Everything was quiet for a few minutes and then when I came back and was standing by the table holding a hot pecan pie with two thick oven mitts looking for a spot to put it down, Daddy said, *Well, you girls had better get used to Patti because she's going to be my wife.*

"I thought I would faint. Then, Gracie said, *Oooo-kay! That's it! I'm fucking out of here!* She pushed back her chair and ran out of the house.

"God help me, Momma, I didn't do it on purpose but I dropped the pie right on the floor."

We started to laugh and couldn't stop laughing for the longest time.

"It was a good thing Buster liked pecans," Lindsey said.

"It's a good thing we're moving," I said, "and speaking of moving . . ."

"Yeah, I know, Mom, we've got a lot left to do."

I wouldn't miss Patti and Fred for two seconds. I knew that Patti could've been a good influence on both my girls in all kinds of ways, but I was feeling selfish. Too many years had passed with me out of their lives during the critical parts of their days. I didn't need any more reminders of my shortcomings or any opportunities for my girls to make personal comparisons between plain old me and the fabulous Patti.

Five

"JACKSON HOLE, BRAD SPEAKING"

I T was early Monday morning and I was sitting in my soon-to-be-former office, shooting the breeze with Robert. We were waiting for Linda to arrive and assume the reins of manager, liberating me from the drudgery of accounts payable duties and the myriad small duties that consumed my day.

"I can't wait till she gets in here and changes my world," I said. "She claims she loves this detail stuff. What time do you have to be in court?"

"Not in court today. I'm driving up to Pawleys Island to take depositions from my latest client. Seems their connubial bliss is losing altitude and gaining speed."

"And you're representing the bride or the groom?"

"The bride and God help her, her husband's got money hidden all over the islands and he's, shall we say, *not cooperating* with the discovery process?"

"Wealthy?"

"Listen, as long as they pay the bill, do I care? I never take a client based on how much *money* they have! Jesus man! I take them based on how interesting they are!"

"I'm just giving you a little grief, Robert. Want some coffee? They just made a fresh pot."

"Sure, why not?"

We were on our way to the kitchen when the phone rang. Someone in the front answered it. As soon as I saw the flashing light, I figured it was for me so I grabbed it.

"Jackson Hole, Brad speaking."

"Brad? Brad?"

It was Loretta, calling from Atlanta. My lovely, unfaithful, soon-to-be ex-torturer. The way she screamed on the phone, I would have sworn the woman was hard of hearing.

"Yeah, it's me, Loretta. What's up?"

"It's Alex! I just got a call from the *police* department. . . ."

Alex was our son, who would soon be sixteen.

"Is he okay?"

"Oh, he's *fine* but he's in *big* trouble."

"So, are you going to tell me what happened or do I have to wait and watch it on CNN?" I couldn't help being sarcastic. One syllable from Loretta's lips and I was instantly irritated.

"Very funny, Bradford. He was caught shoplifting a DVD from Tower Records."

"Well, go get him out of the cooler and read him the riot act, Loretta!"

"I can't . . . I just can't . . . someone might see me there and . . ."

I couldn't believe my ears. She was worried about *herself?*

"Loretta! Have you lost your mind? *Go get Alex!*"

"What if he gets suspended from Lovett? What if he can't play football? Do you understand what I'm *dealing* with?"

Her voice quivered and I knew that any minute she was going to break down.

"Loretta. Calm down. Call Archie. He'll tell you what to do."

I turned to Robert, who was listening to my end of the conversation and biting his lip not to laugh. Linda arrived and walked up to where we were standing. I held up two fingers to let her know I'd be off the phone as fast as I could. I could see she and Robert liked each other right away, which was good.

Loretta had mumbled something and because I was distracted I had missed it.

"What did you say?"

"I said, I *can't* ask Archie anything. We broke up!"

I wasn't about to ask her what happened to *Archie*. I was ready to die laughing at the thought of her wounded pride, but she was so distraught, I held back.

"Then call Theo!" Theo, my wonderful father-in-law, was the guy who had sold me out and bankrupted me without any apologies.

"Who's he talking to?" Linda whispered to Robert.

"Shhh!" Robert said. "He'll be off in a minute."

Loretta continued to whine in my ear. "I can't call Daddy! He'd just *die* if he heard this!"

"Then Loretta, what do you want me to do? Get on a plane?"

"Would you?" she said in the tiny voice of a minx.

Outrageous!

"Loretta! You listen to me and hear me good, okay? Alex is your responsibility! You have full custody! So, *get* your behind down to the police station and get my *fifteen-year-old* son and take him home! Then, if you want me to, I'll call Alex and talk to him."

"I'm putting him in military school, Brad! I mean it!"

"You'll do *no such thing!* Alex has never done anything like this in his life! Now, *get going* and tell Alex to call me later!"

I slammed the phone down so hard Loretta's earring probably fell off. Taking a deep breath, I extended a hand to Linda, forgetting that the last time she had nearly broken my fingers.

"Hey! Welcome on board, Linda! I see you've already met Robert? He's the wallet behind this glamorous establishment. . . ."

She shook my hand hard and I winced.

"And, his best friend of his entire life. . . ."

She turned, shook Robert's hand and he nearly buckled at the knees.

"Some grip! God, woman! Don't hurt me!"

"Oh, God! I'm so, so sorry! I keep forgetting. . . ."

I threw my hands in the air and Robert shook his head. Linda was mortified but recovered quickly, saying, "Who's Loretta? Who's Alex? Is everything okay?"

"Should we tell her about Xanthippe?" Robert said, rubbing his knuckles.

"Who?" Linda was obviously befuddled by Robert's nickname for Loretta.

"Xanthippe was the wife of Socrates, known for her constant nagging. Loretta is my almost ex-wife and Alex is our fifteen-year-old son, whom Loretta can't seem to handle without shrieking. . . ."

"She broke up with Archie?" Robert said. "What happened?"

"Who's Archie?" Linda said.

"Archie is the son of a bitch who broke up my marriage. . . ."

"Who should be *thanked* for it every day for the rest of his life!" Robert said. "I think the gravity of this moment calls for a cigar. Care to join me, Brad? I have some very excellent Cohibas in my briefcase."

"Cigar?" Linda stared at me. "You smoke cigars?"

"What? You allergic? You hate them?"

"No! I love cigars! Smoke your head off! They remind me of my father."

"Oh? Is your dad still alive?" I asked.

"Oh, no, he passed away years ago."

I realized Linda was standing there with her handbag and a box of office supplies and I hadn't even told her it was okay to put them in the office. Robert had two cigars in hand and was fishing around in his brief-case for a cutter and I, so far, had done nothing to make this woman feel welcome, except to allow her to remangle my hand and confuse her with a bunch of names that made no sense to her.

"Linda? Why don't we go into your new office and I'll get us some coffee. Then I'm gonna tell you the story of Loretta and Archie and how I ended up here."

"Fine! I mean, you don't have to tell me. . . ."

"It's best she knows," Robert said, and began the process of circumcising the cigars with his Swiss Army knife.

I brought three large mugs on a tray back to the office, where Robert was flirting like Casanova with Linda. She knew he was just kidding around, and in fact she was giggling like a schoolgirl.

"He's harmless," I said, putting the tray on the empty desk.

"Unfortunately, that's true," Robert said, feigning the most infinitesimal sliver of shame. "Susan would obliterate me off the planet if I ever *seriously*, I mean . . . you haven't met her yet, but when you do . . ."

"Oh, stop blathering, you old woman, and let me give Linda the salient points of my heroic adventure," I said. "Okay, first there came Loretta. I married Loretta straight out of business school and knew right away I'd made a huge mistake. Her father owned a small but prestigious investment banking firm in Atlanta and I, being the son of a farmer and a schoolteacher, wanted nothing more than a life of glitz. . . ."

"Here's a light," Robert said, lighting my cigar. "But what he got was a life of grunt!"

I inhaled and coughed and then I groaned.

"You okay?" Linda said.

"Yeah! Whew! Man! Every time I think about the hell I went through and for what?" I said. "Anyway, it was pretty dismal. I worked and worked these ungodly hours and the old man was always breathing down my neck, second-guessing every decision, every plan—it was just awful."

"Tell her about Amy!" Robert said, "Amy was *hot*, bubba! That's why the whole thing started to unravel. . . ."

"You had a *girlfriend?*" Linda said and blushed.

I didn't know if she said it that way because it was impossible to believe I'd consider adultery or because she thought it was impossible that anyone would find me attractive. I decided to defend my viability as an object of desire and tell her the story exactly as it happened.

"Ah, Amy!" I rolled my eyes. Linda must've thought I had a twitch because she didn't smile. "Okay, it was just last November, and I was having a perfectly nice lunch with Amy, my secretary. We had just ordered. A fist slammed my table and the next thing I knew, Theo, my father-in-law, was leaning over me and the hissing began. *I never should have let my only daughter marry you. I knew it was a mistake then. And, I know it now.*

"I felt like saying, congratulations—we were both right. Anyway, Theo, who was one inch from my face, was whispering, may I add, very unsuccessfully. I could tell from the creeping scarlet of my secretary's neck and face that she was mortified. Our captain scurried away, leaving us to sort out this simple misunderstanding.

"I stood up. *Theo?* He was firmly planted in his spot, ready to launch something nuclear my way. Naturally, when he did not reply in a timely fashion, I spoke. *Theo, it's Secretary's Day and I am merely having lunch with my secretary.*

"*You don't fool me for a minute*, he said. Theo looked at Amy in disgust and then back to me. *No one takes their secretary to the City Grill. You must think I'm an idiot.* I said, *No, I think you owe the lady an apology.*"

"Yeah, you see, Theo is Atlanta's authority on where you can take your secretary to lunch," Robert said. "He's got a plaque from the mayor in his office. . . ."

"Yeah, sure. So, did he apologize? God! I would've died on the spot!"

"No, he didn't apologize and Amy just left the table."

"So tell her what Amy looked like!"

"Okay, okay. Amy was a willowy, redheaded, green-eyed gal with this face that was like, I don't know, a porcelain figurine or something. It looked like she had the dust of crushed pearls on her skin. I swear . . ."

Robert and Linda were staring at me as though I were overdosing on psychedelic mushrooms from Thoreau's forest and that at any second I would begin to spasm and writhe in erotic ecstasy. I cleared my throat.

"Anyway, as she escaped to the ladies' room, she sidestepped the arm of Theo's suit, as though it was dipped in anthrax."

"Good Lord! I would've been shaking and fainting!" Linda said.

"Not her. Here's the kicker. When she glanced back, I saw that her face was void of any emotion and I thought that was odd. In the same instant, Theo blew his stinking breath in my face and stormed out, leaving me there, holding my cloth napkin, completely mystified by what had just occurred. I thought, wait! *Great God!* Was it *possible?*

"Had I missed something about her feelings? After all, it was Amy who had asked that we have lunch. She had made the reservation, chosen the provocative blouse she wore, and she who had doused herself in perfume that day. Amy was hot for me and I hadn't even suspected it. Or *was* she hot for me?

"I took my seat again and continued to consider it. No, I began to *relish* the possibility. Someone was hot for me? Someone found *me* attractive? No, it was impossible. I was the most married, albeit frustrated, man I knew!"

"SNL did a skit modeled on Brad's life called 'The King of the P. Whipped,'" Robert said and snorted with laughter.

"Up yours," I said to Robert and then looked quickly at Linda. "Sorry."

"Puh-leeze!" she said, not offended in the least.

"Come on, man, tell her how you got hammered!"

"Okay, so, Albert, our captain, appeared at my side, placed a large scotch on the rocks right next to my okra soup and corn bread and said, *Mr. Jackson, on the house.* I said, *Did you hear my father-in-law? He must be insane!*

"Albert held his small silver tray behind his back with both hands and said, *April.* And I said, *What are you talking about? April?*

"I could see Amy coming toward us then. *Sir, Secretary's Day is in April. This is November.*

"I just said, *Oh, shit.* So, old Albert held her chair for her and winked at me before leaving us to examine the calendar year and ruminate about its holidays. *I'm really sorry about Theo,* I said. *He's a, pardon me for saying this, windbag of the first order and I don't know why . . .*

"Suddenly I was riveted to the rise and fall of her, um, chest? I just sat there wondering how they, um, *she* managed to be so lovely and why had I never noticed them, um, *her* before?"

"She just smiled at me and said, *Mr. Jackson?* I took a long drink and looked at her, trying to concentrate on the issue at hand and not become completely entranced by the curve of her full mouth. She was so young! I couldn't help but wonder if she had ever been really *ravished* by a man before."

"You're a pig, Jackson!" Robert said, grinning from ear to ear.

"All men are pigs," Linda said.

"Well, instead of asking her, I cleared my throat and got back to Theo, saying, *I mean, I don't know where he gets off . . .* and she says, *Brad? You don't mind if I call you Brad, do you? I mean, if you'd rather I didn't . . .* Then, she reached across the table, her long red curls tumbling over her shoulder in this *holy hell* landslide of sensuality, and placed her hand over mine. I just looked at her hand there, laying over mine in a gesture that on any other day would have seemed to be just friendly concern.

"Such a young hand! Probably not a day over twenty-two. It was soft, silky in fact. Unlike Loretta's hand, which wore the contents of Bailey Banks and Biddle and was tanned to a leathery finish, hers were naked of any jewels. So, then my brain starts driving me crazy! My head says, *Naked? Nice choice of words, Brad.* I knew I was heading for trouble if I didn't take control of things. But, to tell you the truth, I didn't *want* to take control of things with Amy.

"Our eyes met and I knew I was correct about her intentions. Where was this heading? All at once, I was thankful my hand wasn't hairy and that it didn't have liver spots.

"I said, *No, of course, uh, I mean, yes, you can call me Brad, why not? I call you Amy, don't I? I mean, we're not in the office, right?* I was telling myself, that's it, man, keep the decorum thing working. But she can see I'm a bit of a wreck and she says, *Are you sure you're all right?*

"I sat up a little, sliding my hand away, and said, *Of course. I'm fine. I'm sorry about Theo. He's an ass, that man, to think that I had you out here trying to seduce you. It's outrageous! Don't be mad at him.*

"Amy then said, *He's just being protective of his daughter. And, anyway, it doesn't matter.* She smoothed her napkin in her lap and picked up her fork, pairing a bite of her fried green tomatoes with the mozzarella burratta and the grilled Cippolini onions."

"Leave it to you to remember exactly what she was eating!" Robert said.

"Whatever. So, she put it in her mouth as I scooped a spoon of soup. I watched her chew slowly and suddenly, God help me, everything about her seemed erotic. In my mind, we were already in a room at the Ritz-Carlton in Buckhead! Can you believe that? Here I am, this very married guy, one lunch with my secretary and I'm actually thinking about doing something so, so . . .

"But, I didn't *do* it! Think about this . . . the one time in your life you actually get propositioned by some gorgeous young girl and you're so out of it in your head, you can't even pay attention to what she's saying! I remember Amy leaned over and said, *Did you hear me? You're not even listening, are you?* I was completely lost in this fantasy of actually, you know . . . but then, reality came crashing back and once more I was across from my secretary, the heretofore virtuous and demure Amy who had never done anything inappropriate in her life, as far as I knew. What was wrong with me?"

"Hello? You're normal!" Linda said.

"Right! So I said, *I'm sorry, Amy, I was still thinking about killing Theo with my bare hands. Save your strength for better things,* she said."

"Ha! Better things! Don't you love that? Ah, God . . ." Robert could not contain his running commentary.

"Shut up, Robert! So I said, *What do you mean? Better things?* Was she going to announce some illicit intention? Not possible, I thought. And then she says, *Well, the merger you're working on, the millions of things you've got coming up, you know. . . .*

"God! She looked so innocent! Was she waiting for me to make the first move? But then, she said, *Your son? I mean, he must take a lot of energy, right?* I breathed a little easier then. See? Unfortunately and fortunately, she was a nice girl. Not some tramp looking for an older man to take care of her so she could acquire, God knows, whatever it was that girls of her age acquired. Anyway, I don't know why I said it but I said, *Well, my son is a great disappointment to me, actually.* Don't ask me why I told her that. Anyway, I remember taking several sips of water and she said, *What do you mean a disappointment?* Well! She began eating with this enthusiasm seldom displayed by the fair sex, slathering her bread with butter. . . .

"Get a grip, bubba! I said to myself, and cleared my throat. So, I said, *Well, he's so busy . . . I mean, when I was a boy I did all sorts of things with my father and my son has so many scheduled activities sometimes I feel like I hardly ever see him.* And she says something like, *Well, why don't you just put him in the car and take him somewhere?* Anyway, I realized right then and there that I should have just demanded that Loretta make it possible for me to have more time with Alex. They finally bring the entrees and Amy is giving me all these looks and I am *still* wondering if she has, you know, *designs on my body,* and then I decided to just say very little, keep the conversation light and wait for her to make a move. Just act normal. She couldn't be old enough to hold back her cards for long.

"I was right about that. It took about one minute. She's cutting her steak and all of a sudden she says, *Can I ask you something, Brad?* And, I said, *Sure. Shoot.* So, Amy says, *Are you in love with your wife?* And, I said, *What kind of a question is that?*

"About two seconds later she looked at me and said, *I see you looking at me and wondering what it would be like to make love to me.* Then I realized what a chicken shit I was because I launched into this whole speech about how I was committed to Loretta and how the commitment was the thing and how I had never stepped out on Loretta and all that stuff."

"Wait!" Robert said. "Here's the point to this whole story! Brad never laid a finger on Amy but he may as well have because Theo went right to Loretta and told her he had practically nailed Brad in flagrante delicto!"

"Pants down?" Linda said.

"You got it," Robert said and laughed so loud and so hearty that we all laughed. "Come with me, Linda. Let's get Louise to give us a sandwich. You want something, old man?"

"Nah, I'm good, thanks."

"I don't want bread," Linda said, "counting carbs, you know. But I could go for soup?"

For the next few minutes, while Robert and Linda were away, I relived the rest of the conversation with Amy and how, at that moment I had wished I had the balls to take her up on her suggestion.

I just want to get laid, Brad. Get laid by a gorgeous man like you with your beautiful eyes that crinkle a little looking down at me, with your gorgeous blond hair . . .

It's thinning, actually.

Shush! It's beautiful. And I want to feel your breath in my ears. I don't want the burden of a personal relationship. I like things the way they are and don't want to mess that up. There it is, plain and simple.

It had taken me a minute to catch my breath.

Well, I guess you couldn't paint it much more transparent than that, could you? Look, Amy, let me be honest here, okay? Were I single and we didn't work together? We'd be in bed as fast as I could take us there. But, we work together and there's the issue of being married.

What if I change jobs?

Please don't do that, Amy. You're the perfect secretary. My whole business would fall apart without you. You know that.

I had looked at her for a long time and she stared at me. What had become of the world? Amy was a stunning young woman who could have had any man she wanted. Except me. I didn't have the stomach for something as tawdry as an affair. I just wasn't wired that way.

What are you thinking? she had said.

I'm thinking that I am very flattered and that I wish things were different. . . .

You must have seen me looking at you, no?

Yes, but I wouldn't have known you felt this way in a million years. You have to understand that I have never stepped outside of my marriage, ever.

Never?

Never.

Well, there's a first time for everything.

Her light green eyes had sparkled with danger and mischief and I knew I would have been well advised to run like hell. I should have run like hell and laughed like hell at the same time. But all I had said was, *I think we had better get the check.*

I was combing my fingers through my hair. I remember that I leaned forward in my chair and tried to organize my thoughts before I spoke. *Amy. Listen to me. I think you are so beautiful, which I'm sure you already know, because everyone has probably been telling you that since you could understand what it meant. And . . .*

Brad! It's okay! I swear! But don't you ever wonder what it would be like to sleep with somebody else? I mean, do you realize that if you spend the rest of your life married to Loretta, that her lips are the only lips you'll ever kiss again? I mean, isn't that a little scary?

She had me on the ropes with that. Of course, I had thought about it. Over the past few years, Loretta had only delivered the perfunctory variety of kisses—skin stretched over teeth—but that lack of wild passion wasn't something that had kept me awake at night. I had grown accustomed to what we had and didn't have.

Look, of course I have wondered what it would be like to sleep with someone else. I've been wondering about it intensely for the past few minutes. But that's what you get when you sign on for marriage—that old till death do us part thing, you know? Virtue is its own reward crap? And, then there's the office problem. You just can't have an affair with someone who works for you—remember Monica? There are laws—stupid laws—but laws.

Well, I say bull to all that and I think I'd like the chocolate cheesecake with chocolate sauce and whipped cream and a double espresso.

Amy, you are the most desirable of all women but this is the wrong time and the wrong situation. . . .

Like the song, right? Okay, enough said. For now, anyway.

I put my fork and knife on my plate and smiled. She was right but she'd never hear me admit it. I had my high moral ground staked out and I wasn't about to budge.

Had Amy ever called? No. Had anyone? Only Loretta when she didn't want to act like a parent. I rarely saw Alex. Loretta saw to that. I was alone. Maybe that was the way things were meant to be.

Six

BOATHOUSE

———•◆•———

"SO, this is what two hundred thousand dollars buys today? A gentrified but ramshackle two-bedroom carriage house in the old village?" I said.

"Linda! Look! It's got a view of the harbor," Mimi said.

"Yeah, if I hang out the window by my knees, lean to the left and risk my life. . . ."

"And, the kitchen's bright and sunny!" the broker said.

"If you overlook the flocked metallic neon wallpaper," I mumbled.

"I'll repaper the kitchen for you," Mimi said. "Hey! We can teach the girls to hang wallpaper! These are good things to know."

I wasn't even sure if Mimi had heard me. She was lost in dreams of feathering the perfect nest for her sister and her two nieces, one she visualized and decorated, a home whose door held a wreath for every season, accented with beautifully varnished pinecones, satin wired bows stretched like arms to welcome all comers, and lush pots of flowers and ferns on the stoop, clean gutters, swept porches, lavender-scented pillows and linen closets. All I would need to complete her vision was a Labrador a big black one with a long pink tongue, named Beauregard to honor one of our most auspicious Confederate generals.

I watched her for a few minutes—her laser eye like a measuring tape, already calculating yardage for kitchen curtains. And, would the trim be ball fringe or rickrack? For all her good intentions, I was afraid the answer was no. It would be neither one.

"Mimi?"

"Yeah, baby?"

Her smile was so loving and generous, it would be hard to say that I didn't adore her, even when it was obvious she meant to position me front and center in her life. I should have been more grateful for the attention, and I *was* grateful. It was just that Mimi had yet to grasp that I wasn't coming home to retire or that I felt defeated in the least. I was coming here for a fresh start, mainly because I was sick to death of the miserable winters and I wanted Gracie to see the world from another point of view. But her nurturing, while unexpected, was actually, in small doses, rather nice.

"I gotta go to work," I said again, and smiled at her.

"I'll follow you out," she said and turned to the broker. "This is sweet? But, um, I think we probably want at least three bedrooms, you know what I'm talking about?"

"Uh-huh," said the broker, nodding, "I'll call y'all if anything new comes on the market."

"Too small?" Mimi said, after the broker had closed her car door and started her engine.

"Yeah, too small and too *old*. I want squeaky clean and all that new stuff, you know? I am all over *drafty* windows, *uneven* floors, *leaking* gutters, *cracked* asphalt driveways, *unreliable* furnaces . . . I want *central* air, *central* heat, new *windows! I want to flush my toilets with confidence!* I want a dishwasher that lulls me to sleep, *not* one that sounds like a 747! Do you know what *I'm* talking about?"

"Gotcha!" she said, her index finger pointed like the barrel of a revolver.

I opened my car door, threw my purse over to the passenger seat and got in. Mimi leaned in the window. "How's this Brad person?" she said.

"Brad's great! The job's great! But I gotta find a house, you know?"

"I'll comb the *Moultrie News!*"

"Thanks," I said and blew her a kiss.

There were so many choices of where to live in Mount Pleasant. And, I suppose like everyone else all up and down the coast, I would have loved to own a home with a view of something besides my neighbors. The harbor, the Cooper River, a creek—any of them would have been fine. But, not knowing how much I could spend put me in a weird position. It meant that I had to look at houses from the point of view of what would be sufficient. In spite of everything, my heart was leaning to living in the old village where I grew up, even though that choice would never deliver a house with *new everything* in my imagined budget range.

Yesterday, I learned Brad lived in Simmons Pointe, right by the Ben Sawyer Bridge. He was lucky enough to run into a furnished, year-round rental. Even though Brad was a partner in the restaurant, he hadn't been in business long enough to earn enough money to buy anything. He said he felt like he had definitely hit the jackpot with his three-bedroom house on stilts, a new kitchen, two and a half bathrooms, and a marsh and water view for which there was no price tag on the face of this earth.

He had invited me to come see it, saying there might be another one available, and I had thanked him and had said I would but, in reality, the last thing I wanted was for my boss to have access to my privacy. I mean, what if I decided to let Antonio Banderas sleep over? Did Brad need to see his limo in my driveway? No. And did I want to know who was hanging around him? No thanks. Life was complicated enough as it was.

I pulled into the parking lot of the restaurant and, getting out, the smells of the creek startled me. How powerful! And, how reminiscent of my childhood. I could close my eyes and be seven years old again, my hand in my dad's, tromping over to Magwood's to buy five pounds of shrimp, the soles of my sneakers crunching along the broken oyster shells that covered the ground. After a good soaking rain, there were puddles wide enough for zigzag navigation and jumps that resurrected the boy in my father as we leaped over them together, whooping with laughter. Even hours later, long after the mud in the treads of my shoes was dry and fallen away, the smells of salt and sea remained. That same fragrance was linked to good memories like a bookmark. In some remote part of my psyche, I believed that to be surrounded by it again would bring me happiness.

It was in that dreamy state of mind that I began my workday, shuffling through a mountain of bills, organizing them on the computer by category, backing them up on disc. Certain things stood out as too expensive, others as bargains. I would have to think about all of it and apply some kind of analysis to it. One thing was certain—the produce bill was in the stratosphere. Others were unclear. Such as, I couldn't understand the process for verifying the bills for seafood or why we used rentals for special events. It would all be sorted out in due time. My first order of business was to get everything entered in a bookkeeping software program that would produce checks.

Louise appeared at my door and cleared her throat. She was holding two mugs of steaming coffee and placed one in front of me.

"Some people come say hello in the morning and I reckon some others don't!"

"Oh! Louise! I'm so sorry!"

"Everybody comes in and says hello to Louise, even Mr. Brad and he owns the place."

"Other than that, how am I doing?"

"Guess we thought the place would fall apart until you got here this morning, that's all!" She smiled at me, her dimples showing.

"You are so wicked! Come on, sit down and talk to me. How's everything in the kitchen? What's Duane up to?"

"Humph! That man drives me crazy! Now he's wanting to do all kinds of raw fish—something called *carpaccio*. I can tell you right now that people don't come to Shem Creek to eat no fool *carpaccio*. They want a clean piece of fish out of the waters of Charleston and they want *you* to tell *them* to eat it *fried* so they don't have to feel guilty about it. The most exotic thing they order is oysters on the half shell. Isn't that right?"

"Well, carpaccio *is* Italian and Brad's got his Italian thing going on everywhere else around here."

"Humph! So, I'll let him put it on the menu for now."

I thought about what she was saying and essentially, she was right. Most of the restaurants along the water served more fried seafood than broiled and I couldn't remember anyone serving raw seafood, with the exception of oysters.

"There's a restaurant in New York—Greek or Italian, I can't remember—but they serve mostly seafood, pretty much like us. But what's different is that the customer picks out their own fish. They have a huge presentation of iced-down fish in the front and what you do is go with your captain, pick out your fish, and then they only cook it one of two ways. Either they put it on a bed of rock salt and bake it with olive oil and lemon juice or they fillet it and sauté it in butter and olive oil."

"Fish just sits out there?"

"Yeah."

"You know what? You might have something there! That might be the scratch for Doo-wayne's itch! There ain't nobody over here doing that! That would, you know . . ."

"Make us look like our seafood was fresher? Give us a little style!"

"I gotta go find out how much one of them things to show the fish would cost." Louise stood up and gave me a little pat on the shoulder. "You know what?"

"What?"

"I like you. You ain't stupid!"

I hollered after her as she left my office, "Thanks! I think?"

The day was flying by and I didn't see Brad until well after lunch, when he stopped in.

"Hey! Welcome to your second day in the asylum."

"Thanks! I am so excited! I have a new job, I have a new life!"

"Um, Linda?"

He was leaning on the frame of the door and if he had not been my employer, I might have been thinking some lascivious thoughts. I didn't know why but, during the interview, his appeal had gone unnoticed.

"What?" I said, and thought my lascivious thoughts anyway.

"Are you always this upbeat?"

"No." That was the truth. But since returning to the land of my people, I had become undeniably optimistic. In fact, I had stopped taking my happy pills and didn't miss them at all.

"And, so what's happening with your domestic arrangements?"

"Oh, that! Well, I, that is, we are still hanging in my sister's crib."

"Ah," he said, taking a moment to digest the meaning. "Well, this may or may not be of interest to you, but Robert has a client who owns a property in the old village that used to be a farm. One outbuilding—a boathouse—still exists and he wants to rent it. I know the guy—very nice guy—nice wife, all that. I think he would even consider selling it if he could get the variance and found the right person, but you might like to have a look."

"How many bedrooms?"

"I don't know. I'll call him if you want."

"Sure. Why not?"

Brad whipped out his cell phone, one that sent and received pictures, and called Robert for the number and then got his friend on the line. "Lowell? You still interested in renting that little cottage?" Pause. "Uh-huh, uh-huh. No, she works for me." Pause. "Two teenagers, one going to college this fall. Yeah. NYU. Yeah, no kidding. Okay, sure." Pause. "How much? What? Hey, didn't I tell you she worked for *me*? She ain't related to Donald Trump, okay?" Brad covered the mouthpiece and said to me, "Don't worry." Pause. "Okay. Five o'clock. Sure. I'll bring her around. Yes, I'll bring some wine!"

Brad turned to me.

"Okay. Here's the vital stats. It's on the bank of the harbor and used to be a caretaker's cottage slash boathouse. It's been renovated, has three bedrooms, a sort of living room, dining room, kitchen, two-bathroom combination but it's got light and a fireplace and enough storage—so he says. We can see it at five. Want to do it?"

It had been a very long time since a desirable man had thrown out the phrase *Want to do it?* I took a deep breath, steadied myself and said, "Sure, why not?"

Who was I kidding? He was not interested in me in the least and I would be well advised to get over myself. I immediately switched gears to Little Miss Pragmatic, and began making a list of the features of living so close to work.

The biggest advantage of living in the old village was that driving to work would take less than five minutes, even if I caught every single red light. That was certainly a plus. But the truth was that as long as I stayed east of the Cooper River, the most time it would *ever* take was fifteen minutes, even from the islands.

I continued to dig through the pile of papers on my desk, deciding to withhold judgment until I actually saw the place. The afternoon glow began to cover the dining room in deep shades of pink and I looked at my watch. It was four-thirty.

I thought Brad was probably in the kitchen and went to look for him.

"Seen Brad?" I asked anyone in earshot.

"He's up on the sunset deck," one of the guys said.

I said something like *Okay, thanks* and climbed the outside stairs to find him with a hose, spraying the deck with a vengeance.

"What in the world are you doing?"

"Well, it's a thousand degrees up here, right?"

"Whew! No kidding!"

"And, we get about a hundred to two hundred people up here every night for happy hour, right?"

"Yeah, so . . ."

"Well, hosing down the floor, or the roof, depending on your point of view, cools it down about ten degrees." He continued to spray for a minute and then realized I was standing there for a reason. He turned off the nozzle and looked up to me. "Um, want to take my car?"

"Sure."

He grabbed a bottle of white wine and we were off. Without a lot of conversation beyond the usual niceties, we drove from the parking lot to the house of his choosing, which worried me. After all, what if I didn't like the house he thought I should like? But when we pulled into the yard of the big house and drove down the live-oak-columned gravel drive to the back, every hair on my body stood on end. This was it. I knew it, even before I saw the inside. This was my new home. This might be my home forever. How could he have known?

"It's beautiful," I said.

"Yeah, it's pretty cool. Love the location."

"Me too."

We climbed the steps together. As though I owned the place, my hand reached out to the flower boxes overflowing with the palest lavender petunias and fragrant blooms of yet another something I didn't recognize. The owner, Lowell Epstein, was waiting inside for us. He had turned on the lights and Rod Stewart's new CD of ballads filled the air. And, there was a smell of something familiar but then I knew that every house had its own perfume.

"Hey, Brad! Gimme that and I'll open it."

"Thanks," Brad said. "Lowell, this is Linda Breland."

"Hey. How are you?" I said.

We shook hands, and I was careful not to wrench his hand. I took the glass of wine he offered. When he turned his attention to Brad, I began to snoop.

The rooms were furnished as though someone was living there full-time. The master bedroom was cozy with its big brass bed covered in layers of handmade quilts. An old wardrobe with a mirrored door guarded the corner on its great ball-and-claw feet. The end table held a stained-glass lamp, the type made by Tiffany a century ago. Stacks of books were piled on the floor. When I pulled back the curtains, light flooded the room and I saw that there were sliding glass doors that led to a tiny balcony.

The other two bedrooms were large enough for trundle beds, a chest of drawers, a small desk but not much more. There was a well-designed bathroom in between with a shower and a tub. The master bathroom had a brown granite countertop that sparkled with flecks like diamonds. The hall had a large walk-in cedar closet combination linen press and the kitchen was in the front, facing the water. The kitchen was open through to the

living area and the sliding glass doors on the far end opened to the balcony
shared with the master bedroom. I stood there thinking how nice it would
be to have breakfast at the little café table, even though it was encrusted
with the dust and dirt of one hundred storms. Of course, blooming flower
boxes lined its rails, overflowing and trailing down the front of the house.

Situated between the kitchen and living room was a fireplace fash-
ioned of ancient bricks. I could envision myself reading a book, curled up
on a sofa while a great pot of stew simmered on the stove. This tiny place,
of less than, I guessed, eight hundred square feet, was like a New York
apartment but all the windows made it seem endless. I *had* to have it.

"This is very charming," I said, putting my empty glass down on the
counter.

"I usually don't rent this place," Lowell said. "My father lived here until he passed away and since then I've just used it for friends and family.
Barbara and I spend most of our time on Pawleys Island now. I'd just like
to have someone around here, I think."

"Well, that's probably a good idea. God, I haven't been to Pawleys in
years," I said.

"Yeah, well, it's the same as it was when you last saw it," he said, "and
that's probably why it's so appealing."

"I told Lowell that you have two daughters, one going off to college in
the fall," Brad said, "and no pets. Am I right?"

"That's about it," I said. "Um, are you thinking of renting this furnished or unfurnished?"

"As you wish. Brad tells me you're an old Geechee girl, so I guess I'll
have to rent to you, and actually, putting all this stuff in storage isn't a big
deal. In fact, my kids would probably love to have some of these things for
themselves. Think about it."

"Great," I said, "I just want to bring my sister over to see it before I sign
my life away. Is that okay?"

Lowell looked at me, then to Brad and shook his head. "Here's the key,"
he said, handing it to me, "don't throw any wild parties until we have a
deal, okay?"

I had to smile at Lowell's trusting nature. "Yeah," I said, "this is just how they do things in New Jersey." They looked at me in surprise. "Don't y'all have a sense of irony down here?"

"I just figured in that Liz Claiborne outfit, you probably weren't a flight risk, that's all! Sensible women wear Liz."

"Is it Liz? Shoot! How did you know?"

"He's a retailer," Brad said, "with an eye like an eagle!"

"How should I know?" I said. "I bought it at Loehmann's!"

"Another quality to her credit," Lowell said to Brad, "doesn't throw money away!"

"Right! Come on, I have to get back to the grind," Brad said. "Thanks, Lowell!"

Driving back I sat in the passenger seat, twirling the key chain around my finger. "I can't believe it! I mean, that little house is a dream!"

"Well, I saw it a while back. Of course, Lowell and Barbara live in the main house, but they don't care who comes and goes from your part of the place. They just want someone reliable and someone who would pick up the newspapers when they're away or let them know if something goes wrong, like a tree falls on the house or something."

"It makes perfect sense, really. I mean, at least I can stay there for a while. I love my sister and all, but it's too much female energy, right?"

"One can only imagine."

"Hey, thanks a lot for taking me over there and making the introduction . . . Oh! We never discussed *the rent!*"

"You *really* don't like to discuss money, do you?"

"Oh! What if it's like two thousand or something?"

"Girl! Stop worrying! I'll negotiate it if you want!"

"Okay! Be my guest!"

We got back to the restaurant and it was already crazy with early diners. I talked to the waitstaff about why it was taking so long to get breadbaskets and water on the tables. My feeling was that every customer should be greeted, seated, and drink orders should be taken within the first three minutes they arrived. Even if the rest of the dinner got tangled up in the kitchen with *Doo-wayne* (I loved Louise's pronunciation of his name), the customers should at least think we were on top of their dining experience and trying to do our best. Besides, the profit margins on tea, soft drinks and salads were a lot higher than anything else. It had taken me one whole day to figure that out! Actually, my annoyance with the slow waitstaff came from my *northern exposure*. If you owned a restaurant in New York or New Jersey and took your sweet, lazy-ass, shuffling time getting water, bread and drinks to the customers, you'd be out of business in twenty-two seconds! Please the customers and turn those tables, baby; that's the name of the game.

"Miss Linda?" Louise came over and said, "Phone! Line two! It's your sister."

"What? My sister? What does she want?"

"A reservation, but she wants to talk to you."

"Probably wants a window table," I said, and walked over to the telephones at the reception area. "Hello? Mimi? Kids okay?"

"Oh, yeah, they're fine. At the beach. Where else? Listen! I've got a date!"

"*What?*" Mimi had a date? With a man? The last time she had a date George Bush's daddy was in the White House.

"Yeah! Can you believe it? You know my friend Maggie? Well, her husband Grant has this doctor friend they want me to meet and they want to have dinner so I thought that we could come . . ."

"What time?"

"Seven-thirty?"

"No problem. Window table for four at seven-thirty. Done!" I typed it in the reservation log, which was like carving something in stone.

The restaurant had a software program that recorded phone numbers, birthdays, anniversaries, seating preferences and, believe it or not, it had a special box for notations such as: special needs (for example, slightly deaf, mobility issues or low vision), allergies, and can you stand this, *cheap tips*, which of course was entered in code as *ppc, punta poco costosa* in Italian. There was a code for drunks—*bt* for *bevande troppo*, also Italian, a code for demanding patrons—*dolore nell'asino* for, you got it, *pain in the derriere*, and even a code for the *never satisfied*, which was *non satified mai*. I didn't know what was up with Brad and this Italian thing, but according to Louise, by the time the hostesses learned it, they usually quit. Anyway, I entered "prefers window table" in my sister's profile.

I decided to hang around and make sure that Mimi got the right spot. I wasn't kidding about my sister and her dating history, which was another reason for us to move out into our own place. I mean, what if she wanted to bring someone home for a little ooh-la-la? She would have this army of estrogen flag bearers waiting for her in flannel pajamas, eating popcorn, watching *An Affair to Remember* for the eighty-fifth time, weeping all over her living room. Not exactly the uber-den of seduction.

In any case, I had mixed emotions about telling her about the boat-house. Part of her would be delighted that we found something suitable that was so close to her. The other part of her would not like to relinquish the control she had over us. But then I realized it was silly to worry and decided the best time to tell her would be as soon as I saw her. She would be delighted and flattered when I asked her to see it before I took it.

I got a call from the front that Mimi and her friends had arrived. I reapplied lipstick, ran a comb through my hair and made my way to their table. The late evening sun was beginning to descend and the heat of the day had broken. For the first time that day, it finally felt like the air conditioner was working. Despite the crowded dining room, it was cool. When I finally got to their side, Mimi stood up to give me a hug.

"Y'all? This is my baby sister, Linda," she said and gave my shoulder a squeeze.

The men immediately stood. Another thing I liked about the south was that gentlemen stood when a lady was to be introduced or when one just entered a room.

"Hi, I'm Grant and this is my wife, Maggie."

"Hey," Maggie said from her inside seat by the window, "Mimi's been talking about you so much, I feel like I know you already! Welcome home!"

"Thanks," I said, "I feel *very* at home with this view all day long! Is the table okay?" And, who was the nice-looking man with my sister?

"Oh! It's perfect! Linda! I forgot to introduce you to my new friend!"

"Hi," he said and extended his hand for a shake. "I'm Jack Taylor. Mimi didn't tell me she had such a beautiful sister!"

"Thanks," I said and blushed. "Y'all sit! Please! Hey! Guess what?"

"What?" they all said, the men settling back into their chairs.

"I found a house! It's adorable and Mimi, we have to go see it first thing tomorrow!"

"How wonderful! Where is it?"

"In a good stiff wind, you could stand on your roof and spit on it!" I realized that wasn't the most feminine thing to say so I added, "Or throw a rock at it?"

They all smiled, and suddenly I felt stupid standing there with them. Mimi had a funny look on her face that made me uncomfortable. Was it because of my poor choice of words or because we were going to be moving?

"Okay! I gotta go! I hope y'all have a great dinner!"

For decades I had been the renegade little sister. Mimi was the only one who had listened and advised me all through each stage of my divorce from Fred, which was the most traumatic event in my life. If I had my own home right under her nose and a satisfying job as well, she might tell herself that I did not need her as much as she thought I did. It was very easy to make someone feel you were too busy to keep them in your daily life. Too easy, in fact.

Here she was on her first date in ages and she had come here for dinner when there were many other options. She had wanted me to see her out with a man, with other friends, doing fine. It had been natural for her to choose my restaurant because it would make it easier for us to dissect her date the next day. Being a sister came so easily for her. I had been away for so long that I had forgotten how to read the nuances of her moods.

I would take a lesson from her and make the effort to help her see that we were moving out, but not away. After all, there was a great difference between being in someone's life by periodic long-distance phone calls and being in someone's life in person. We had both been lonely, which next to poor health was the worst condition for the human heart. I told myself that I would remind her of her significance and that I would welcome and consider any advice she had for me or Lindsey and most especially for Gracie.

Take each day as it comes, I told myself.

SEVEN

MIDNIGHT PLANE
TO GEORGIA

I T was Thursday night and I was still at the restaurant talking to Mike O'Malley, the bartender, who was a true sweetheart. He took a phone call from his girlfriend, whose eight-year-old son had broken his left arm playing football. She wanted him to go with her to the emergency room.

"O'Malley!" I said, "Go! Don't even think about it! I can pump beer and open mini-bottles with the best of them! Louise and I can handle the bar. Right, Louise?"

"Humph," Louise said, "go on and we'll take it out of your hide later!"

"I owe y'all one," he said, "thanks!"

"You take the roof bar and I'll see about this one," Louise said.

I grabbed an apron and climbed the steps thinking. A lot had happened that week. Most importantly, I had shown the boathouse to Mimi and the girls. Mimi thought it had great possibilities, but just as part of me clung to Lindsey, I could tell she was not quite prepared for us to leave her. Her urge to be a matriarch was Mimi's strength and weakness. The girls had never complained about Mimi and her hovering—snickered maybe, but complain? Never. She was the kind of person who had two pillows on your bed—one down and soft and the other more firm. Each nightstand had a package of tissues and bottled water with a glass. Every bathroom had a nightlight and extra tissue under the sink. Her closets had padded hangers, skirt hangers and, well, Joan Crawford would have approved. In ways that cost so little, she injected a modicum of elegance into our lives, cluttered as they were with a surplus of worries and a shortfall of resources.

There was always a small cut-glass dish of homemade jam on the breakfast table, the ubiquitous fresh pound cake on the counter, a small nosegay of flowers, arranged in a "found object," placed in a spot that surprised and delighted you. When she corrected her posture, you corrected yours. Mimi saw to it that everything we needed was always at our fingertips, including her abundant affection.

This summer had been the only time in my girls' lives that they had experienced the daily benefits of extended family. I only hoped that through my relationship with Mimi and hers with me that we demonstrated to Lindsey and Gracie the importance and power of what being sisters was all about.

The girls thought the boathouse was precious. Despite the fact that its address had a South Carolina zip code, Gracie liked it because we could see the water. Lindsey compared it to a tree house. Best of all, Brad had negotiated a ridiculously low monthly rent with the proviso that we would walk through the big house once a week to check air-conditioning, leaks, mail, and so on for the Epsteins. No problem! I was thrilled!

But there was a problem. Signing the lease put Gracie one step further away from her fantasy of returning to New Jersey. She had pitched one fit after another and I was fast deciding that if she wanted to spend more time with her father, it would've been fine with me. But that was not in Gracie's cards.

I had called Patti Elliott to test the waters with her—actually, I had called Fred, but he wasn't there so I got stuck on the phone with Patti. The conversation went something like this.

"Gracie really doesn't want to live in South Carolina," I said.

"Does she mean she doesn't want to live in South Carolina or that she doesn't want to live with *you?*"

I could hear her chewing on something and I think it was my last nerve.

"I'm pretty sure it's South Carolina," I said, fighting hard to keep the irritation out of my voice.

"Hmmm, well, what does that mean? She wants to live with *us?* How do you feel about *that?*"

How did I *feel* about that? Since when did Patti care how I felt about *anything?*

"I guess it's a case of what's best for Gracie. I mean, she's got two years left in high school. All of her friends are there. I can understand that she's not happy to leave them but life is filled with disappointments, right?"

"You can say that again."

At least we agreed on *something*.

"And, I'm sure she's a little nervous to start over again in a new school with all southern kids, and let's face it, it's not as culturally diverse here. I mean, she's not as likely to have Pakistani friends or Canadian friends or friends from South Africa, right? Society here is a little more prescribed than it is in New Jersey."

"So, she'll teach them something about being more open-minded. Isn't that southern bigot thing over and done?"

"Pretty much, but the pool to draw on is still shallow and I guess it all depends on who you're talking to."

"Well, for my part, I don't care. I mean, I can put up with anything for two years . . ."

"Easily said, Patti. Gracie can be a handful."

"I'm familiar. She doesn't scare me, but listen, here's how it is. I have a store and I work six days a week. I'm not around most of the time. I can give her a room and make sure she's fed and all of that, but play *stepmother?* You must be kidding! Anyway, what makes you think she would listen to me?"

She was right. Gracie didn't listen to anyone. And, what Patti was *really* saying was that she could only provide basic supervision. Fred would only do what he had *ever* done and that was to fulfill the most minimal obligation to his daughter.

"You're right. She's a knucklehead." I sighed so hard that Patti sighed as well.

"Raising teenagers is just hell, isn't it? Listen, after she and that kid drove that car into Edgemont Pond last winter and those other kids got busted for pot, she obviously needs more than I can offer, and Linda, I'm not trying to wiggle out of anything. . . ."

"No, I know you're not. . . ." Remembering the afternoon I spent at the police station was all I needed to feel my pulse race. I had been devastated.

"Daughters need their mothers, no matter how difficult that may be. And, at least you have your sister there. She's pretty straight, right?"

"She's a regular Mother Teresa," I said.

Patti's voice softened in sympathy.

"Look, Linda, you and I have never been best friends but I'm going to give you my honest opinion. I think letting Gracie finish school here would be a disaster. First of all, we don't live in Montclair, so she couldn't go to Montclair High. And second, she probably needs a break from her old friends anyway. They were all headed for trouble."

"Not all of them," I said in Gracie's defense, "just that boy she was mixed up with."

We were both quiet for a minute and I knew in my heart that Patti was telling me the truth. Sometimes the road ahead is as unappealing as trying to shave a bobcat's behind in a phone booth. And that, I'm afraid, was a pretty accurate picture of what it was like to raise Gracie.

"Listen, if you want to send her up here for a couple of days before school starts, we can probably work that out. I can arrange some time off and I'll make Fred do the same thing. Maybe you need a break."

"Some days, life between a rock and hard place just plain old stinks."

I told her that I would think about it but I couldn't see what possible good would come from rewarding Gracie's poor behavior and bad attitude with a trip to see her friends. Besides, I was hoping to cash in my chits with Fred to help get Lindsey settled at NYU. Fred's child support would end if he took Gracie, but it was so small and Gracie was so challenging that I think he would have paid me double to keep her.

I was thinking about all of these things and filling drink orders as fast as I could. By eight o'clock, the sun was setting, the crowd had mellowed and begun to thin out and I was dead tired. Louise suddenly appeared at my side. All the ruddiness of her high color was drained and it alarmed me.

"What's up? O'Malley still not back?"

"No. I just took a phone call for Brad. Do you know where he is? His cell's off and he was supposed to be here by now."

"Louise! What's happened?"

"It's Loretta—his wife. Loretta's dead. Oh my God, Linda, we've got to find Brad. Her daddy called, crying and carrying on. . . ."

"Sweet Jesus! How could that be?"

"Hit by a car crossing Peachtree Street! Big head injury and just terrible . . . oh, Lord! That child! His boy, Alex!"

"Oh, my God!"

Suddenly the thought of Brad having to tell his son about his mother . . . or did he already know? Of course. He already knew. Brad would have to raise Alex now. He would have to go to Atlanta, go through a funeral, take care of her estate and somehow manage to move Alex to Mount Pleasant. Poor Brad! Good Lord! And, what would happen to Theo, Loretta's father? From what I knew, he doted on Loretta. He was a widower and Loretta was his only child. If Brad took Alex to live with him, Theo would have no one. Well, too bad. He was a bastard anyway.

Louise was thinking the same thoughts and both of us were getting plenty upset.

"Call Robert," I said to Louise, "he'll know where Brad is."

Louise went straight to the phone and dialed Robert's number. It rang and rang.

"No voice mail?" I asked.

"Humph. What's the matter with you? You can't leave a message like that on voice mail!"

"Oh, God. You're right. Cell phone?"

"I don't know what's the matter with him and why they never answer the phone in that house! Come on with me! I got his cell number in my purse downstairs."

I tossed my towel to Lisa, the other bartender, and followed Louise.

"Can I do anything?" Lisa said, calling after us.

I turned back to her and said, "Yes! If you see Brad, tell him to find us right away!"

Louise was fishing in her purse for her phone book and her reading glasses. Just as she said, *Okay, I got it right here,* Brad appeared by the office door.

"Good evening, ladies," he said, chipper as usual. But then he saw our faces. "What's the matter?"

"Steel yourself, Mr. Brad, I got terrible news," Louise said and put her hand on Brad's arm. "Loretta done been run over by a car and she's gone."

"What? Loretta dead? How can that be true?"

"Louise, give me Robert's number," I said, "I'll call him."

"Mr. Theo's waiting to hear from you. He's at Grady Memorial Hospital and here's his cell number."

Brad sank in my chair and pulled out his cell phone to call Atlanta. I dialed Robert's cell number and he answered.

"Robert Rosen speaking," he said.

"Robert? This is Linda? Linda Breland from the restaurant?"

"Oh, of course! What's going on? I'm at Cypress having dinner with my lovely wife, Susan, and some friends . . . is something wrong?"

"Yes. Loretta has been killed in an accident and Brad just got the news. I thought you might want to know."

"I'll be right there. Tell him I'll be right there. Okay? Can I talk to him?"

"He's on the phone with her father right now. . . ."

"Okay, I'll call him in five minutes. Wait! I'll see him in ten! Good God! This is terrible! How's he doing?"

"He's okay but it's a horrible shock. . . ."

"Of course it is! Old Xanthippe gone? Well, well. The Gates of Hell are open tonight! I'll be right there!"

If Brad's side of the conversation was any indication of the hysteria taking place in Atlanta, I had to help get him there. Maybe Louise and I could get him packed. No, Robert would probably do that. I decided the best thing to do was get him a drink.

Brad was choking up and any minute the tears would come.

"Robert's on the way," I said and slipped out of the office wondering if I should get him a cup of coffee or a scotch.

O'Malley was back, serving drinks to the crowd of patrons around the bar. I ducked under the service opening and stretched up to his ear.

"We got an emergency," I said as quietly as possible.

"What?"

"Brad's wife just got killed in Atlanta. We gotta get him outta here and on a plane tonight. His father-in-law is on the phone with him now."

"You're shitting me, right?"

"No, I'm not shitting you, O'Malley, just give me a scotch for him, okay? Better yet, give me a bunch of mini-bottles and two glasses. Robert is on the way."

"What happened?"

"She got hit by a car. Head injury, I think."

"Jesus, man! What a stupid way to go. When your number's up, it's up, right?"

"Yeah, I guess so," I said. "I feel bad for him though, you know? He's got a son and all. . . ."

O'Malley reached down under the counter, produced a box of Johnny Walker Black Label minis and put a handful of them on a tray with a bucket of ice and two glasses.

"I'll take it to him," he said. "Cover me for a minute, okay?"

"Sure," I said.

In a moment such as this, it was important not to become a dictator. Let O'Malley take the scotch in to Brad. Let him be one of the first to say that he was sorry about the accident. In fact, let everyone who wanted to say something or do something say it or do it. The most urgent detail was to get Brad packed and to Atlanta as fast as possible. And, I didn't know how that would happen.

By the time I had served two white wines and one Budweiser, O'Malley was back.

"He's shook," O'Malley said, holding the lift gate up for me to pass.

"So am *I*! This is a *terrible* thing! Tragic!"

I wasn't back in the office for more than a minute when Robert walked through the door. He must have been going a hundred miles an hour to arrive so quickly. He went straight to Brad and hugged him.

"God Almighty, Brad! Okay," he said, "what can I do to help?"

"I gotta get there," Brad said. "How am I gonna get a plane at this hour?"

"Let me handle it," Robert said. "Um, maybe I'll have a scotch too?" I poured him a drink and as I poured he was talking to Louise nonstop. "Did anybody call Delta? Somebody call Delta. They fly back and forth all the time. Call US Air and Continental too. Shoot! Call 'em all! Okay! Who do I know with a plane? What's the difference? I'll call the private terminal and see who's there! Maybe you can hitch a ride with someone—a pilot, someone leaving late tonight—let's try!"

"Where's Susan?" Brad said, asking about Robert's wife.

"We're one step ahead of you," Robert said. "I gave her the key to your house and she's over there now packing you up for five days. Don't worry. No one's more organized than Susan. And if she forgets anything, I'll bring it tomorrow. Susan and I are flying in tomorrow."

Brad's voice broke as he spoke. "Thanks, Robert."

Louise put the phone down hard and her anxiety was obvious. "Nothing on Delta or US Air until tomorrow. I *told* them this was a life-and-death thing and you know those airlines don't give a damn!"

Robert was on the phone with Mercury Air. "Yes. Bradford Jackson. Wife just died tonight and he's got to . . . yes, sure. No problem." He covered the mouth of the phone and said, "I'm on hold. I know this guy—did his divorce two years ago. Speaking of hold, how's Theo holding up?"

"Like shit," Brad said.

"And Alex?"

"Like shit too."

"Yes! Okay! Okay! Thanks. Yes. We'll be there at ten-thirty!" Robert hung up and said, "Okay. We've got you on a plane. Some guy from CNN is flying out on a Net Jet tonight after dinner. He said, no problem, glad to help. Let's go to the house now and meet Susan."

"Call us tomorrow, okay? If we can do anything . . . ," I said.

Louise threw her arms around Brad and said, "Now you listen to Louise, son. You go do what you have to do and bring your boy back to me."

We followed them out to the parking lot and watched them pull away in Brad's car. Brad was in shock; that much was clear.

Louise and I turned to walk back to the restaurant and stopped for a moment on the dock to look at the night sky.

"Looks so peaceful," she said.

"The calm before the storm," I said.

"You know, you think you can count on certain things and sometimes you just can't."

"What do you mean? Like Brad counting on Loretta staying alive?"

"Yep. That and a lot of other things too. My momma used to tell me that there ain't no quicker way to bring the devil to your door than for him to think that you are having a party without him. That's right. That's what she always said."

"Suspicious, was she?"

"You can say that again. But it's true. Just as soon as you think you got all your ducks lined up so nice . . ."

"The fox gets in your henhouse?"

Despite the gravity of the night, Louise started to laugh. "Something like that! Come on, girl, let's call it a night."

EIGHT

LINDA AND LOUISE

L OUISE and I opened up the restaurant together, arriving at almost the same time. She followed me to the office and dropped her purse on a chair.

"I couldn't sleep all night," Louise said. "Worrying and fretting . . . we got to find out where the funeral is going to be and send some flowers! I'll call Mr. Robert."

"I'll get us some coffee," I said.

Louise called and as expected, he had all the information we needed. Of course, we wanted the details of Loretta's accident too. As inconceivable as that might seem, our lowly human nature craved the lurid details. We were not disappointed. The facts surrounding Loretta's death were pretty revolting.

It seems she was going to meet Archie, the scoundrel who had lured her away from Brad. The scoundrel and the adulteress had broken up, as previously reported, and perhaps they were meeting to reconcile. Who knew? It was raining like the end of the world and they were to meet at the Margaret Mitchell House to attend a reading and lecture by Anne Rivers Siddons. Loretta was crossing the street and wasn't watching where she was going. A taxi ran a red light, knocked her up in the air and she landed right on her head, fracturing her cervical spine. All of this occurred on the other side of the enormous glass windows of the Margaret Mitchell House Museum, where a sold-out crowd was enjoying refreshments, eagerly anticipating the appearance of Ms. Siddons.

Loretta died instantly. It was the most dramatic moment of Loretta's ill-spent life and no one even saw it.

The least attractive detail was that Loretta's face had suffered severe lacerations and fractures, her left eye was enucleated (fell out) and they were going to have to keep the coffin closed. Her recent eyelift and collagen implants would go unseen and unappreciated.

Naturally, Brad was stunned, his son was bordering on hysterical and old Theo was practically catatonic. Theo had insisted on seeing her body and it had taken years off his life. At least that was what Robert told Louise.

After Louise and I arranged for a large spray of flowers to be delivered to Patterson's Funeral Home, we began to gossip, as only women in those circumstances can do.

"That's what happens," Louise began, "when you live a life of sinning like that."

"Oh! Shush! Louise! You know it's bad luck to speak ill of the dead!"

We looked at each other and grinned, neither one of us showing the slightest sign of remorse.

"Poor old Mr. Brad. Look at him! He marries this Loretta, she's got all this money and her daddy's got all this money and neither one of them got a stitch of class! You should hear what Mr. Robert say about them people!"

"Tell it, sister! I'm here till five! You want a doughnut? Somebody stopped at the Piggly Wiggly and got a whole box of Krispy Kremes." I had two glazed ones in paper towels. They were still warm.

Louise pursed her lips at the doughnuts and cut her eyes at me. "*Only* because this is a special occasion. Usually, I never touch this kind of thing!" She took hers and continued. "Well, first you have to know the story of Mr. Bradford Jackson. He's this nice young man from south Georgia. His daddy was a farmer and his momma was a schoolteacher. They were good folks, you know?"

I shook my head. "Regular people." I pressed the button to turn on my word processor and all its sounds filled the air like background music. It was a gentle reminder for both of us that at some point we would have to get some work done.

"That's right, just regular people. Anyway, Mr. Brad meets Loretta right after he gets out of graduate school. He's got himself a master's degree in business and he was the first person in his family to have one too."

"His parents must have been awfully proud of him."

"I imagine so. He moves himself up to Atlanta and gets hired by old Theo, because Theo's looking for a young man to help him run his business—some kind of buy and sell thing where they help little businesses find big buyers and everybody makes a lot of money."

"Sounds good to me!" I began opening the mail with a letter opener and stacking it to read later on.

"Well, as I understand it, Theo always wanted Loretta to marry this Archie fellow but once she saw Mr. Brad, she set her cap for him and that was all she wrote. The old man wasn't too happy about it, but what's he to do when his only daughter says she's in love?"

"Was Brad in love with her? I mean, what do you think?"

"Ha! You see, this is why I can talk to you! You get the picture, don't you, girl?"

"Well, some days are better than others," I said and smiled back at her. "But tell me, do you think our boy Brad was a little bit of a gold digger?"

"Well, Mr. Robert prefers to put it like *this*—he says that Mr. Brad was *blinded by the lights*—all that highfalootin' living with fancy clubs and big cars. . . ."

"All that glitters ain't necessarily gold, right?"

"Ooh! Chile! You said it! Anyway, Mr. Robert thinks the only reason Loretta gone and married Mr. Brad is to prove to her daddy that he can't *make her* marry his friend's boy, Archie. Well, this Archie is so high and mighty that he starts flirting with Loretta."

"Because he can't stand it that Loretta didn't want him?"

"That's it! Well, Loretta's momma's been dead for a thousand years and the old man's been staying in the house up in Buckhead, but as soon as she's pregnant with Alex, her daddy says he'd rather live downtown, closer to the office. Next thing you know, Loretta's got Brad living in that house."

"Well, actually that sounds like Theo did a generous thing, no?"

"No! Every child gots to have his own, Linda! It's in the Bible, for heaven's sake!"

"So, you mean, they held it over Brad's head that he got the plum daughter and she even came with a house?"

"Honey, if you ask me, poor Mr. Brad was just a substitute for Loretta's daddy! Wasn't *nobody* in love with *nobody!* Loretta wasn't ever anything but a daddy's girl and her daddy never remarried after her momma died."

"That's a little sick, Louise."

"Humph! You telling me? Listen, Mr. Brad gets a big sale and the company makes a lot of money, okay?"

"Yeah, so?"

"Well, instead of giving Mr. Brad a big wad of money or a raise or something, that Theo goes off and buys Loretta a diamond bracelet or earrings!"

"*What?*"

"I'm telling you what's for true! Next, they got Mr. Brad running the business while Theo's off at the Piedmont Driving Club—that's this very uppity place for *white* people, with *too* much money who like to drink bourbon with their lunch. . . ."

"Or, perhaps, *all afternoon?*"

"*Exactly!* So, Mr. Brad's working like a dog, they got a nanny raising their boy, Alex, Loretta gets herself on all these committees that get her picture in the newspaper, and that bad Archie is still flirting up a storm with Loretta like an old tomcat."

"Jesus, Louise! This is a regular soap opera!"

"Hang on! I ain't finished! Get me some more coffee! This is the best part!"

"Don't move!" I dashed to the service station, poured the coffee and dashed back. "Here!"

Louise chuckled and said, "Oh, Lord! People are so crazy!"

"Amen to *that*," I said and settled myself back into my chair. "Come on! I gotta pay bills!"

"Okay, okay!" She took a long sip and stared at me, her dark eyes twinkling with mischief. "So, according to Mr. Robert, Mr. Brad's just a working fool! Always at the office, coming home late, just not paying attention, you know what I mean?"

"Yeah."

"So, one day Mr. Brad's secretary, this woman, Amy—"

"Amy! Oh, yeah! I heard about her! She's a little *ho*."

"And, *she* gone be showing up here someday too, soon's she find out Loretta gone to God, and that might not be where she gone."

"Yeah, but wait, I *know* this part! Brad takes her out to lunch at some hot spot and runs into Theo and he pitches a fit! Right?"

"Humph! That meddling old fool goes running to Loretta and *tells* her that *Mr. Brad* is running around!"

"No way!" Of course I had already heard that part, but I wanted to hear Louise's version.

"Yes, ma'am! He sure does! So Loretta, who ain't got the brains God gave a garden pea, she turns around and tells Mr. Brad that she's been shacking up with that Archie fellow and how does he like *those* apples?"

"But, Brad *never* went to bed with his secretary!"

"Yeah, I *know* that, but that stupid Loretta believed her father and spilled the beans on her own self!"

"What an idiot!"

"And, listen to this . . . that *Archie?* He's married, see? And guess what?"

"I can only imagine!"

"His wife is going through chemotherapy for *breast cancer!*"

"Nice guy, this Archie, right?"

"Humph! *Dog meat trash*, that's what! Anyway, Loretta goes crying to her daddy, Theo sells his business to Archie's daddy, which was really run by Archie Junior, and Mr. Brad quits, because he ain't going to work for some man who's bedding his wife all over Atlanta. He walked out without a penny to his name! Didn't even take a car!"

"How do you know all this?"

"I know all this because I was working at the Rosens' house when all this talk was going on. Mr. Brad? He called Mr. Robert every single day! Finally, Mr. Robert says to him, *You get your behind out of there! Come stay with us! We're gonna figure this out!* And, that's just what they did."

"Whew! That is some pile of mess, Louise! Man! And now, Brad's on his way to bury his ex-wife and face Theo again and probably Archie too!"

"Nope."

Obviously, Louise had one more bomb to drop.

"Tell it, sister."

"Yeah, he's gonna see Theo and you know that Archie is gonna be there, but that ain't his *ex*-nothing! They ain't divorced yet!"

"Holy hell!"

"Now, I gotta get out of here and get some work done! Gots to see what that crazy Doo-wayne is planning to cook next to ruin our reputation!"

"Probably octopus cocktails!"

"Don't give him any ideas!" Louise got up to leave and said, "You tell *a living soul* what I told you and I'll cut your neck!"

"Not me, sugar."

"Humph!"

Long after Louise was gone, I couldn't get Brad out of my mind. Had he really married Loretta for her money and had Loretta married him to defy her father? And, what was Brad to Loretta? A sperm bank? And to Theo? A workhorse? I would never complain about Fred again.

It was around eleven when O'Malley showed up for work and he stuck his head in my office.

"I've got the liquor orders done. You want 'em?"

"How do you usually handle it?"

"Brad orders it, but I can do it. No sweat."

"Yeah, just do it. Give me a copy of the order and a copy of the invoices when it comes in. I'll pay it and file it."

"Man, this place is going to be so organized nobody's gonna believe it!"

"How's your girlfriend's boy?"

"Oh, he's fine. Hey, anybody hear from Brad?"

"Yeah, we sent flowers from all of us. Funeral's tomorrow. Brad will probably be out for part of next week. He's got to organize his son and all and probably Loretta's estate and all that stuff."

"I hadn't even thought about his son. He's gonna have to bring him here, huh? It's not bad enough that Loretta drops dead, now he's an instant full-time parent."

The phone started ringing. First, a waitress called in sick. Then, a dishwasher called in sick. By the time everyone was supposed to be in for the start of the lunch shift, we were short three people. I called Mimi.

"Hey! I'm in an awful pinch. The help is like . . . dropping like *flies* around here and I need waiters and dishwashers on the double. Where are the girls?"

"Sleeping. Wait! Here's Gracie! Gracie, come here, honey. Your momma wants to talk to you."

Traitor! Why couldn't Mimi just handle it? Sure! Put the Demon on the phone! Thanks a lot!

"What? I just woke up."

It was the gravel voice of my darling daughter.

"Gracie! I need your help!"

"What?"

"I'm short dishwashers and waiters all over the place! I need you and Lindsey to come down and help me, so get dressed, wash—"

"*No way! No way!*"

"You want to eat?"

Silence.

"You want spending money?"

Silence.

"I have *plans*, Mom. You can't just *call* me like this and wreck my day!"

"*Yes*, I can. *But*, I'm not wrecking your day. I'm making you a better person by giving you the chance to help your mother and I *know* that's what you want to do!"

"Fine."

Mimi took the phone at that point.

"So?" she said.

"Yank Lindsey out of bed, stuff a Pop-Tart in their mouths, clean them up, get them over here as fast as you can and I'll be your slave."

"No problem. Consider it done!"

"And if Gracie wears shorts, make sure her little behind isn't hanging out, please?"

"Are you kidding? Don't even worry about *that* for a second!"

When Lindsey and Gracie arrived with Mimi thirty minutes later, Gracie had left her attitude in the car and Lindsey and Mimi wanted to work too. Mimi must have given them the dickens on the way to the restaurant.

"How much?" Gracie said, money being the first concern on her mind.

"Depends," I said, "you wash dishes, you get minimum wage. You wait tables you get the minimum and tips. You bus tables you get minimum wages plus a tip from the waiters."

"I'm waiting tables," Mimi said. "I've always wanted to do that! Oh! Y'all! I'm so *excited!* I can't wait!"

"You'll get over it," I said. "How about you two?"

"What's the easiest?" Gracie said.

"Bussing."

"I'm bussing."

"Lindsey?"

"I wanna be the hostess," she said.

"We have a hostess," I said.

"Okay, then, um, okay . . . I'll wash dishes, I guess. You need a dishwasher too, right?"

"Bless your heart, honey!" Mimi said.

"Yeah, *right!*" Gracie said in exquisite Jersey-ese, switching to redneck southern in her next breath. "Her brain's so teensy-weensy, that if you put it on the head of a pin, it would roll around like a bowling ball, *bless her heart!*"

Then even I had to laugh. Gracie *doing southern* was something to behold. At least she was approaching it from a humorous angle and the good Lord only knew how much humor we were going to need to survive the next few days.

My prissy sister, Mimi, a waitress? Skinny little Gracie bussing tables? And the long-suffering Lindsey washing mountains of dishes? I got on the intercom and called Louise. Not one of my recruits would listen to me on how to do their jobs. But they wouldn't dare cross Louise!

NINE

LIFE GOES ON

———◆————

LOUISE and I were waiting for Brad to appear. He called us from his house at Simmons Pointe, where he had just dropped off Lupe, his Costa Rican housekeeper. Bringing Lupe back from Atlanta was an intelligent decision for many reasons. It was tragic enough that Alex had suddenly lost his mother, and in such a catastrophic circumstance. Losing a parent was horrible at any age, but for a young man of fifteen it was especially saddening. And naturally, there was a considerable difference between Brad and Alex on the feelings they held for Loretta. I suppose Alex loved his mother as any child normally does and Brad, well, it was easy to imagine that his emotions ran the gamut from complicated grief to guilt-ridden hatred.

The inclusion of Lupe was given the nod of consent by Louise and me on that morning, long before we laid one eye on her. We wanted to like her because we liked Brad. Alex had suffered the worst week of his life and Lupe represented normality. She could help Brad settle Alex into his new life. And, if she decided to stay, she could keep his house neat, drive Alex wherever he needed to go and keep an eye on him too. I was a little jealous because I'd never had a housekeeper, but I did have Mimi and she was already onto Gracie's whereabouts and social plans like shrink-wrap.

We were discussing all these things while having a cup of coffee at the bar with O'Malley.

"Don't you know Brad's been through hell the past few days?" I said.

"Let's just hope his child's grieving isn't too terrible," Louise said. "I lost my momma when I was sixteen and there's never a day that I haven't missed her and wished I could bring her back."

"Yeah," I said, in full agreement, "but don't you know this is some kind of soup because Brad wasn't exactly in love with Loretta anymore. It might be hard for him to be sympathetic with Alex, right?"

"Don't assume to know a man's heart," O'Malley said, "sometimes they show one thing but feel another."

"You are too right!" Louise said. "But at least we can say that we held this place together while he was gone."

"Well, I just hope that when he walks through that door, that he realizes he owes you a kidney and me half his liver!" I said to Louise.

"Humph. He ain't gone realize *nothing,* honey! He's a man!"

"Ahem!" O'Malley said, clearing his throat. "Ladies? He did just bury his estranged wife, ladies. Have a heart."

"Sorry, O'Malley, you're right," I said. "But you have to say that my sister gets the award for most bizarre waitress of the year! Who knew she could calculate fat grams and carbohydrates in her head?"

"Who knew she would tell the customers?" O'Malley said.

"Well, at least she was *polite,*" Louise said. "And I thought for sure that Gracie would be dropping dishes everywhere with those little chicken arms she's got, but she's *strong!* And, you had better shush your mouth, talking about your family like that! Are they coming to work today?"

"Just Gracie. Mimi is taking Lindsey to get her hair cut! She wants her to have a good haircut to start school. What that really means is that Mimi thinks a good haircut will help her get a good boyfriend."

"Lindsey ain't gonna have no trouble whatsoever! I think she can have any boy she wants."

"Well, she's very smart and that threatens a lot of boys, but the funny thing is that Lindsey could already have had boyfriends and I never would have known it. She's very private."

"Good for her!" O'Malley said.

"Gracie is *so* jealous but you know Mimi will do something good for Gracie if she can behave herself for five minutes. And, Gracie says she's sick of carrying trays. She wants to wait tables. So what do you think? Think she's old enough, Louise?"

"No, she ain't *old* enough, but she's got *nerve* enough," Louise said.

"You don't know the half of it," O'Malley said. "What do you think she said to me Saturday night?"

"There ain't *no* telling," I said.

"Well, the place is packed and I'm serving drinks right and left. It was about eight-thirty and I've got one of the waitresses—that girl, Erica? The one who goes to Winthrop College?"

"Yeah, yeah, we know her—the one with the long hair all fluffed out crazy like a Renaissance portrait, right?"

"Right. She's helping me . . ."

"She's as thick as a post," Louise said.

"True, but most of the dinner crowd is finishing up but the bar is getting wild and Gracie comes by with a bin of dirty dishes and says, *Hey! O'Malley! Come here!* She's calling me over like I'm her *friend* or something."

"Maybe she thinks you are," Louise said.

"She knows better," O'Malley said, "I'm old enough to be her father! Anyway, I say, *What is it, kid?* and she says, *Look, I get a buck from the waiters when I clear their tables, wipe it down and carry all their nasty dishes back to the kitchen. You get a buck for just pouring a beer. So, if you need help, let me know. I can dump this bussing gig with no problem. So, I said, If you serve liquor, we lose our liquor license, honey. You're underage. Does this kid have some guts or what?"

"That kid of mine! I'll tell y'all this—she's the one who's gonna make my hair fall out one of these days."

"She's as cute as a bug," Louise said. "I got one like her. She's grown now and got three children! I thought I would never live to see the day."

"Listen, when Gracie goes into labor, I'm going to Canada! Married? I can't even imagine who on earth . . ."

"Would have the courage to take on Gracie?" O'Malley said, laughing.

"Pretty much," I said and turned around to see Gracie standing there, furious, having heard everything.

"Thanks, Mom," she said, spinning on her heels, heading for the kitchen.

"Ah, shoot," I said, "busted! Thanks, O'Malley! Good job watching my back!"

"Hey! She knows you were kidding."

"Bull! She's got a temper like all the furies in hell!"

"I'll go see about her, Miss Linda, and assign her a wait section. That should cheer her up." Louise stood up from the bar stool, winked at me and followed Gracie into the kitchen.

"Where would the world be without Louise Waring?" I said.

"In the sewer," O'Malley said.

It was after eleven in the morning and people were starting to arrive for early lunch. Connie, the hostess on duty that morning, seated the first few people and gave them menus. Louise came back through the swinging doors, pushing Gracie with gentle taps on her back.

"Go on, now," she said, "and wait on those people. Remember the soup special is tomato basil and the special pasta is angel hair with shrimp. . . ."

"I know, I know—with a light creamy tomato sauce and the sandwich special is fried grouper, right?"

"Right," Louise said, "with a small house salad."

Gracie scowled at me when she passed but I could tell she was over it.

I looked up and saw Brad coming through the door, and on impulse I went to him and gave him a huge hug. Poor devil.

"You okay?" I said. "Welcome back."

"Thanks. Yeah, I'm okay."

In just about the time it took Gracie to leave the customers and arrive to the point where we were standing by the reception desk, Alex appeared with an old basset hound on a leather leash. Gracie took one look at Alex and nearly dropped dead. Alex was gorgeous. He was tall with black spiky hair and deep blue eyes. Alex was a refugee from the pages of an Abercrombie & Fitch catalog. Slack-jawed Gracie had been smacked up side her hard head by Cupid's arrow. I grabbed her by the arm to introduce her to Brad and she did not resist.

"Brad? This is my daughter Gracie. She's helping out until three of our waiters and one of our dishwashers return to work."

"Hi, Gracie. This is my boy, Alex. He's going to be living with me and probably going to school with you. And that's Bogart, our best friend," Brad said. "What happened? Did we have a mutiny?"

Alex and Gracie bent down to pet Bogart and made some small talk, during which Gracie actually had the poise to offer condolences for the loss of his mother.

"No mutiny—there was a three-day rock festival out at Charles Towne Landing that coincided with an alleged stomach virus and we're expecting the return of the crew sometime today. Meanwhile, my daughters and my sister have been doing the heavy lifting. No big deal. We're just glad to see you, that's all."

O'Malley shook Brad's hand and gave him a few words of sympathy. Louise gave Brad a warm hug and then she hugged Alex too.

"Now, Mr. Brad? Everything around here is just fine. I just want you to know that we are all here to help you and Alex get used to all the changes and all you gots to do is ask, all right? And, Miss Gracie? You had better *move yourself* and get their order in the kitchen!" She pointed her thumb to Gracie's customers, who were thus far water-less, bread-less and drink-less.

"Oh!" Embarrassed, Gracie scooted through the kitchen doors, giving Alex a little wave.

Alex was delighted and Bogart, a true male, gave her an approving woof.

It was not long before the telephones started ringing for dinner reservations and the lunch crowd was swollen to the point of a twenty-minute wait.

"Line two," Louise said, "it's Lindsey."

Lindsey was euphoric.

"Mom! My hair looks fabulous!"

"Woo-hoo! That's wonderful!"

"Mimi wants to talk to you. Hang on!"

"Hey!" Mimi said. "Remember that cute doctor I went out with last week?"

"Yeah," I said, with no clue of what was to follow.

"Well! How's this? He's got a friend he wants you to meet! A *date*, Linda! He's gonna call you this afternoon!"

I broke out in a sweat and I couldn't think.

"Who?" I said. "Who's going to call?"

"His name is Jason-something and he's this environmental scientist or biologist or I don't know . . . anyway, he came to Charleston to work at the aquarium but he wants to teach and so now he just took a job teaching at Wando High School. So! He's gonna call! *Be nice!"*

"Fine!" I said. *Be nice?* What did she think I was going to do? Go through the phone, bite his neck and suck his blood?

"Let me know when he does, okay? Oh, and wait until you see Lindsey! Don't you know she . . ."

All I could hear was *blah, blah, blah* . . . a man was going to call me and ask me for a date. Okay. Okay. I could handle it. As long as he wasn't married like all those bastards who had—

"Linda? Answer me!"

"What? Listen, I can't talk right now. Brad just got back and—"

"Oh! How's he doing? Did you meet his son? That was just awful, wasn't it? I'll tell you—"

"Mimi! I love you madly, but I gotta go! I've got piles of work here!"

"You know what, Linda? Sometimes you can be just a little bit coarse, do you know what I'm talking about?"

"Yeah. Sorry. I'll call you later."

I went back to entering data on the word processor. I was setting up a directory with contact information for everyone we did business with— fishmongers, kitchen supply companies, plumbers, greengrocers, electricians, cleaning supply houses—not very sexy, but it had to be done. And, I had to do payroll.

Brad did the rounds, checking out everything and talking to everyone and then came to my office, plopping himself in the chair opposite my desk.

"You okay?" I asked.

"Yeah, I'm okay. Just tired."

He did look tired, especially around his eyes.

"Funeral went all right?"

"It was horrible. First of all, Theo must have taken a Xanax or something like it because he could hardly speak. Then, Archie, my worst enemy of my entire life, comes up to me and says he's sorry for my loss."

"Holy hell! What did you say?"

"I wasn't very nice, I'm a little ashamed to say."

"Let's hear it word for word."

"I said, My *loss was your gain, wasn't it?*"

"Good for you! Nobody ever says what they think!"

"Yeah, well, I was so completely pissed off to be back there and reminded yet one more time that those three had brought so much pain and confusion to Alex's life, I just wanted to kick him in the teeth."

Brad had crossed his legs and his arms and it was clear he was still deeply upset.

"You know something?" I said. "I know we are all entitled to the pursuit of happiness, but I don't think it should be at the expense of somebody else's."

Brad stared at me for a minute.

"Look, if Loretta wanted Archie, that wasn't exactly fine with me, but our marriage was such a tangled web of duplicity and psychotic behavior, it didn't surprise me that it fell apart. I guess what bothered me was that Loretta never showed *any* remorse. And, Theo knew he was wrong about me and that he hadn't been fair with me on any one of a thousand issues over the years, and he never showed any remorse *either*."

"Well, you know what they say; the nuts don't fall very far from the trees."

"I think it was apples, but whatever. I just feel bad for Alex, you know?"

"Well, sure! Of course you do. He didn't ask for any of this to happen."

"Exactly. Anyway, horrible as it all was, Alex is probably better off with me. I just didn't like going through seeing that asshole Archie. And, you know? I actually felt sorry for Theo."

"Well, he's an old man and nobody, no matter how awful they are, should ever have to bury their child."

"Yeah. That's true. I'm just glad that part is behind us. Now there's the estate stuff, but thank God for Robert."

"He's taking care of it?"

"Yeah, he's got a cousin in Atlanta who's an estate lawyer, got a big firm and all that. I could not care less, but if Alex has any inheritance coming to him he should have it, right?"

"Right." I could sense that Brad had discussed the whole disaster as much as he could endure and I didn't want to pry. "Where's Alex now?"

"He's out on the dock with Duane, learning how to cut a deal with a longline guy."

"What's he got?"

"A load of blue mackerel that could feed half of Charleston County."

"I love blue mackerel—baked with crab meat? Yum!"

"So, what are you up to?"

"Organizing everything, a dull and dreary job to be sure. You know what I was thinking?"

"What?"

"That once a year we should put all our vendors out to bid, you know? Keep them honest so they don't inch up their prices and we get gypped?"

"Well, some of these guys are friends, so that makes it sticky, but some of the others aren't. I mean, they're nice guys and all . . ."

"Yeah, but isn't this a *business*? Come on, Brad! This isn't a frat house, is it?" I thought that a little teasing was in order, something that would get his mind back on work and lift his spirits.

"Well, we don't walk away from the kitchen supply guys so fast because they're invested in this restaurant! Before you go off and pull a vendor, you'd better let me know who it is."

"Ah! I see. Oopsie?" It had never occurred to me that some of the vendors might be investors. I hated to get caught being stupid. "You're right."

"This time, but not always. So tell me what went on while I was gone."

"Well, the cleaning service sent us this new man who looks like somebody from a rehab center for hard drugs."

"I'll keep an eye on him," Brad said. "By the way, your Gracie is a very pretty girl. I think Alex is a little taken with her."

"Thanks. And she's already gasping for air. Maybe they can go to the movies or something or the beach? Hey! I just remembered, I have to register Gracie for Wando High School next week. God, school starts so early here! Want me to take Alex too? Oh! Have you thought about where he's going? I mean, you might want to put him in Porter-Gaud or something."

"I'm a big believer in public school education," he said. "My mom was a teacher for thirty years. Taught English and American literature. Gee, God. I didn't even think to bring his transcript."

"I can call for it, if you want. Just tell me where he went to school and I'll do it right away."

"He went to Lovett in Buckhead."

"Private school?"

"Thought you had me?" He gave a small grin.

"Just kidding!"

"Lovett was Loretta's doing, not mine. Anyway, things are going to be very different for him now."

"As they are for Gracie too." I looked at him and he seemed so subdued. "Look, anything I can do to help . . ."

"The school thing would be great—where is Wando High School anyway?"

"Out on Mathis Ferry Road—hey, we can carpool!"

"Excellent. We can meet at the Piggly Wiggly."

The office phone rang and Brad picked it up.

"It's for you," he said, holding his hand over the mouthpiece. "It's a man named Jason. Who's Jason?" He narrowed his eyes in suspicion.

The old Brad was back, at least for the moment.

"My next husband," I said. I held out my hand to take the receiver and he held it over his head out of my reach. "Oh, *grow up* and give me the phone!"

He handed it to me and said, "Someone you met in a chat room?"

"Hello? This is Linda Breland speaking," I said, in my very professional voice.

"Hi! This is Jason Miller calling—I'm a friend of Jack Taylor? He said I would call?"

"Yes! Of course! How are you?"

"*How are you?*" Brad said in a little girlie voice, teasing me.

"Great!" Jason said. "I thought maybe we could meet for a drink or something?"

"Sure! That sounds fine! When?"

"*Sure! That sounds fine!*" Brad said, then whispered, "You'd better make sure he's not a serial murderer, you know."

"I'm sorry, what did you say? I missed it because I have a juvenile delinquent in my office harassing me!"

"No problem," Jason said. "I said, how about tonight around seven? How's the Shem Creek Bar and Grill? We can spy on the competition!"

"Perfect! See you then."

I hung up and looked at Brad, who was pretending innocence.

"I have a life, you know," I said.

"I hope so," Brad said.

"Hey, Brad? You okay?"

"Yeah, I'm fine. Seriously, I am." He stared at me for a minute and then said, "This weekend is gonna be crazy—Fourth of July and all that. You'd better get your rest."

"What do you think I'm gonna do? Carry on with this guy all night?"

"No. Of course not. I just . . ."

"Don't worry, I'll be home before curfew."

I had a date. Brad was teasing me about it. Was he jealous? Was that it? Not a chance. Maybe Jason Miller *would* be the man of my dreams. Who knew?

TEN

SOUTHERN ITALIAN
WEDDING PLANS

———◆———

I went to work early the next morning because I had a ton of phone calls to make. Louise had to run up to Pawleys Island to take care of her cousin who was recovering from an emergency appendectomy. Fourth of July weekend and we were shorthanded again.

"I feel terrible," she said.

"Don't think a thing about it," I said.

I was in my office, drinking my third cup of coffee for the morning when Brad arrived.

"So, how was your hot date last night?" he said.

I was reasonably sure that his question, his itsy-bitsy innocent question, was intended as polite. But the prior evening's close encounter had been one of the terrorist kind. Reliving any part of it put me in a foul humor.

"That guy can kiss my endangered species," I said. "Would you like to hear why I'm gonna be single for the rest of my life?"

Yes, Brad was mourning but all the signals he was sending my way said that he wanted life to be normal around the restaurant, and as normal as humanly possible when dealing with him. If he wanted to talk about Loretta, he would probably do so with Robert and with his son. Or if he wanted to talk to me, I would gladly listen.

"Sure, why not?" He sat opposite me. "We got any fresh coffee around here?"

"Oh, sure! I juss run fetch 'em fuh yah, massah!" It was not evolving into one of my better days. The feminist bitch in me climbed not quite all the way back in its cage. "Let me get you a cup."

I leapt from my seat, bolted from the office, poured him a cup of black steaming coffee and presented it to him, bowing low, indicating my grasp of my lowly stature. A serf. A peon. An indentured servant. An untouchable. A little joke.

"I like a shot of half-and-half in mine," he said, shooting me a grin of mock disappointment.

"Get it yourself," I said and sat back down in my chair.

He sort of laughed and I pretended to be wildly irritated, making the same kinds of teeth-sucking sounds my daughters made when I served Brussels sprouts. *Snnnk! Snnnk! Snnnk!*

"Ooh, hoo! *Somebody* didn't have fun last night! What happened? Rape artist?"

"I wish! Listen . . . oh, God! Can I just tell you something? Ever since I divorced Fred, if there's a *psycho*, or a *nut bag*, or a freaking *maniac* out there on the loose, he's got my phone number and I've been out with him at least once!"

"Come on, tell Uncle Brad what happened."

Uncle Brad. I thought, well, he wants a diversion so I'll give him a story to lighten things up.

"You're not going to *believe* . . . okay, so I'm supposed to meet this guy Jason Miller at seven o'clock at Shem Creek Bar and Grill, right? I walk in and there are three guys at the bar. One of them is wearing a suit and has a briefcase, so I say, nah, not him. The next one is wearing camouflage and rubber boots—not him. And the *third* guy is wearing khakis and a knit shirt. . . ."

"So you go up to the guy in the khakis and . . ."

"Right! Guess what? Jason Miller is wearing camouflage and rubber boots to meet me for a drink. Nice?"

"Very polished! Suave fellow, this Jason."

"Sure! Snicker! Go 'head! He looked like he had been crawling around in the freaking swamp! In fact, he had been! Anyway, he starts impressing me right away by telling me what he does for a living. . . ."

"Reenacts war games?"

"Worse. He just moved here from North Carolina, where he got himself in trouble—almost—for being a political activist. Seems they've got some kind of problem with the runoff of hog waste from farms that's trickling down to the Cape Fear River. You may not know this, but if you pile enough hog waste in the river, it can kill everything in its path."

"I'm just . . . shocked! Do I look shocked?"

"Exactly! Like who cares, right? I just sat there, drinking my miserable little glass of white wine listening to his whole way-too-well-rehearsed lecture on watersheds and waste management, thinking I might throw up any second."

"Hog poop is some toxic shit."

"Very funny, boss. Anyway, that was my date with Mr. Wonderful. You know what I think?"

"Let's hear it."

"I think that even though it's not fair, that love is for young people. You know?"

"That's pretty depressing, don't you think?"

"No, yes, maybe . . . but it sure seems that way. I mean, I have two almost grown daughters, spider veins in my ankles and little wrinkles around my eyes. I know that I've got mileage and that should be okay, but it's not."

"Of course it's okay! What kind of a mood are you in?"

"Look, Brad, on the rare occasion when I meet someone who is available, I look at every possibility and try to see myself in that person's life. But you get to a certain age and your own world is already so orchestrated, there's almost no room for somebody else and their whole load of stuff. And, you know what else? I'm tired."

"Tired? Tired from what? One date with a tree hugger?"

"No, I'm just tired of the whole mental exercise of sifting through other people's minds and struggling to see myself with them or that I'm like them—it just never works. For me, anyway."

"Well, Robert actually has a woman he wants me to meet. She's supposed to be gorgeous."

"She's probably just out of high school."

"Oh, come on . . ."

"So, call her up!"

"Sure. Easy for you to say. Loretta's not even cold yet!"

"True, but listen, you hadn't lived with her in ages. You're entitled to some female companionship. If you've got the strength."

"I've got the strength, Miss Jersey, thank you. But, Alex just got here and I think it would upset him, you know? I'm just going to wait for a little while, that's all. Besides, I'm not ready for women yet and this may sound funny, but I don't think Alex realizes that Loretta is really gone. And in a little ironic twist, here I am divorcing her for adultery and she dies before I have the pleasure. There's just no justice in the world anymore."

"Boy, you can say that again."

There was a long pause in our conversation then. I was thinking that my girls probably still viewed being in South Carolina as a temporary vacation. Moving into the boathouse would alter that for sure. When I looked at Brad again I sensed that he was confiding things that perhaps he would not have told someone else. I was getting to know him and we were becoming friends.

"I think losing parents is hard enough when you're our age, you know? I mean, Alex is young and Loretta didn't exactly die easily. You know, it was pretty tragic."

"Yeah, tragic for her and for her father. I couldn't tell you what Alex is thinking for the life of me."

"Well, boys are notorious for not talking about what's bugging them. I mean, that's what they say, anyway." I waited a moment before speaking again. "About boys. Have you heard from her father?"

"He calls Alex every night."

"That's intense."

"Yeah." Brad breathed a deep sigh. "Yeah, it is."

Brad got up to leave and begin his workday.

"Hey, Brad?" I said. "Maybe you should have Alex see a therapist for grief counseling? I mean, it's done all the time . . . very normal and all that."

"Maybe in New Jersey," he said.

"Oh, fun-gool!"

"Um, that's Italian for something very bad. . . ."

"So what? And, how do you know?"

"I'm Italian."

"Yeah, right, and I'm the Queen of England."

"I became Italian when I moved to South Carolina—at least in my brains. I decided they have a better attitude. You know, about life."

"You're a little odd, you know. Anyway, my sister knows all these doctors and if you decide a counselor might be a good thing . . ."

"I just want to get Alex settled in school. When does it start?"

"August the eleventh."

"That's soon! By the way . . ." Brad reached in his shirt pocket and pulled out a piece of paper, handing it to me. "Here's the name of his guidance counselor at Lovett . . . you had mentioned you might . . ."

"Sure, no problem. I'll call him first thing. I'm taking Gracie in to register at Wando next Tuesday at noon—want me to pick up Alex?"

"Sure. You know what? Let's go together—Alex would probably feel better if I'm there too."

"You're right. I'll arrange it."

Needless to say, the weekend was crazy on Shem Creek. Countless boats decorated with red, white and blue balloons and crepe paper, and of course American flags, floated by the restaurant and the take from the sunset bar broke all records. That night on the sunset deck, you could see fireworks from every direction, and although my feet were aching, the display was so fabulous that I was exhilarated and giddy every time another blast of fire and color would explode in bursts and waterfalls all over the dark sky. We all were. Brad was up top with O'Malley and while none of us were the types who would wax patriotic, all of us were misty-eyed by the depth of the meaning behind the holiday.

O'Malley said, "Thank God for the Chinese!"

To which Brad added, "Thank God for our forefathers!"

I just remember nodding my head and continuing to take drink orders.

I was exhausted by Tuesday, but ready and determined to do battle again. One of the wonderful things about public schools was that they were very accommodating. I had set everything up at Wando in less than five minutes, including an appointment with a guidance counselor for Gracie's curriculum planning. Getting the copy of Alex's transcript was more problematic.

The gargantuan endowment funds of private schools landed me on the other end of yet another experiment in technology. First, I had the pleasure of listening to an electronic laundry list of what extension I wanted and none of them fit the bill. I redialed the number and sat on hold for so long that I forgot who I was calling, who it turned out was not there anyway. I finally got somebody in the guidance department who said Brad had to sign a release form and then . . . I mean, the whole world had become so suspicious . . . I mean, were they really worried about identity theft of a fifteen-year-old boy? Probably.

I was trying to think about my blessings and finally finished preparing the bank deposit from last night's business when a flashy blonde appeared at the reception area with an old geezer who was at least twice her age. Not only was she flashy, but she was buxom. Now, I'm not an expert in plastic surgery, but I would venture a guess that she was something of a graduate from a spot on *Extreme Makeovers*.

We were not open yet, but the front door was, so occasionally someone would wander in, looking lost. It probably wasn't a good idea to leave the door wide open until I returned from the bank, just for security reasons. We took in a large amount of cash every night, especially at the bar because some patrons didn't want their watering habits to show up on their credit card bills.

"Can I help you?"

"Hi!" she said and stuck out her hand. "We're getting married Labor Day weekend, that Saturday—just a small wedding and my fiancé and I— um, this is Douglas Lutz. . . ."

When the old man smiled, twenty years fell away from his face. He was mad for her. I thought she said her name was Lucy.

"So, Doc and I thought it might be fun to have a little dinner reception here."

"Sure!" I said. "What's the date?"

"Saturday, August thirtieth."

"How many people will you be?"

"Oh! I think around twenty to twenty-five. It's not exactly our first waltz around the barn, if you know what I mean?"

I just nodded my head and thought, well, there's hope for everyone.

"I'll be right back," I said, "why don't y'all just look over the menu for a minute."

Shoot, I thought, Louise usually handled private parties. I had zero experience with special events. But how complicated could it be? I decided I would show them around and give them a menu to take home. Then I would call Louise and find out what to do.

I was on my knees, putting the bank deposit sack back in the safe because I had decided to go to the bank after the bride and groom left or maybe on the way to Wando High School, when Gracie and Alex bounced in. Gracie's bounce nearly scared the liver out of me.

"Hi, Mom! Waddup?"

"Good Lord, honey! I didn't even hear you come in!" I threw the sack in the safe, which was hidden in the closet. I turned the key to lock it and returned it to its hiding place on the top of the door frame. "What time is it?"

"We're early, but I figured if you weren't busy maybe we could go get this root canal over with. Besides, I'm starving to death."

"Well, we have an appointment. We can't just go walking in. Go get yourself a crab cake or something."

"You want a crab cake?" Gracie said, turning to Alex, who was leaning against the door to the office, exuding young masculine scent, which I could not have caught a whiff of in a thousand years but which had Gracie thoroughly intoxicated. "I mean, we should eat something before we go sign our lives away to this redneck hell."

"Sure," he said.

"It's not hell. Hell is no air-conditioning and I'll be about ten minutes—just finishing up with a bride and groom."

"Okay," Gracie said. "Come on, Alex."

"Okay."

This Alex kid may have been short on conversation but he was way long on dangerous good looks. And although Gracie was still taking cheap shots at the south in general, the arrival of Alex had mitigated her pain.

I found Lucy and Douglas out on the dock. There they were, just as I was every day, completely mesmerized by the continuous rhythm of Shem Creek's dance. They were holding hands and cooing like young lovers. They were thoroughly adorable. A shrimp boat was attempting to tie up at the far end of the docks. Several small fiberglass boats were motoring by, barely observing the *no wake* rule. Pelicans and seagulls swooped all around while others stood guard on the pilings. It was a gorgeous morning with a sky so blue and the air so sweet with salt and breeze it would have lifted the heart of the worst curmudgeon. Even mine.

"It's beautiful out here, isn't it?" I said.

"I was just saying to Doc that I could feel my soul flying all around, like it had thousands of eyes and just wanted to take it all in. Do you know what I mean?"

"Yeah," I said, "I do. Everything here is so alive, right?"

"Yes," Lucy said, "like us."

I smiled at that. "Sometimes I try to memorize it and I can't hold it all in my head. When it rains and it's overcast for a few days, I forget how everything just sort of pulsates when it's clear because it's all moving, all the time—the water, the birds, the sun—well, it really is something."

"It's just what we wanted," Doc said, "someplace unpretentious, lively and romantic all at the same time. And, slightly Italian. No better spot that I know of."

"Me either," I said. "Tell me. If you don't think I'm being nosy, how did y'all meet? I love stories about brides and grooms."

"I'm marrying the girl next door," Doc said. "Well, actually, she lives next door to my daughter on the Isle of Palms."

"I went over with a casserole the day she moved in and we met. I took one look at him and my heart just started *raaacing!*"

"See? Southern hospitality!" I said. "You never know, right?"

"Yep! It's a good thing I had something in my freezer!" Lucy said and brushed Doc's hair away from his forehead. "And we've been together ever since!"

"That's wonderful," I said, handing them a card with my name and phone number and also Louise's name. "Louise will be back tomorrow, I hope. Anyway, if you'll give me your phone number . . ."

We exchanged contact information and talked about a few other things like flowers, a wedding cake and the frozen margaritas Lucy wanted to serve for sentimental reasons.

"I know you don't have the final say-so on this," Lucy said, "but Doc and I were just talking and we thought it would be so romantic if we could use the roof bar for our dinner. You see, that's how we fell in love . . . on my widow's walk where we used to go to watch the sunset, gosh . . . remember?"

She raised her chin to Doc, who looked down at her like Romeo to her Juliet.

"All those blender drinks? I sure do, kitten," he said.

"And don't you think we should have Italian food?"

"Whatever you want, kitten."

What could I say? Meow? We were not truly an Italian restaurant, but we could fake that part. And, I knew that Brad would kill me if I let them take over the sunset deck for their dinner, because that was the cash cow of all times. It easily held a huge crowd and that would be a lot of money to flush in the name of love. So I weaseled around with my answer.

"You know what? I can't commit for that because of the size of the space, but let me ask. Maybe we could work out something special for a cocktail hour and then dinner downstairs with a little privacy. Maybe if we book it before the regular dinner hour begins? I don't know. But I'll ask."

"We could always invite more people," Lucy said.

Doc just grinned at that, patted her arm and said, "We'll call you to-morrow."

We shook hands and they left with menus under their arms. I could see them smiling even though their backs were facing me. Their happiness radiated with each step in the same way the haze of morning mist rose from the water. It was impossible to grab the mist or their happiness, but all the same you knew it was there. They had something so hopeful and beautiful and I wanted them to have whatever kind of dinner would make them happy. Italian? Why not?

Kitten? Ah, well. I wasn't and never had been anyone's kitten.

But, maybe the day was not turning out so bad after all. One date should not have turned me sour on the idea of a relationship. If there was hope for a dingbat like her, there was definitely hope for a slightly aged Jersey magnolia like me. At some point.

I found Brad with Gracie and Alex in the kitchen.

"Guess what?" Brad said.

"They found out who was buried in Grant's tomb?" I said.

"Oh, that's pathetic, Mother."

Mother?

"Okay, I give up. What?"

"I just hired Alex and Gracie to work in the kitchen after school. They're gonna prep vegetables for Duane. Minimum wage, three hours, three days a week. Unless of course Alex plays football and Gracie becomes a cheerleader, that is."

"I'd rather take a needle straight through my eye than put on a short skirt and act like an ass," Gracie said, waiting for a reaction.

"I don't know," Alex said. "Some cheerleaders are hot."

"Do you play football?"

"Yeah, for two years. Quarterback."

"Gosh."

Brad and I exchanged the nod of parental recognition that pompoms and splits were in Gracie's future and ball games were in ours.

"Let's go, you two." I said, "Time's money."

We took Brad's car for the short drive to Wando High School. The entire back of my Blazer was still crammed with boxes from New Jersey. What was the point of unloading when I'd be moving soon? I was conserving energy.

The front office directed us to the guidance counselors assigned to our children and we agreed to meet in the lobby when we were finished.

"Well, this all looks in order," Mrs. Hagerty said, going over Gracie's transcript. "Here's your schedule. You're signed up for driver's ed, in case you're curious."

"Sweet," Gracie said.

"In fact, some of your new teachers are still in their classrooms today 'cause summer school's in session. Why don't you have a walk around and introduce yourself?"

"I can't believe we have to go to school in *August!* I mean, in New Jersey we never went to school until after Labor Day!"

"Well, sugar, you're not in New Jersey anymore," said Mrs. Hagerty. "Now, go on and move yourself!"

Gracie shot me a look of insecurity.

"Do you want me to go with you?" I said.

"Gracie! How old are you?" Mrs. Hagerty said, taking off her reading glasses.

"I'll be sixteen in two months."

"Well, honey, if you're going to be driving around the countryside in a few weeks, you ought to be able to find your way around a building now."

"I can go with you if you'd like. . . ."

"Mom! I can handle this!" Gracie leapt to the door, turned back and spat, "She thinks I'm a baby."

"I do not," I said, and then regretted even answering her.

"Do too!" came the voice from a distance.

When there was silence in the hall, Mrs. Hagerty said, "Why should your teenager be any different than the rest of them?"

We swapped horror stories for a while—tales of drugs, safe sex, sex at all, college planning, clubs and sports—and when Gracie still had not returned, I decided to go and find her myself. I had lingered long enough in Barbara Hagerty's office, not that she was fidgeting over it.

"Listen, thanks a lot for all your help," I said. "I would like to be an involved parent, so if you ever need anything . . ."

"I'll let you know," she said, adding, "Don't worry about Gracie. I'll keep an eye on her."

"Thanks." I meant it.

I wandered down the halls, passing open classrooms, remembering being a high school student and all the anxiety of starting a new school year. What would the girls be like? Would I find a boyfriend? How hard would my classes be? Would I like any of my teachers? And, that had been decades ago. The stresses facing Gracie here and Lindsey at NYU were monumental compared to how the world had turned on its axis in my day. Gracie had her picture taken for an ID badge that she was required to wear at all times on school grounds—for security reasons, Mrs. Hagerty had said, but I suspected it was to deter drug dealers and weed out troublemakers.

I stopped to read a poster on a bulletin board in the hall.

BE GREEN!
JOIN THE OCEAN CLUB TODAY

Save the Environment by Becoming an Advocate!
Just like humans, the ocean's population needs oxygen to breathe!

ENEMIES:	ALLIES:
Developers and Big Business	Ecologists and Biologists
Motor boats and Jet Skis	Better Government
Pesticides and Asphalt	Maybe YOU!

See: Mr. Miller in Room 318 for more information. TODAY!

Mr. Miller? I thought, no way, it couldn't be Jason Miller, could it? I moved myself as fast as possible to Room 318 and sure enough, Jason Miller was behind his desk, folding paper. He looked up and saw me.

"Hi!" I said, not knowing exactly what to do. "Remember me?"

"Of course. Come in."

"Oh, no, that's okay. I was just looking for Gracie."

"That's your daughter? I just met her. She's a very bright girl."

"Thanks."

"She's in my marine bio class. I think she'll do very well."

"Good. Well . . . nice to see you again." I was hemming and hawing all over the place.

"I think she took a left out of my door. . . ."

"A left?"

He pointed and I pointed and after some consternation I figured out which way left was. I gave him a little wave and escaped, thinking about what a creep he was.

I found Brad, Alex and Gracie in the lobby as planned. All the way back to the restaurant, the kids talked nonstop about their teachers and schedules, bragging to each other about what a piece of cake the year was going to be, compared to the horrible burdens they had borne at their prior schools. Even though I knew better, I was relieved to see the enthusiasm in both of them, and when I would glance at Brad I could see that he was too.

Everything was fine until I went to Gracie's room late in the evening to say good night.

"Love you, baby," I said.

"Me too." She said, "Mom?"

"Yeah?"

"Didn't you have a date with Mr. Miller?"

"For about twenty minutes," I said, "he's not my type."

"Too bad," she said, turning out her light. "He's a genius."

"Hey, Gracie? You okay about going to Wando?"

"Do I have a choice?"

I was standing there beside her bed in the darkened room, feeling very insecure. I wanted her to like it here so badly and I was worried. Worried that she would rebel and not study and ruin her future. Worried she would run away. Worried that it would be over before it began.

"Well," I said, "let's give it a try, okay, baby? For all of our sakes."

"Oh, Mom, don't be so dramatic. It's not the end of the world, for God's sake."

"Thanks, honey," I said and leaned over her, giving the top of her head a kiss. "It means a lot to me."

She didn't answer me, but I could almost read her mind. On one hand, she was stuck in what she viewed as Confederate mud. On the other, maybe it wasn't as terrible to be here as she had thought it would be. I hoped that over the next few weeks, she would come around. After all, she wasn't the only urban expatriate—now there was Alex.

ELEVEN

LINDSEY'S LAUNCH PAD

OVER the next four weeks, we had established a routine and Mount Pleasant was starting to feel like home. The Epsteins had promised the boathouse to some friends for two weeks but after that they promised to give it a fresh coat of paint and get it ready for us. Moving day was scheduled for August twenty-third. I thought we would all have pushed Mimi to the edge of her sanity by then, but she insisted that she loved having us around.

Lindsey had been helping around the kitchen at the restaurant, along with Alex and Gracie, peeling mountains of onions, potatoes and shrimp in the final weeks leading up to her departure, which was a good thing as the work gave her spending money for school.

On their time off, the three of them went to the beach on Sullivan's Island and saw every movie released during July and August. They were the most tan I had ever seen them, in spite of the fact that I was always warning them to use sunscreen. When the same full tube I had bought them in July appeared on the floor of my car in August, it was obvious they were not using it. But they were happy and earning money and I thought it was probably the best summer of their lives.

Speaking of annoyances, my next job of the day was to call good old

Fred and make sure that he would pick up Lindsey at Newark Airport on Friday night of the following week. If I wanted Fred to do anything, he wanted plenty of notice. I decided to do it early in the day to get it over with. I dialed his cell and he answered.

"Fred Breland."

I loved that. Not *hello* or anything remotely friendly. Just *Fred Breland.*

"Hey, Fred, it's me."

"Oh. Hello, Linda."

Sure, inquire about my health or general well-being, why don't you? Ask about your children!

"The reason I'm calling you is about Lindsey? Remember she's arriving a week from Friday?"

"Airline? Flight number?"

I gave him the information and hung up. Talking to Fred was like inhaling a big bottle of ammonia. Every time I had to speak to him, I always wondered how I had ever managed to get excited about sleeping with him. Only the good Lord knew what Patti saw in him.

Fred had not made a single remark to inquire if Lindsey was excited or nervous. He had not said, *Is there anything else I can do?* Hell, no. For Fred, that would have been tantamount to giving blood.

On the other side of the spectrum, Brad decided we should do something nice for Lindsey before she went off to school, and naturally a big dinner was his choice. It had to be early, because we all had to work the dinner hour, but that didn't bother anyone.

It was Friday the twenty-second. Brad and Louise set up a table for us by the windows. Helium-filled foil balloons were attached to the backs of the chairs. They had messages on them. *Bon Voyage! Congratulations! Good Luck!* I guess he couldn't find ones that said *Ciao!*

Anyway, it looked very festive, considering how rustic the restaurant was. Can we just pause for a moment to say that the term *rustic* was probably generous? I had never said anything to Brad about it because I would not have wanted to hurt his feelings. I mean, he thought it was fabulous!

Can I tell you something? No one but *no one* would ever have accused his decorator of setting his budget on fire.

In New Jersey, this place would have been under the watchdog eye of the state health department. But in South Carolina, a ramshackle old dump was where you would find the very freshest of fresh seafood. Weird but true. Martha Stewart would have taken one look at this place and hyperventilated herself into oblivion.

The dining room walls were constructed of salvaged woods probably found in construction Dumpsters and the same could be said of the floors, except for the stretches of mismatched linoleum hammered in place and secured by duct tape along the edges. Old tin signs advertising everything from eggs to gasoline covered the walls, interspersed with football jerseys hung on dowels from all the colleges in South Carolina. Across the ceiling and around the perimeter of the room were ropes and ropes of every variety of retired buoy you can name—small ones from crab traps, big fat ones from lobster traps—all of them with chipped paint scars, remnants of old fishing dreams.

Even the doors to the kitchen were appropriately humble—heavy red plastic sewn to metal rods that swung open, dancing with the bustle of passing waiters or swaying in a strong breeze. Everything was alive and breathing, right down to the growing collage of business cards stuck to the bulletin board by the front door and the pictures of customers from the opening party that were affixed to the bar under layers and layers of clear polyurethane.

Jackson Hole felt like it had always been there, very much like an old friend waiting to throw an arm around your shoulder and offer you a cool drink. And, since we all worked there, it was the perfect place for a going-away dinner for Lindsey.

The day, like the entire month, had been a scorcher with temperatures in the high nineties. The humidity was performing unspeakable acts on my hair, which annoyed me to no end. In fact, the humidity of South Carolina's Lowcountry in August was the reason God invented ponytails.

I was feeling exhausted, cranky, sticky, ugly, fat, old and moody. And, I am ashamed to admit this, but the last thing I wanted was a party.

I realized the real reason I was so off-kilter was that Lindsey was leaving me. All along I had been so thrilled that Lindsey was accepted to NYU that I hadn't stopped to consider what her leaving would actually feel like when it finally happened. And of course, we were living in New Jersey when she was accepted, not seven hundred miles away. With the passing of each minute, I was becoming increasingly weepy. It was a lot like nursing a terminally ill family member. During the illness you were completely obsessed with meeting their needs. But when they closed their eyes for the last time, you were shocked by the fact that your diligence and affection had still led up to their demise. I had cared lovingly for Lindsey every day of her life, preparing her for this moment. She was excited and I was depressed. I just wasn't ready. It was yet another test of my stiff upper lip, which betrayed me with quivers every time I tried to speak. And my stupid eyes—no matter how I struggled to maintain my reserve, they would well up. Intellectually, I knew it was ridiculous. Emotionally, I was a two-year-old, bordering on a tantrum.

We got together at four and everyone found a place at the table. Duane announced that he had prepared a special dish for Lindsey, who, all summer long, had shown strong support and sympathy for his most bizarre medleys. This announcement, of course, produced heavy eye-rolling from Louise, which led to stealth rib-poking and guffaws followed up with Louise cutting everyone her most threatening eye. But we began our meal with our trademark crab dip (ours actually had crab meat in it) and Waverly crackers, a basket of steaming hush puppies and cups of peppered seafood chowder. It was delicious and we were all eating like starving fieldhands.

Brad tried to offer a toast, but the racket coming from our table was so loud that it took him a few minutes to get our group to settle down.

"I just want to say . . ."

Ping! Ping! Ping! He tapped his glass with his knife.

"Ladies? Gentlemen?"

Finally, everyone became quiet.

"I just wanted to say how much I have enjoyed getting to know you, Lindsey. I remember the day I left home for Emory University. My stomach was all in knots and my mother was a mess, all weepy and moody like your momma is today. . . ."

"I am not. . . ."

Yes, you are! came the resounding chorus.

Oh, fine, I thought, trying to collect myself before I started to wail like a baby. Mimi passed me a tissue and I took it, knowing I would probably need it.

"Anyway, I just wanted to say something about the importance of this occasion. Too often we take things for granted—a holiday meal, someone's birthday—you cook, you run out and buy a gift and then it's over. Many of these occasions are not life-changing, but this one is. Lindsey, you've arrived at a threshold and, once you pass through, the world will consider you a young woman. That may not sound like news, but life after high school is very different."

Brad stopped talking as though he hadn't really finished his thought. He just stood there at the head of the table, glancing in the direction of Alex, who seemed slightly more somber than usual. Speaking about pivotal moments had surely reminded Alex about his mother's death, and being somewhat selfish, I hoped Loretta wouldn't become a topic of conversation. Brad spoke again. However forced it was, he grinned from ear to ear while speaking.

"Anyway, I just wanted to encourage you to savor the whole experience. Now I realize you spent the first eighteen years of your life in the New York area, but living in the city is a horse of another color. Join a sorority or some clubs, see all the sights—it's a very exciting place—try different food and get the recipes for us. . . ."

Everyone chuckled at that and the gray mood floated away. Brad wished Lindsey good luck, gave her a peck on the cheek and a card with a fresh hundred-dollar bill inside.

"Oh! Gosh! Thanks!" Lindsey said. "I didn't expect this! I didn't expect anything!"

"It's WAM," Brad said, and when it became obvious that no one knew what he meant, he said, "*Walking around money*. Don't ever go walking around without a little WAM in your pockets."

"Brad's right," Mimi said, "you don't want the robbers to go away disappointed!"

Classic Mimi.

Mimi had brought Lindsey a pink wool muffler she had knitted that must have been ten feet long. "It gets mighty cold up there in New York," she said. When I looked at her like she must've thought we were complete ignoramuses regarding real live full-strength winter weather, she added, "Y'all! I watch Willard Scott every day!"

Louise had a gift for Lindsey too—a digital alarm clock like those sold in the drugstores.

"Listen, this way you won't be late for class, and if you break this, let me know and I'll send you another one. Remember, you never be flashy because people will judge you by your possessions. It ain't right, but that's how it is."

Lindsey blew Louise a kiss and said, "It's perfect!"

O'Malley gave her a dictionary and thesaurus, saying, "I know they'll have these at school, but it's good to have your own, you know? I wrote something in them too so you won't forget me or this summer."

"I'll be back, O'Malley," she said and leaned over to hug his neck.

The generous gestures brought a glow to Lindsey's face that reminded me it had been too long since she had been singled out for recognition. I was very grateful to Brad and to everyone else too.

Duane had baked flounder stuffed with lump meat crab for the table and served it all around with fresh asparagus sautéed in lemon and butter. Then with great flourish, he placed his pièce de résistance in front of Lindsey. It was a tower of shellfish and fish separated by paper-thin wafers that appeared to be made with cracked pepper or maybe sesame seeds. There was a red satin sauce drizzled all over the plate in a looping design and everything was sprinkled with minced parsley and dill. I wished I'd brought my camera.

Louise's eyeballs had mysteriously tripled in size, bulging in their sockets. "Just what the heck do you call that, Mr. Doo-wayne?"

"Tour de Mer," he said, with a slight indignant hiss.

"Tour de *who*?" Louise said, with a grunt.

"*La mer, la mer!* The sea, the sea!" There was nothing Duane liked better than to torture Louise. "That's your whole problem, Ms. Louise. No imagination."

"I don't need imagination when you got enough for *all* of us!" she shot right back. But in a moment of curiosity, she stuck her finger in the deep red sauce on Lindsey's plate and literally purred when she tasted it. "What's that? Tomato?"

"Coulis of pomegranate," he said, smiling his most superior smile of food snob victory.

"Well, if that don't beat all. . . ."

We began to eat amid snickers and chatter about what Lindsey thought NYU would be like, and eventually the talk turned to Alex and Gracie's experiences in their new school.

"Football practice is rough," Alex said. "I thought Lovett was tough but these guys are animals."

"But, it's good, right?" Brad said.

"Yeah, if you like the taste of your own blood," Alex said.

"Ew! Disgusting!" Gracie said.

"You're just pissed because you're not a cheerleader," Alex said, "but you can join dance team."

"Whatever," Gracie said, "you're just pissed because you're still playing JV! Besides, I'm auditioning to take modern dance lessons at Charleston Ballet, and in between I'm working on a river sweep with Mr. Miller."

"Would someone like to tell me what a river sweep is?" I said.

"Mom, you have no idea what's going on around here. I mean, did you know that Shem Creek is dead?"

"What are you talking about?" Louise said. "Look down there on the dock. See that big old pelican? What's he eating on?"

We glanced outside and sure enough, there was an enormous pelican tearing the insides out of a huge fish. Not exactly a lovely sight to behold from the dinner table, but if Shem Creek was dead, where did he get the fish? Simmons Seafood Market? No, not likely.

"That fish came from a fishing boat," Gracie said, "and it might have come out of these waters but I'll tell you this. There's no shrimp and no oysters here anymore."

"I'd still like to know what a river sweep is," I said and was completely ignored.

"Where'd they go?" Brad said. "Murrell's Inlet?"

Naturally, Mimi, Louise, Brad and I thought that was a clever enough remark, but I've also learned that what an adult may find amusing a teenager may use to skewer you. I looked at Gracie and saw that she was about to take to the pulpit for a sermon to educate us.

"Look," Gracie began, "you guys might not think—"

"*You guys?* If you want them to listen," Alex said, "don't talk *Yankee.*"

"Oh, puh-leeze," Gracie said. "Look, *everyone!* Good enough, Alex?"

He shrugged, indicating it was not exactly what he expected, but he didn't know my Gracie. She would only say *y'all* on her deathbed pleading to the southern saints for time off in Purgatory.

"Anyway, there's a whole environmental disaster growing all over South Carolina and if something's not done about it, it's gonna be bad."

"What are you talking about?" Brad said. "I mean, over the last twenty years all these laws have been passed about clean water and recycling. I thought things were getting better. Can somebody pass the tartar sauce?"

"Sure," Mimi said, handing the squeeze bottle to Louise to pass to Brad. "Brad's right, Gracie darlin', I mean everybody recycles now."

"Well, maybe you do, but there are still plenty of people who dump their garbage in the creek. That's what the river sweep is about. Picking up garbage," Gracie said. "Anyway, the bigger problem is about all these new developments. You know that parking lot at the Kmart? The one out on Highway Seventeen?"

"The one as big as Alaska?" Lindsey said.

"Yeah, that's the one. So, every time there's a big rainfall—which is about every other day all summer long—there's nowhere for the water to go, since asphalt doesn't absorb water?"

"So what?" Alex said.

"So what? So *what?*" Gracie said, so excited that she was momentarily unconcerned about losing Alex's favor. "I'll tell you *so what*. How about that all that water runs into a little tiny tidal creek along with petroleum, chemicals from cars, garbage people toss like cigarette butts and soda cans and kills all the baby shrimp and fish that used to get hatched there?"

"And, that tidal creek feeds into Shem Creek?" Lindsey said.

"You got it!" Gracie said.

"And you learned all this from Mr. Miller?" I said.

"Yep," she said. "He's amazing, Mom. He showed us this film about these guys throwing a net to catch some flounder in Shem Creek at high tide. So they left the net there until low tide and all the fish died. Wanna know why?"

"Actually, yeah," Brad said. "I'd like to know."

"Because at low tide there's not enough oxygen in the water for even flounder."

"Gross," Alex said.

"Yeah, gross," Gracie said. "So anyway, that's what I learned in my life-altering experience in school today. It's pretty intense and I don't think people know about it."

I was about to say that Jason Miller was a wacko but then I thought better of it. Maybe this was a good thing, even though I suspected that one reason Gracie was aligning herself with Miller was because I had rejected him. But, maybe having Gracie involved in a community project would raise her consciousness above the usual teenage rebellious garbage she brought home to my doorstep like the neighborhood alley cat dragging in a dead something that thrilled the cat but left you disgusted.

"Well, Gracie, maybe all us old dogs can learn a few new tricks from you!" I said.

Gracie sat a little higher in her seat and Alex shook his head in approval.

Lindsey, who was always the least talkative of all of us, cleared her throat.

"What, baby?" I said.

"Well, I was just thinking that it might be interesting to take some courses in marine biology. You know, I was just running it around my head, that's all. I mean, if South Carolina is really going to be our home from now on . . . maybe someday Gracie and I could figure out how to, I don't know, educate the public and do something about it too."

"Ah! The Mighty Breland sisters conquer the world!" Gracie said. "I seriously doubt it."

Later that night, Lindsey, Gracie, Mimi and I were sitting around the kitchen after packing the last of our clothes in both cars, preparing for the morning's move to our new home.

"Let's get ourselves a glass of tea and sit on the porch," Mimi said. "This is our last night together in the house and—"

"The last one where you don't have to kick your way through our dirty clothes to find the bed," Lindsey said.

"I have loved every single kick," said Mimi, "and I'm going to miss seeing your faces when you get up in the morning. I really am."

"Wow. That's pretty masochistic, Aunt Mimi," Gracie said.

I smiled and in the dim light of the kitchen, I saw Mimi's smile too. There was recognition. In the same way Gracie had supported Lindsey's harmless barb, my smile connected with my sister's heart.

We sat on the dark porch until our eyes became accustomed to the light of night and our ears attuned to the sounds of the woods and nearby marsh and we talked. At first we spoke of the dinner, Alex, Brad and the loss of Loretta and how Alex seemed to be adjusting so well. We moved on to Louise and Duane and the whole hilarity of their friendly fire. Then our minds turned to other things. But not our mouths. That was how we were. Our family preferred not to speak of things that were uneasy to hear. We would hem and haw around them like a patch of green stickers in the grass and we were the barefoot children, unprepared for pain, unwilling to give pain a chance to teach us something.

So, there was small talk about Lindsey leaving. Small talk about our new home. Small talk about how it all felt—these changes in our lives. Little jabs and tidbits about life that should have kept us up until the break of day. But not us. No. We said we had to get up early. We said tomorrow would be very tiring indeed. We said good night.

But we said *thank you* a thousand times to my sister (who had promised to make us biscuits in the morning) and we told each other we loved each other, and even though an onlooker would have said it was a routine deliverance of a polite requisite, we knew we meant it—meant it that we loved each other. We knew that the hearts of women knew no generation or borders, that love was complete. It was.

Twelve

MOVING

———◦◆◦———

THE sun rose sooner than I wanted to see it, but there it was, creeping through the venetian blinds of Mimi's guest room, where I had been holed up since the middle of June. It was a landmark day because up until then we could have told ourselves that we had just been trying this new life on for size. Having decided it fit pretty well, we consented to sink new roots in the Lowcountry. Even Gracie, who said she didn't understand why, was comfortable here and felt safer than she did in New Jersey. After all, the Lowcountry was the land of my ancestors and one we could claim with no apology. It was not a runaway destination. Rather, it was where we had begun, generations earlier. The Lowcountry belonged to us and us to her.

All that said, moving back to Mount Pleasant was still the single largest defiant act of my adult life. Giving Fred his walking papers was big, but moving us over seven hundred miles away was more impressive, at least in my mind. I think it had shocked everyone so much that no one had really fought me on it, besides Gracie, that is. And, the greater hand of life had been kneading our hearts ever so gently, giving us the courage to rise to the challenges and changes.

Gracie's stubborn determination to prove she could fit in anywhere on the planet, and in a front seat, thank you, had served her well so far, except for her one drunken incident when we first arrived and her sassy mouth. She was involved in school, flirting with Alex—although she would have vigorously denied it—and her environmental interest was her new cause célèbre.

Lindsey was ready to leave, but in Lindsey's normal low-key style, she repressed any expressions of wild enthusiasm. She probably knew that if she reveled in the family headlines, Gracie's ego would demand that she do something more spectacular and dramatic to secure center stage. We all knew and accepted that Gracie just had to have the spotlight. From the day she was born, she had always been just the kind of kid who clamored for attention. Although no one said it, there was still the worrisome thought that if Gracie became rattled, she would take off for New Jersey and wind up a drug addict, living in the streets of Newark or Paterson. As long as we focused on the positive aspects of our new life in Mount Pleasant, Lindsey's stellar achievements could quietly glow under the bushel. While that wasn't quite fair to Lindsey, families did things that weren't quite fair in the name of peace.

I was fully entrenched in my new job and there were many things I liked about it. The hours were flexible and I knew what had to be done. As long as I did everything, no one seemed to care when I did it. Louise wasn't quite ready to relinquish control of the staff, which was fine with me, because I could not quite see myself executing orders with the same authority she possessed. We were operating like co-captains and it was working out well. When Louise needed me to fill in, I would act as waiter or bartender but I had yet to trespass into the inner sanctum of the kitchen. O'Malley's whole personality was a combination of professionalism and pleasure and the drama of Duane's kitchen kept us all in stitches—except for the occasional outburst of anger, which was unnerving. The restaurant was always busy, which made the days go quickly. Brad was nice to work for, although he rarely said anything that sounded like instructions. When he was there, which was about half the time we were open, he sat at the end of the bar and shot the breeze with customers. From that perch he had the ideal view of Shem Creek, which was music for my eyes at every glance, no matter what the weather.

Overall, life was better than I had dreamed it could be and all over the course of a summer. Basically, I had stepped in it, if you know what I mean.

I stretched under the sheets, wanting to linger for few more moments, linger to search for a deeper read on our new life, and I decided, while in the midst of a smell fest with the sweet jasmine-scented water my sister used to wash her linens, that I had made the best possible call. It didn't matter that the call had been made in a moment of panic, brought about by the antics of my youngest. I thought about that old *retreat to the familiar* and decided that it had nothing to do with us beyond the obvious. We had few alternatives. Given that, we, that is *I*, had chosen a sensible solution. I mean, was I expected to move to Duluth?

I stretched again and even before I wiped away the sleep from my eyes, I allowed myself to be happy, just a little. It was important that my daughters felt I was in charge of our little family and so what if I had enlisted the aid of my sister? It had given my sister purpose, my girls a chance to know her again and the work I was doing had brought them jobs and a sense of usefulness too. No, all these things were good.

My morning adrenaline kicked in and I was getting anxious to get the day moving so I rolled over and looked at the clock. It was only six forty-five. If I got up, surely no one else would be awake, so I laid there for a few more minutes. My first thought was that I would preheat the oven for Mimi's biscuits. It took a while for her oven to reach four hundred and fifty degrees. I would wash my face, pick up the newspaper from her front walk and dress myself. I was compiling a list of things to do and more came with each thought. I threw back the sheets and said in a whisper, *Thank you, God. Thank you for everything.* It was not the prayer of a devout *anything* but only of a woman relaxed and hopeful for the first time in years. Wasn't it funny, I thought, that sometimes you didn't know how miserable you had been until you weren't miserable any longer.

I was brushing my teeth and thinking how sparkling and perfect the basin was. Although I cleaned up after myself and wiped the sink and faucet to a spotless shine each morning and I would always encourage the girls to do the same, I knew that Mimi came behind us with a sponge and a bottle of disinfectant. Soon, that evening in fact, we would begin to encrust our new sinks with little bits of toothpaste and clog our new drains with hair. I laughed to myself, thinking I wouldn't have a clean house like my sister until the girls were both gone and that then I would no doubt hate the cleanliness.

I dressed myself and went about, beginning the day at the kitchen table with the newspaper. I was reading "Dear Abby" when Lindsey appeared with a glass of juice.

"Morning," she said, "wanna know what I just thought of?"

"Morning, baby," I said, folding the paper and putting it away. "Listen to this. Here's a letter to Abby from a twelve-year-old girl with a big bust. She wants to know why the guys don't like her for her brains. Want some eggs?"

"Who cares about her? I get to move twice in one week! How disgusting is that? You're gonna die without me around to help you, you know."

I looked up at my beautiful daughter and the reality of her leaving me grabbed my heart for the millionth time. But I wouldn't let her see that. It was too early for tears.

"There's no doubt that I'll be at enormous risk," I said. "Want some eggs?"

"Eggs make me gag, Mom, you know that."

"Pour your poor old mother another cup of coffee, sweetheart."

She took my cup, refilled it and gave it back to me. "I'm gonna go get dressed."

Soon the kitchen was alive with activity, Mimi's biscuit preparation carefully monitored by each of us.

"Mom? Can you make biscuits like Aunt Mimi?" Lindsey said.

"Not if my life depended on it," I said, stuffing a hot one in my mouth, dripping with fig preserves she made from figs she grew.

"Oh, man! These things are banging!" Gracie said, buttering at least her third if not fourth one.

"Banging?" Mimi said and looked in my direction.

"Gracie, in our day that term had another meaning."

The girls giggled, knowing exactly what I had meant.

After we had consumed enough carbohydrates to fuel every runner in the NYC Marathon, we stripped the beds and threw all the sheets in the washer.

"Don't want to leave you with a big mess," Lindsey said to Mimi.

I was coming through the kitchen with an armload of damp towels and almost knocked Mimi over.

"Here! Lord! Don't worry about all that!" She took them from me and marched to the laundry room.

"I need the exercise! Seriously!" I said.

"Look! Why don't you all just take the first carload over to the new house and I'll be right along!"

I hugged her neck and said okay.

"You don't mind?"

"Git!"

We were so excited to begin moving in; it was ridiculous. The car was stuffed to the hilt.

"So, where am I supposed to sit?" Gracie said.

Lindsey patted her thighs and a groaning Gracie crawled in. We backed out of Mimi's yard.

"I can't believe we're really doing this," Gracie said.

"Did you brush your teeth?" Lindsey said to Gracie. "Your breath smells like shit."

"Yes, I did. And, by the way, yours smells like ass!"

"Girls! Do you mind? Jeesch!"

For the duration of the short ride, Gracie exhaled in Lindsey's face, Lindsey exhaled on Gracie and both of them argued over what radio station they were going to blast. I was so obsessed with a list of what we had to do that I was almost oblivious.

"I called SCE&G, the phone company, the water bureau," I said out loud and to the interest of no one. "And, I ordered the *Post and Courier* for Sundays, and put in a change of address with the post office."

"I'll be in the club, with a bottle fulla bub . . . ," Gracie rapped along with the radio.

I just rolled my eyes and pulled into the yard of our new house. As we moved down the long drive, the girls got quiet.

"Wow," Gracie said, "it looks smaller than I remember."

It did to me as well.

"Well, we'll just make do, that's all. We have to wait until we sell the house in Montclair and then we can buy something. In the meanwhile, we'll manage."

We began unloading the car, carrying clothes over our arms and tromping up the steps. I opened the door and we were home, at least for the short term. I had asked the Epsteins to remove the bric-a-brac, and without all the framed pictures, books, area rugs, potholders and so on, the place looked completely unloved. On the other hand, they had put a fresh coat of paint on the living room/dining room/kitchen and that brightened things up considerably. We were keeping the beds and the rest of the furniture until we could move our own and figure out where we would be long term.

"You can have the larger bedroom," Lindsey said to Gracie. "Since I'll be gone and all."

"Oh, thanks a lot, Miss Generous!"

This kicked off another spirited exchange of comments regarding the frugal nature of one versus the martyr status of the other, but it was all a big joke because one bedroom was a matchbox and the other one was a shade smaller.

"Just hang your stuff up and let's keep moving!" I said.

We must have gone up and down the front steps a thousand times that morning and the screen door slammed so many times, I thought I would hear it in my sleep.

Mimi arrived around ten with groceries, specifically salt, flour and sugar.

"It's bad luck to buy your own or maybe it's bad luck to sleep in a new home on the first night without it. Whatever! I can't remember! I just know you're supposed to have it, that's all."

She had also brought diet soda, chips, salsa, microwave popcorn, canned soups, frozen pasta and pizza, bread, and eggs, basically one of everything from the grocery store. She also brought a flashlight and extra batteries.

"Hurricane season?" I said, holding up the shiny aluminum beacon.

"You got it, baby cakes!" she said.

"Did you call Mom *baby cakes?*" Gracie said.

"Yeah, I'm her baby cakes!" I said and giggled.

"Come on, baby cakes," Gracie called to Lindsey, "let's get the last load!"

"What did you call me?"

"Just move it, lard ass," Gracie said.

"You know, Gracie, you are going to have to tone down your language if you want the nice girls to be your friends!" Mimi said.

"Um, bad news, Aunt Mimi," Lindsey said in the doorway, "she doesn't *want* the nice girls to be her friends."

"Don't slam—" I said.

Slam!

"Oh, my," Mimi said, in a defeated tone that lasted about one second, adding, "Well? Every flower blooms in its own time."

Mimi assessed the kitchen and began wiping down the countertop, the insides of the cabinets and the stove. When she began to tackle the refrigerator, I stopped her.

"The cleaning service did all this, you know," I said. "You don't really have to do it."

"How do you know where their sponges have been?"

I just shook my head and smiled.

"Smirk if you want, but I read this article that said your sponge is a bacterial nightmare and you should microwave it for a minute every day!"

"Okay, okay! I'll microwave my sponges!"

About noon, I looked out to see Louise's car pull into the yard and park next to ours. She had somebody with her—a Spanish woman.

"Anybody home?" she called out.

"Get on in here!" I called back.

"This is Lupe! She made lunch for y'all 'cause I know you ain't gone feed nobody 'less we bring it!"

Louise came up the steps smiling, followed by Lupe, who carried a cardboard box filled with food I had never seen before. She had made fish salad in pita bread, grilled eggplant with mild chili peppers and marinated jicama rollups, and a sticky rice and mango pudding.

"Hey, Lupe!" I said. "It's nice to see you someplace besides the Piggly Wiggly parking lot and have a chance to talk."

Well, that was all I had to say and then Lupe took over. Here was a woman starved for conversation and believe me, she talked nonstop for two hours. While we stuffed our faces and returned to unpacking, we learned all there was to know about Loretta and her daddy fixation, but mainly she talked about Brad and Alex. It became clear that Lupe was more than a little dedicated to them.

Lupe, Louise, Mimi and I were standing around the kitchen counter eating, using paper towels as plates. The girls were setting up the bathroom and the music from their boom box was so horrible that I had to ask them to turn it down twice.

"I can't hear myself think," I said.

"Mom! You need to learn to appreciate—"

"Turn it down!" I said and then whispered, "It sounds like screw music!"

They giggled and when I went back to the adults, Lupe was still talking.

"I say to *heem*, Mr. Brad? Lupe fix home for you and Alex. I sleep in teeny bedroom, and they sleep in the other two. I don't mind. I just glad Jesus put me here to take care of them."

"Amen!" Louise said. "God's got his plan."

"Humph," Lupe said in a grunt. "Plus, I know plenty that nobody knows."

"Like what?" I said.

"Like his secretary, thees Amy who try to get him in the bed, she's in town and been watching hees house. She come every single morning and sit outside in the car, jess watching."

"Good Lord!" Mimi said. "That's stalking! Isn't it?"

The talk went on well into the afternoon while I rushed around trying to make an instant home. I tried to ignore Lupe, unsure exactly what it was about her that irked me so much. Maybe it was that she worked her jaw like a jackhammer. I could see that it had annoyed Louise, but Louise was very old school, believing that we all had a place in the world and should stay in it. Mimi, however, hung on Lupe's every word. If Lupe was suffering audience deprivation, Mimi was suffering from the confines of her narrow world. I didn't like the fact that Brad's old secretary was hanging around and spying on him. That made me nervous. Finally, I couldn't stand Lupe's gossiping any longer so I went to Louise.

Louise was on the balcony, wiping off the plastic table, which had not seen a squirt of Lysol in ages. There was a pile of dirty paper towels next to her.

"Louise! You don't have to do that!"

"This thing is filthy! Besides, if that woman doesn't shut her mouth, I'm gonna lose my mind."

"Just tell her you have to go. Seriously! I can do this and the girls can help too!"

"You stupid? She in there taking the oven apart and cleaning it while your sister is lining the shelves! You got more free labor today than—"

"Listen, Louise," I said, looking back to the kitchen through the sliding glass door at Mimi and Lupe going to town on the kitchen, "it ain't worth it. Lupe's gotta go. Now."

Louise just stared at me and then said, "I don't know how Mr. Brad can stand it. That man's a saint. But between us in the daytime and Lupe at night, Mr. Brad is safe."

"With a stalker?" I added.

"Yeah, that ain't no good."

"I'll tell him," I said, and in that statement there was a slight shift in the world between Louise and me.

As a rule, everything that reached Brad's ears passed through Louise. She was very protective of him. Now it had become acceptable for me to step in the circle, and on a personal matter.

"You just make sure you *do* tell him," she said. "And fast."

"Count on it."

I thanked her profusely for lunch and she said, *Thank that Lupe with the motor mouth, I just wanted to see what kind of mess you got over here, that's all.*

I knew that wasn't true. I knew Louise had come out of friendship.

I stayed on the terrace and continued cleaning the table until it was white again, which took large applications of elbow grease.

Finally, when Mimi was happy with the kitchen, she came to get me to show me what she had done. It was marvelous to have a sister like her.

"See? All your glasses are here and the plates are in this cabinet. I ran them through the dishwasher because they had been lying around in newspaper since you got here."

"I don't even know why I bothered to bring them. Ah, well. Mimi? How can I thank you?"

"Don't worry, I'll figure out how to get even later." She picked up her purse and ran her hand through her hair. Her forehead was laced with perspiration and I knew she had pushed herself. "By the way, I gave Lupe twenty dollars. I hope you gave Louise something."

I just stood there, shocked.

"No, I didn't, I mean, I don't think . . ."

"Honey, you think those girls don't expect to get something?"

Then, she looked at me with the funniest expression, realizing that Lupe was Brad's housekeeper, but Louise was my friend. Needless to say, Mimi did not have a single friend with walnut-colored skin.

"Well, maybe Lupe did but . . ."

"No, of course, you're right." She gave me a peck on the cheek. "I think you're in pretty good shape now. I'll call you later."

I could read her mind. She was thinking that something terrible had happened to my social sensibilities during the years I had lived in the north. Something had happened all right, but it wasn't a terrible thing.

The phone rang, which almost scared me out of my wits. Gracie answered it.

"Sure," she said, "definitely!" Then she turned to me. "Mom? It's Alex. Can we go to the movies tonight? Lindsey too? Mr. Jackson said he would drive us there and pick us up."

"Sure."

The worst of the work was over. Not having a lot of possessions was strangely liberating. It didn't take weeks to unpack. I checked the linen closet and wondered why I had bothered to bring my ratty old sheets and towels from New Jersey. I decided that when the house in Montclair sold, I would have a yard sale for all the things I had left behind and use the money to buy new down pillows and three-hundred-count sheets, whatever that meant.

Within the hour, a horn was honking in the yard. It was Brad and Alex and the girls were off. They asked me if I wanted to come but I was so tired I couldn't have stayed awake long enough to watch the previews. I pressed twenty dollars into each of their hands and told them to have fun.

When they were gone, I sat down in Mr. Epstein's recliner chair, lifting the footrest. My legs were throbbing from going up and down my steps. My hands ached from overuse. I rubbed them with some lotion, giving each tired knuckle a little pressure.

It was twilight, my favorite time of day. When we were little girls, Mimi and I called it *the magic hour*. We knew that our parents and their friends were all gathered on their front porches for a gin and tonic or a bourbon and branch, long after the supper dishes were washed. In our seersucker pajamas, hair still damp from our baths, and barefoot, we would run across the yard for one last moment of play. On the horizon there was always a freighter that we would imagine was headed for some exotic port. *Take us to Zanzibar!*

I didn't have to get up to see that the sky was streaked with red or that the blue was deepening. I knew the evening star was out along with a sliver of the new moon and that the tide was coming in. I must have been dreaming because there was an older man by my side, squatted on the brick hearth of the tiny fireplace. His hair was white and he wore a camel-colored cardigan sweater with gray trousers. His hands were folded across his lap and he seemed very pleased. He was telling me what a nice place this was and how good it was to see it filled with life and the laughter of young women. He asked me about Lindsey and I told him all about her.

Then he asked me about Gracie and his face became very serious as he listened. I worried about his concern but I couldn't remember if I had asked him why he looked so somber. Then he left the room and I remember curling up on my side, thinking I would just stay there until the girls got home. I wasn't really hungry, just exhausted.

It was pitch-black dark when I heard someone coming up the front steps.

"Who's that?" I called out.

"Just your dinner delivery, ma'am!"

It was Brad. I looked at my watch. It was nine-thirty. I had slept for over two hours. I scrambled out of the chair to the door, smoothing my hair and turning on lights.

"God! It's dark! I fell asleep! Come on in!"

"Look at you! Go wash your face! You're a wreck!"

"Right!"

It was awfully nice of Brad to bring dinner, I thought. Definitely above and beyond the call of duty. I looked at my face in the bathroom mirror. The buttons in the tufting of the chair had left marks on my face. I splashed water on my face and gargled with mouthwash to get the taste of sleep out of my mouth. Where was my brush? I opened the top right-hand drawer of the sink's vanity and there it was, right where I must have put it. I stopped for a second, because I had no memory of having unpacked my cosmetics and bathroom things. Well, I thought, maybe one of the girls had done it. I would thank them.

"Whew!" I said, coming back to the kitchen. "I fell asleep in the chair! What a day!"

"Glass of swill?" he said and offered me a goblet of white wine.

"To be sure! Thanks!"

We raised them to each other and he said, "Congratulations on your new home!"

"Thanks! I'd never have it if you didn't find it!"

"Glad to be of service." He took a sip and offered me the cardboard-covered aluminum container. "Fried shrimp, French fries and coleslaw."

"Perfect! Let's go outside on my huge terrace, uh, palazzo!"

"Palazzo. Um, I'm not sure about that word. Well, this place sure shaped up in a hurry," he said.

"We're working on it, but we got rid of most of the boxes today and that's always the worst thing. Tomorrow we have to hang pictures and organize things a little more. I still have tons of stuff in New Jersey that I'm seriously considering abandoning." I pushed the sliding glass door opened and placed my dinner on the table. "Come sit! Hey! Guess who showed up today?"

"Louise? She told me she was gonna check on you to see how it was going."

Brad sat down at the table with me and put the wine bottle between us.

"Yeah, she came over but she brought Lupe!"

"Lupe's a trip, isn't she?"

"Well, I've been assigned the task of telling you something you probably won't like, but here goes. . . ."

"What?"

"First, Lupe drove us crazy today, but so what, right?"

"And?"

"And, because she's got a tongue as long as the Amazon she told *us*, but she doesn't want *you* to know that your old secretary has been sitting outside your house for the past few days, watching you come and go."

"Amy? Amy's here?"

"Apparently."

"Well, why doesn't she just knock on the door?"

"Because she's a sociopathic lunatic?"

"Why wouldn't Lupe just tell *me*?"

"Maybe she doesn't want to get in the middle of something that's really none of her business?"

"Maybe. Are you sure it's Amy?"

"No. How would I know? But Lupe seems convinced. Anyway, just thought you should know that."

"Boy! No shit! How weird is this?"

"I don't know, but I think I'm gonna hear?"

I munched away on the shrimp and fries and watched Brad's face as he told me the story of Amy in full detail for the second time.

If I had ever learned anything about men, I knew this. You could predict with the precision of Doppler radar where their britches would fall when opportunity came knocking on their zipper. They would fall in the first available location.

Brad was going to connect with Amy as fast as possible and take full advantage of her, um, availability. Just when I was starting to flatter myself by imagining that Brad might have had some interest in me, Amy had to show up and put the kibosh on that. The brazen slut. So, he had brought me shrimp. Big deal. I could tell by his face he had something much more meaningful in mind for her.

THIRTEEN

FOUR WOMEN AND A FAREWELL

THE days lumbered along until Lindsey's final day with us arrived. They had seemed like rows of dominoes standing on their edges, arranged so that when the first one received a slight tap they would collapse to the tune of their design. *Click, click, click* went the days, slipping away in normal rhythm, too quickly for me and I was sure, too slowly for Lindsey.

It seemed that a teenager's life was one of waiting for their *real life* to begin and they were tortured by the anxieties of what the future would allot them. Every adult understood that the future entered history with each passing minute and that time was relative. Teenagers felt they spent the better part of their time languishing in an unjust limbo. They had to wait to get braces removed from their teeth to be able to smile with confidence. They waited to get a license so they could drive to the movies or a friend's house. Which college accepted them would predict—not with certainty, but to a point—who their friends would be for the rest of their lives and where they would land in the economics of career reward.

I had watched Lindsey as she pored over the curriculum guides, looking beyond the freshman core requirements and trying to figure out which electives could lead to which kind of degree. She was a math and science wizard with a curiosity and thirst to understand everything, and with her wonderful mind she could probably become anything she wanted to become. The horsepower was there, but it would take time and waiting.

My life was exactly the opposite of my girls' lives. Each hour of my day was filled with something that had to be done and my days passed with such frightening speed that I was always astonished.

It had been a wild summer and as could have been predicted, a wild week. Several weeks ago, Lindsey and I had arranged for her to have a bankcard and it had shown up in the mail on Monday. We agreed that a bankcard was much safer than keeping cash in her dorm room and more practical than checks. On Tuesday, we had taken her boxes to Pack Mail. She was shipping things like books, a boom box, her CDs, and enough clothes to last her until Thanksgiving. On Wednesday, we bought phone cards and a great pair of shoes on sale at Bob Ellis.

We were walking back to the parking lot on George Street.

"Thanks for everything, Mom," she said. "I know we spent more than you wanted to."

"Oh, honey, it's okay," I said, "but the truth is we didn't spend enough."

"What do you mean?"

"I mean that it makes me crazy that I can't help set up your dorm room. I keep seeing us going to the big Bed Bath and Beyond in the city and taking all your pillows and towels and things back to school, all crammed in a taxi, and now I'm not going to get to do it. Miss Perfect gets to help you and I don't. It just frustrates me, that's all."

"You mean Patti?"

"Yeah. Her."

"Momma! She hasn't said a word to me about doing *anything* to help me! And, if she does, I'll tell her it's all handled, okay?"

"No, no. Let her help you. But, she'll probably do your whole room in monkeys."

Lindsey elbowed me in the ribs and I laughed a little with her.

"Mom! You're terrible!"

I stopped, took off my sunglasses and searched Lindsey's face for loyalty.

"I hate missing anything that has to do with you or Gracie taking a new step in life, you know? Rites of passage? I've never missed one and now I'm gonna . . . oh, hell, Lindsey, I shoulda put a brick on your head years ago so you wouldn't grow up!"

"Ah, Mom!"

"What am I gonna do about it now?"

"Ain't nothing to be done now. Too late." She threw her arm around my shoulder and gave me a one-handed hug. "I grew up anyhow."

"No, baby, you grew up wonderful."

"How about this? How about I get a digital camera and take before-and-after pictures? I can e-mail them to you at the restaurant, right?"

"God! I hadn't even thought of that! And, yeah! You can e-mail me at the restaurant every day!"

I felt better, until the next day, that is.

On Thursday, oh yes, it was Thursday for sure when I met Amy.

Brad came to work that morning looking like, as he would say, the dog's breakfast. His lips were puffy, his eyes were puffy and his hair was knotted in the back.

Louise and I were in the kitchen with Duane, solving the problems of the world when he stumbled in, looking for hot coffee. Louise looked at me, I looked at her, and we burst out laughing. You know me by now. I didn't need anybody's permission to give the boss a little heat.

"So, Brad! Rough night?"

"Oh, my God," he said. "I'm too old for this."

"Mr. Brad! You sick?"

"No," he said, "just a little tired, I think. I didn't get much sleep last night."

We knew he had a date with Amy because he told us so the day before. He had said, *So I just went up to her car and said, Amy! How nice to see you!*

Aren't you concerned that she was just sitting outside your house? I had said. *I mean, in my world that would be bizarre!*

I know, I know, he said, *but anyway, I'm taking her out for dinner tonight.*

Yeah, young woman make an old fool anyhow! Louise had said.

"So, how was your date with Amy?" I said, pushing a little further.

"If she shows up, tell her I'm not here, okay? I'm serious, y'all."

He looked at us, from face to face, as we nodded our consent.

"No problem," Duane said.

"Good Lord!" I said.

"Humph," said Louise.

Brad was obviously no Marathon Man. Duane handed him a mug of coffee and Brad pushed his way through the swinging door, heading for the dock and fresh air. I followed him outside. He was standing by the railing, staring down at the water.

"So what the hell happened?"

"What the hell happened? What the hell happened? The woman is a raving screaming sex machine of death and destruction! *That*'s what happened!"

"Holy hopping hell! I told you she was a freak!"

"She's a freak of nature! She had to take me to the emergency room. . . ."

"What?"

"Yeah! The emergency room!"

"Do I get to ask why or do I have to wait to read it on your insurance claim?"

"We don't have insurance yet and let's just say that I was having some heart palpitations brought on by a combination of things, but they said it wasn't a heart attack."

"And the combination of things was?"

"Stress . . ."

"Well, of course you're stressed." I felt my *nervous babble thing* rearing up and decided to let it rip. "You move here, you open a business and the next thing you know, your wife has the bad manners to get herself run over and bam! You're a full-time parent! That's enough to make anybody's heart palpitate. Right? Am I right?"

He was now watching the birds and thinking about something that was most probably none of my business. That didn't matter to me one bit.

"So what did you do? Something stupid like take Viagra? That stuff kills, you know."

"Shit! Viagra?" He burst out in a laugh. "What are you? Crazy?"

"I've been called worse, lemme assure you!"

"No! I drank red wine and ate chocolate! It set off an episode of tachycardia!"

"What the hell is that?"

"Don't know. Some bullshit thing. Makes you feel like your heart is gonna explode."

"Ah! I see. A bullshit thing." I gave him a knock on the arm. "How about we find you somebody at the Medical University and get you checked out?"

"Yeah, maybe that's a good idea."

"Okay, I'll do that. First thing."

Of course, the first thing I did was to tell Louise everything.

"You think he was in the bed with that woman?"

"Where else would you be with chocolate and red wine?"

I called Mimi.

"So, listen, remember that doctor you went out with a couple of weeks ago?"

"Was he in the restaurant with another woman?"

"No! What kind of a doctor is he?"

"Why? Are you sick?"

"No!"

"Do you have basal cell carcinomas?"

"Ah ha! Dermatologist?"

When I told her the reason for my call, she went into Mimi overdrive and I knew Brad would be in the hands of a renowned cardiologist within twenty-four hours.

I left my desk to find Brad and tell him what Mimi had said. I came around the corner of the bar and almost knocked down a customer.

"Oh, sorry!" I said. "Can I help you?"

"I was just looking for Brad?"

I took one look at her short white shorts, skimpy top, perfect tan and pedicured toes and knew exactly who she was. Amy. Did I mention that her shorts were short?

I stuttered around like I always do when I'm nervous. "Um, he was here earlier but um, gee, um, I think he might be out back. Uh, I'll go look. But! He might have left! I think he had to go to the bank or something. No! Not the bank. Lowe's! That's it! I think he went to Lowe's! But! I'll just go and check."

Well, this little tramp, Amy, who was at least fifteen years younger than I was, just stood there and looked at me like I had lost my mind. Let me assure you my brain was only missing temporarily. I didn't like her vibe. Too aggressive. I didn't like her. I walked in the kitchen, around the huge center island and right back out to the dining room.

"Nope! He's out. Went to Lowe's. Like I thought. Yep. Went to Lowe's."

She knew I was lying, but I'm not a very good liar anyway. Just then, Brad came in the door behind her. My eyes got big as I tried to signal him not to come in farther, her head turned around and Brad was busted.

"What's the *matter* with you?" she said to me and went to Brad's side, giving him a kiss on the cheek. "How are you feeling, sugar?"

"I'm fine, fine," he said, "really." They walked outside together and I was left there feeling like an idiot.

My face must have been purple. I turned to O'Malley, who was setting up the bar, and said, "Nice one, right?"

"Yeah, those Jersey women are slick! Let me tell you. . . ."

"Oh, bite me, O'Malley! He *told* me he didn't want to *deal* with her!"

"And, you did one helluva job keeping her away from him."

"Whatever. You got receipts?"

"Yeah," he said, "I'll get them for you right now." He stopped lining up mini-bottles on the shelves, reached under the counter and handed me an envelope.

I sat up at the bar and started going through them, thinking that the amount of rum we were selling was surprising, but then, there was the heat to consider. They were probably running blenders making frozen daiquiris, piña coladas, and rum runners for the masses. And, naturally, I told O'Malley about Brad's heart palpitations. He said it was very common. I said I had never heard of it. We agreed on one thing though: Brad was going to have medical attention whether he liked it or not.

"Isn't it amazing how relieved you are once you decide to see a doctor?" he said.

"Yeah," I said, "it's like we think there's a cure for everything. Just go see any old guy with an M.D. and he can fix it, right?"

"Exactly."

After a few minutes, Brad came back inside, sailing across the dining room floor with way too much swagger, and positioned himself by the bar, leaning on one elbow. O'Malley and I looked at each other.

"Um, excuse me, sir!" I said. "You don't look like somebody who wanted to avoid someone!"

"I told her to go back to Atlanta," he said, "I said I wasn't ready for a relationship."

"No way!" I could smell a lie. "What did she say?"

"She said that she had just come down here to make sure that I was all right. I don't know if I told you this or not, but she had seen Loretta's obituary in the *Journal,* and she was concerned. That's all."

"You're lying like all hell," I said. "That woman planned to come down here, move in with you and take over your life."

"I hate to say it," O'Malley said, "but I'm with Linda on this one. I saw the way she sneaked in here dressed for the hunt."

"Well, I think she expected to find a glamorous restaurant, a huge house and a stud. Oh, yeah, and I think she thought that Alex would be in boarding school or something. And, I think the deal with my heart last night scared her."

"You think, you think, you *think?* Well, *good!* I'm glad you can think!" I said very emphatically, and I wasn't even sure why. Suddenly, I was embarrassed by the way Brad and O'Malley looked at me. "Wha?" I delivered that *wha* in my best New Jersey trucker accent.

"Nothing!" O'Malley said and turned back to his work.

"Yeah! Nothing!" Brad said and walked away.

I knew they were smirking. Especially Brad. Even from the back of his head, I could tell that his cheek muscles were tightened into a smile.

"Oh, fine!" I said and went into my office, closing the door hard.

I buried myself in work for the rest of the day, answering the phone when it rang more than four times. Mimi called for Brad. She had found a doctor and the appointment was set up.

"This guy's from Duke," she said with the authority of a physician. "They're the center for any kind of arrhythmia problem in the whole country. Anyway . . ."

She ran on and on, I thanked her and transferred her to Brad.

Gracie called in at the end of her school day. "Do I have to work today? It's Lindsey's last full day and we thought maybe we could go to the beach one last time?"

"Better check with Louise," I said, "your behind belongs to her, you know."

"Oh, hell, I'll come in."

"That's up to you," I said.

"Are you mad at me?"

I assured her that I was not angry with her but she could read in the tone of my voice that I did not approve of blowing off work for play when other people were depending on you.

Finally, the day ended and I said good night to Louise.

"Your girl going tomorrow?"

"Yeah, God, I can hardly believe it."

"Why don't you take the day off?"

I thought about it for a minute. I was considering committing the same crime I had discouraged Gracie from committing. "I'll work half a day. I have to do the banking and all that stuff."

"Yeah, okay. Hey, that contraption you and Doo-wayne ordered for the fish is coming in tomorrow."

"Excellent!"

"Oh, yeah, and um . . ."

"What?"

"I didn't get to see that Amy thaing. Spill it!"

"Ho from hell," I said.

Louise's eyebrows took a trip to the rafters.

"Young enough to be his daughter."

"Humph," Louise said, and her eyebrows went through the roof again.

She smiled at me and I thought about how much I liked her. Louise was a good woman.

The next afternoon, Mimi, Gracie, and I drove Lindsey to the airport. Considering that the car was filled with chatterboxes, it was almost silent. There was not the usual fighting over the music—the radio wasn't even turned on. There wasn't even the usual bickering from the girls about who sat where. We pulled into the passenger drop-off area and I got out to help Lindsey with her bags.

"I'll park and meet you at the restaurant?" Mimi said.

"Perfect," I said.

"I'll go with Aunt Mimi," Gracie said. When Mimi turned around to pat Gracie's leg in affection, she added, "Well? She's old! She might get lost!"

Mimi gave her a little slap and shook her head at me. "Who's old?" she said through the window and pulled away from the curb.

Mimi was winning over Gracie's stubborn little heart.

Lindsey showed her identification, checked her bags and got her boarding pass. "Let's get a Coke or something," she said.

As soon as our waiter placed our drinks in front of us, Mimi and Gracie appeared.

"Here," Gracie said, dropping an armload of magazines in front of Lindsey. "Don't say I never gave you nothing!"

"Good English, dumb ass," Lindsey said.

"Up yours, you'll miss me," Gracie said, sitting and taking her menu. "I'm starving!"

Mimi said, "The only good thing about Lindsey running away from home—"

"I am not!"

"We know that, darlin'!" Mimi said and winked at her. "As I was saying . . . the only good thing is that Gracie won't have anybody to cuss with!"

"Ha!" Lindsey said. "You should hear her and Alex!"

The inane conversation lasted through burgers, pie and the check, but that was normal for us. Chitchat, time passes and the dreaded moment arrives and leaves without us giving it more than a cursory nod.

"We had better go to the gate now," I said.

I paid the check and walked arm in arm with Mimi, Lindsey's tote bag slung over my shoulder. Gracie and Lindsey were in front of us.

"There's nothing like sisters," I said to Mimi.

"Look at them," she said.

"Look at us! I mean, where would I be without you? Seriously!"

"It's the truth! You'd be dead in a ditch for sure! But you know what?"

"What?"

"Gracie's gonna miss her Lindsey."

Mimi was surely right about that. I could see Gracie's shoulders shaking and I thought they were laughing about something. In the next second, she stopped, Lindsey threw her arms around her and I knew she was crying. That was it. I ran to them, Lindsey started to cry and I was next. It was impossible for us not to be emotional, but crying in public was not on Mimi's list of acceptable activities.

"Y'all! Get a grip!" she said, and started pulling tissues from her pocket. "People are staring!"

Her eyes were brimming with tears too. How could they not have brimmed with tears? We were going to be short one person in the daily body count until Thanksgiving. I was miserable!

"Baby? Come here!" I put my arms around her.

"How will you stand Gracie? You'll murder her and have good cause!"

"Shut up, jerk."

"Hush, Gracie! No. I won't. I promise. You'll see. Just go. Study! Make A's! Make us proud!" I sniffed so loud the carpet ruffled. "I love you. We all do. So much."

Lindsey shifted her tote bag from one shoulder to the other. She hugged Mimi and Gracie and then came back to me. She looked at me as though she was trying to memorize every detail of my face.

"I'm gonna be fine, Mom. Really."

"I know."

"I'll call you tonight?"

"You better."

We watched her go through security and walk halfway down the long corridor leading to the gates. She stopped, turned and waved to us. I blew her a kiss. She seemed so young to me. Mimi put her arm around my shoulder and Gracie put her arm around my waist. I stood there until Lindsey rounded the corner and was out of my sight.

"Let's go home, Momma."

Whether it was on purpose or not, Gracie called the Lowcountry home. It was then that I knew we were going to be fine.

PAR-TAY TIME

M Y house was so quiet that when the phone rang it sounded like a fire alarm. It was after ten o'clock and Lindsey finally called to let me know she had arrived safely. Fred and Patti had picked her up at the Newark Airport and taken her to dinner at Knickerbocker's, a neighborhood haunt close to her dorm. Her voice crackled with excitement.

"So, I wasn't really hungry, because I had just eaten with y'all, but I ate anyway."

"I don't want to sound like an old poop, but it's almost midnight! I was getting worried!"

"Mom! It's only like ten-fifteen or something!"

"Still!"

"Okay, sorry. I should've called you when I landed but we were talking and all. Anyway, freshman orientation is on Tuesday and classes don't start until Wednesday, so tomorrow I'm gonna work in her store and make some *di-ne-rrro*. Monday, I'm gonna help her do inventory and come back here after dinner. Her store's closed for Labor Day, right? *Hopefully*, my roommate, who I pray to God isn't a raving *lunatic*, will show up by then and at least I'll be unpacked and all, which is why I decided to stay here tonight. Patti's gonna pay me ten dollars an hour! Isn't that great? Oh! I am so psyched!"

"Yeah! It's great. How are you getting back and forth to Essex Fells?"

"I'll take the bus from the Port Authority. No biggie."

"Lindsey! You be careful! The Port Authority is crawling with perverts and derelicts! It's filthy! You have to wash the bottom of your shoes!"

"Mom! I've been taking the bus back and forth to New York since I was twelve!"

"You have not!"

"Yes, I have! So has Gracie!"

Well, *that* little revelation took ten years off my life. And, Patti sucking up to Lindsey was making me uncomfortable. Maybe I was a little bit jealous. Who knows? Better yet, who cares? About Patti, that is.

"Are you there? Mom?"

"Yeah, I was just thinking about something. . . ."

"What?"

"My thighs. I have to go on a diet."

"No, you don't. You're fine. Most women your age look like, I don't know, half-dead cows."

"Great. I feel much better."

"Stop! Where's Gracie?"

"Out. She went to the movies with Alex, I think."

"You think? What do you mean, you think? Mom! You'd better watch her, you know."

"Oh, honey, she's fine. But I will tell her you called. Oh, shoot! Do you have a phone yet?"

"Yeah, here's the number."

"What's the deal on computer access?"

"The room is wired for ethernet and I'm just hoping my roommate has a laptop or something. If not, I can use the tech room. There's a whole IT office and everything. Don't worry."

Don't worry? I had a vision of Lindsey walking across campus after dark and getting killed—how's that for don't worry? I took her number and e-mail and she promised to call Gracie Sunday morning. We hung up and I decided to take a bath and go to bed early with a book. The good Lord knew it had been a very long time since I had indulged myself with a good long soak and even longer since I had read something besides the newspaper. Gracie's curfew was midnight and I would stay awake long enough for her to come in and to see that she was all right.

I was up to my nose in bubbles, reading a book that had won some big award that was the most boring story ever written. Basically, this woman was in her house, looking out of her kitchen window, thinking about her miserable life and so far, in the first twenty-five pages, nothing had happened, except she worried about every single stupid thing that crossed her mind. If I had her life, I'd kill myself, I thought. I tossed it across the floor and added some hot water to the tub. If I had one secret guilty pleasure, it was turning the air conditioner way down low and then soaking in a bath hot enough to cook shrimp.

I had just leaned back and had closed my eyes when I heard a car crunching across the gravel outside. It was probably Gracie. Shoot, I thought, I wasn't even wrinkled yet. Back in New Jersey, I would have let her cruise past the bathroom door and I would have called out a greeting. But because Lindsey had just left I thought Gracie would be happier if I got out and came to welcome her home.

I threw on my robe and opened the front door.

"I need a hand here!"

It was the voice of Alex. He was panicked.

I opened the screen door and saw Alex and a friend struggling to get Gracie out of the car. I nearly fainted from the sight of her limp body. He held her under her arms and struggled to pick her up. Her shoes were missing and her arms were thrown back.

"Oh my God! Oh my God!" I hurried down the steps to help him. "Gracie! Baby! What happened?"

"She's okay and she'll be okay," Alex said. "Let's just . . . here, Steve, take her feet."

What was he saying? Gracie was *not* okay! Steve carried Gracie's feet, and Alex had her under the arms. I ran up the steps to open the door, struggling to keep my bathrobe closed, talking the whole time.

"I thought y'all were going to the movies," I said.

"We did, but everything we wanted to see was sold out."

"How did this happen?"

"We met some guys from the football team at Millennium Music and they were going to a party . . ."

Gracie groaned and said, "Where am I?"

"You're home, Gracie," I said. "So, you went and there was booze, right? Am I right?"

"There was a *lot* going on," Alex said.

I got the screen door opened and together we managed to get Gracie to the couch. I knelt down beside her and it took about one minute to see that there was more at work than liquor. "What else did she do, Alex? Tell me! You have to tell me!"

"I'm gonna take off, Alex," Steve said, "I've got curfew. Y'all okay?"

"Yeah, we're good," Alex said. "Thanks."

"Who was he?"

"A senior . . . Steve Michel . . . he's a good guy. . . ."

"How did this happen? Tell me!"

"I don't know, Ms. Breland! I swear! I don't know! I was in the living room of this house and she went off with some guys and then I was watching a game on the tube. I went looking for her and found her in not very good circumstances and got her out of there and brought her home right away. That's all I know!"

He was telling the truth. At least, at that moment, I believed him. I opened Gracie's eyes to see what her pupils looked like and they were a little enlarged. Her eyes were bloodshot.

"Was she smoking pot? Just tell me!"

"Um, I don't know, but some of the other guys were, so, maybe. I don't know."

"Your knuckles are bleeding. Go wash your hands good and get some ice from the freezer. Why are your knuckles bleeding, Alex? What the hell happened?"

"They hit this asshole's, um, sorry . . ."

"That's okay," I said.

"They hit this creep's jaw a couple of times. I'm gonna call my dad to come get me, okay?"

"Sure. And give me a cold washcloth!"

Gracie's hair was a mass of tangles. I took the wet cloth from Alex and began wiping her face, over and over, trying to bring her around. Then I wiped her hands. She moaned and said something I couldn't understand.

"What is it, Gracie? It's Momma. Talk to me."

" 'Sokay, Ma."

It was not okay.

"Gracie! Let's try to sit up! Come on!" I got her to almost sit by pushing pillows under her shoulders. "Come on, Gracie! Talk to me! What did you take? Why are you in this shape? Did you do any drugs?"

"No! Oh, oh . . . I don't feel so good . . . Momma! Help me!"

One of the few blessings of a small home is a short path to the bathroom. I held her head while she was sick, and in between bouts of nausea I let her rest on the bathroom floor.

I heard Brad come in and I could hear him talking to Alex through the walls but I couldn't make out what they were saying. Alex had seemed sober enough and I tried to think of why he had called his father when he could have just gone home with his friend. That had to mean that something else had happened and that Alex had not told me what it was.

"Gracie? Gracie? Let's try to get you to your bed, okay?"

"Okay," she said and then she started to cry. "Oh, God, I hate those boys! Redneck assholes!"

"Do you want to tell me what happened, Gracie? Or do you want to tell me in the morning?"

"Tomorrow, 'kay? Gotta sleep. I feel awful!"

I pulled back her covers and let her tumble into her bed, smoothing her hair away from her face. On another night, I would have been furious with her. But my maternal instincts told me that she had fallen victim to something I hoped Alex could explain.

I turned off the light next to her bed and left her door ajar, so I could listen for her. I tightened my robe and went to face the rest of my *Little Night Music.*

Brad was in the kitchen leaning against the counter and Alex was leaning in the refrigerator.

"I told him he could have a can of Coke," Brad said. "How's Gracie?"

"She's seen better days," I said. "So, does somebody want to tell me what's going on with my daughter?"

"How cold is it in here?" Brad said. "Do you want me to adjust your thermostat?"

On any other occasion I would have read something lewd into that, but this was no time for jokes.

"I'll do it," I said, and slid the thermostat bar to the right. "You're right; it's freezing."

Alex closed the refrigerator door, popped open the soda can and cleared his throat. "Ms. Breland? Here's the story. I know we never should have gone to this guy's house in the first place, but we did and I just want to say that I apologize for taking Gracie there."

"Your apology is accepted," I said, thinking this was a very formal sentiment for a young man of his age.

"Yes, ma'am, I appreciate it. You see, there were about fifty or a hundred kids there . . ."

"Where was the house? And, whose house was it?"

"Uh, well, the house was out Mathis Ferry Road, in one of those subdivisions and I don't know who owned it . . . one of the guys who plays defense for Wando. His parents were out of town."

"That figures," Brad said. "Linda, do you want coffee or anything?"

"No, it's late, but thanks."

"Anyway, what happens is one cell phone calls another cell phone and the next thing you know there are cars and people coming from all over, looking for a party," Alex said. "Somebody brings vodka and somebody else has beer and then some idiot has pot and another one has something else . . . you get the picture, right?"

"I think we get the picture," I said. "So how come you're straight and Gracie's in the state she's in?"

"Because I didn't stay with her and when the house got crowded, we got separated. Some girl said to her, *Come on to the kitchen. Somebody brought jots and brownies.*"

"Jots?" I said.

"Yeah, you mix like cherry Jell-O with vodka or rum and jell it in these little plastic cups. So, Gracie must have had a bunch of them and eaten some brownies too."

"The brownies were loaded with pot," Brad said.

"Did you eat any brownies?" I said.

"No way," Alex said, "I had six tacos before we got there. I wasn't hungry. If I hadn't been stuffed, I might have though."

"Did Gracie know they had pot in them?" I asked.

"No. I'm sure of that. Ms. Breland, look, Gracie and I are new at Wando. Those girls never said a word—not that I heard anyway. They don't like Gracie because she's good-looking and she's got this big personality and they're just a bunch of jealous bit—"

"Alex!" Brad said.

"Sorry," Alex said. "Anyway, if I want to get tanked, I'll do it with Dad. If I get caught drinking, I can't play ball. And, I don't know all these people yet, so I don't trust them. Dad says you never drink with people you don't trust. I mean, Gracie's different. She thinks everybody's nice and all."

"And, they're not," I said.

"That's right. They sure are not. That's a lesson I had to learn the hard way. When I was in Atlanta, I wanted to join this club in school. And to get in you had to shoplift something. So I took this DVD from this store and got caught. The one time I did something like that in my life and I got caught. It was pretty . . . well, it was terrible for my mom. I could've gotten kicked outta school, but I didn't because my mom went down there and begged and I had never been in any trouble before. . . ."

There was silence for a moment as Brad and I let Alex relive the moment and think about his mother. We were not surprised to see him get choked up as he tried to continue. It was high time he showed some emotion.

"Then Mom got killed and I just couldn't *believe* it. She was *still* pissed off at me and had just screamed at me for the hundredth time right before she left the house . . . it was raining and I told her to be careful and she gave me this look, this look like she *hated* me and . . . and I don't think I'll *ever* forget that. . . ." Alex's voice trailed off into a whisper.

"Alex, you never told me that," Brad said. "But, I can promise you your mother did not hate you. She loved you very—"

"I know, I know. It was just a lousy coincidence or something. Anyway, that's when I learned the awful truth about life being unpredictable and all. Oh, hell, and the next thing I know I'm in Mount Pleasant, South Carolina? I mean, where the hell am I?"

Alex's face was filled with anxiety. Brad put his arm around Alex's shoulder and hugged him. Alex crumbled into a mass of tears and sighs. The poor kid. He had been carrying all his grief and trying to be so stoic. Kids weren't supposed to have to be so strong all by themselves.

"I'm sorry, I just . . ."

"Alex," I said. "Please don't worry about it. . . ."

I grabbed a tissue and handed it to him.

"It's okay, son," Brad said.

Alex blew his nose and took another tissue and blew his nose again.

"Anyway, Gracie needs someone to look out for her and I was supposed to be that person tonight and I didn't do a very good job and that's why I stayed around here . . . to tell you that I'm sorry."

"Why did you call your dad? I mean, you could've had that other kid take you home."

"Because Gracie had me *scared*. You know? I mean, she could've dropped a bunch of bad acid or X for all I knew and I got scared. I always, well *now* anyway, I call my dad."

I could hardly believe my ears. The teenagers I knew hid everything they could from their parents. Here was this kid who fessed up and took the rap when I wasn't going to blame him anyway. But Alex had been thoroughly traumatized by his mother's death. I could see that he was suffering from trying to be perfect—the perfect son, the perfect friend, and the all-around perfect kid.

"Alex, listen to me, sweetheart," I said. "First of all, we have never talked about your mother's death and I never knew your mother, but I can promise you this. Her annoyance with you over the shoplifting incident had nothing whatsoever to do with her death. Everyone feels guilty when someone dies in an accident. It's *normal* to feel that way."

"Yeah," Alex said, quietly, "I guess so."

"Linda's right," Brad said. "Look, son, you know your mom and I had some serious problems, but when I heard about her accident I knew that it was just that. An accident. But I felt guilty anyway."

"*You* did? Why? I thought you must've been happy to see her get hers!"

"No way." Brad took a deep breath. He looked at me and said, "You got any beer?"

"Sure," I said and reached in the refrigerator and took out a can. "You want a glass? Why don't we sit down for a minute?"

Before Brad could answer me I had already taken out a glass and begun pouring. They sat at the table—Alex with his Coke and Brad with his thoughts. Brad began to talk.

"Look, don't you think that I feel responsible for leaving your mother?"

"You weren't fooling around, Dad. *She* was. And *I* got stuck living with her."

"Yeah, I know. I think we all thought that she would let you see me more and I had intentions of bringing you down for the summer anyway. I thought that summers would make up for not seeing you so much during the school year and I know now that was wrong. I mean, in some ways, I think I should have stayed in Atlanta until you went to college, but I couldn't. I just couldn't. . . ."

"Dad! It's okay! Really! If I had been you, I would've left too!"

"Well, thanks for saying that but that's what pride will do for you. Anyway, ever since our marriage blew up I always felt like if I had been a better husband—you know what I mean, right? I was always working, always on a plane, always closing a deal, always looking for the next one—anyway, if I had been around more, maybe your mom wouldn't have become involved . . . you know what I'm saying, right?"

"Yeah, sure."

I poured myself a glass of wine from the oversized bottle in the refrigerator and sat down next to them.

"So, if I had been a better husband, she wouldn't have been all tangled up with Archie and then there wouldn't have *been* an accident! See what I mean? It's sort of like you saying that if you hadn't ripped off the DVD, she wouldn't have been angry and she might have seen where she was going and then . . . follow me?"

"Yeah," Alex said. "But I didn't send her downtown to go meet him that day. That was her choice. Is that what you mean?"

"That's exactly what I mean," Brad said. "Choices have consequences."

"And some choices have serious ones," I added.

"Boy, you can say that again. Mom's dead, Gramps is drinking himself into oblivion and I'm in Mount Pleasant. Not that it's so bad, because it isn't. In fact, it's really a lot better than I thought it would be."

"We should try to do something for ol' Theo." Brad sighed and shot me a look that said he was thinking it would be good if Theo dropped dead too.

"Well, I am sure that you and Gracie have talked about being here a lot. She didn't want to live here either. But your mother's death brought Gracie a great friend who she surely needed, especially with her sister leaving and all. You know?"

"And, son, time heals. Look, as time goes on and you and Gracie make other friends, you'll see."

"Yeah, I guess," Alex said. "It's just been rough. Losing Mom, coming here, I don't know anybody really. . . ."

"We'd better go, son, that is, if you think Gracie can just sleep it off, Linda?" Brad said.

"She threw up her brains tonight," I said, trying to lighten things up. "I think she's gonna have a big head tomorrow but she'll live."

"Okay," Brad said. He got up, put his glass in the sink and walked to the door. "Then, I'll see you tomorrow."

"Um, tomorrow's Saturday. I'm not working tomorrow. I took the day off."

"Oh. Right. I forgot."

"I'll see you Monday then."

"Okay, well . . ."

I opened the door for him and he looked at me as though he was expecting something else. I stuck out my hand to shake his in thanks. He eyed it with suspicion and extended his hand. I shook it but not like a trucker. He smiled with relief, and of course the back of my neck got all clammy with embarrassment for some stupid reason.

"Yeah, see? Not so dangerous! Hey, Alex?"

Alex was already halfway down the steps but he turned back to me. "Yes, ma'am?"

"Thanks, Alex. Gracie should have known better. And she's awfully lucky to have you for a friend. So am I."

Even in the darkness, I could see him smiling. I knew I still didn't have the whole story, but I would wrench the rest of it out of Gracie by Sunday.

I did not want them to see me watching them turn their car around. I stood there behind my screen door like a puppy until their taillights were out of sight. So! They saw me. Big deal! Why would they care that I was wearing the tackiest terry-cloth robe in captivity. I was thinking about Alex and Brad and how their life had been hacked to pieces but they had just carried on.

I slipped into Gracie's room to see how she was doing and don't you know my little lamb was fast asleep, her breath rising and falling like all innocence. I just shook my head. This child was a mule. It was time for us to have a serious discussion about her trusting nature, her morality, drugs, alcohol and a few other topics as well.

I tossed and turned in my bed thinking about a million things at once.

Loretta could not have been such a terrible mother if she turned out a fine boy like Alex. But then, maybe Alex was just born good in the same way that Lindsey was and that Gracie had been born with a little devil in her. He was going to be a great man when he grew up—he already was. Poor kid! I was glad that he felt comfortable enough to unburden himself in front of me. I decided that he must have wanted me to know him and that pleased me to no end.

And wasn't it interesting that Brad thought he would see me tomorrow. Well, he probably did forget I had taken the day off. Why did he have that funny look on his face when I went to shake his hand? Was I supposed to kiss his cheek? No way!

Was it because I had not asked him about his doctor's appointment? Couldn't be. But was a late-night visit the time to do that? Was it my business anyway? Didn't we have enough going on as it was?

Maybe he thought I was interested in him, and I did care about him but the last thing I was going to do was screw the boss. That might be the trashiest thing a woman could do. What was the matter with me? Did I really think the widower of an Atlanta socialite would be interested in the likes of a gal like me? *Don't flatter yourself, Linda.*

FIFTEEN

PLANTED SEEDS

I T must have been around eight in the morning when I heard a car door slam and bolted out of a sound sleep. I had been dreaming about a party and had no intention of leaving. Was that it? Yes, it was a party for me, for my birthday. It was not my birthday but I didn't want to tell anyone because they had gone to so much trouble. Someone I knew was in the kitchen making hamburgers and hot dogs and handing them to everyone wrapped up in paper napkins. I thought they should have at least bought paper plates but I kept that opinion to myself. Suddenly the crowd thinned and there were only a few people left. I apologized for being late and then someone said to me that I *wasn't* late. No one had shown up. I said, you mean you invited a bunch of people and they didn't come? Someone said, *Yes, no one came to your party.* Then the old man with white hair showed up, the same one I had dreamed about before. He was wearing the exact same camel-colored cardigan and gray trousers. I said to him, *Well, you sure were right to be concerned about Gracie!* He seemed to still have great concern for her. His expression frightened me and I started running and ran the whole way to the causeway leading to Sullivan's Island. I ran and ran until I heard a loud noise.

Now the trunk of a car slammed and I was wide awake, glad to get up, and not missing my dream. What had it meant? Was Gracie in trouble? That I had no life? That I was pathetic? I didn't want to think about it.

I went out to the kitchen and looked down into the yard. Mimi was there in her gardening clothes, surrounded by flats of plants, ready to go to work. I opened the door and called down to her.

"What in the world are you doing at this hour of the morning?"

"Good morning, sunshine!"

Sunshine, indeed.

"Hey yourself, sunshine! You want coffee?"

"Why not?"

Mimi smiled wide and once again I loved my sister like crazy. I had no idea why she had shown up like this but I knew her well enough to accept that whatever she had planned, it was for my own good. In the process, she would also make herself feel better. When Mimi decided to do something, you may as well just stand back and let her go to it.

While the coffeemaker dripped, I threw on a pair of khaki shorts, a knit shirt and sandals. The day was expected to be a scorcher. September was hotter than August but only the locals understood that. All the tourists would be leaving after the Labor Day weekend and hurricane season would begin. I could not have cared less about hurricanes. Maybe it was the salt in our genes. Besides, the really big storms hardly ever actually occurred with the same intensity as the geniuses on the weather channel would predict. They blew out to sea, they stalled off the coast and lost their strength, they took a turn and set a new course to ram Cape Hatteras or they simply never materialized. The majority of hurricanes were merely an inconvenience, except for the one sleeping in Gracie's bed. That was the one I had to watch like a hawk. I peeked in her room. She was still sleeping and probably would be for hours.

I poured two cups from the pot before it finished its cycle and wiped up the drips with a million paper towels. Why was I so impatient? I couldn't even wait for the coffeepot to finish brewing.

I went outside and brought Mimi's to her.

"Here you go," I said, handing her the mug. "So, what's all this?"

"They had cabbage and kale plants on sale at the garden shop at Kmart, so I got you some too! I just thought we could cozy up your path, you know what I'm talking about? Make it *say* something."

"Like what? Let's eat?"

"Linda! Are you okay? Get up on the wrong side of the bed?"

"No, I just had all these screwed-up dreams and I was up late last night and I had a little drama with Gracie and oh, hell, I don't know. . . ." I looked at the sky and could see dark clouds. Storms were building everywhere.

"Tell me your dream and I'll tell you what it meant," she said. "I got this book on dream interpretation and I'm pretty good at it."

That was Mimi in a nutshell. She could read a book, hang a shingle on her door the next day and she actually would make a living from it.

I took a deep breath and told myself to be nice to my sister. After all, it didn't pay to nitpick with the Rock of Gibraltar.

"It's so Irish to tell your dreams," I said and giggled. "Momma used to say that if you told your dreams before breakfast, they came true."

"Momma was a superstitious Irish Catholic with a loose screw too!"

"Mimi! You've never said . . ."

"Ssh! Don't say I said it or I'll call you a liar! Now are you gonna tell me your dream or what?" She put her mug on the bottom step and began laying out the pots.

"Okay," I said and repeated as much as I could remember.

After only a short pause she said, "Honey, that ain't nothing but you thinking about your work. You're surrounded by all these people and you don't know them yet. And the party where nobody shows up? That's just you trying to get a new life together. I mean, if you had a party now, who would you invite? You need to do something to make some friends."

"Probably, but I have you and work and not much time left over. So what do you think about the old man? That's not the first time I've dreamed about him."

"Maybe he's your daddy figure? I don't know what to tell you about that one. What did you dream the last time?"

I told her the dream and the subsequent episode with Gracie of the night before and she got the shivers, which was particularly notable since the thermometer had already climbed to well over eighty-five degrees.

"What's wrong?" I said.

"Girl! You might be getting a message from the Great Beyond!"

"Yeah, right! Now I'm the freaking Sylvia Browne of Mount Pleasant. Let me help you with this stuff."

"You got a hose?"

"I wouldn't even know! I'll go look under the house."

I had yet to roam around in the garage. I guess I felt like it wasn't part of the living space and therefore it wasn't part of what I had rented. But maybe it was. I would have to call Lowell and ask him. I pulled open one side of the double doors and squinted to see what was inside. It was filled with every kind of household debris you can imagine. Rusted bicycles, old lawnmowers, a mountain of paint cans, boxes of books, a high chair, an old rollaway bed with a mildewed mattress, and an endless stream of useless rakes, worn-out brooms and other gardening equipment. Everything *but* a boat. Some boathouse! And no hose.

I looked around and all I found that would help was an ancient galvanized tin watering can. It was covered in cobwebs, so I knocked them off with my sandal and looked inside for spiders. None found, I gingerly lifted it from its grave and went back outside to look for an outdoor spigot.

"Oooh! That garage is disgusting with a capital *D!*"

Mimi looked up and said, "I'll bet it is! Is it yours too?"

"Jesus! We even think the same thoughts! I have to ask. But if it is, it could sure come in handy! When the Montclair house sells, I'll have to find a place for all my stuff! God knows, it won't fit upstairs."

"Speaking of which, any nibbles?"

"Not yet, which reminds me to call my broker and see what's going on. Anyway, I'm gonna find a spigot."

"Yeah, there must be one since they used to store boats here."

Sure enough, I found one but it didn't work. It was probably turned off

and if I could ever kick my way through the museum of decay in the
garage, maybe I could locate the main valve and get it working again. The
more I thought about the garage, the more I wanted it. I could use it for
storage for sure. But I could also get new bicycles and some decent gardening equipment. I could pull my car inside so it wouldn't get bombed
with the calling cards of birds. My old Chevy Blazer was ugly enough as it
was.

Walking back to Mimi, I could see a storm coming. It was going to rain
and soon.

"I don't think we have to worry about watering those babies today," I
said, calling out. I pointed up to the darkening sky and she looked up,
shaking her head.

"It was so beautiful when I got up! I'm telling you, all you have to do is
wait five minutes and the weather changes. Let's go make some eggs," she
said, "I'm finished anyway."

I was embarrassed because Mimi had done all the work herself.

"Talk about perfect timing," I said, "I'm sorry . . ."

"What? Honey, I came early to do this and surprise you!" She threw
her arm around my shoulder and we went up the steps together. "Come
on, I'm starving!"

Within minutes, I had bacon sizzling in the pan and four eggs cracked
into a bowl.

"Gracie still sleeping?"

"Are you kidding? Still unconscious is more like it."

"Hmm," she said and poured herself another cup of coffee. "Guess
what? I went out with Jack Taylor again. Last night!"

"And . . . ?"

"And, we had a very nice dinner and a very nice bottle of wine and a
very long kiss at my front door!"

"Ahhhh! You kissed a man! How was it?"

"You know what? It's been so long since I laid my lips on a man, I
couldn't tell you if it was good or not!"

She burst into a fit of giggles and I, the sophisticated city slicker, spit my coffee through my nose, laughing and coughing at the same time.

"Stop! Augh!" I said. "Oh, my God! How ridiculous are we?"

"Very! So, tell your Mimi! When's the last time you laid those collagen lips on a stud muffin?"

"Collagen? Sister? If I could afford collagen, don't you think I'd have a better wardrobe?" I blew my nose and sighed deeply, thinking about all the married rats I had dated one time and never again. "God, wait! When was the last time I kissed somebody? And, how are we qualifying the kiss? Does that have to be a romantic kiss or can it just be a kiss to get on with business or what?"

"Ahem! Just what is a *get on with business* kiss? Is this something they do up north?"

I turned the bacon onto the three folded paper towels next to the frying pan and thought for a moment before answering. Was I going to horrify my sister with the truth or sugarcoat the facts of life to keep her estrogen levels in check? Aw, what the hell, I thought as I stirred the eggs around.

"Up north? Don't they screw just for the fun of it in the south?"

"Yeah, but they usually get twenty dollars for it! What are you telling me? All y'all Yankee girls go hooking for fun?"

"Yeah, right. Come on! Haven't you ever been out with some guy and just gone to bed with him because it had been a zillion years since you'd been to bed with someone?"

"Nevah! Nevah! Nevah!" Mimi said and clutched her bosom for effect. "Okay. Maybe one time, but it was a long time ago and I was drunk, so it didn't count, I think, I mean, it was Captain Somebody Rum! Yes! I remember now! I never drank rum again! But do that on a regular basis? Nevah!"

"Right, sure, whatever. Throw some white bread in the toaster and I'll get these eggs."

"Okay." She unwound the twist tie on the bread and placed two slices in my toaster oven. I could tell from the curl of her lips that there was something brewing in her frosted blonde head. "Don't you know that when a southern woman has unintentional sex, it doesn't count?"

"Really? And for men?"

"It probably doesn't count for them either—at least it shouldn't! After all, it's the twenty-first century! You have to let go of that old double standard thing, Linda!"

"That is the most stupid thing you have ever said. But! I like it. And, I may adopt the philosophy."

It was so easy to have breakfast with my sister, and just plain old regulation fun had been scarce in my personal life. For years! Until recently, how many times in the last ten years had we shared a meal? Two? Three? What had been a rarity had now become something I could have almost any time I wanted it. That tiny benefit lifted some part of me that I couldn't explain.

I set the table for us with place mats and paper napkins and she came right behind me, folding the napkins and rearranging the flatware. I cannot help a little sidebar notation on the fact that if I lived under the same roof with her permanently, it wouldn't be long before she would witness the deep furrowing of my brow.

As we sat down and began to eat, the skies began to rumble. The first crack of lightning burst over the water of the harbor and it began to pour. The storm was so loud we could hardly hear each other speak. The rain was coming west to east and sliding down the terrace doors in sheets. I kept watching the floor around it to see if water would seep in and it did not. Well, I thought, this may not be the grandest palace I have ever lived in but so far it doesn't leak. In Montclair, I had a collection of special plastic buckets stacked in the basement for heavy rain.

"I can't believe Gracie is sleeping through all this," Mimi said as the storm raged on.

"No kidding! It sounds like Zeus and Hera are having an intergalactic domestic dispute, but that's what you get for marrying your sister!"

"Redneck mythology? Where'd you get that tidbit?"

"Gracie did a paper on Greek myths last year so actually—"

"You did a paper on Greek myths?"

"Yeah," I said, "I got an A. Listen, speaking of Gracie, maybe you can give me a little help here. I'm worried about her."

"Honey? That girl is gonna be just fine!"

"Easy for you to say," I said. "You want more coffee?"

I started the water running and picked up our dishes to scrape.

"No, thanks. Don't run the water and the garbage disposal when it's lightning!" Mimi said. "You might get electrocuted!"

"What? Are you crazy?"

"Don't you remember Momma used to unplug the television and make us say the rosary? Don't you think it's dangerous?"

"She was crazy too, okay? Anyway, back to Gracie . . ."

"Yeah, and what happened last night. She came home a little toasted?"

"Yeah, but she was drugged too and she got very sick."

"Drugged?"

"Yes, at least I think so. She went out with Alex—"

"Brad's Alex?"

"Yeah, they were supposed to go to the movies but apparently the show they wanted to see was sold out and they met up with some football players from school and—"

"Football players are the worst! I mean, their whole thing is about physical aggression! But drugs and alcohol? I would think they would be worried about getting kicked off the team! School coaches are super strict about curfew and everything! Even grades!"

"Well, anyway, Alex brought her home and she was in quite a state. After I got her to bed he said he thought the girls had set her up because she's new and they were jealous and didn't want her to think she could just march in and be one of them or something."

We talked about Gracie and Alex for a while and Mimi almost had me convinced that what had happened to Gracie was within the range of normal. She reminded me that when we were Gracie's age, we had our share of fun and mishaps. But that didn't mean that accidents couldn't happen and I didn't recall any teenage girls I knew who were willing to feed pot brownies to another girl without her knowledge.

Mimi was quiet for a few minutes and then she said, "God! Girls can be so mean. Is Gracie all right?"

"We'll see when she gets up. Brad came over to pick up Alex. When he left it was a little strange."

"What was strange?"

"Because Alex hung around saying he stayed because Gracie's condition had frightened him and he called Brad. I mean, I think he was trying to let me know that someone had tried to maybe take advantage of Gracie. He socked this guy in the jaw and got Gracie out of this party as fast as he could and a friend of his drove them here."

"But he didn't tell you exactly what had happened?"

"I don't think he knew. But his knuckles were all cut up. And he was pretty upset."

"Good grief. Oh Lord! Raising a child in this world today is so complicated! All this glamorized sin on television . . ."

"You said it. Well, I'll get the whole story from Gracie but I just wanted to tell you this so that maybe you could just say to her that she really needs to be more careful with herself."

"So, what did Brad have to say for himself?"

"We actually had an interesting conversation—well, mostly the conversation went on between him and Alex, but I got an earful on Loretta. I think he came in case it was necessary to go to the emergency room or something and anyway he had to drive Alex home. Speaking of which, remember he was just there himself for that racing heart thing? You got him the cardiologist? Men! He thought he was having a heart attack but what he was *really* having was a twenty-two-year-old former secretary."

"Oh, swell. What's the matter with men?"

"They don't like getting old. Neither do we. Anyway, he hung around and left."

"What's the matter with that? *Hmmm?* Did you want him to stay?"

"Oooh! You are so bad! Hell no! He's not for me! Good grief! Mimi!"

"Well, good, because Jack has someone he wants to introduce to Brad."

"But he doesn't even *know* Brad!"

Mimi got this very strange expression on her face and I thought she was about to say something and then she finally did.

"Look, available men are pretty hard to find. This gal is the widow of a young doctor who died last year from an aneurysm. According to Jack, she's about your age but she has three small children and she's supposed to be really, really beautiful."

"Well, that's nice, but I don't think Brad wants to meet anyone yet. Anyone serious, that is."

"Linda? Are you maybe a little bit sweet on Brad yourself?"

"Who are you sweet on, Momma?"

We turned to see Gracie in all her early morning splendor—terry shorts up to here and down to there, a T-shirt up to here and pushed over there and hair going every which way but where it should.

"I ain't sweet on *nobody!*"

"Hey, baby! Come give your Mimi a kiss!" Mimi said.

"How are you feeling this morning?"

"Terrible! My mouth tastes like crap. . . ."

"Couldn't we say something like *my mouth tastes like the bottom of a bird cage?*" Mimi said, trying in vain to instill a little gentility in Gracie.

"Ooooooh, Momma!" Gracie groaned and fell into old Mr. Epstein's recliner, curling up into a ball. "Last night? Thanks."

"Hey, I'll hold your head over the john anytime, kiddo, but we have to talk. Why don't you go brush your teeth and I'll make you some pancakes?"

"Okay," she said and turned to Mimi, "then I'll give my Mimi a smooch. Who can sleep around here anyway? Between the storm and y'all yakking at the top of your lungs?"

Did Gracie say y'all?

We didn't respond to her complaint about us and the storm was on its way to Georgetown by that point. The rumbles were less frequent and in the distance. There were small razors of lightning in the sky, dancing like swizzle sticks—not the earsplitting crackles of the last hour. The rain had softened but was still coming down in a steady pace. I went back to the business of the kitchen, putting together some instant batter for Gracie's pancakes, wiping the grease from the bacon pan and soaking the pan from the eggs.

"Look!" Mimi said. She pulled a credit card from her wallet, dumped the water from the frying pan and scraped it clean with her Visa card. "It's a little trick I learned from a cooking program." Then she rinsed it off and put it back in her wallet.

"Will wonders never cease?" I said and put three strips of bacon in the pan for Gracie. "You kill me."

The phone rang, scaring me half out of my wits. It was Gretchen Prater, my real estate broker from Montclair.

"I think we might be getting an offer for your house!" she said.

"Really?"

She told me that a couple had seen it, liked it and wanted to see it again.

"The wife's pregnant with their second child and he works in the city," she said. "He does very well. And listen, I just got a contract for the Hollanders' house—"

"Larry and Denise? They're moving?"

"Oh! You probably didn't hear. He took a job in L.A. Anyway, their house was built in the same year as yours. Same amount of bathrooms and an old kitchen and guess what? They had it listed for four eighty and they got four eighty!"

"No kidding!"

"Yep! I told you that the train station location makes all the difference. Anyway, as soon as I know something, I'll call you right away. I'm showing it to another family this afternoon too."

"Okay, this is gonna sound really stupid but what did we list the house for?"

"Well, that's the thing. You and I are so thickheaded and all, we spent all our time thinking about what we were gonna do about decorating the front entrance. I have to fax you a seller's agreement to sign."

"Oh Lord! And, I owe you money too! For the Pier One stuff, right?"

"Yep. I can fax you receipts for the wicker and the painter's bill and the plants and you can send me a check. It all comes to about six hundred dollars for the whole shebang! Or, if we sell this house as soon as I think we will, you can just pay me back from the sale."

"Whatever you think. Listen, how much should we ask?"

"Based on the Hollanders' sale? I'd ask for five ten. I mean, why not?"

"Holy mother! Well, why not? We can always come down."

"Give me a fax number. . . ."

I didn't have one so I gave her the one at the restaurant. We talked for a few more minutes and then we said good-bye. I was a little dizzy from the astronomical amount she thought we could get for the house. Fred would break out in a sweat if it happened. That thought cheered me immeasurably.

I turned to my sister, whose eyes were as big as bagels.

"Are we selling the ranch?" she said.

"Looks like a solid maybe," I said.

"I'll be right back," she said and went to powder her nose.

I thought for a moment. My insides felt a little seasick. If I sold the house, I was letting go of New Jersey forever. Was that what I wanted? Yes, I told myself, it is what I want. There was no longer any reason to go back. Even Fred had said nothing about us leaving.

Despite last night's incident, Gracie's friendship with Alex was a consolation to me. At least she finally had a friend who seemed to care about her welfare, a young man with a sense of morality and the courage of his convictions. And, Gracie had an after-school job that would help to keep her out of trouble. Of course, there was Mimi. Finally, there was my job on the lovely sparkling waters of Shem Creek with the sun and wildlife and oh, what was I doing? This constant inventory was enough to drive anyone right out of their mind.

"Whew! You sure are deep in thought! What is going on in that head of yours?"

I poured some batter in the skillet for Gracie's breakfast. "Well, it's like this, O wise and wonderful sister of mine. I'm about to cut my umbilical cord with Yankee territory and I'm a little bit nervous."

"Honey? You can always go back and shovel snow and throw bundles of newspapers any time you want."

"Life there wasn't *that* bad."

"Life there wasn't this *good.*"

And, *that* was the whole point.

Lucy & Douglas's Wedding Menu

Cocktail Hour

Gamberi Grille
(marinated, grilled shrimp)

Tuna Carpaccio Duane
(raw tuna)

Pettini Seared del Mare
(seared sea scallops)

Funghi Cotti di Portobello
(grilled portobello mushrooms)

Crab Cakes Fra Diavlo
(deviled crab cakes)

Minestra del Giorno

Cioppino
(Italian fish stew)

Insalata

Tricolore Insalata con Silenzio Cuccioli
(tricolor salad with hush puppies)

Piatto Principale

Pollo Champagne
(chicken with grapes in champagne cream sauce)

or

Fritto Misto
(assorted fried seafood)

Dessert

Cannoli-Filled Wedding Cake with Lemon Glaze

Sixteen

HERE'S LUCY!

—◆◆◆—

MIMI left after breakfast and I hurried to the restaurant to pick up my fax. When I arrived, Louise was standing by the new fish display case with O'Malley, holding the fax in her hand.

"Hey! Well, will you look at that?"

"I don't like the way that red snapper is looking at me," O'Malley said. "He looks sneaky. Maybe I should check his ID."

"Humph! Glad you came in," Louise said. "We got that wedding today and four waiters, including the Zone Man, called in sick. Here."

The Zone Man was a guy named Mike Evans who we had just hired away from The Trawler, another restaurant on Shem Creek. He called himself the Zone Man because he said that when he was in *the zone*, which we thought was a Transcendental Meditation or yoga/Zen term to mean what *in the alpha state* meant to the rest of the world, he was the best waiter on the planet. His absence was not a good sign.

She handed me the paper and I glanced over it, trying to understand what I was about to sign. "Four waiters?" I said. "Thanks. Are you joking?"

"Do I strike you as the joking kind?"

"We have to do something about them."

"I agree entirely, but today is not the day."

"You're right. Okay, no problem, I'll work this afternoon. But I have to go home first. I can be back by three."

"Thanks, Miss Linda," Louise said. "At least the weather is clearing up."

"Yeah, that's a break," O'Malley said. "I still can't believe that Brad gave them the sunset deck for their cocktail hour."

"Yeah, that was rather stunning," I said. "He's losing money left and right on this deal."

"See?" Louise said, smiling wide. "Y'all don't know all there is to know about him! No, sir!"

"Like what?" O'Malley said.

"Like he's romantic, that's what!" Louise said. "He got to talking to the bride, that Lucy woman, and she says she wants to serve Eye-talian food, because that's the first thing she ever made for her honey. Although she can't be much of a cook if she puts taco chips in a casserole."

"That sounds more Mexican but she didn't strike me as a gourmet either," I said, "more like an aging cocktail waitress." I wiggled my eyebrows at Louise and she covered her mouth, hiding her laugh.

"Don't be so cynical, Miss Jersey," O'Malley said. "If there's a lid for her pot, there might even be one for yours!"

"When my pot wants a lid, I'll let you know."

"Anyway, Mr. Brad, he says, *I think you should absolutely have the sunset deck! I mean, it's a wedding and how many times do you get married?* I was so surprised, I almost dropped my drawers! He knew I was listening to them talking and I hate that—when I get caught eavesdropping—you know? Anyway, he knows I never miss a thing around here. . . ."

"Girl? *Everyone* knows you don't miss a thing around here!"

"Well, I just be telling y'all that this man gots more romance in he head than he know what to do with and he ain't even knowing he got it! And that, my friends, is all she wrote!"

I loved when Louise got excited and lapsed into a kind of Gullah.

"He'll figure out what to do with it," O'Malley said, "as soon as Loretta's been cold long enough."

Louise and I stared at O'Malley for a second and grinned. It was rare to get anything that smacked of catty from him.

"You're a little late," I said. "I think that his *old*—and I use the term to mean *former*—secretary already took a swing at that ball—no pun intended."

"You bad," Louise said.

"But in a good way," O'Malley said.

"Thank you very much!" I folded the fax, put it in my purse and took out my sunglasses. "You know what? I could go for months and months in New Jersey and never need sunglasses."

"Well, if you don't wear them here, you'd have cataracts in about an hour!" O'Malley said.

"I'll see y'all later," I said. I turned to leave and then stopped. "Hey, Louise? Do we need my sister to help?"

Louise and O'Malley looked at each other, remembering what I had forgotten at that moment—how Mimi had lectured the patrons on caloric content. They looked at me, neither of them quite sure of what to say.

"Uh . . . uh . . . ," they said, in a chorus.

I just said, "Well, if you're desperate, let me know."

They smiled in relief and gave a little nod.

I picked up the dry cleaning, went to the gas station and returned home. Gracie was in front of the television set, flipping channels with the remote.

"Hey, honey! Whatcha watching? Anybody call?"

"Hey! Nothing *to* watch! And, nobody called."

I noticed that the counters were sparkling, all the food was put away and the dishwasher was humming. I knew I would be wise to acknowledge it. "Good. Hey, thanks for cleaning up the kitchen."

"Well, this place is so small every little mess really sticks out. I washed everything but the coffeepot—I ain't touching wet coffee grounds. Ew!"

"I don't blame you. It's pretty gross. I'll be right back."

I was pulling the plastic off the clean clothes and hanging them in my closet when Gracie came in and plopped herself on my bed.

"Wassup, baby doll?"

"Juss chillin' with my momma. Wanna go see a movie today?"

"Oooh! I'd love to but I have to work! Four people called in sick."

"Yeah, there's a concert out in Awendaw this afternoon. Is this a cosmic coincidence?"

"I'll tell you what. Brad's gotta stop hiring these kids and get some real waitstaff."

"No shit, Mom. . . ."

"Language!"

"Sorry, but you should hear them talking—half of them are a bunch of stoners anyway."

"They don't smoke pot at work, do they?"

"No, they burn a little bud in *church* and *then* they come to work," Gracie said.

"Smart-ass!"

"Mommy! Such language! I'm telling Mimi!"

"You go right ahead and tell her," I said and pinched her bottom. "So, what's up with you today?"

"Well, I've basically recovered from last night, which is a good thing because I've got that river sweep late this afternoon. I thought for a while it would get rained out, but no such luck!"

"I thought you were so enthusiastic about it! What happened?"

"*Mom?* What happens in the creek after a big rain?"

"Um, eighty billion, kazillion mosquitoes hatch?"

"*Exactly!* And, they love the back of my knees for some reason. God, I hate mosquitoes."

"Honey, nobody likes them but they feed the fish and the bats—food chain, you know."

"And tadpoles, dragonflies and sweet little girls like me too, okay? I do my homework, you know. Anyway, Lindsey left a pair of drawstring pants that I can stuff into waders, so I guess I'll go. I mean, I said I would. Maybe I can talk Alex into coming with us! Then Lupe can bring us and I'll have a ride! Excellent idea!"

She bounced from my bed, was out the door in the blink of an eye, and once more I was left to marvel at the energy of youth, and as my mother used to say, it was most surely wasted on the young.

I dressed for work and when I was ready to go, I stopped by Gracie's room. She was on the phone.

"Gimme two seconds of your time, okay?"

"I'll call you back," she said. "Alex is coming with me."

"Good. Um, listen, Gracie, we didn't really talk about last night and I didn't want to say anything in front of Aunt Mimi, but what do you think actually happened?"

"What do you mean?"

I leaned against the door and found myself drawn in by the details of my daughter's face. Her features were almost perfectly symmetrical and her eyes were so expressive, her smile so perfect . . . had I ever looked like her?

"Mom?"

"Oh, sorry, baby. I was just thinking that if I had known at your age what I know now I could've changed the world."

"Probably. So, waddup?"

"Um, can I ask you something? When did *wassup* become *waddup*?"

"When people *your age* started saying it," she said.

"I see. Thank you for that enlightenment."

"On the house."

"Listen, last night, Alex brought you home and then he stayed for a while."

"While I was having my NDE?"

"In English?"

"Near Death Experience."

"Yeah, okay. Anyway, Alex never said anything directly but he implied that the girls who gave you the brownies knew they had pot in them. I guess one of my questions is did *you* know?"

"Not until my head started spinning . . . do you mean they did it on *purpose*?"

"Yeah, that was what Alex seemed to think and he didn't like it very much either."

"Oh, my God! Mom! That completely *sucks!*"

"Exactly. Anyway, there was apparently some funny business with the boys that Alex rescued you from. Um. I guess what I'm getting at is that, you know . . ."

"That's right! Oh, God! Now I *remember!* Look, Alex is a little bit of a worry wart too, Mom. I mean, I was glad he cared but he totally didn't have to hit anybody. He just went nuts. I think he thought we had a *date* or something. Anyway, things got a little out of control."

"So, you're satisfied that none of the boys tried to get you to do something you didn't want to do?"

"Are you asking me if one of those little assholes tried to like rape me or something?" She looked at me and when she sensed that I wasn't breathing in a normal manner, she said in her usual Gracie speak, "Mom! Do you think I'm completely stupid?"

I knew that what she said had been intended to assuage my fear and panic. For a moment, I felt like an airline passenger in a nosedive, grabbing her words like an oxygen mask, then coolly laying it aside when the terror of a crash had passed. I took a cleansing breath as discreetly as possible. Remember: when dealing with teenagers, most especially your own, always appear unflappable.

"Okay, I just wanted to be sure that you were all right. That's all. I love you, you know."

"Mom! *Stop!* I'm fine! Listen, all these *southern boys?* They talk with this sweet accent and everything? But boys are the same *everywhere*. Believe me. I can handle myself. What *really* pisses me off is that the *girls* would do that. Girls are supposed to stick together."

I didn't say anything to her about her language. I was so relieved that she wasn't compromised, that is, beyond what I had seen. I mean, every, well not every, but most teenagers do something stupid at some point and suffer for it. I knew that. It made no sense to be a prude—it was about the same as being delusional, because believing *your own* idea of their reality came at a much larger price.

"Well, now you can remember this and don't trust those girls so fast. I gotta go."

I gave her a light kiss on the top of her head.

"Ah, hell. I guess I'll spend the afternoon in the marsh, picking up beer cans."

"It's a worthy endeavor! I'm very proud of you!"

When I got to the restaurant, the dining room was almost empty. I went to my office, read over the real estate agreement, and having no freaking idea what I was signing, I signed it and faxed it back to Gretchen in New Jersey after making the sign of the cross three times. The three times was a Romanian superstition I had acquired from my New Jersey days in the dark with a coworker, trying to start a truck with a dead battery. *Three times is the charm,* he had said. Okay, I thought, the truck started and I never forgot it.

I took a bin of bar supplies up to the sunset deck and found Louise there with Duane. She was draping white tulle all around the banisters and tying it up at the columns with white ribbons and bunches of daisies. Duane was rattling off the menu and she was arguing with him as usual.

"Doo-wayne? What the devil is Key o Pino?"

"*Cioppino!* It's fish chowder, Louise! The only significant difference is some red wine in the stock base and that you leave the clams in their shells!"

"Gonna be clam shells all over kingdom come too!" Louise said and looked up to see me. "Come here, Miss Linda. Look at this fool business! Doo-wayne's printing up menu cards for the table with all these Eye-talian names and I ain't letting him do a thing without me seeing it first!"

"I swear! Y'all are like two cats in a bag! Whatcha got, Duane?"

He handed me the draft for his printed menu, sighing with frustration. "You know, you try to add a little sophistication to this dreary world and you're met with nothing but derision!"

"Poor Duane!" I said. "Listen, honey, every act of true genius requires courage. You know that, don't you?" I gave him a little elbow on his arm and although he continued to pretend to be insulted, he knew his ally had arrived and would save him from Louise.

"Well, this time my precious mettle has been tested nearly beyond my endurance!"

"Oh, shush! Let's see. Okay. *Cioppino*—I heard about that one. Okay, what's Fritto Misto?"

"Fried seafood," Duane said, "on plates, not in a basket! It *is* a wedding, after all. And during the cocktail hour we have platters of roasted *funghi* . . ."

Louise's eyebrows, which got a lot of exercise on any given day, were arching, dipping and stretching all over her forehead. "Foon gee, my big fat foot," she said, under her breath, "sounds like something you can only do in the eyes of God if you're married!"

"Sounds like something that grows under your toenails," I said, laughing.

"I *heard* that!" Duane said. "*Funghi cotti di portabello, gamberi grille* . . ."

No one was paying attention to Duane and naturally he was miffed. He probably spent two days on the Internet finding all the correct Italian spellings.

"Sorry, Duane! How do you say puppies in Italian?" I said.

"*Cuccioli*, I think," Brad said, coming up the steps. "What's going on up here?"

"Hey, there! Afternoon comedy hour! And, how do you say quiet?"

"Ah! That one's easy! *Silenzio!*"

"Ha! I see where you're going! Let's put that on the menu! *Silenzio cuccioli!*" Duane said. He grabbed the menu from me. "Oh, God! I *love* it! Linda! If you ever leave, I *definitely* quit! The rest of the menu is *tricolore* salad and cannoli wedding cake. And of course there's *pollo champagne* if somebody is allergic to *fritto misto*. Does that meet everyone's approval?"

He didn't wait for nods. He just spun and flew down the steps.

"What kind of fool thing is he talking about now?" Louise said. "Silen-zero Cucco? *What* did he say?"

I was dying laughing and so was Brad. "Hush puppies, Louise. *Silenzio cuccioli!* He's serving just about the same thing we always serve—fish chowder, fried seafood and hush puppies with a green salad. I think we should serve *mucca pazza bistecca*," Brad said.

"What kinda fool. . . ?" Louise's agitation had disappeared and she was laughing now too.

"Mad Cow Steak, with an amusing *fungi* sauce on the side, of course!"

"I love this job," I said. "There's a store in Ridgewood, New Jersey, called The Nut House. I always thought it would be funny to work there. But this is way better!"

"Yeah, this is some nut house, all right," Louise said. "I'm going downstairs. We got flowers and ferns coming. Better see about that and make sure the Fat Bastard got here too."

"Louise!" I said, shocked by her language. "Who are you talking about?"

Now it was Louise's turn to laugh along with Brad.

"What?" I said. "What's so funny?"

"Fat Bastard is the brand of wine they insisted on serving," Brad said. "Lord only knows why! It's terrible! But she wanted Fat Bastard and frozen margaritas. Some sentimental thing, I guess."

Louise started to leave again but Brad stopped her. "Louise? This looks awfully nice. Isn't it great to have a wedding here?"

"Yes, it surely is," Louise said, and disappeared down the steps. "Bring us all good luck!"

Brad and I were left alone for the next ten minutes or so and I decided it was a good time to thank him for his concern last night. I had the bar almost ready to open.

"Hey, Brad, um, well, thanks. You know? For last night and everything." What was the matter with me, stammering all around?

"Oh, shoot. It was nothing." He grabbed a handful of pistachios from the bowl on the bar.

He stared at me the same funny way he had the night before. I was glad that at least this time I had on makeup.

"Yeah, it was. It was a big deal to come out at that hour. Thanks." I leaned down and pulled up a handful of ashtrays to put around the deck on the odd chance that someone still smoked.

"No problem. Everything okay today?"

"Yeah," I said, and went behind the bar to unlock the liquor cabinet. "In fact, Alex is going with Gracie on this river sweep thing."

"Cleaning up the riverbeds?"

"Uh-huh," I said. Jeez! Why did I always talk like such a moron around him? I could do better! "Uh, actually I think they're onto a good thing actually. Learning about the environment is surely more beneficial than sitting in front of a television. Don't you agree?" With the exception of that one *uh* and the two *actually*s I felt better about my facile use of the language.

"Definitely," he said, with a smirk. "Hey! Here comes the bride!"

I rushed around to the railing to see the long white movie-star limousine pull up in front of our poor little dump of a seafood joint. Her bill for the car would probably be twice as much as the dinner. O'Malley was right—I was too cynical. But the romantic in me waited to see the bride emerge and when she did, what a sight she was.

She was wearing a skintight white spandex halter dress to her knees with a veil that went to the ground. She had more cleavage than Dolly Parton and more razzle-dazzle fake diamonds than all the vendors on QVC! Wow! Four other cars were behind her, loaded with guests, and I suspected there were more to follow.

Brad looked at me with his jaw hanging and said, "Well?"

"Well, what? I say, gentlemen? Start your blenders!"

The sunset deck was bulging with wedding guests within minutes and it was all I could do to keep up with the drink orders. But everyone seemed to be having a wonderful time. O'Malley had come up to help, which I appreciated very much. Erica and Lisa were passing hors d'oeuvres on bamboo trays.

"Thought this was a party of twenty-four," he said quietly. "So far, I've counted over fifty people."

"Well, that's typical," I said.

"Yeah, I'll go tell Duane to add water to the soup."

"Get another blender!"

So far, it didn't appear that Brad was going to lose one dollar on the cocktail hour judging by the rate of consumption. There was an excitement in the air that only comes with a wedding reception. One of the guests was leaning on the bar, trying to get my attention.

"Hi," I said, "what can I get for you?"

"A glass of white wine would be great," he said. "Hey, do you need a hand back there?"

"Are you a bartender?" I put the goblet in front of him and filled it.

"My dear lady, I happen to be the Cheese Whiz of Charleston!"

"What? What are you talking about?"

"I'm Arthur Fisher, by the way." He extended his hand; I gave it a good shake, and he winced. "Some grip!"

"Sorry." Unfortunately, first impressions are sometimes all we are given and I decided this fellow was a little peculiar.

A great-looking blonde woman who must have been his girlfriend came through the crowd and took his elbow. "Don't bother the nice lady, Arthur."

I giggled and said, "Glass of wine?"

"Sure, thanks," she said, "he's really harmless. Did he give you a whole cheese education yet?"

"No," I said.

"I actually offered to help her, Anna," Mr. Whiz said. "She's running this whole bar by herself and I just thought . . ."

"Actually, the other bartender will be right back. So, where do you perform your cheese wizardry?"

"I just left High Cotton downtown and I'm at Cypress for the moment."

"Never been there," I said. "I just moved back here a couple of months ago."

"That's the thing, isn't it?" Anna said. "Once you get the South Carolina sand in your shoes, you always come back."

"Sure seems that way," I said and turned to help some other guests, but Arthur kept talking.

"Come see us at Cypress," Arthur said, "I'll make you a green apple martini and dazzle you with dairy."

"How cheesy can you get?" I asked, and put a batch of margaritas in the blender.

Arthur would have been happy to stand there all day making cheese jokes but Anna finally pulled him away.

Finally, the bride approached.

"Hi! Congratulations!"

"Thanks! Isn't this just wonderful? Isn't life wonderful? Isn't the world wonderful?"

I smiled and just shook my head. "Yes, it is. Can I get something for you?"

"Yes! I believe I'm gonna have me a big old martini! But, don't tell Doc!"

I crossed my heart and opened two mini-bottles of gin.

"You married?" she asked.

"Nope?"

"Got a man?"

"Not right now," I said, shaking the gin and vermouth.

"Well, you should go on and find yourself one and take the plunge! There ain't nothing in all this cotton-picking world like being in love!"

Lucy, the bride of Doc Lutz, dressed like, saints preserve us, a pole dancer from a border town, was dead serious. And, I suspected she was dead right. In a peculiar twist of Lowcountry artistry, the beaming light behind her made her look radiant. In that moment, she looked absolutely angelic despite all her wardrobe and cosmetic attempts to appear otherwise. Maybe that was what made me really hear what she was saying. I poured her drink into a glass, added two olives on a toothpick, and placed it before her.

"Mrs. Lutz . . ."

"Call me Lucy, darlin'! But I *do* love the sound of Mrs. Lutz!"

"Lucy then. Lucy? I believe you. How do you know when it's the one?"

"Oh, honey, that's easy. You find the right man when you put out the vibe that you're the right woman! And, one other thing, you have to be ready."

She raised her glass to me, took a very large gulp and moved back among her guests.

Dinner was announced and everyone slowly drifted downstairs. O'Malley and I stayed behind to clean up and get ready for the regulars to arrive. It was barely five o'clock, and within the hour we would be packed to capacity again.

"Louise has got the downstairs bar under control," O'Malley said, "and Brad's there to help her if it gets crazy."

"Good," I said. "With all the extra wedding guests, our regulars are going to have a fit!"

"That's the beauty of a preplanned menu," O'Malley said, "Louise will have them fed and out of here in an hour."

"This I gotta see," I said. "I think that crowd takes their partying seriously."

I looked out at the bridge over Shem Creek. Under it, I saw a group of about twenty people with black plastic garbage bags, stooped, picking up garbage. It had to be Gracie's river sweep team. I spotted Jason Miller and thought about my prejudice toward him. Just because I didn't like him did not mean that he wasn't a good influence as a teacher. Indeed. If anyone had told me three months ago that my Gracie would spend a glorious afternoon picking up beer cans and cigarette butts I would have laughed. Now, if the beer cans were full? Then, yes, Gracie might have been the first to sign up.

"What's going on?" O'Malley said.

"You won't believe this, but that's Gracie and Alex and a bunch of kids from Wando. They're doing community volunteer work to clean up Shem Creek."

"No way! When I was that age I would've screamed my head off if somebody made me do that."

We looked down again and Jason Miller was coming toward the restaurant with the kids. Directly below us was the main dining room with an enormous open-air porch, probably crammed with early diners, as were all the other restaurants along the creek. He was carrying a tube that he stopped to open. He pulled out and unrolled posters, giving one to each student. They climbed up on the dock and proceeded to the area just below the porch and lined up. The hair on the back of my neck stood up and my heart began to race. They held up their posters for the diners to see. They said, *Shem Creek is dead and it's your fault! Boats kill habitats! Stop supporting restaurants that poison the water!*

Before I had the time to faint, I said, "I gotta get Gracie and Alex out of there."

I hurried down the steps and out to the dock as fast as I could, and by the time I got there Brad had Alex's arm and was already in the middle of the group. I grabbed Gracie by the hand and pulled her away.

"Have you lost your mind?" I said. "I *work* here!"

"I didn't know he wanted us to protest, Mom," she said, "I swear! Neither did Alex!"

"Well, there went *your* after-school job," I said, moving back in the group to hear what was being said.

"I'm just trying to make a living here," Brad said.

"Yeah? And, I can show you statistics that prove you and all the others along here are killing the water," Jason Miller said.

"You're a little aggressive, okay? Let's move along and not disturb my patrons any more than you already have," Brad said. "Okay, pal?"

Then I heard the sirens. I took Gracie and Alex back inside and put them in my office.

"Do not leave this room, do you hear me?"

Gracie glared at me and Alex stared at the floor.

The dining room became a little chaotic and many people were asking for their checks all at once. Others were standing along the porch railing, watching. One thing was certain—this was not good for business.

I went back upstairs to the sunset deck, where O'Malley was serving drinks as quickly as he could. Quite a crowd had gathered there, most of them hanging over the side, gawking at what was going on below. I saw Jason Miller taken away in handcuffs and the kids were apparently free to go home. At that point, the posters had been put away, probably stuffed in their garbage bags or taken in for evidence. I called Louise on the intercom.

"Hey, it's me. Listen, Gracie and Alex are in my office."

"No, they ain't," she said.

"What?"

"They're washing dishes with Lupe! I told them they were getting demoted!"

"Good! Lupe's here?"

"Honey, it's all hands on deck today!"

"How's the bride? Do you need a hand down there?"

"The bride is leading a conga line around the dining room, twitching around like she's got fleas and kissing all the men. On the lips. And they're not her guests."

"I'll be right down."

WHIRLPOOL

came into work in the morning, said hello to everyone and began
what had become my morning routine. First thing, I checked the
restaurant's e-mail. There was something from Lindsey for me. *Hi,
Mom! I'm fine! Did you kill Gracie yet? Ha ha! Love you, L.* I sent her one
back. *Dear Lindsey, Love you! Love your e-mail! Gracie's not dead, but I plan
to kill her soon. Call her and tell her to watch herself! Miss you madly! Mom.*

E-mail? I loved it.

I started downloading yet another version of some bookkeeping software and decided to get something to drink from the kitchen while the
download continued. It occurred to me that if I received a dollar for every
minute I waited for something to download or for every minute I waited
on a telephone for a human voice, I would be a very wealthy woman. It
also occurred to me that if I would stop searching for the latest version of
this and that, I might actually get my work done in half the time.

Louise and Duane were together at the back door, checking the
amount of the produce delivery against the invoice. It may have been Labor Day, but that didn't mean it was a holiday for us. Thanksgiving,
Christmas and New Year's Day were it. There were stacked crates of lettuce, onions, carrots, celery, string beans and herbs all over the porch in

the delivery area. Once they had counted them and signed off on them with the trucker, they began bringing them indoors and opening them to check the contents.

Louise and Duane never argued over the quality of food—it was perfect or back it went. I had come to understand that despite their bickering, their shared view on quality was why Louise tolerated Duane's other eccentricities and why Duane tolerated Louise's meddling. Louise understood that Duane ran a kitchen so clean that a doctor could perform emergency surgery there without prior notice. And Duane knew that on his days off Louise would leave it even cleaner. They may have had disparate personalities but their souls were grown from the same seed.

The slightest question over the smell of a fish or the blemish of a vegetable would provoke a great discussion between them and remind them they were comrades in the war against mediocrity. Louise needled Duane without mercy but she would be the first person to say that he was a talented chef of very high standards. And, he might say she was like gnats at sunset, but she was the only person whose opinion he sought in all matters pertaining to the kitchen.

"They call this beat-up thing a Vidalia?" Louise said, holding an onion with a large soft spot in front of his face to inspect. "I wouldn't feed this to the rats!"

"Oh, Lord!" Duane said. "You're right. That won't do." He began digging through the onion crate.

"Morning, all!" I said. "Is Brad in yet? Y'all have a good weekend?"

"Hey! Morning! Some weekend! One day!" Louise said. "Ain't seen hide nor hair of him so far."

I poured myself a glass of iced tea. Although it was not yet ten o'clock, it was very warm. It was the kind of day you prayed the air-conditioning system would behave itself.

"About half of these onions are rotted!" Duane said. "But that was some wedding this weekend, huh?"

"Forgive me," I said, "I know that bride was a little bit tacky but didn't you love her?"

"Oh my, yes! Here," Louise said, and handed me the produce invoice. "She was tacky as white shoes after Labor Day, but she loves that old man so much, well, it just did my heart good to see all that happiness."

"What happened to that crackpot, Jason Miller?"

"Who knows? I heard they gave him a ticket and released him," Duane said. "Yes, there's nothing like a wedding. It's just such a hopeful thing to do, you know? And, they loved the *cioppino*." Duane waved his arms in the air like a rave as he over-enunciated the *p*'s.

"Yes, they did," Louise said, with a chuckle. "It's a good thing you made plenty! Doo-wayne? You are so crazy. Do you know that?"

In Louise's secret language that meant that *she* was crazy about *him*.

"Y'all need a hand?" I asked.

"No, thanks," Duane said, "but I do need the number of the produce guy from Wentworth Farms. They must've left their onions in the sun too long. And Vidalias rot faster than you can whistle Dixie."

"I'll get it for you in a flash," I said and went through the swinging doors.

There, at the reception area, wearing a celery-green T-shirt and matching Capri pants, stood Amy. Her princess slides were the same color, but the toes had pale pink leather flowers. Needless to say, her toenails were painted the exact same shade, like a teacup poodle from Marilyn Monroe's era. There was something sickening about the grooming politics of that time.

"I thought you were going back to Atlanta," I said.

The tone of my voice said it all. It took two seconds for the lit fuse to reach the cherry bomb, but when it did, she had a retort at the ready.

"And, I thought *you* worked in the office," she said, "and, I don't suppose you would tell me anyway if Brad was here."

"I work all over this restaurant and, no, Brad's not here."

"Well, is Louise here?"

"Sure! You just stay right there and I'll go get her!"

That was perfect. Louise would nip a chunk out of her carcass before she knew what hit her. I swung open the door to the kitchen. Louise was standing next to the island, holding a head of romaine lettuce, pulling back the leaves.

"Filthy!" she said. "So nasty you gonna have to throw away more than you can use! Looks like they froze it."

"Hey, Louise!" I said.

"You got that number?" Duane said.

"No, but there's a number in the dining room," I said. "Amy's here and she wants to talk to *you*, Louise."

You could've heard a leaf of parsley drop in the following moments.

"What's she want with me?"

"I think she thinks I'm unreliable in the message department."

"I'm coming too," Duane said, "I always miss *everything!*"

"You just stay put!" Louise said.

Louise's face took on the glaze of a partner in crime and together we went out to the dining room to ruin Amy's day.

"I'm Louise," she said. "What can I do for you?"

"I'm Amy. . . ."

Louise drew herself up to her full height and her face turned to stone; her jaw in particular was a wedge of granite.

"Um-hmm," she said slowly, "I'm well aware of that."

Not one to be summarily dismissed, Amy put her hand on her hip and glared at Louise, drawing her line in the linoleum. Louise, at the same time, gave Amy the head-to-toe traveling hairy eyeball. Amy was messing with the wrong person.

"Look, I just want to leave Brad a message," she said and turned to me. "Don't you have something else to *do?*"

Louise and I exchanged looks of surprise.

"No, I don't guess I do," I said and raised two of my fingers to my lips in mock embarrassment.

"No, I guess she doesn't," Louise said, and did the same thing.

Amy took the one-two punch and didn't even bat an eye.

"Oh, fine," she said. She opened her purse and pulled out a business card and a pen and wrote something on the back. She handed it to Louise. "Please tell Brad that this is the address and phone number of the house where I'll be for the next thirty days. I'm staying with my old roommate. Please ask him to call me, okay?"

She sashayed out the front door and Louise took a seat at the bar.

"Come here," she said to me. "You got an ashtray back there, Mr. O'Malley?"

O'Malley gave a low long wolf whistle and put the ashtray in front of Louise.

"You taking up cigarettes?" he said.

"Yeah, that's right. I'm gonna smoke something but it ain't tobacco. Matches?"

"She's at 1212 Thompson Avenue on Sullivan's Island," Louise said, "isn't that nice?"

I climbed on the bar stool next to her. I knew exactly what Louise was up to. She tore the card into four pieces. One by one, she lit each square, dropped it in the ashtray and watched it burn.

"I don't *like* that woman," Louise said. "I just don't *like* her."

"Me either. Not one bit. But did we think Brad could get rid of her that easily? He told us she was going back to Atlanta."

"How old are you? Men lie," Louise said. "You should know that by now."

"Well, Brad doesn't own Charleston County. Maybe she decided to hang around and work on him."

"Yeah, that's just what he needs is a little redheaded Jezebel to work on him."

We both sighed hard enough to rattle the hanging racks of O'Malley's wine glasses.

"Can I get you ladies something?" O'Malley said. "Serious times call for serious solutions."

"No, thanks," I said. "Just get rid of the evidence. We don't want anyone to find out we were burning garbage. I gotta get a phone number for Duane."

Louise followed me to my office. I wrote the number of Wentworth Farms down on a piece of paper.

"I'll give it to him," she said.

"Thanks."

"So, that was Amy."

"Yeah. That was Amy."

Our eyes met, we pursed our lips and shook our heads in mutual disgust.

"She's a little too bold for me," Louise said.

"Honey, she ain't nothing. Just another amoral, overgroomed, self-absorbed numb nut from a TV reality show starring sex addicts."

"Um-hmm. That just about covers it. I'm going back to work."

I worked through the bills and just before we opened for lunch, Louise and I hosted a little "Come to Jesus" meeting with the four waiters who had bailed out on us for the rock festival. Sullen and generally uninterested, they sat before us at a table in the corner of the dining room.

"Here's the deal," I said, "you ladies and gentlemen can be replaced in a heartbeat. If you do this again, you're gonna get replaced."

"No, Linda, you're being too soft on them," Louise said. "Look, I remember what it was like to be your age. If I wanted somebody to hire me and they said *okay* and gave me a chance, showing up and doing what I was supposed to do was the bare minimum. I was also expected to act like I *enjoyed* the job and *appreciated* the job and wanted to *keep* the job! You folks don't seem to abide by that concept. You don't just show up when you feel like it and go off to a concert when we have a wedding going on."

I looked across the faces, which didn't seem penitent in the least. Two of them were chewing gum, one was staring out the window and the other was listening so intently it made me nervous. Cokehead? (And I don't mean the carbonated variety.) Louise sighed and looked at me for help.

"Listen up, okay? It's not *fair* to the other people who work here for you just to bail out on them. We find ourselves short of hands, the customers don't get the service they deserve and then they go someplace else next time they go out to dinner. Your choices jeopardize our business and the livelihoods of all the other employees. I mean, look, y'all might be going to college and still getting some help from your parents. We're not. This is it for us."

The Zone Man, Mike Evans, spoke up. "Uh, we know you're right and I guess we just didn't think about it from that point of view. I think I can speak for all of us that it won't happen again."

I didn't have faith in him for a single minute. Besides, who had elected him spokesman?

"Okay. If you want time off, just ask for it. You know? Then at least we have a chance to find someone to fill in for you."

"Okay," Louise said, "nuff said. Let's get to work."

The lunch hour came and went and there was a slight but persistent wafting of sour discontent surrounding the waiters. At one point when I was bartending with O'Malley, I said, "So what do you think? Think the Brat Pack will shape up after the little therapy session Louise and I gave them?"

"Nope," he said, "I wouldn't waste my breath on them."

"Really? Not even the Zone Man?"

"Except him. He's cool. I'd probably try to keep him but I would dump the rest of them. They don't get it."

Around three o'clock, Brad moseyed in with Bogart and stopped at the front desk, where I was going over the dinner reservations with Connie, the hostess.

"Hi! Do I have any messages?"

"Is this your dog?" Connie said. "What's his name?"

No, I thought, that is a kidnapped dog, you moron. Call the authorities. I said nothing.

"Bogart," he said. "I'm taking him to the vet for a checkup. Messages?"

"Oh! Sorry! Yep, here they are. Theo called once, Robert called and said he and Susan are coming for dinner and someone named Amy called four times."

"Only four?" I said.

"Oh, swell," he said, "she didn't leave."

His chin was tucked because he was reading the messages, but even from where I stood on the side of him I could see delight sneaking across his face. He could say whatever he wanted but I knew that, on some level, he enjoyed the attention Amy gave him.

"So, where have you been?" I said.

"Can I use your office for a minute?"

"Sure," I said and followed him there. Bogart settled himself next to the wall as though he'd been in the office all his life.

"Well, as incredible as this may seem, I was out kayaking with my son."

"No kidding! How was it?"

"Incredible. Just incredible. Right over there on the other side of the bridge, right past Shem Creek Bar and Grill, is this place called Coastal Expeditions. I'd seen it but I never looked into it for some reason. Too busy, I guess. Alex found it on a place mat at Billy's Back Home Restaurant, where I took him for breakfast this morning. One of those little ads?"

"Right, right. So?"

"So, he said, can we go check it out and I said sure, why not? We went over there and hired two guides and went all over the other side of Shem Creek, out in the harbor and out to Crab Bank Island, which is this truly amazing bird sanctuary. It was beautiful!"

"I've never been kayaking. It sounds like work."

"Come on! You can't live here and never kayak! That's a sin! Think about it, you're in this little boat, paddling along, right at water level and here come the dolphins, swimming right next to you. Amazing."

"That would scare the living daylights out of me," I said.

"No, it wouldn't. They don't get that close to the kayak and besides, they have more to worry about than you do. You might eat them or stuff them and hang them on your wall. Anyway, it's perfectly safe."

"Gracie would probably love it. But, like, what if it turns over? And your legs get stuck? And, you can't, you can't get out? And you're hanging upside down in the water? And you drown?"

"Then, you die."

I looked at him and there was a grin across his face as wide as the Cooper River.

"Very funny."

"Are you always this big of a nervous Nellie about trying something new?"

I cleared my throat and stood up straight, realizing my hands were damp. "No. I am not. It's just that I like to know what the odds are on life and death before I get in the water. There are sharks all over the place, you know. Didn't you ever see *Jaws?*"

"Big deal. That's Hollywood. Well, suit yourself but I think you would really love it. If you could get someone to repair that broken-down dock on the Epsteins' property, you could put a boat in right there."

"Well, the pilings are still there . . . it's worth a thought . . . probably cost a million dollars to rebuild the dock."

"How about no? It wouldn't? Maybe Lowell would split the cost with you. Anyway, try it first. It's a healthy sport."

"Well, maybe I will."

We stared at each other for a minute while I was just standing there like a tobacco-store Indian, waiting for someone to move me to another room. He had wanted to use my office to have a moment of privacy and I continued to stand there.

"I'll just be a few minutes," he said.

I recovered and said, "Oh! Take your time. By the way, speaking of Lowell, if you happen to speak to him would you ask him if the garage is included in my rent? Tell him I'll get it emptied if he wants. It's full of junk."

"Sure. I gotta take Bogart and then I'll be back later on."

"Okay. See you later."

I left and went to find Louise.

"Who's cooking tonight?" I said.

"Yours truly," she said, "I figured Duane could use the time off. He just left. I mean, the man has worked the last eight days straight. Want to help?"

"Sure, why not? Gracie's coming in anyhow so there's no reason for me to rush home. You know, Louise . . ." I lowered my voice to a whisper. "I don't know how to cook, really. I mean, I make breakfast and hamburgers and meat loaf and spaghetti, but that's about it. Mimi's the cook in our family."

"You must be pulling my leg!"

I shook my head.

"Lord, help us! She can't cook. No wonder y'all are so skinny!" she said. "Okay, you got decent knives?"

"I ain't got squat."

"Mercy!" she said. "Okay. First thing you need to know about working in a professional kitchen is that every chef has their own knives. Knives are expensive, so you keep them locked up in a toolbox and take them home with you at night. But since this is your first time, you can use mine. Then, if you like cooking and you want to rotate with me in the kitchen, you got to go buy your own. Okay?"

"Okay."

And that marked the beginning of my training in the slice-and-dice club.

I was slicing onions the exact way Louise had shown me and scooping them into a metal bin that was used only for onions. There were many of them, all lined up in the same order every day. They held sliced onions, diced onions, garlic, green bell pepper, red bell pepper, watercress, chopped parsley, lemon wedges—they all needed to be filled and refilled. I had that knife rolling back and forth over fresh chives until they were minced like confetti.

The more I looked around the kitchen the more I learned. For example, they used three frying pans to every one pot. Things like potatoes were parboiled and then reheated in a pot. But string beans, carrots, asparagus, and any number of side dishes that were served along with entrees were blanched and reheated in butter or olive oil in a frying pan. That partial cooking and reheating routine sure got the food out to the dining room a lot faster. And the kitchen was in high gear long before the first customer would arrive for dinner.

"It's all about preparation," Louise said. "Once this place starts to rock and roll, there ain't no time for starting from scratch."

"I see that! This is like warming up the orchestra, right?"

"You got it! Now you're cooking with gas!"

Gracie was back and forth from the dining room to the kitchen, wiping down tables, setting up for dinner, and Alex was sweeping the floor. Lupe had dropped them off.

Louise and I were talking about Lindsey and her classes at school and then we rolled back around to Amy and how much we didn't like her. Alex and Gracie seemed to have a running commentary going about Gracie's passion for the water.

"It's about drainage!" she said, leaving through the swinging doors, carrying a rack of glasses. "You gotta have drainage!"

"That's what ditches are for!" Alex said, coming behind her with a broom and dustpan. "Don't you think the developers plan these—"

"No, they don't! They don't even monitor the water quality of Shem Creek and it's got the lowest rating . . ."

"Well, you'd be an idiot to drink it . . ."

When they were out of earshot, Louise turned to me.

"I heard her say that she joined a new club at school. In my day, clubs were for fun. I think they make these children too serious, 'eah?"

"You're right about that. You wouldn't believe some of the stuff they talk about. When I took health in high school, their idea of teaching reproduction was watching flowers bloom. On a good day, you got to see bees pollinating. That was considered wild and we were supposed to fill in the blanks. Now they practically hand out how-to videos."

"Humph," Louise said. "I don't know what this world is coming to."

Alex came back through, behind Gracie, stopping to empty his dustpan. "If you go to that rally, you're nuts."

"*Wha evah!*" said the young lady from New Jersey.

"Miss Gracie? What's got your bloomers all in knots? Tell Louise!"

"It's this Jason Miller guy," Alex said. "He's a creep!"

"Is your name Gracie? He is not," Gracie said. "He's one of the smartest people I have ever met. And, you don't even know him."

"Um, excuse me? Was I not here when he pulled out all those posters right in front of my dad's restaurant? The guy's a freak!"

"Okay, he's a little bit of a nut. I'll give you that, but I have learned more from him in just a few weeks than I ever knew about watersheds and how to protect my hometown than I learned in my whole life."

"Fine, you go with Jason Miller to his stupid rally and don't call me to bail you out of jail," Alex said.

"Fine," Gracie said and took another rack of glasses back to the dining room.

"What's this rally?" I said.

"You know that place up the creek where they're building the new restaurant?"

Louise and I nodded our heads.

"Well, I think he wants to plaster environmental posters all over it or something."

"Good Lord," I said.

"He's a busybody," Louise said. "And, maybe dangerous too, 'eah?"

"I think he's more of a jerk than a mastermind criminal. I gotta hose down the sunset deck," Alex said, and went out the back door to the service steps.

We watched him go and then I went back to chopping mushrooms. I didn't like what I had heard. I could not allow Gracie to protest against the businesses that put the clothes on her back and the roof over her head.

It was around four-thirty when Brad came back. We had just given the waitstaff the list of the dinner specials—Louise's specialties—benne seed shrimp for an appetizer, Carolina crab cakes for an appetizer or a main course, okra gumbo with Carolina white rice, baked flounder stuffed with crabmeat and grilled orange chicken with ratatouille. The dessert special was fried bananas over homemade vanilla bean ice cream. I got hungry just listening to them.

Brad was having dinner with Robert and Susan at six and when they arrived I made sure they were seated at the best table, which I had reserved for them. I went over to say hello.

Robert and Brad stood but I motioned for them to sit back down. I had never met Susan before and she looked exactly as Robert had described her— gorgeous. And, she was nice.

"It's so nice to meet you at last," I said, "Robert has said so many wonderful things about you."

"See? I'm a fabulous husband! Am I a fabulous husband or what? Right? Right?"

"You're fabulous," Brad said, shaking his head.

That Robert was hilarious.

"Oh, thanks!" Susan said. "And he's said some pretty terrific things about you too! It's nice to finally put the name and face together. Is Louise here?"

"Yeah, of course! Do you want me to tell her to come out or do y'all want to come back and say hello?"

"Tell her we'll pop our heads in, okay?" Robert said. "And, tell her I'm dying for her crab cakes, I've been thinking about them all day."

Men and their stomachs—you could write a book.

I gave Louise the message and went to check on the kids.

Gracie had decided to stay until I finished that night and was in my office doing homework. Alex was doing his on the other side of the desk. They seemed quiet and happy. Around nine when almost everyone had left, I got them some dessert, took the cash from O'Malley at the bar and went to my office to put it in the safe overnight.

"Here, I brought you something."

"Oh, man! Thanks, Mom!"

"Gosh, thanks!"

"Excuse me, sweetheart, I have to get in the closet behind you." I took the key from the top of the door frame, opened the closet door and knelt to open the safe. Gracie and Alex were watching me.

"Mom? Is that really smart? I mean to leave the key just right up there?"

"Well, honey, nobody knows it's there except Brad, Louise and me and now y'all. But if I can't trust you with that information, you should tell me now," I said, standing up and replacing the key in its spot.

"Cross my heart," Gracie said.

"I don't know, Ms. Breland, now that Gracie knows, I'd put it somewhere else," Alex said and winked at me.

"Alex! Finish your math or just give it to me and I'll do it! Let's get out of here. I want to go home and vege."

It had been a long day and I was tired too. Alex went to find Brad. Gracie and I said good night to O'Malley.

"I'm packing it in for the day," I said, "see you tomorrow."

"Yeah, we're closing soon. Pretty slow tonight."

Gracie and I walked across the parking lot and from there we could see that most of the other restaurants were nearly empty too. Most kitchens closed at nine and most people ate supper early. Even on the nights I stayed beyond my shift, it wasn't that late when I got home.

"Whatcha thinking, Gracie?"

"I don't know," she said, "a lot of things."

"Did you talk to Lindsey today?"

"Yeah. She's fine. I miss her, you know?"

"Me too." I gave her shoulder a rub. "Next year we start looking at colleges for you. Can you believe that?"

"I'm not even ready to think about it."

I unlocked the car with the remote and we got in, slamming the doors. All the way home, we were quiet. I was thinking about my girls and how unprepared we all seemed for life. How did anyone prepare for life? I was going around, acting like a great stoic, when most of the time I was shaking inside. Was Gracie shaking inside too?

Before I crawled into bed, I turned out the lights and went to her room to say good night. She was propped up on her pillows with her stuffed animals all around her and she seemed so little to me. And young. Her old pink-and-white quilt was pulled up over her waist, even though the house was warm.

"Want me to tuck you in?" I said.

"Yeah. Will you scratch my back?"

"You bet."

Gracie turned over on her stomach and pulled up her T-shirt for me and I began to run my nails across her bony ribs and shoulder blades.

"You know what? We need to fix up this room a little. Maybe we should take some pictures and frame them and cover that whole wall. What do you think?"

"Sure. Right in the middle," she said. "Ahhhhh! Gaaaaa."

"That means it's good?"

"Yeah."

"Gracie?"

"Hmmm?"

"How are we doing here?"

"What do you mean? How are we doing in South Carolina versus New Jersey? Or you and me or what?"

"I guess I mean, what's going on in Gracie's heart?"

"I'm okay," she said, but I could tell in the tone of her voice that something wasn't quite right.

"Come on, tell your momma. . . ."

She pulled down her top, rolled over on her back and chewed on her lip a little before speaking. Then she propped herself up on one elbow and looked in my eyes with an intensity I had only ever seen when it came from anger. This time though, it came from another place.

"Mom? It's different here, you know? I mean, Mount Pleasant has some things that Montclair didn't and Montclair has some things that Mount Pleasant doesn't. Kids are kids. There might be more white girls in my class, but they're just as bitchy as the girls I went to school with in New Jersey, except they're not as up front about it, but I think that's just their style. All teenage girls stick it to each other and especially outsiders. I'm still an outsider."

"Well, that won't last forever."

"It doesn't really matter. I just hang around with Alex anyway. And in classes, the girls are okay. And, academically I'm a little ahead in some subjects and behind in others, so I have a little catching up to do."

"Well, do you like Wando?"

"You want the truth? School sucks wherever you go."

"You just want to dance, right?"

"Yeah, but that's not all I want."

"What else do you want? A sports car? A million dollars?"

"That would be fine, but that's not what I was thinking. I was thinking that I want to see you happy like this for the rest of your life."

"What?"

"Look, you may not know it but everybody else does. You're the happiest I have ever seen you in my whole life. That's why I quit complaining about being here."

"What are you saying?"

"I am saying, Mom, that I would put up with anything to see my momma this happy."

"Yeah, but if my happiness comes at your expense, I can't be happy."

"Ma! Stop! I'm a teenage girl and all teenage girls are a pain in the butt! Now go to bed! We have to get up early in the morning and I don't want to see you dragging around like an old dog. I love you. I do."

"I love you too, honey. Good night."

I gave her a kiss and a hug and she hugged me for the longest time I could remember her hugging me in years. She got down under her covers and I turned out her light. I went to the door and turned back to look at her again. I loved her so much at that moment I thought my heart would burst.

EIGHTEEN

CRYSTAL BALL

T HEY say that danger lurks behind complacency and I say, oh, go needlepoint that on a pillow and sit on it. Oh, yes, Louise said things like that, making reference to the devil banging on your door if you neglected to send him an invitation to your party. She believed that bad things happened in threes and that you could predict rain by the shape of a new moon. If it was a bowl with its edges up, it was holding water. If the bowl was tipped, it spilled rain.

I would have to agree that generally, most people who were born and raised in the Lowcountry believed in something more than what they heard in church or learned in Sunday School. Too many inexplicable things happened and were reported by perfectly sober, intelligent and reasonable people. There was the story of the Gray Man of Pawleys Island, the story of Alice and the Summerville lights. The Lowcountry probably had as many ghost stories as the Tower of London.

Gosh, I remember when Mimi and I were kids, there was a girl in her class who swore her house had a death knock. If there was a knock on the front door three times and no one was there, someone in the family would be laid out at McAlister's Funeral Home within the month. Even her mother said it was true. We would beg her to let us come spend the night but I regret to report that we never heard anything except crickets.

For myself, I believed that my dreams processed all my daily stress and happenings and let them go. But, I was becoming suspicious that maybe there was more meaning to them. The concept of collective unconscious was intriguing to me, that you could somehow inherit the experiences of all your ancestors or all of humanity and that your dreams were filled with symbols that could tell you something, if only you knew how to break the codes. I had no clue on the codes but I knew there was something larger.

It had never been enough to only believe in what could be proven by science. Apparently, it wasn't enough for a lot of people, or how could you explain the bulging parking lots in the many churches every Sunday morning? If you asked the average churchgoer what kept them in the pews, they might say that weekly services kept them in step with the goal of righteous living and reminded them that they had a community to which they belonged. And, of course they went to church in an attempt to connect with whatever their concept of God was.

Gracie told me I seemed happier than I had ever been and I thought that I knew why. With all the difficulties her young life seemed to attract, for the first time in years I was finally in step with her. I liked it very much that I knew more about her now, even though I did not always like *what* I knew.

The distinct pace of the Lowcountry had reset my clock. I had found a community of people where I felt at home. I had a job that was all about making people happy. But I loved my job best when the day ended, and the customers had long gone home to their beds. I would climb up to the sunset deck on the excuse of double-checking the battened hatches. I would stop for a minute to feel the breeze, have a nightcap of salt air and marvel at the enormity and astounding beauty of the skies overhead.

I was not an unusual specimen. Any morning or evening all year long, people paused to watch streaks of jewel-toned opalescence of color scream across the sky, sighing and remarking at the magnificence of nature's outbursts. Visitors, residents and natives alike never took these things for granted. You did not dare. Mother Nature's spoiled inner child could read your thoughts. If you ignored her she would slam the Lowcountry with a storm so great that it rattled your teeth, or weather so hot that you laughed at the face of hell. No, we were all well advised to nurture a *generous* respect for Mother Nature's nature.

A healthy imagination naturally resulted from living in this tiny corner of the world. It was commonplace to spend some time looking for signs or warnings from nature about what was in your future beyond the weather. The old man had returned to my dreams and while his dour expressions were worrisome, I could not carry his chains in addition to my own and those of my daughters.

It was Sunday morning. Gracie was over at Alex's house allegedly studying. He was supposed to be tutoring her in Spanish and she was to help him with a poster for some history project.

Mimi was at my house, measuring for curtains, when I answered the phone in the living room and took it out on the balcony. It was Gretchen from New Jersey.

"Hey! What's going on?"

"I got an offer for your house!"

"What's the offer?"

"Four ninety-five!"

"What? Woo-hoo! I can't believe it! Gretchen! That's wonderful!"

"Time for a yard sale? I have these girls who can organize it for you. . . ."

"Yes! By all means. Good Lord! I have to come back and take out what I want, right?"

"Yes, and the sooner the better. This couple wants to close by the end of October. They don't think they will have a problem selling their co-op in Manhattan—the market's very hot right now because of interest rates and all. But, one thing, there's a problem with the roof," she said. "My Sandy got up on the extension ladder and he says the flashing around the chimney needs to be replaced. The good news is that if his guys do the work it's not going to cost you an arm and a leg."

"That roof has been leaking since the day we bought the house. Fred had at least ten different companies look at it. Does Sandy really think it's just a flashing problem?"

"Linda? If Sandy Prater says it's a flashing problem, then that's what it is. How old is the roof anyway?"

"Probably twenty years or more."

"Probably time to replace it but you know what? Let the next owner do it. Just fix the flashing. I mean, the buyer isn't asking you to replace the whole thing."

"Yeah, if I put up gray tiles, they'll want beige."

"You're absolutely right."

"How much does Sandy think it will cost?"

"I don't know; I'll have to ask him. But we could take the offer contingent on you paying for the repairs. What do you think?"

Four ninety-five! Four ninety-five! That was all I could think about. Holy Mary. It was a fortune.

Gretchen went through all the details I needed to know for the moment and we said good-bye.

I went back inside to the kitchen and poured myself a glass of water, adding some cubes of ice. My mind was racing. Was there anything in that house that I needed? The furniture was old, the pots and pans were old, the rugs were worn out, and the linens were practically rags. There wasn't a lamp in the whole house I was emotionally involved with or a table or chair that I missed. Old Mr. Epstein's furnishings suited me fine. I knew I needed to go through the house again just to be sure, but I was almost certain that beyond the things I had brought with me, I could leave the rest behind. The cost of moving everything would probably exceed the value of it. Besides, none of what I had would fit in this little house. If and when I moved, I would buy what I needed to fit the new space.

"I'm thinking a pretty chintz for your bathroom window and the sliding glass door in your bedroom," Mimi said, coming in. "You know? Something cheerful! Who was that on the phone?"

I held my hand across my heart. "Four ninety-five," I said.

"For what? Four ninety-five what?"

"Four hundred and ninety-five thousand dollars for the house in Montclair!"

"Lord have mercy! Mother McCree! Linda! Honey, I was gonna take you to GDC and buy remnants but now we're going to Southeastern Galleries! Four hundred and ninety-five thousand dollars! That's almost half a million!"

I did not make the smart-ass remark on the tip of my tongue but said instead, "I gotta sit down, and GDC is perfect. I can find everything I want right there!"

"Why, with that much money you can buy a gorgeous house and furnish it too!"

"Yeah, but I shouldn't spend it all. I should save some of it, right?"

"Except that you'll have to pay capital gains taxes. And why in the world would you want to give all that money to the government? Don't they have enough?"

"Well, I can't think about that right now. Anyway, for the moment I'm very happy right here in this little spot."

"Maybe we should go to a spa! You know? Get wrapped up in seaweed and mud and sweat out our toxins?"

"That's disgusting!"

"We could get massages. Oh! Wouldn't you love to have someone rub your back and feet? What have you got to eat? I'm starving!"

Massages? I didn't want some stranger putting their hands all over me. Too weird. Doctors were bad enough.

"Let's go out," I said. "I'm in the mood for a burger."

"Great! Now that you're rich, you're buying! Let's take my car."

"Yeah, and after lunch we can buy me a new one. My poor Blazer has eighty-three thousand miles on it."

"Save it for Gracie and get something nice for yourself—maybe a convertible!"

I stopped to lock the door behind me and thought about myself in a convertible. I suddenly realized I had never envisioned myself in something sporty like a Mustang or another car with any kind of pizzazz.

"You know what? You're right! Let's go to Poe's Tavern over on Sullivan's Island and we can pick up Gracie on the way back."

I had yet to visit Brad's house other than picking up or dropping off Gracie and Alex. There was no reason that I should have gone inside. It was important to keep my professional distance, and if Amy's reappearance at the restaurant was an indication of how well I was doing, I was not doing very well. Although, technically, Louise was the one who had burned Amy's card. Fat lot of good it had done. She called Brad all day long anyway.

Amy did not count Louise and me among her treasured friends and we didn't care. Brad merely thought our attitude was amusing. And most importantly, to our mutual delight, we could tell that she was driving him a little crazy.

We arrived at Poe's and were seated right away. The bar area was crowded and most of the tables were filled. We sat for a moment, reading the menu and commenting on Edgar Allan Poe's short life.

"He used to live on the island, you know," Mimi said.

"Um, I know that," I said.

"Well, you've been gone a long time. I thought you may have forgotten. He wrote 'The Gold Bug' here, you know."

"Um, I know that too."

When she spoke to me like that, I wanted to reach across the table and smack her. Isn't that awful?

"What's it gonna be, ladies?"

"I'm gonna have the Tell Tale Heart Burger," I said, "with a side of Edgar's Drunken Chili."

"That's with a fried egg, Applewood bacon and cheddar cheese. And how would you like that burger prepared?"

"Medium, please, and mayonnaise on the side."

"No problem. Coleslaw, potato salad or French fries?"

"Fries. Show me no mercy." I handed the menu back to her.

"And for you, ma'am?"

"I'll have the Pit and Pendulum burger with fries too."

"Medium?"

"Perfect," she said.

We ordered iced tea and as soon as it arrived, the gossip began to flow. In the next minute, our waitress put the chili in front of me and I all but dove right into the bowl. With the news from Gretchen, I was suddenly ravenous. The day was hot and humid, but fortunately we were sitting in a small booth, in the back of the restaurant under a ceiling fan where it was a little cooler.

"So what are you gonna do about your trip?" Mimi said, reaching over with a fork and helping herself to a bite.

"Mmm. This is so good! I'm gonna talk to Louise and work it out, I guess. Here, take all you want."

"Thanks. I am so thrilled that you're going to get such a great price for your house," she said. "Fred would die if he knew."

When she spoke about Fred like that, I wanted to reach across the table and kiss her! Wasn't that awful too?

"Then let's tell him!"

"You're bad," she said.

"I know."

We chatted for a few minutes, devouring the chili. The burgers arrived and we proceeded to devour them too.

"I haven't been over to Sullivan's Island hardly at all since I got here," I said. "This place is getting packed! Is it too cheap?"

"No!" Mimi said. "It's too good! And, darlin', you've got burger dripping down your arm."

"Oh, great. Think it would be gross to lick it off?" I used my napkin and my sister looked at me in utter disgust. "Sorry. Anyway, I've just been too busy to do anything and now I have to go back to New Jersey and move out of there whatever I want to keep and sell the rest."

"Well, check out storage because you have two girls who are going to have their own apartments soon."

"Bite your tongue!"

"Well, it's true! Do you think Lindsey is going to want to stay in a dormitory forever?"

"When she finds out what it costs to rent an apartment in Manhattan? Yes!"

"Well, it won't be long and I wouldn't throw away anything you might be able to recycle. Besides, she might find a place in Brooklyn. Who knows?"

"Brooklyn? Lemme tell you something, rent in Brooklyn is about the same as the city. Everyone commutes by subway and—"

"Doesn't the thought of Lindsey going down in a subway all by herself scare the turkey stuffing out of you?"

"Yes, it does and thanks for bringing it up."

Sometimes my sister said the most insensitive things. Did I worry about Lindsey being in New York City by herself? Was she kidding? My face must have transformed into the reflection of maternal frustration and resignation to a life of futility, anxiety, despair and all the other charms of motherhood because she piped up.

"Oh! I didn't mean . . ."

"Mimi? If you had one daughter in New York on her own and the other one was like Gracie, you'd be looking for a liver donor."

"And a wig maker! You said it. Gosh, it's got to be a terrible source of stress for you. . . ."

Sure, remind me again.

"If I had the time for the luxury of a nervous breakdown, I would have had one years ago. You know what I do? I don't think about it. I pull a Scarlett. If I worried about everything there is to worry about concerning their safety, I'd never sleep. And, I don't sleep that much as it is. Or well. Pass the ketchup. Please."

"Well, darlin', there's always me. I don't have kids to worry about, so why don't you let me take over for Lindsey. I'll say a novena every day."

"Okay, deal. Perfect. Lindsey is now officially your cross. But while you're on your knees, say two for Gracie. She's enough for ten women to fret over."

"Momma always said she could raise one hundred sons for the strength it took to raise one daughter."

"Half the planet says that! How would she have known? She only had us! Anyway, back to Brad . . ." I squirted a puddle of ketchup on my plate and dunked my burger in it, and to my sister's horror I took a bite large enough to satisfy a starving gorilla and continued talking. "So, apparently Amy lost her job when Brad's enemy took control of the firm and then, when she found out that Loretta got her head cracked open like a coconut . . ."

"You do have the most delicate way of putting things," Mimi said and giggled.

"*Wha evah!* So, she follows him down here and is staying with some friend of hers—probably another little slut—and now she's looking for a job."

"What do you care?"

"You know what? You're right! I guess I just feel protective of him like everyone else in the restaurant does. I'm sure we'll all relax when he gets all his blood work back. He's awfully young to have anything serious the matter though, don't you think? Anyway, the problem is that she calls him all day and she wants to push her way into his life. I mean, his son's not ready for another woman hanging around, especially considering her age. She's only twenty-two! Anyhow, I *know* Alex! He's sensitive . . . what?"

I looked up to see that Mimi had stopped eating and was grinning from ear to ear. My face was turning bloodred; I could feel it.

"What?" I said again.

"I theenk my sustah ees a leetle beet beetten by the looove buuug!"

Her Spanish accent needed work.

"That's absurd. That's positively absurd."

"Girl? It ain't absurd at all. Look at you! You're as red as every Chanel lipstick and nail polish on the cosmetic counter at Saks Fifth Avenue!"

"I'm just embarrassed, that's all."

She started to giggle and I could feel the beginning rumbles of a temper tantrum coming on. I sat up straight, took three sips of my tea and took a deep breath. I felt better then, knowing I was back in control.

"Okay," she said. "You don't like him one little eyedropper full, you and your Tell Tale Heart Burger. You're just pals."

"He's my boss, Mimi. Can you think of anything more pitiful than getting involved with your boss?"

"Yes, I can. Watching someone you love with a stupid girl closer to his son's age than his own as she occupies all his free time, convinces him he's a God, and screws him so wildly, madly and frequently that he winds up in the emergency room—that, my dear sustah, is pitiful. You may not know it and you may never know it but you are dead in love with Brad Jackson and I can see it all over you—not just your face. It's in your words, your eyes, your complexion and even your mannerisms change when you talk about him. You're a dead duck, honey chile. So, you gonna let that common whore just have him without a fight?"

"Mimi! You are so off base here, you don't even know it!"

Was my sister losing her mind?

"Tell me your sad story when Amy walks by you sporting a diamond from Crogan's as big as a kumquat! I love you but you're in denial. When is the last time you had to compete for anything?"

"I don't know. I . . ."

"That's what I thought. Linda, I love you. You know that. But besides taking Gracie off your hands so that you can race back to New Jersey and transport the family heirlooms ready to take their rightful place in the paradise all around us, I'm gonna tell you something you might not like to hear."

"Do I have a choice?" My appetite disappeared.

"No," she said and leaned forward across the table so close I could smell the artificial sweetener from her tea on her breath. "In all my life I have never seen you fight for anything except to make a good home for your daughters. What in the world are you afraid of? Do you really imagine that this little tart has one half to offer him of what you do? She hasn't lived long enough to learn anything except that by lifting her skirt she can get some attention."

"Well, bully for her."

"Listen to me. You and I were not brought up that way and yes, the world seems to have gone crazy sometimes with everyone having sex like it's the same thing as a hello, how are you. I don't behave that way and neither do you—and if you do, you shouldn't. . . ."

"Don't worry. The closest thing I've had to a sexual encounter lately was the PAP smear I had before I left Montclair."

"Good Lord! Anyway, anybody can screw like a little tramp these days. All you have to do is watch one episode of *Sex and the City* and you can learn everything you need to know. But with a young girl like her, she wants to be taken care of. Women take care of men, not the other way around. Believe me, from what you've told me about Brad and Loretta, he's never had a real woman in his life to take care of him. He's got a son and a business and he needs a woman, not a tramp."

"That's probably why he loves Louise so much."

"And why you love Louise too. You're all in love with the same person. Brad Jackson. Now we just have to get Mr. Jackson to realize that he's in love with you."

I was eyeing a passing plate piled high with nachos. Me in love? It was time to start eating neurotically.

"Let me ask you something. How come if you know so much, you're still single?"

It was time to change the subject. I knew that was not the nicest thing to say to my very well intentioned and only sister, but it just slid right out. Mimi, to her credit once more, let my zinger pass over her like a breeze.

"Because when your ex-husband gives you enough money to live, you don't get off your fanny to meet anyone, number one. Number two, it's a heck of a lot easier to see what to do to fix someone else's life than your own. And, last but not least, I have another date with Dr. Wonderful tonight. I'm cooking him dinner."

"Well, good for you! What are you cooking?"

"Roast beef stuffed with garlic, mashed potatoes, gravy . . ."

"Man trap!"

"You got it! Onions, carrots, string beans, biscuits . . ."

"Your biscuits will make the man cry for his momma."

"I hope not! And my pound cake with lemon glaze for dessert."

"No appetizers for cocktail hour?" I was joking, of course.

"Think I should make something else? Cheese straws?"

"I think you should get your legs waxed and change the sheets! Now, about me going back to Montclair . . ."

We decided that as soon as I could find a palatable fare that I would fly to Newark and rent a car. When I could figure out what I was bringing back, if anything, then I could arrange for it to be shipped. We estimated three days for the trip if I left early and returned late. I had an attic of things to sort through and a cellar too and although I had been moaning that it was all junk, it still needed to be sifted through. Mimi agreed to take care of Gracie in my absence and she even offered to help at the restaurant once again.

"I'll tell Louise and make sure she has your number." I knew Louise would never call Mimi unless a plague ripped through our ranks, but then I had an idea. "Are you thinking you might like to work? I mean, have a job?"

"Heavens, no! Well, that's not entirely true. I would like to have something to do that would give me some pin money. . . ."

"You mean shoe money?"

"Lord, isn't it the truth? I could shop for shoes all day long! Anyway, I don't know. You work, everyone works, you know what I'm talking about? I worry sometimes that I'm getting a little dull."

"Make Louise and Duane a cake."

"What? Is it their birthday?"

"No, it's not their birthday. Make one with lemon glaze and the other one with your caramel glaze. And let's see what happens. I guarantee you that you'll be making pound cakes for the restaurant in the time it takes them to swallow one bite. Heck, it's what you like to do anyway, right? Look, Louise and Duane can cook like nobody's business, but they can't bake for beans. Their pies all come from some nasty distributor and they're worse than Little Debbie."

"I love Little Debbie and Hostess and all that stuff."

"Oh, so do I but they don't taste like what comes out of your oven. Not even close."

"Well, there *is* a difference. Maybe tomorrow. I'm cooking for Dr. Taylor tonight."

"Well, it was just a thought."

Maybe Mimi making pound cakes for the restaurant was as convoluted as me being in love with Brad. I didn't believe that I was even in the remote areas of that kind of risk. As long as I kept my distance, I was safe.

Nineteen

DUCK!

YEARS of fiscal constraint, the politically correct way to say I had been a tightwad by necessity, had taught me many valuable lessons in life. One of the tenets of any shopping expedition was that I never spent a dime that I did not have to spend. So when I began my search for a low fare back to New Jersey, I did not book the flight until I was sure I had come away with the least amount of bloodletting to my wallet. When you're willing to leave at an ungodly hour and return on a late flight, there were still a few bargains to be had. My next step was to clear it with Louise.

Monday morning, bright and early, I met Lupe at the Piggly Wiggly and picked up Alex. While he was getting out of her car and into mine in the Chinese fire drill mode of our carpool, I lowered down my window to say hello.

"Hey, Lupe! How's it going?"

That was a dangerous question and one that could have kept us there until Christmas if I didn't stay on guard.

"Good, good! Mr. Brad ees fine and I'm just doing God's work. And you? Everything ees good?"

"Yep! I'd better get going or they'll be late. See you soon!"

I raised my window and looked at Alex in my rearview mirror.

"So, how's school going, Alex?"

"Gotta game after school today."

Notice, I had asked about school, meaning academics, and the answer came in the form of a sports announcement.

"Oh! I want to come!" Gracie said. "Who are we playing?"

"We're going to kick the ass offa St. Andrews," Alex said. "Sorry, Ms. Breland."

"That's okay, kick them good. You're not working this afternoon, Gracie?"

"It's Monday, Mom! I work Tuesday, Thursday and Saturday, unless I have a test. I have it all worked out with Louise. Don't worry."

"Okay. Gosh, I have so much on my mind that I forget my own name half the time."

I dropped them off at Wando and told Gracie to call me if she was going to the game. The way we had it arranged, I drove them in the morning and Lupe handled the afternoons, but still, I just wanted to know where Gracie was.

My first order of business was the bank deposit. After a weekend there was a hefty amount of cash in the safe and we all felt better when it was neatly tucked away in our account at PNC.

I arrived at eight forty-five and went to the kitchen to see who was in. There was Mimi sitting on a bar stool drinking coffee while Duane and Louise were inhaling thick slices of Mimi's pound cake. She had probably crawled out of her bed at dawn to bake, but never mind that, she had made the recipe so many times, she could have thrown two cakes together in her sleep.

"Morning, all. Hey, Mimi." I poured myself a mug of coffee and gave her a hug around her shoulder. "Are you trying to fatten up Louise and Duane? What's going on?"

"Well, I just wanted to thank them for being so good to you and the girls so I decided to bake them a cake." She winked at me. "And you won't *believe* what they want me to do!"

"Let me guess," I said.

My clever sister! I just didn't expect her to do it so soon.

"This is the most delicious pound cake I ever had in my entire life," Louise said. "I can't stop eating it and you know I'm not crazy for sweets. It's like satin and velvet and butter all at the same time."

I giggled because it was a well-known fact that Louise had a sweet tooth.

"That goes double for me," Duane said, "it reminds me of my grandmother's!" He pretended to be wiping away tears.

"They want me to bake cakes for the restaurant! Can you believe that?"

"No kidding," I said.

"No," Louise said, "you're *going to* bake cakes for the restaurant or else things are going to get ugly around here. I'll have to beat your sister every day until you say yes! Don't *make* me take my wooden spoon to her backside!"

Everyone was amused because Louise was demanding the cakes or maybe it was the idea of her chasing me around with a wooden spoon or because they were just enjoying a little sugar high to begin their day. No, it was the sugar. I was not about to touch Mimi's pound cake because I had already gained six pounds since I fled New Jersey and my clothes were tight.

"Well, y'all work it out. I'm going to the bank."

"I put everything in the safe last night," Louise said.

Of course she had. Louise was beyond dependable.

When I returned, Louise was waiting for me.

"How come you didn't tell me your sister could bake like that?"

"Well, it never occurred to me, I guess. She's something, huh?"

"She don't belong in the dining room, but she can work in my kitchen any time she wants. She's gonna make us ten cakes—four plain, two with lemon sauce, two with caramel icing and two all chocolate. Once people get a taste of them, we're all gonna be rich! I mean *rich!*"

"Good! By the way, she makes killer biscuits, corn bread, shortbread and pies too. Did she tell you about them?"

"No, she did not! I'm gonna call her and have a word with her on with-holding information!"

I giggled, imagining the tirade Louise was going to deliver to Mimi. "Wait!" I said. "I gotta talk to you about something."

"Sure, what's going on? Tell me quick 'cause I have a million things to do."

"I'm getting an offer on my house in New Jersey. . . ."

"Hallelujah! Praise the Lord!"

"You said it, sister! And, so I have to go back to New Jersey again and empty the house."

"When are you leaving?"

"Well, I have a flight Friday that's the right price but I know it's short notice."

"Girl, if it's the right price, it's the right flight—go on and make your plans and I can cover for you. Shoot, I'll get your sister in that kitchen yet!"

"I told you she could cook!"

"You were right too!"

I called Mimi.

"So, is Betty Crocker there?" Wiseass. All in caps. On my tombstone.

"Don't you just loooove it?"

"Amazing. Isn't it great to get paid for doing something you like to do?"

"Well, we'll see. I mean, I just have this old stove, but let's see how long it lasts."

"Louise has even had *me* in the kitchen a few times. She taught me how to make her crab cakes. The secret is as little breading as possible and to sauté the green peppers and onions in a tiny bit of butter before you add it in. Then let them sit in the fridge and get cold. Then they won't fall apart when you cook them."

"Is that all? Glory! I think picking crab meat is too much work, much less all you're talking about. So, you're *cooking*?"

"Only in the loosest definition of the term. Hey, tell me about your date last night! How did it go with old Jack?"

"Well, he's a good eater and an excellent snorer. I fed him two full plates of food and he sopped up the gravy with six biscuits. I was going to serve him dessert while we watched a movie on television. So, he went into the den and turned the television on and I went to start the coffee. By the time I got there, which was all of four minutes, he was snoring so loud and with so much force my curtains were waving back and forth with each snort. But, he did bring me flowers."

The vision of this man shoveling down a mountain of food, who then falls asleep in front of her television, snoring like a barnyard full of hogs, was very funny indeed.

"That's some groovy hunk of burning love you got there, sister. What kind of flowers?"

"The kind they sell at the grocery store for two dollars."

That wasn't a good sign. "No moofky poofky?"

"Not diddly. Nada. Goose egg."

"Rats. You cook all day for two dollars' worth of flowers and no seduction."

"Seduction. Humph. And, you know what else? This is going to sound really peculiar."

"Not to me, honey. You can tell me anything."

"Well, here's this nice-looking man, he's a doctor, has nice manners, I mean, he's got everything you could want but there's no . . . I don't know . . ."

"No heat? No hot and heavy? No urgent desire for a little ooh-la-la?"

"Yeah, I guess that's it. And, you know what? He's kind of boring too."

"So are you gonna see him again?"

"I guess so, I mean, why not? It's not like there are a thousand guys trying to take me out."

"That's why I decided to be celibate. It ain't worth it."

"Come on. That's some bull, girl. As soon as we figure out how to get rid of Amy, you won't be celibate anymore."

"Forget it. I thought about what you said and I just don't see it. Anyway, I have other fish to fry, like they say over here on Shem Creek. I'll talk to you later."

I hung up the phone and looked at it for a few minutes, thinking about what we had just said. As usual, what was unsaid was more interesting. How was it that there were so many people who wanted to be with someone and yet there were so many people alone? Never mind how many people were rotting away in lackluster marriages that should have ended when their kids went to college. Or men my age chasing girls who still got pimples. Sure, there were legitimate reasons why people had less than optimal personal lives—extensive business travel, demanding careers, narcissism, momma's boys, daddy's girls, impotence, uncontrollable flatulence, chronic halitosis, neurological disorders such as Tourette's syndrome, Obsessive Compulsive Disorder, being incarcerated, and heroin addiction, to name a few. And let us not forget—you could have just been born with a face as ugly as a mud fence.

But still. There were too many people in unsatisfying relationships and too many with no relationships at all. This did not apply to me, of course, because I had solved the problem of desire by simply lowering my expectations. If I did not expect anything I could not be disappointed.

I checked the e-mail for word from Lindsey and there it was again. *Hi Mom! College is fab! Did you kill Gracie yet? Love, L.* I answered her, *Hey baby! All's good. Gracie breathes! Love you! Mom.* No one would ever accuse us of replacing a lengthy phone call with electronic messages, but a blurb from her was all I needed. I just wanted to know she was all right.

I was finishing a phone call to one of our vendors, asking for a duplicate invoice, when Brad appeared in my office doorway.

"You busy?"

"No, I'm on hold. Come on in—sit a spell." The man I was talking to came back on the line and gave me some jazz about our payment being late. "If you want to fax a copy of the invoice, I'll get the check out to you today. Okay, thanks." I hung up the phone and looked at Brad. "What a jerk! How can we pay him if we don't know how much we owe?"

"Good question. Hey, how come you never told me that Amy came by?"

Shit! "Um, I thought Louise told you?"

"Funny. She said the same thing about you. Do you have the card she left?"

Shit! "Um, I think Louise has it." I was blushing very hard and very fast and very deep, which sounds like more fun than it was.

"Funny. She said you had it. Is there something going on around here that concerns me that I am unaware of?"

It's important to note here that Brad was not angry, annoyed or irritated in the least. In fact, he seemed to be up for a little cheery verbal spar.

"We, that is, Louise and I are concerned about your *health*. Did you hear back from your doctor?"

"My health? Yeah, I heard. I'm fine. Gonna live to be a hundred and two. I just have to avoid red wine and chocolate."

"*And,* that Amy."

"Yeah, well, she's tough to avoid. I don't think there's ever been a man who told her no besides me and so she just keeps calling and calling and calling. She's driving me a little crazy."

"So, why don't you just tell her to buzz off?"

"Because, Miss Jersey, that's not how I do things."

"Well, I'll tell her if you want me to. It would be a pleasure!"

"Louise said the same thing. You two *really* don't like her, do you?"

"That's riiii-ght."

"I don't care, but can I just ask why you ladies harbor such ill will for a girl you don't even know?"

Ladies? Girl? I didn't like the implication of the difference in our ages.

"Because she's a slut, whore, gold-digging bitch from hell, that's why. Louise and I know what's best for you and it's *not* Amy. I don't like a thing about her from the top of her dyed red hair on her too-big head to the tip of her manicured and polished like a stripper toes. Even the sound of her voice rankles my nerves. So, now you know."

I said all this in a perfectly calm voice as though I had said, *Pass the peas, please.* Also, delivered in one breath.

"Now I know. Gee."

There was the hint of a smirk on his face that I suddenly felt like wiping off with a backswing of my right hand. I decided to give him something to think about. "And doesn't it bother you that she could be Alex's sister? Isn't that a little sick?"

"No. I mean, yes, of course, that would offend a woman *your* age."

"My age? My age? I'm *your* age! Probably. Well, close anyway."

"I'm forty-two."

"You're older. And, it *is* offensive. But not for the reasons *you* probably think."

Now the air in the room sizzled with the electricity between us. I only ever argued to win.

"The fact is that she still has a hard body and you've had two children that, let's face it, can dramatically alter certain internal aspects of your physiology."

I could not believe my ears! He could not have meant what his words implied. But if he did, what had begun as teasing would escalate into a contest for each other's jugular. For a moment I was unsure how to answer him. We were on the brink of some barroom trash and even I, the one who had worked with teamsters in New Jersey, was not going to take a ride on the elevator down to that gutter. But I wanted to be certain that he had been that explicit.

"Let me understand this. Are you saying what I *think* you're saying?"

"What do you *think* I'm saying?"

"I think that you are saying that women who have given birth are not as, um, the same as women who have not. Am I right?" My face was so hot you could have baked macaroons on my cheeks.

"That's correct."

I became infuriated with him and did not care if he fired me on the spot.

"That is about the most disgusting thing I have ever heard from your mouth and if you want me to continue to have the smallest shred of respect for you, you had better take it back and say you are sorry. And, this is not a joke, Brad."

He realized that he had crossed the line and now his face turned red. I thought it was admirable that he had the decency to blush but I was not backing down.

"Linda, I . . . come on! Don't be mad at me! I was just shooting the shit with you. Come on!"

"No. You meant what you said! You really believe that, don't you?"

"Um, well, isn't it true?"

"Would you like me to come around this desk and pop you one?"

"Simmer down, Jersey! Jeesch! No sense of humor!"

"Listen, Brad Jackson. In the first place, it is an affront for men of my generation to go out with little girls. Where does that leave us? Bait for geezers? We are the ones you choose to give you children and then we are discarded only to be replaced with a younger version so that you can all tell yourselves that you're still young too. Well, guess what? There's something terribly wrong with those girls who date men your age! They're looking for a meal ticket, a daddy, or an excuse to never have to do anything with their lives except trade on their youth. And as a woman, I find it appalling. I do. It's not unlike prostitution. Really. Sorry I went off like that. No, I'm not."

"Guess I touched a nerve. I apologize. Seriously."

"Get the hell out of here and leave me alone."

"Can I buy you a cup of coffee?"

"Very funny."

When he left the office, or I should say slithered out, I closed my door. What in the world was the matter with me? Why did I lose my temper like that? Five minutes later, there was a slight *knock, knock, knock.* I ignored it and the door opened slowly. A bottle of olives on a tray came in followed by Brad's arm.

"I couldn't find an olive branch, so I'm making do."

"No, thank you," I said. "Go away. Some of us have work to do."

Two minutes later, there was a *knock, knock, knock.* I ignored it again and the door opened slowly. In came the same tray, held by Brad. This time it held a fat slice of Mimi's pound cake with lemon sauce.

"Have you tried this cake? It's incredible!"

"Yes, my sister made it and no, thank you."

"Oh," he said and closed the door again.

About five minutes later, the door opened and he held inside a piece of cardboard on which he had drawn—poorly, I might add—a picture of a basset hound with a bubble above his head. In the bubble, with letters printed backward like the dog wrote it himself, was the sentiment *Bogart says, Brad is a dog and he knows it. He put himself in doghouse.*

I started to laugh. I couldn't help it.

"Can Bogart's best friend come in? He wants to thank you for not suing him for some violation of behavior in the workplace."

"Oh, come on in," I said.

He came in with a tray and on it were two cups of gumbo and two wedges of corn bread. He had brought salt and pepper shakers and even one of the bud vases we had for the tables. It held three blooms of yellow daisies.

"Peace offering," he said.

"Thanks. Just remember, I can always be bribed with food." I could smell the gumbo from where he stood. "Wow, that smells so good. Louise make it?"

I cleared away the folders in the middle of the desk so he could put the tray down.

"Yeah, Duane's gumbo can't touch Louise's."

We got organized for a desktop lunch and began to eat.

"I'm really sorry about what I said before," he said, and his cell phone rang. He pulled it off his belt and looked at the caller ID.

"Who's calling?"

"Who do you think?" He shook his head and put his phone back on his belt. "Fifth time today."

"Well, you're gonna have to speak to her."

"I know. I just hate confrontation. I figured if I just ignored her, she would give up."

"*Normal* people would," I said, and stared at him until he noticed that

I was dead serious. "Hey! Did you hear that I got an offer on my house in Montclair?"

"Fabulous! Good one? Gonna take it?"

"Yeah, it's very good and I'm grabbing it! But I have to go back and empty the house."

"When are you going?"

"This Friday. I worked it out with Louise. I'm flying up very late Friday and coming back Monday."

"Well, good! Then I take it that, besides the fact that your immediate boss is a horse's patootie, you plan to be with us for a while?"

"Yep, you're stuck with me," I said and relaxed.

We were talking about the kids when O'Malley's head appeared in the doorway.

"Sorry to interrupt," he said. "Brad, there's a lady out here to see you."

Before Brad could respond, Amy pushed her way by O'Malley and into the office. She was in a very agitated state.

"Why aren't you taking my calls?" she said, and she saw we were having something to eat. "Well, isn't this just precious?"

Brad stood up and reached out to take her arm but before he could take her outside, she turned to me.

"Well, now I know why Brad's not calling me back!" Then she faced Brad and said, "You know, I was calling you to tell you that I had a job offer."

I inhaled sharply—gasped, actually.

"Well, that's great," he said. "Here or in Atlanta?"

"Would you *rather* it be in Atlanta?"

Now I really gasped. You could tell by the timbre of her voice that her anger was expanding by exponents of ten. O'Malley and I exchanged looks. I had no escape and I thought he stayed there to make sure she didn't lose it.

"No . . . I just thought . . . ," Brad said.

"Oh! So that's *it!* You thought I was leaving Charleston, right? Well, let me tell you something . . ."

That was when I should have remained quiet, but foolishly did not. All I said was, "Hey, Amy, we've got customers out there having lunch, so why don't you bring it down—"

Before I could finish my sentence, she picked up Brad's gumbo and hurled it at my head, hitting me full force across the bridge of my nose. The cup broke, soup went everywhere and blood began gushing from my head and nose.

"Oh! God!" I said quietly. I could barely see with all the blood and soup. I grabbed the napkin from my lap and held it to my head. "I'm hurt!"

"Oh my God," O'Malley said.

"Get Louise!" Brad said and pushed Amy down in his chair. "Are you out of your fucking mind?"

O'Malley took off.

Amy struggled to stand and get out, but Brad held her by the arm.

"Let her go!" I said. "Just let her go!"

He released her and she flew out the door at about the same moment Louise flew in.

"Great God in heaven! What has that crazy woman done to you?"

Louise came around behind the desk and gently took away the napkin. My whole body was shaking from head to toe from the shock of what had happened and I felt faint.

"Go get me some clean towels and some warm water, and a bowl of ice and call an ambulance," she said to Brad and O'Malley.

"Jesus my King! You're gonna be fine, Linda, but you definitely need stitches. I'll go with you to the hospital."

I started to cry, which only made things worse. "Call Mimi, okay?" I could no longer breathe through my nose and I knew it was broken. "Damnit!"

"You can say that again," Louise said. "Listen, sugar, I don't want you to worry about a thing. I'll call your sister and tell her to meet us there, okay? God! That woman is so evil."

Two hours, fourteen stitches and a reset nose later, courtesy of the talented hands of a plastic surgeon, I was home in bed, furious. Mimi, Brad and Louise were in my kitchen ranting and raving under their breath. They had given me pain medication at the hospital and it was supposed to make me sleep, but it wasn't working. I had an ice-cold wet cloth over my eyes held in place by two small bags of frozen peas. Mimi said it would keep my eyes from turning black and blue and keep the swelling down. I hoped it was working. I couldn't put pressure on my nose as I had two plastic stints in there holding my nose together. My upper lip was swollen and I resigned myself to drinking from a straw and having bad breath for three days until I could have the stints removed. At least it was a clean break and predicted to heal well, and that was the only break I had caught that day.

Mimi peeked in.

"You sleeping?"

"Hell no! I'm too angry to sleep! As soon as I can get up, I'm gonna find Amy and kill her!"

"You'll have to get in line. You want some tea?"

"Sure."

"I'll be right back."

Mimi returned a few minutes later with a glass of iced tea and a straw.

"How are you feeling?"

I took a long drink and was surprised by my thirst, but breathing through my mouth had dried my throat.

"Actually, it's just the fact that I can't breathe normally and I'm groggy from all the medicine and my head hurts like all hell, but other than that, I'm fine."

"Good Lord. Well, I suppose we should say prayers of thanks that the crazy lunatic didn't knock out your teeth."

Before I could tell her what an idiotic thing I thought that was to say, Brad and Louise appeared in the doorway. By the expressions on their faces, I knew I looked horrible.

"Don't worry about Gracie," Louise said, "Lupe said she would pick her up after the game and bring her home with Alex. And we'll see about her supper."

"Okay. Thanks."

"Listen, Linda. I spoke to Robert," Brad said. "If you want to press charges, and I think you should, we can. This whole thing is so incredible. And, I am so sorry."

"No, I think I'll just sleep now. We can talk about it later."

"Okay. Well, then, I guess we should be getting back to the restaurant now. If y'all need anything at all, I expect y'all to call us. Okay? We'll check in with you later. Oh, Linda, by the way, I spoke to Lowell. The garage is yours."

"Well, *that's* good news," Mimi said.

I nodded my head and inched down under my covers, moving carefully. Mimi got the message.

"I'll just see them out and then I'm gonna sit in the living room and read. Just holler if you need anything, okay?"

I began to drift off to sleep but as soon as a dream would begin to materialize, I would wake up again. My head hurt so much I knew this had to be the worst point of my injuries—recovering from a gash in my head and a broken nose and then the surgery it required to put me back in one piece. Everyone had been so nice to me. Everyone felt terrible that this had happened. It was so ironic that through all the years I had lived surrounded by terrorists, muggers, rapists, drug dealers and every kind of vermin that occupy the lowest rungs of society, nothing had ever happened to me. I had never even had my pocket picked in Times Square. It was incredible that something so violent could have happened here. I was completely and thoroughly stunned. Not only that, how in the world would I go to Montclair in four days? In a mask?

I thought I smelled pipe tobacco burning. Not a powerful odor, but something distant and sweet. I thought well, maybe it's just in the wood. Houses built of wood absorbed odors. When you least expected it, you would catch a trace of something in the air, even if it had been from years ago. I began to think about the old man in my dreams and wondered if his somber expressions in my last dream of him had been related to Amy's violent assault.

For some crazy reason, and it was most likely linked to the painkillers in my bloodstream, I could almost feel the old man in my room, sitting in a chair next to my bed, watching over me. Yes, there was a distinct presence nearby.

Through the haze of drugs and ice packs it came to me that I had truly brought the entire episode with Amy on myself. If I had not been so obnoxious to her, she never could have singled me out as an enemy. Why did I do these things? I consoled myself that it was the human condition to cause your own trouble, but that was a very small consolation to my throbbing head. My nose would have been fine if I had simply minded my own business. I took an oath with no witnesses that from that moment forward, I would never be a busybody again. Maybe I had saved Brad from something worse later on. Maybe I had cut a cosmic deal with Brad somewhere out there in the ethers.

I was thinking crazy thoughts. It was time to rest and let my body heal.

TWENTY

GRACIE WANTS TO TALK

HEN you have a big trauma in your family, you want to be sure you can dig up an aunt like my Aunt Mimi. I got home from the ball game around five and at first, when I saw Aunt Mimi's car, I didn't think a thing about it. But when I came up the steps in my usual regal manner—that is, two at a time, swung open the door, slammed it and announced my presence in a song at the top of my lungs—Aunt Mimi leapt from the couch to the door and gave me a huge *shhhh! Your momma's asleep.* Well, old Linda ain't been asleep at five in the afternoon in my whole life, so I knew something big was cooking.

"Hey!" I said. "Why's Mom in the sack?"

She then proceeded to tell me the story, which let me tell you, scarred me for life. There is nothing worse in the entire world than something happening to your mother. I mean, if you look back at every childhood story from Hansel and Gretel to Sleeping Beauty to Snow White—name one, it doesn't matter—the mother is dead. That's why kids are completely freaked out when their mother goes to bed off schedule. By the time she was finished giving me the details, I was shaking all over from head to toe.

"Is she okay?"

"Of course she's okay! Listen, come sit. It's one of those things where you look worse on the outside than you are on the inside. Anyway, I'm sure she's gonna wake up soon and when she does, she's not going to be very happy. Her head took quite a hit."

"Did you call Lindsey?"

"No, I didn't. Why don't you take my cell outside and call her yourself?"

"First, I'm just gonna look in her room and see if she's awake."

I opened Mom's door slowly and when I saw her, I thought I was going to faint. My knees got weak and my hands became clammy. Poor Momma! She had ice packs over her eyes and cheeks, a bandage on her forehead and she was breathing through her mouth. And what in the hell were the plastic things in her nose?

"Mimi?" she said.

Well, at least she sounded normal.

"No, Momma, it's me. Gracie."

"Some mess, huh?"

"Man! That woman ought to be put away! Seriously!" I tiptoed to her side and took her hand. "Does it hurt?"

"No, not too much. It's sort of like somebody hits you across the face with a baseball bat, that's all." She sat up a little. "Here, help me, honey. I want to powder my nose. I took all these pills and I'm still a little wobbly."

I leaned over and helped her untangle her feet from the covers and brought her up to a sitting position.

"Well, first of all, Mom, you should not be wearing a long nightgown. You'll trip and bust your behind! Don't you have enough trouble as it is?"

"Do I look really terrible?"

Was she kidding? "Uh, no, you look fabulous! We should take a picture right now and put it up on match.com."

"Yeah, I'll bet. A real beauty queen, right?"

"Hey, you got a broken nose and a ton of stitches, what do you expect?" I led her into the bathroom. "Um, do you want me to help you . . . ?"

"No, thanks, honey. I can handle it now. Tell Mimi that I'm up, okay?"

I went back into the kitchen, where Mimi was digging around in our cabinets, presumably to concoct some creation that would cure the world and feed us at the same time.

"Mom's awake," I said, "she's in the bathroom."

"Oh! How's she doing?"

"Like crap, but who wouldn't be?"

"I just want her to keep her eyes iced so they don't turn black, but they probably will anyway. Do you want to split a Coke?"

"Sure, do we have diet?"

"Yep!" She popped the top and divided it between two glasses filled with ice. "So, that was some story, right?"

"Like no other. I mean, you can't make stuff like that up! Is Mom gonna press charges?"

"I don't know. I don't think she's had time to think about it yet. Can I tell you how bad Brad and O'Malley feel? They were standing right there when it happened. Brad said he thought she was just going to take a look at what he was eating."

"Yeah, right." I imitated the attempted murderer's voice. "*This needs salt!*"

"Exactly. And, O'Malley said he was standing there because he thought something might happen and then, when it did, he didn't do a blessed thing to stop it!"

"Another tale of failed macho hoo-rah," I said.

"Well, that's not entirely fair. I think the whole incident happened so fast that there wasn't time to react. Anyway, your momma is supposed to go up to Yankee territory this weekend and empty the house, but I think she should wait until next weekend. Do you know where her ticket is? I'll call Louise for her, see if it's okay to change her time off and then I can change her reservation for her."

It was just like Aunt Mimi to think of the next step. It was just like me to be clueless about the next step. I guess I wasn't quite the adult I liked to think I almost was, but I figured the mere fact that I recognized my limits was progress.

Mom gave Mimi her flight information and Mimi got busy coaxing the reservation agent into changing Mom's ticket and waiving the change fee. Naturally, she had to talk to her supervisor and explain why Mom couldn't travel and even the supervisor gave her a hard time.

"I can send you a copy of the report from the emergency room if you want," Mimi said, shaking her head. "Of course, we can get a doctor's letter!"

People probably made up crazy stories all the time to try and get out of extra charges, but the drama with the airline sure seemed like a lot of unnecessary aggravation to me. When she finally convinced the supervisor she wasn't lying and was given a new reservation number, she hung up the phone and turned to me.

"That was ridiculous," she said and sighed hard enough to move the furniture. "Well, let's call Lindsey and then I have to go. I put a frozen lasagna in the oven for you. Take it out in fifty minutes. I have to go home and bake! Did your momma tell you I was baking cakes for the restaurant?"

Big surprise.

We dialed Lindsey's number and she was actually in her dorm room, studying. Of course she was studying. That was all she ever did! I could tell from Aunt Mimi's end of the conversation that Lindsey was very upset, but when she finally talked to Mom she calmed down.

"We all need to learn when to hold our tongues, right?" Mom said.

Lindsey must have felt that Mom wasn't in any danger because Mom said, "Oh, I'll be fine." And then they started talking about her classes and her roommate—a girl named Naomi from Wyoming—and after a few minutes, they said good-bye.

"Hey! I didn't even get to say hello!"

My complaint fell on deaf ears, as most of them did, but I didn't rag on them. Mimi was leaving and I could see that Mom was exhausted. I told her to go back to bed.

That night I made Mom sip some chicken noodle soup through a straw and I put the noodles on a spoon and into her mouth. I fought my way through some of the lasagna, but I didn't have much of an appetite.

Around nine-thirty, there was a knock at the door. I was doing geometry homework, cussing my head off over the areas of triangles. Imagine my shock to see O'Malley and Duane standing there with flowers.

"Is your Mom awake?"

"I think so. Come on in."

O'Malley was wearing a knit shirt and khaki shorts and Duane still had on his chef's jacket and black-and-white check pants. They had both combed their hair, which seemed a little strange to me. I mean, wasn't Duane a queen? And didn't O'Malley have a flame? Maybe they thought they were coming to a wake.

They stood inside the door like they didn't know what to do with themselves and so I said, "Lemme see if she wants to get up. . . ."

"Oh, no! Don't make her get out of bed!" Duane said.

"Okay. I'll just tell her you're here."

I opened Mom's door and she wasn't in her bed where I had left her. So I tapped on her bathroom door and heard her muttering to herself.

"Mom? Mom?"

"Yes?"

"Duane and O'Malley are here to see you."

"Oh, God . . ." The bathroom door opened and out came Mom with a very swollen upper lip and the beginnings of black eyes. "Look at me. My eyes are turning purple."

The purple was just in a couple of spots and her cheeks were a little yellow. Overall, I didn't think she looked that much worse than she had earlier that afternoon.

"Come on," I said, "you're gorgeous."

I followed her out to the hall and living room.

"Hey," O'Malley said, and handed her a little book that was gift wrapped. I could tell he was shocked that Mom looked so beaten up. "I brought you a bartender's guide. Figured you could use some fun reading? How're you feeling? Did you get the license number of the truck?"

"Thanks a lot," Mom said with a very lopsided grin. "It was a big redneck Amy truck."

"Jesus!" Duane said. "Girlfriend! Don't you worry! I've got this little compact from Chanel—it's not mine; it belongs to my sister; she left it at my apartment—anyway, it's got four kinds of cover-up in it and we can hide everything! But *what* have they stuck up your nose?"

No one believed for a makeover minute that Duane didn't have his own compact of cover-up.

"Splints," Mom said, "comes out Thursday."

"Well, that can't feel so great," Duane said. "Here. I brought you something to start your collection. And there are flowers in the sink from both of us. Connie and the Zone Man send their love too."

He handed her a small box from Williams-Sonoma. Mom opened it and lifted out a paring knife.

"Oh, y'all, this is so sweet of you to do this, you didn't have to. . . ."

I could see Mom was really moved by what they had done. It was completely unexpected and very thoughtful.

"Um, do you guys want something to drink?" I said.

"*You guys?* Lawsamercy, Gracie!" Duane said, with this look on his face that seemed to say that saying *you guys* was worse than using the F word.

"Okay, okay. Do *y'aaaall* want something to drink?"

They laughed and said, *That's better,* and I knew the reason they were laughing was because they were uncomfortable. It was funny that they were so relaxed in the restaurant but so awkward in our house. Or maybe it was because Mom looked worse than they thought she would.

"No, thanks, Gracie, we gotta get going," O'Malley said. "It's late. We just wanted to come by and say we were sorry this happened, Linda. I feel terrible that . . ."

"Don't even think about it," Mom said. "Amy was so quick, no one could have done anything."

"Thanks for saying that. Brad's seriously pissed. He's been on the phone with Robert all night."

"You know what?" Mom said. "I think we're better off just letting it go. I don't want a lawsuit. If this whole crazy incident gets her away from Brad and all of us, then that's really what we want."

"Well, you can discuss that with Brad," O'Malley said. "We just wanted to make sure you were all right."

"I'm fine. I swear," she said.

"Okay, if you say so. But if you want me to kill the bitch, just say the word," Duane said. We all smiled when he said that because Duane was about my size. He cleared his throat with the realization that everyone knew he wouldn't mash a bug and said in the most tender voice, "I just wanted to see with my own eyes that you were okay. That's all." He shrugged his shoulders. "You know, we're sort of like a family at the restaurant—a weird family, but a family nonetheless. And now you're one of us, you know? If I had been in that office I would have slapped her face off. I'm not kidding."

"Oh, Duane," Mom said, smiling all crooked because of her big lip, "there wasn't an instant that anyone could have, even if they had thought of it. Really. But thank you. And you too, O'Malley."

They left, Mom shuffled back to bed and I put the flowers in a vase. That night I was the one who turned out the lights and locked the door. I went to Mom's room to check on her and was happy that she was sound asleep. I put the flowers on the dresser in a spot where she could see them when she woke up in the morning. I went back to the kitchen and called Lindsey.

"Hey, got a sec?"

"Sure. How's Mom?"

"Mom's fine. She just has to heal. Needless to say, she ain't coming to New Jersey this weekend. She's got splints up her nose and stitches and everything. Aunt Mimi changed her trip to next weekend. Maybe you could go out to Montclair and help her?"

"No problem. How does Mom really look?"

"Well, she's on the way to two black eyes, which she's not going to like one f-ing bit, and her cheekbones are bruised too. I think it's one of those deals that's gonna get worse before it gets better. But she will survive. You know Linda!"

We said good night and I thought about school for a few minutes. We had a field trip the next day. I was trying to figure out what to wear. I took Mom's alarm clock, intending to let her sleep. I made one more phone call to ask Alex to ask Lupe to pick me up in the morning.

"No problem," he said. "How's your mom?"

I guess the whole world knew.

"Okay. You know what's really kinda odd about this?"

"What?"

"Who does something like really throw stuff except for the bad guys on a show like *Law and Order*? I mean, that's pretty crazy, right?"

"Yeah, you would think that by the time you're grown up, you're civilized."

"Yeah. No kidding. Okay, well, I gotta close up the house and all . . ."

In the morning, I tiptoed out of the house and left Mom a note to say that I would be home by four. I drew a big heart on it and left lots of X's on the bottom so she would know I was thinking about her. In a rare act of maturity I even put my cereal bowl in the dishwasher and left home feeling pretty good about myself.

It turned out we were going to the aquarium for the field trip and I was pretty psyched for it. We rode on the big yellow bus like a bunch of first-graders, laughing and carrying on. Mom may have been right that Mr. Miller was a bit of a jerk, and I agreed with her that his protesting in front of the restaurants was a little psycho, but at least he got us out of classes for the day.

We arrived and were milling around the lobby waiting for our guide to show up and enlighten us on ecosystems and watersheds. Miller was getting antsy and kept asking the receptionist to call the office and tell them that we were on a schedule. Well, after about ten minutes, this nice little old lady with a cup of coffee came waltzing out from the staff offices and I thought old Miller was gonna need resuscitation. I guess he was figuring, what could an old biddy like her know? We couldn't have cared less if she was a hundred years old. As long as I got to skip geometry for the day I was happy. Turned out she knew plenty.

She began her talk with a lecture on the Sustainable Seafood Project, which actually made my ears perk up. Turns out a lot of restaurants in Charleston no longer served Chilean sea bass, orange roughy and shark. Well, I never ate shark anyway. I was dangerous enough as it was. You are what you eat, right? But Chilean sea bass was delish! Then she told us that orange roughy lived to be a hundred years old and I looked over at Alex.

"You want to eat a hundred-year-old fish?"

"Are you kidding me? I'm strictly a burger man myself."

"Yeah, sure. Mad cow. Have a ball." I had seen him put away massive quantities of anything that was put in front of him. He probably didn't even know what he ate.

She continued to talk and I was surprised to hear that they were endangered and all the better restaurants in Charleston were not going to serve them until their population was replenished. I wondered if Duane and Louise knew about that. They probably did. I thought it made more sense to use local seafood at the restaurant anyhow. Even at my age, I didn't think people came to Shem Creek for exotic fish from Japan or something. Besides, if we bought fish from the men who had been fishing the waters around Charleston for years, we helped support them. Wasn't that better for the economy?

Every time the guide made some statement about conservation you could see Jason Miller's little heart pump right through his shirt. Any reference to the environment got his motor going and we thought that he was acting very, very stupid.

"That old lady was pretty smart," I said to Alex when we were riding back across the Cooper River Bridge.

"Yeah, she was."

"You know, my mom had a date with Jason Miller."

"No shit?"

"Yeah, no shit. She didn't like him. She thought he was a whack."

"Well, he is a whack."

"Yeah, but you can't dump people just because you don't agree with their politics, you know? I mean, he might not be her—whatever, man of her dreams or something—but that doesn't mean he isn't really, really smart, right?"

"Hey, Gracie. Know what? I think this is one of those classes where you just get your grade, get out and don't look back."

"You sound like my mother, Alex. You guys are like *way* too conservative."

"Who? *You—who?*"

"Fine. *Y'all.* Happy? I just don't think anyone sees the big picture here."

TWENTY-ONE

ENCORE

―――◆◆◆―――

HE phone rang all day long like the thing had nothing else to do. First, Mimi called. *How did you sleep?* Fine, I said, fine. Then Louise called. *How are you feeling?* I have a headache, I said. Headache was an understatement. I didn't know that you could get that much pain into a single head and no matter how many aspirin I took, the pain was so distracting I could barely concentrate on anything. But Robert and Susan had sent an enormous bouquet and that somehow made my head feel a little better. Brad came by at lunchtime and brought me a cup of soup and a shrimp salad sandwich.

I answered the door barefooted, wearing sweatpants and a T-shirt; my bed hair was up in a ponytail and my eyes were now an official reproduction of a color wheel. If Steven Cojocaru had been on the other side of my screen door instead of Brad Jackson, he would have said, *Girlfriend, I am too sorry, but put yourself in a box and seal the lid.* But Brad had his own comment.

"Well! Don't you look fetching!"

"Please," I said, opening the door. "Like I don't know it."

"I didn't mean to get you up, but I thought you probably didn't feel like cooking." He dropped the bag on the counter and opened it up. "Here, eat something."

"You didn't get me up. I was just lying in bed thinking about life."

I wasn't really hungry until I started eating. But there wasn't much for me to do besides eat, as Brad talked nonstop.

"Ah, life. Yes, a worthy cause to ponder. Look, I talked to Robert last night and again this morning. We can sue her for assault and Robert says it's a slam dunk. You're entitled to all the medical bills, lost wages . . ."

Lost wages?

"And, something for your pain and suffering. Now I don't want you to worry about any of that because the business will cover your medical and Robert agrees with me that we should cover your salary. I mean, that's the least we can do."

Whew!

"Now, in terms of a pain and suffering award, there's probably not much to get, but you could press charges and have her locked up. In the least case, I think we should have the court order a psychological evaluation and maybe ask the court to consider some anger management training. . . ."

As I finished the soup, sandwich, the pickle and every last French fry, he slowed down. I was finally able to squeeze in a word.

"Brad? I am not suing anybody and I am not pressing charges. It just isn't something I would do. I don't like her. She knew it. I was in the wrong place at the wrong time and opened my big mouth. I appreciate the offer to cover my hospital bills, but I'm still on Cobra. Remember? However, if you want to pay me for the week, I would really appreciate that and we can just call it vacation or something."

"Let's not count this as a vacation. Let's count it as battle pay."

We were sitting at the table by the window and Brad had the strangest expression on his face.

"What?" I said.

He reached across the table and took my hand in his and covered it with his other hand.

"I am just so sorry this happened, Linda. I wish it had been me instead."

"Well, I'm just glad the crazy maniac didn't hit my temple. I could have been dead."

"God. Don't even think that." His hand pressed mine and he stood to leave. "You get some rest now."

The pressing of my hand was very sweet. Obviously, he had no interest in seducing me, unless he had a thing for sideshow freaks with black eyes and bulbous lips. No, he was just a friend, but a very special friend who really cared about me.

Bummer.

It was probably time to admit to myself that I would love to be his, I don't know, girlfriend? Lover? Wife? I didn't really know what I wanted from him but what he had given me so far was the treasure of his confidence. His friendship. His caring. As I tried to nap I could not help but wonder what it would be like to lie next to him—not with any *you know what* going on—but just to rest by his side. I thought it would be wonderful.

By the time Gracie returned home, I was up, showered and dressed. But like we always say in our family, decent people get up, shower and dress.

I was lying on the couch, watching the news, when she walked in. She tossed her backpack on the floor and opened the refrigerator.

"Hi, Mom! You're up! You must be feeling better, I hope?"

"I'm alive. I think I'll feel a lot better when these stupid splints are out and I can breathe normally, you know? There's a pitcher of tea in there. Help yourself."

"Uh-huh. Those things would drive me right over the edge. You want tea?"

"Sure. So, how was school?"

No answer. I looked up to see Gracie's knitted eyebrows and I knew something was bothering her.

"Spill it, Gracie. What's going on?"

She put my tea on the coffee table and sat on the end of the couch by my feet.

"You're not gonna like this. You've got some serious black eyes now."

"Yeah, lovely, huh?"

"Well, that woman makes me sick."

"Forget her. Anger is like a cancer, you know. She's just crazy."

"I guess, but if I were you, I'd sue her for a million dollars."

"You can't get blood out of a stone, Gracie, and she hasn't got a million dollars to give."

"Then at least send her to jail."

"Why is everyone so intent on me doing something about this woman? Can't I just get better and go on with my life?"

"God, Mom, you're like so passive about this."

"No, I just don't want all the negative attention it would bring, that's all. It's not good for the reputation of the restaurant, she's got nothing to sue for anyway and I'm still getting my salary. So, bump her!"

"Well, I think she needs like a lobotomy or electroshock therapy."

"It sure couldn't hurt. But you know what? If I hadn't been such a wiseacre to her, she wouldn't have thrown the soup at me. And if Brad had just been honest with her, she wouldn't have come in the restaurant ready to kill somebody."

"Where did she come from anyway and who is she?"

"She used to be Brad's secretary in Atlanta and she has this crazy obsession with him. She's been stalking him ever since she got here a few weeks ago. Louise and I can't stand her. So every time she showed up at the restaurant, we gave her some lip. And she was calling Brad all day and night and he wasn't returning her calls, so she was plenty pissed, pardon the term. But no one ever expected her to go crazy as a result of it."

"You know what? Grown-ups are just as screwed up as teenagers."

"You're right."

"And, if I ever get the chance, I'm gonna go all Jersey on her. Like stomp her foot or something."

"You will do no such thing. She'll get hers. Karmic rule number one."

"Yeah, sure. So far all my enemies are living long and prospering. But I actually did learn something today."

"About what?"

"Endangered fish. Turns out there are like forty varieties of sharks that are disappearing along with Chilean sea bass and orange roughy. We don't serve any of those, do we?"

"Sometimes."

"Well, we had better take them off the menu or Jason Miller and his environmental goons might come back."

"I'll tell Louise. Speaking of goons, how are the girls in school behaving themselves?"

"I don't talk to them and they don't talk to me. I'm just doing my time and getting out. I hang with Alex. By the way, I dropped out of his club, Mom."

"Miller's?"

"Yeah. Too militant. Besides, that whole scene he pulled that day weirded me out." Gracie took the channel changer and started surfing the stations, stopping on the Style Channel. "That's what we need, Mom. We need makeovers."

"We need more than makeovers. Well, *I* do anyway. Why don't you join the debate club?"

"It's all nerds. Besides, I start modern dance lessons with the Charleston Ballet this Friday. Don't stress. Mimi said she would drive me back and forth. You know what? As soon as you get the splints out, let's go to Saks and get our makeup done."

"That is an excellent idea! Actually, it might have to wait until we close on the house in Montclair, but let's put that on our list, okay?"

"We don't have to wait that long, do we? I mean, you don't have to buy anything. They just do your makeup and you can just say, *Well, thanks! Bye!*"

"Honey, those ladies make their living on commission and it's not nice to ask them to do your makeup for free."

"Whatever. I got homework. What are we doing for dinner?"

"Pizza? Call Domino's?"

"I can handle it. And, hey, Mom? I can get my driver's license by Thanksgiving!"

"Excellent! Know what? I was thinking of trading my car, but I thought I'd save it for you. What do you think?"

"The Blue Buzzard? The one with a billion miles on it? Ah, Mom, come on. It's too good for me."

"Well, you can always buy your own."

"Did I tell you how much I love the Blue Buzzard? How sentimental I am about it?"

"Ingrate. But I'm glad you're starting dance again."

"I'll call Domino's."

That night and for the rest of the week, we ate pizza, Chinese food and whatever anyone brought us. I wasn't going anywhere, even in sunglasses. Mimi was in and out of our house with her war chest of cosmetics, trying to figure out how to help me hide the black eyes. There just wasn't much that could be done.

The splints came out, and a few days later so did the stitches, and I was left with some bruising and a bright red scar between my eyebrows, which I covered with a small Band-Aid. I was feeling much better by the following Tuesday and wanting to return to work. At least by then I felt like my face wouldn't traumatize small children. And, let's be honest—I was bored silly.

Tuesday afternoon, Brad brought Gracie home from school with Alex. It was a good thing I was dressed because they all just walked in the door. I was sitting on the terrace, reading the newspaper, enjoying the mild weather.

"Hi, Mom!"

"Hey! How was school?"

"Life-changing! How are you doing? Hey, Alex! You want popcorn?"

"Sure," Alex said.

I came inside to greet them and Brad was positioned by the door.

"Well! You look much better!"

"Thanks! I feel much better. It's just these freaking black eyes that are driving me crazy. Have you heard from Amy?"

"They're not so bad. Yeah, Amy went back to Atlanta."

"Hopefully forever."

"Yeah. She's not right in the head."

"Yeah, you think?"

"Yeah. I think. Hey, want to go look at the garage? I was thinking about it. If you're bringing furniture back from New Jersey, you're gonna have to put it somewhere and maybe we could get it emptied out before then? Come on, let's have a look."

I didn't feel like moving my bones anywhere but I did it anyway. Staying home for a week had made me very lazy. Brad was right. I might need the space sooner than later, so I said, "Okay. Let's go."

I opened the side door and he opened the large doors. Light came flooding in and the massive collection of junk looked worse than I remembered.

"Good grief!" he said. "This is some gold mine you've got down here!"

"Disgusting, right?"

"Yep. Hey, I have a friend who's gutting a house and he's got a Dumpster leased. I'll bet you for fifty bucks we can get a couple of his guys to come over here and liberate all this junk from the snakes and spiders. What do you think?"

"I say definitely, yes! You can have all the wildlife. That's a roger, good buddy."

Brad snickered. "Roger, good buddy? Are you a closet CB kind of gal?"

"Yeah, that's me. My handle is Black Eyed Babe. You know, it attracts the more manly man."

"You're a little twisted. Anyone ever tell you that?"

"Those rough-and-tumble sorts who appreciate a girl like me . . ."

"What did Fred do for a living?"

"Fred? My Fred? I mean, my ex-Fred?"

"Yeah, that's the one."

"Who wants to know and why?"

"I was just thinking about what kind of guy you were married to, that's all. What did he do?"

"Oh, well, Fred was and still is a certified public accountant."

"Ah! A certified public accountant? Wow. That's exciting."

"Yeah. Mr. Excitement. That's him."

"A real risk taker, a devil-may-care type—probably wild in the sheets, no?"

I stopped and stared at him. "Know what? You're pretty nosy. Did anyone ever tell you that? You're not supposed to ask me about my sex life! It's very inappropriate."

"Oh, come on! I'll tell you about Loretta if you tell me about Fred."

He picked up a rusty bicycle and pulled it outside. He was laughing at his own boldness and I was a little confused. I mean, was this some kind of flirting tactic?

"Okay, tell me about Loretta."

He stopped, put his hands on his hips and looked up at the trees for a minute. Then he said, "Okay. Here we go. Making love to Loretta was roughly the equivalent of taking my best friend and sticking him in the freezer, okay? How's that for romantic? How about Fred?"

Can I just take a moment here to discuss how I felt about that remark? I was having serious problems. I felt like a teenager, all silly and dying to hear every repulsive detail of what Loretta did and did not do in bed. However, sex with Fred? Who remembered? So, I made something up.

"Fred never brushed his teeth," I said, "so we didn't have sex a lot and when we did it was mercifully short."

"*That's* enticing—a short hitter with bad breath?"

"Pretty much. Let's just say I don't miss it."

"His bad breath or sex in general?"

"His bad breath." There was no reason in the world why I was engaging in this kind of talk *except* flirtation, which made me a nervous wreck. It was one thing for me to daydream about Brad, it was another to become so personal in real life. "Sex can wait."

"How long?"

"I don't know. When the issue presents itself, I'll figure it out. Now, back to my junk heap."

"Well, here's a piece of good news."

"What?"

"It appears to be watertight, which means you could use it as a room. Or you can use it as a garage, obviously. But you could build a big closet to hold clothes."

"I don't have any; haven't you noticed?"

"Okay. Well, you could make it into a den, or a big bedroom and bathroom for yourself. You'd just have to sheetrock it and extend the plumbing, drop a staircase—you could do a little spiral job—run the wiring, seal off the garage doors . . ."

"Oh, that's all? Well, then, let's go to Lowe's. Right now."

"Women. No vision."

"Bump you, bubba. You wouldn't believe the things that fly across my radar screen."

"I'll bet. You keep your cards pretty close, don't you? I always wonder what's on your mind."

All I do is think about you.

"I think it's best that we operate on a *need-to-know* basis. Now can we please call your friend with the Dumpster?"

"Okay. You win."

Wednesday, I went back to work, and when I walked into my office, it was clear that someone had cleaned it all up. Probably Louise. There was a stack of mail on my desk and enough catalogs to wallpaper the inside of an airplane hangar. I went looking for Louise and of course, she was in the kitchen disagreeing with Duane. Big surprise.

"Fennel stuffed in fish? Doo-wayne? There ain't nothing better in this world than fresh, plain red snapper just pan roasted with lemon juice, olive oil, salt and pepper. Welcome back, Linda! What's the matter with the fish? Ain't fresh enough?" Louise came to my side and gave me a hug. "You okay?"

"The fish is perfection!" Duane said. "Linda! You look faaa-bulous! Come see this."

"Thanks," I said and tossed my hair around, which went completely unnoticed, except by Miguel, the new dishwasher, who spoke approximately two words of English and to my surprise winked at me.

Duane opened the door of the mammoth oven, removed a copper pan and immediately the fragrance of fennel filled the air. Personally, I detest fennel, so I could not imagine that it would taste good with anything.

Duane put a fork into the fish, lifted up a steaming bit and came toward me.

"I'll pass," I said.

"Oh, all right. I'll taste the daggum fish," Louise said, in her most disgruntled voice. She worked it around her mouth for a minute and then burst out laughing. "Doo-wayne? Gimme that fish!" She looked at me and said, "Dee-licious!"

Those two were some pair.

"By the way, Louise, thanks for cleaning up my office, the soup and all."

"What are you talking about? I went with you to the hospital, remember? Must've been O'Malley."

I worked my way through the mail and decided to help O'Malley at the bar during happy hour.

"So, you feeling okay?"

"Better than ever. Hey, thanks again for the bartender's guide. Now I can make Side Cars and Pink Squirrels. Nothing like a little education, right?"

"Right."

"So, what's new around here? What did I miss?"

"Not a thing. You going up to New Jersey on Friday?"

"If Friday ever gets here! By the way, thanks for clearing away the debris from the war zone in my office."

"What are you talking about? I didn't do it. Must have been one of Duane's guys."

I asked Duane and he said no. In fact, every single person in the restaurant said they had not even been in my office. Sometimes, the bizarre just happened.

By Friday, I was so excited you would have thought I was going to Paris.

I had packed very little so that I could carry everything on the plane. Mimi and Gracie drove me to the airport. On the way there we discussed all sorts of things, the way desperate people do when they think they may not see each other again. Maybe it was just because it was another separation and leaving Gracie made me worry, although she was in perfectly safe hands with my sister. We talked and talked, filled with some kind of urgency to bring each other up to date on everything.

We talked about the garage and tried to decide what to do with it, coming to the conclusion that for the moment it would be used for storage. We decided to buy bicycles, now that we had a place to store them safely. They were relatively inexpensive and a great way to get exercise. Mimi and Gracie said they would pick them out the next morning. We listened to Gracie as she told us about her first dance lesson in ages.

"I am so completely out of shape! I haven't danced in months but oh, God! It felt so good to stretch. And, I felt so good when it was over!"

"She was dripping wet!" Mimi said.

"Well, if you aren't covered in perspiration, it means you didn't work hard enough."

We even talked about Mimi's half-baked relationship with Jack Taylor, and half-baked would be the operative term because all she ever did was cook for him.

"No nooky again?"

"Mom! Ew!"

"Nope! Did you ever think about how much of our lives revolve around food? I mean, it is the craziest thing! All we do is talk about it, buy it, cook it, serve it, clean it up and then stress over how much we ate and how much we weigh. It's a little stupid, isn't it? And on top of it all, you work in a restaurant and I bake for them!"

"It's what women do," I said, and we all agreed that it was true.

We were on Route 526, passing over long stretches of marsh and water for as far as you could see. The water was so glassy and still that it mirrored the docks and mossy live oak trees that hung over its edges. I wished we had time to stop and just stare at it.

The marsh grass showed the beginnings of fall, as its bright green shards faded into tan and the tide left deep brown watermarks all around its base. Snowy egrets, maybe a dozen or so, were scooting across the shallow water, chasing their dinner, which I assumed were little schools of minnows or shrimp. I spotted a peregrine falcon, circling for a kill.

"Look, y'all! It's a peregrine falcon!"

"I'm driving. You want me to go off the road?"

Gracie started complaining when I lowered my window to watch it spiral.

"What is the big deal about a dumb bird?"

"Well, missy, they almost got wiped out from DDT! See! You're not the only one who knows this stuff! There's a lot to learn around here. We should go up to Bull's Island on one of those eco-tours. You'll see birds so gorgeous it will stop your heart."

"Well, then let's do it when you get back."

"Deal."

"I want to come too," Mimi said, with a little whine.

"Absolutely! We'll see plenty of osprey and oyster catchers and . . ." The memories of all the birds of my childhood came back with their names and habits—I thought I had forgotten all of it, but I had not. It was something I could pass on to Gracie as my father had given the knowledge to me. When I was little, very small, he would point out a kingfisher, great blue herons or the white ibis, whose legs turned red during their breeding season. Sometimes on a walk on the beach of the Isle of Palms, he would point out boat-tailed grackles, raiding waste bins. They had a prissy strut that amused us. *He thinks he's a big shot, but he's having dinner in a garbage can,* he would say and we would laugh. "Yes, as soon as I get back, we're all going to Bull's Island."

It was well past seven o'clock, the time when the sun and moon often occupied the sky together. I was thinking about how grateful I had become to the Lowcountry and all its landscape. It seemed like I had been here forever and that all the years in New Jersey had happened to someone else. It would be strange to be in my old house, but at least I would be with Lindsey and I couldn't wait to see her.

We arrived at the terminal and all of us got out of the car.

"Y'all don't have to come in," I said. "I'm fine. Really."

"Are you sure?" Mimi said.

"Absolutely," I said. "If you get out of here now, you can still have something of a night left. Go to the movies!"

"Excellent idea! A chick flick!" Gracie said. "Make sure to hug Lindsey for me. Tell her to call me!"

At the last minute, Mimi pulled her cell phone out of her bag. "Take this," she said, "you need to have a phone and the battery is good and strong."

"Thanks. It's probably a good idea."

We said good-bye and hugged and kissed and I told Gracie to behave herself, even though, for the first time in her life, it seemed unnecessary.

My flight was delayed because of thunderstorms in the D.C. area. The ground crew made announcements as they received updates. First, it was going to be a thirty-minute wait. Then it was an hour. I bought a maga-zine from the kiosk, made myself comfortable and started reading.

At last, we boarded the plane and actually took off. I was on my way to say good-bye to my house and the town of Montclair for what I thought would be forever.

Lindsey was taking the bus out to Montclair after classes and opening up the house. How wonderful it was to have a daughter who could actu-ally do a few things to make your life more pleasant! Many people had said that after your daughters reach college age they became your greatest blessings. It certainly seemed to be true in my case.

Even Gracie. She was becoming a lovely young woman. Oh, she could still be sassy and I knew that her hijinks were not entirely over, but in the past weeks she had shown great promise. She had become more consider-ate and kind, doing many small things for me. Aside from her trouble with the girls at school, she seemed to be doing well in her classes, which she took more seriously than ever before. She took her work schedule to heart and she earned every penny she received.

I thought that Alex had a lot to do with her settling down. He was a serious kid. Gracie was crazy about him and she knew she had to clean up her act to hold his attention. He didn't like girls cursing or wearing skimpy clothes, and to my surprise, she had all but ceased cursing like a sailor and dressing like a tart. That did this mother's heart good.

Gracie seemed to have concluded that there were many ways to get attention, and it looked as though she had finally figured out that positive attention was better than negative. These days she seemed to place more value on earning and receiving respect.

If I had to venture a guess, I'd say that spending more time in the company of adults had left its mark on her. For the first time she heard a chorus of people—Louise, Mimi, Brad, O'Malley and even Duane—agree with something I said. The isolation we had known in New Jersey had always put us at odds with each other. Having the solid support of our little community of foodies had been beneficial.

I was looking forward to seeing Lindsey and hearing about all her professors and classmates. I wanted to tell her how well I thought Gracie was adjusting and blossoming. I hoped we would find a few hours to run to the city and see her dorm room. She was front and center on my mind as the plane circled Newark and prepared to land. It was almost midnight and the city twinkled below. Now it was Mount Pleasant that seemed to be a million miles behind me.

I picked up the rental car and drove home on the Garden State Parkway and then down Bloomfield Avenue toward Park Street. I was so tired. I couldn't wait to climb in my old bed, but only after I had a good look at my girl. As soon as I could spot my house, I could see that all the lights were on. I couldn't wait to get in the door and throw my arms around her.

She must have been sitting in the living room window watching, because as soon as I pulled into the driveway, she ran out the door.

"Mom!"

She came flying across the yard into my arms, and of course I began to cry.

"Baby! I missed you so much! Good Lord!"

"Oh, Mom! Don't cry! Are you okay? Let me see your head."

"I'm okay, I'm just happy to see you."

I pushed back my hair. Although the light was dim, she could see the scar. I had gone to great lengths to cover it but nothing seemed to work.

"Man! That bitch! I want to hear the whole story, with every detail!"

"You know what? She is a bitch!" I dug in my pocket, found a tissue and blew my nose. "Well, let me grab my things and let's get inside. It's late."

The minute I stepped inside the door, I knew I was not meant to be in that house any longer. It felt like a stranger. I got goose bumps all over from the surprise of it. Gretchen had done everything she said she would, but the combination of fake plants and the absence of family photographs and magazines made it feel sterile. It didn't feel like my house anymore. I couldn't wait to clean it out and put that part of my life in the past where it belonged.

"You hungry?" Lindsey said.

"Not really."

"Good, because there's nothing here except my leftover pizza and some Diet Coke."

"In that case, I'm hungry." I dropped my bag in the living room. We went into the kitchen and once again I felt like an intruder. It really wasn't my kitchen anymore. I took a slice of Lindsey's pizza and put it on a paper towel, unscrewed the top of the plastic bottle, and sat at the kitchen table. "So, does it seem bizarre to be back in this house, or what?"

"Uh, yes! First of all, there are a number of issues. The television's still here, but you canceled the cable, so no TV. The telephones are still all around, but you canceled the service, so you can't call anybody."

"Correction! I have a cell!"

"What?"

"It's Mimi's."

"Of course it's Mimi's. The Breland women don't do techno."

"Oh yeah? Well, I've got news for you! I was thinking about this on the plane. As soon as we close on the sale of this house, I'm buying you a cell, me a cell and Gracie a cell."

"Are you kidding?"

"No, I'm talking Christmas presents."

"Awesome! Can I pick out my own?"

"You can pick out all three. Just find a plan with nationwide minutes and we can talk about it. And, here's the big one, I'm buying you and Gracie laptops."

"Mom! You are like . . . *wild!* What's happened to you?"

"Nothing. I just think that it's time we joined the twenty-first century and all that. Besides, if we have laptops, I can e-mail you from home. And, if Gracie has a flat tire, she can call me. I mean, it just finally makes sense and for once, I will soon have a little money."

"Can we talk car?"

"Sorry, baby. You'll have to talk car with your dad."

"You look tired," Lindsey said. "There's still bruising in your cheeks."

I put my hand to my face and felt the area that had bruised the worst. It was still tender.

"I am tired. No, I am beyond tired."

"Well, let's go to sleep then," she said. "I made up your bed."

Well, how about that?

In the morning, we went to the Montclair Grill for breakfast and fattened ourselves on pancakes and sausages. Then we picked up a few groceries and returned home to begin the battle.

"You take the kitchen and I'll take the bathrooms," I said. "Throw away any spice bottle that looks like it's a year old and pack everything else in boxes. We can take it all down to the soup kitchen."

I sorted through bottles of almost-empty shampoo and conditioners of the same brand and combined them to give to Lindsey to take back to school. The same went for aspirin and tampons, and suddenly I realized why I never had any cash—the girls spent it all at the drugstore!

By dinnertime, we were exhausted. Lindsey was stretched out on the old couch in our living room and I was in the big overstuffed armchair, thinking I would miss it, even though the arms were frayed and the print was faded.

"You want supper?" I said, hoping she didn't want to cook.

"No. Too tired to make anything."

"Let's call Villa Victoria and get penne vodka and a salad."

"Perfect. I'll even go pick it up."

I tossed her Mimi's cell. I didn't care that she wasn't covered on the rental car insurance. How's that for living in the fast lane?

By Sunday night, the job was done. I had tagged everything for the yard sale, and divided the rest between what Lindsey could use, what I was sending back to South Carolina and what we were giving to charity. I was taking no furniture, no linens except for a quilt that I loved, a few winter clothes, raincoats and a couple of jackets. I packed up some pots and pans, a few small appliances, all my decent knives and some other kitchen tools. Every time my hand touched something the girls had made for me in school or at camp, it went in a special pile. Those would be bubble-wrapped along with all of our Christmas ornaments.

Lindsey and I were feasting on what we could scavenge from the salad bar at King's and just talking about everything. The next morning we would dispose of the boxes and take the train to the city.

"I can't wait to meet your roommate and see the campus," I said.

"It's incredible. Not my room, but the campus."

As we closed up the house for the night, I thought about how much more mature she seemed. She had assured me that she was fine, that Fred and Patti were not driving her crazy, and she was relieved to hear about Gracie allegedly growing up. Classes were tough but she loved the challenge and everything in general was going along according to plan.

She took Mimi's cell to call her roommate and I said good night. It was almost midnight again. I remember my last thoughts as I lay down were about how the time had flown by in the past few days and then I fell into a deep sleep.

I was dreaming about the old man again. He was holding my hand and patting it, much like Brad had done. He said, *I'm the one who cleaned your office. I wanted you to know I was real and that I am watching over you.* Then Lindsey burst into my room and threw on the overhead lights.

"Momma! *Wake up!* It's Aunt Mimi! The restaurant's burned to the ground and Gracie's in the *hospital!*"

I was on my feet in a heartbeat.

"What? Mimi? It's me! What's happened? Is Gracie okay?"

"She's fine. Well, she has a broken ankle and a concussion and some minor burns and scrapes, but she's going to be absolutely fine. Right now she's still unconscious, but the doctors expect her to wake up any time now."

My heart was pounding so hard I thought I would have a stroke before I could get the full story.

"I'm coming home. Please don't leave Gracie until I get there. Who's there? What happened?" I glanced at my watch. It was almost four o'clock.

"Get hold of yourself, Linda! Everybody is fine! And, you may as well get dressed because I have you booked on the five-thirty flight. I knew you would want to come back right away."

"Thanks."

"Anyway, the restaurant is covered by insurance. The one next door burned down too. It's some mess, Brad says. I haven't seen it yet. And, they brought Alex in too because he dragged Gracie out of your office and he was sick from the smoke. Alex said that he had heard from some kids that Jason Miller was going down there tonight to plaster posters all over the buildings with Gorilla Glue."

"What the hell is the matter with that man?"

"Honey? He's going to the slaaaa-mah?"

Jail?

"Oh my God. I can't believe my ears. He must be completely crazy."

"Brad saw him leaving with the police. When the fire alarm went off, the alarm company called Brad. But Gracie and Alex heard the sirens, hopped on the new bikes and beat him there. They were here watching a movie and I was asleep, for which you can punish me severely. I never heard a thing until the phone rang and it was Brad. I nearly died, I can promise you that."

"Mimi? Why in the world would anyone have thought that something like this could happen? I mean, it's not a great idea to leave them alone in a dark living room with a television, but no one would dream in a million years that they would get caught up in a fire. Don't spank yourself. You're sure Gracie's okay?"

"Yes. And, I won't leave her side."

"Why in the world did Gracie go in the office?"

"To get the money out of the safe. She thought the restaurant was being robbed."

"That girl will be the death of me yet," I said.

"That girl was doing something she thought was noble and brave. That's what you should think about."

TWENTY-TWO

BRAD WAITING

———◦✦◦———

I wanted the sun to rise. If the sun came up, the world would look better to me. I sat by Gracie's bedside with Mimi, Louise, Alex and Robert. Robert called O'Malley and Louise had called Duane to tell them all the news. They said they would come by in the morning. I told them to check with the ER nurse's station first, because we may have left by then, God willing.

Alex was still feeling terrible from all the smoke but they said he was going to be all right. I wanted him to go home and rest but he insisted on staying by Gracie's side. I didn't even argue with him.

The neurologist had just left and pronounced Gracie fine too, but part of me still doubted his judgment. I couldn't quite believe, looking at Gracie lying there unconscious, that she was fine. Unconscious was not fine.

Mimi followed the neurologist down the hall to double-check, triple-check and quadruple-check that what he told us was true and that he wasn't holding back anything. That Mimi was one terrific woman.

I thought about Gracie. What a spirited child she was! I knew that she loved to dance and I was concerned how her broken ankle would affect that in the long run. I would see to it that she got all the physical therapy she needed and then some. I had always wondered what it would be like to have a daughter, and because of her personality, wit and spunk, Gracie had become sort of a surrogate. I really loved this kid, no, this young woman. God forbid, if she had died, *what* would I have done? What would have become of Linda?

"What are you thinking about, Brad?" Robert said.

"I'm thinking I wish Gracie would wake up. I'm thinking I wish it was daylight because I always feel better when the sun's out."

He slapped me on the back in a friendly gesture of agreement and said, "This is unbelievable. So wrong. I'm so angry that this happened. I mean, who is this maniac? This Miller guy? He's got a mental problem, that one. I hope he goes to jail for a thousand years and you can take it to the bank that I'll do my part to see that he does."

"Good," I said and took Gracie's hand in mine. "Come on, sweetie, let's wake up, okay?" But there was no reaction. "I wish Linda was here."

Louise said, "She'll be here soon, Mr. Brad. I just keep thinking what it would be like if she lost her girl. Oh, God, I wish this child would wake up. Just wake up and say something."

"I'm going out for coffee—anybody want something?" Robert said.

"Yes, just black," I said.

"Me too," Louise said.

Alex just shook his head and went back to staring at Gracie's face. We sat in silence for the next few minutes, all of us waiting, wishing something would change.

"She looks like she's just sleeping," Alex said.

"Well, she is, in a way. Alex, I am so proud of you, son. You saved her life, you know."

"Amen," Louise said. "You are a real true-to-life hero, Alex."

"I just did what anyone would have done," he said. "I told her not to go in there but she was determined to get the cash from the safe."

"God, what a great kid," I said. "She couldn't have known it was fire-proof. Can you imagine if you hadn't pulled her out? Can you imagine us telling Linda that Gracie was gone? I don't think I have ever seen a woman who cares more about her kids than Linda does about hers. You know? I mean, her Lindsey is a wonderful girl. Wonderful! Dependable, smart—all that. But this one is a spitfire and you know, I can't wait to see who she becomes someday. I think it would truly kill Linda if the worst had happened." I thought about it for a moment and then spoke again. "I mean, Alex, you don't understand. You didn't just save Gracie, you saved Linda and Lindsey and really, all of us, because I know I would never have got over it. And you know what else?"

The door swung open and Robert came in with a cardboard tray holding our coffee.

"Here," Robert said, putting the cup down on the table next to her bed. "Watch out. It's hot."

"Thanks," I said, but I couldn't bring myself to release Gracie's hand to remove the lid and take a sip. "I can't imagine the world without Gracie. It would be so empty."

"Tragic," Robert said. "It would be absolutely tragic. But don't think about it. It's not gonna happen."

I looked over at Louise and she was watching me intensely.

"What do you think, Louise?"

"I think you have more feelings for Linda and her girls than you know. That's what I think."

"What do you mean?"

"She's saying you're in love with her, pal," Robert said. "You're in love and you don't even know it."

"No, I'm saying that you're in love with all of them," Louise said. "Let me tell you gentlemen something. Linda Breland is a warrior. She loves with a fierceness I haven't ever seen in anybody except myself. That's just one reason why we get along so well. She is loyal to a fault and as hard-working as anyone I have ever known. She says what she thinks and I agree with almost every word that comes from her mouth."

"Me too," I said.

"She's a helluva gal," Robert said.

"Well, when you find somebody who's got qualities like Linda, you love her. That's all."

Finally, I put Gracie's hand down on her blanket and stood up. I was stiff from sitting for so long and I stretched a little. Mimi came back in and took my seat, so I picked up my coffee and decided to go outside for some air.

"What did the doctor say?" Louise said.

"How's she doing?"

"No change," I said. "So, what did he say?"

"Nothing. You would think that with all the education these guys have that they could think of something more than *Why don't you go home and get some rest and come back in the morning?* First of all, it is morning—almost. Basically, he repeated everything he said when we all heard him. He said Gracie is fine and that she will come around."

"I'll be back in five minutes," I said.

I walked down the short corridor and the doors opened automatically. It was around five-thirty and the eastern sky was streaked with the beginning of dawn. The early morning air was damp but more comfortable to me than the air-conditioning. I put my cup down on the low wall and rubbed my arms to warm them up. As I moved along a few steps toward the parking lot, I realized how exhausted I was. I couldn't wait to see Linda arrive and I knew that I would be a wreck until she did.

Our children had accomplished something that night that adults would never have even considered trying. I wondered where Alex got his strength and where Gracie got hers too. But I didn't wonder for long.

That night Alex had reminded me of my father in the way that he simply jumped in and did what needed to be done. Another man, maybe even Robert or me, we might have weighed the odds first and then decided it was a job for a professional.

And Gracie? She was Linda all over again. I smiled to myself thinking about what Linda must have been like as a teenager and thought that she probably gave everyone a good run for their money. I remembered the day she had given me hell for making that raunchy remark about hot babes versus mothers and even still, I could not help but smile again at her nerve. She would not have cared if I had fired her; she wasn't staying if I didn't apologize. God. I loved that!

And that Lindsey. I would have bet that she was as mad as a hornet for being left behind to return to school on her own, not being here, not seeing what was really going on.

First, Linda had been assaulted and now Gracie had this accident. I would ask Linda if she wanted to fly Lindsey home next weekend. I would pay for it. No problem. No, they were too close a family to be separated at a time like this. At the very least I would make a video of Gracie first thing and send it to Lindsey FedEx. Then she could see her sister and hear her sassy mouth. Yes, that was a good idea. I would do it.

The doors behind me opened and Robert appeared.

"Hey, Robert? Do you have a video camera?"

"Yeah, why?"

I told him my plan and he laughed at me.

"What's so funny?"

"Ahem, Bradford. Do you think that your thoughts are the ordinary thoughts of an *ordinary* employer? You're gonna *fly her daughter in*. No, wait! First, you're gonna make a *video* and FedEx it to her and *then* you're gonna fly her in—I mean, come on!"

"No, I mean, it's just that . . ."

"Right! You kill me!"

"What?"

"Remember the old story about the guy rearranging deck chairs on the *Titanic?*"

"Yeah, so?"

"Well, you're going down! Ah ha ha! You're going down!"

"I'm sinking? You know what? You and Louise drive me crazy sometimes."

"Hey! Say whatever you want! It doesn't matter. The truth is the truth." He began walking toward his car and then stopped. "Things will happen as they should, when they are *supposed* to happen. I'm going to go grab a couple of hours of sleep and I'll be back to look over the mess later on."

"Give Susan my love," I said. "Call me when you get up."

"Okay. And, call me when Gracie wakes up."

I nodded, watched him go and thought it was probably time to go back inside. Maybe Louise was right. If I was already in love as Louise said, it was certainly powerful stuff. I couldn't remember caring so much about another woman. I was very worried about how she was handling it and I was not going to be happy until I knew she was all right. I had to have a part in it.

Linda wasn't like Loretta. I didn't feel about her like I ever had about Loretta—at all. Linda was kind. That's a commonly used description of someone but boy, the world could use more kindness. And, in her way, she was very pretty. In fact, she was really beautiful. And she was funny as hell and as smart as anyone I had ever known. No, she was amazing.

God knows, the thought of my world without Linda and her girls in it was very damn depressing. I hadn't even seen it coming but I knew then that I was fully immersed in her family.

Let's be serious. What did I know about love anyway? Obviously, not much. Linda Breland was right under my nose and I had not even realized until that moment that I was, yes, damnit, I was completely captivated by her. How funny! When I thought about it further, looking back on conversations we'd had about the garage, our children or the restaurant, I could see that we talked to each other like an old married couple anyway. And as these thoughts have a tendency to lead to others, naturally I wondered what it would be like to kiss her. Probably . . . well, let's see? If the energy she exerted for the everyday mundane business of living translated its way into the sack, she could be hot like all hell! I'll bet she was!

Maybe it was time for me to do something brave, like step up to the plate and see what it felt like to really be in love. Let myself go. Really be Italian and enjoy life and truly fall in love. We were already committed to each other. We respected each other too. What would I say to her? I would just tell her the truth. I would tell her how frightened I had been when I saw the fire, and feared for Gracie and Alex's lives and how I just realized I didn't want to live without her. Or Lindsey. Or Gracie.

TWENTY-THREE

LOVE IS ALL THERE IS

———————

L INDSEY had promised to close up the house, call Gretchen to enlist her help with the distribution of the boxes, and get herself back to school on the train. I knew that I could depend on Lindsey and that if there was a way Gretchen could help, she would.

I was coming undone. I knew it. I was close to screaming. No one understood the importance of my daughters to me. They were an extension of the very kernel of flickering light that kept me alive and wanting to live the days left to me. If anything were to happen to either one of them, my own life would have fallen into peril.

There was never a slower plane in Christendom than the one I boarded to return to Charleston. I prayed the entire way. The Lord's Prayer. Hail Marys. Any prayer I could recall. Mostly they went like this—*Dear God, please*. And then through God's mercy, I slept a little as the plane bounced and rolled its way down through the clouds.

The airport at Charleston was already filled with the life of another day's beginnings. I wondered in my panic if anyone else here was rushing to the side of a loved one because of an emergency like mine. No, there could be no one else who felt as I did that morning. My heart was so heavy and my mind so worried that I cannot recall how I found the wherewithal to continue the simple motion of one foot in front of the other. The same force of fear that held me back was counterbalanced by the overwhelming pressure to get to my child as quickly as humanly possible. It would only have taken the slightest brush of another traveler or one question of inquiry from a security guard for me to lash out and wail my story without a breath until I had unburdened myself.

I came through the terminal without incident and Louise was waiting in the baggage claim area. I was so relieved to see her face. I had thought that I would just grab a taxi, but you know Louise by now. She would never have stood for a friend of hers arriving alone, especially one carrying a sack of trouble the size of mine.

"She's all right, Linda," she said. That was all she said.

I burst into tears. Then Louise burst into tears. People passing us probably thought we had no self-control or that we were grieving the loss of a friend or family member. In reality, we cried because we were frightened and because we could console each other in small measures as the magnitude of reality set in.

"Let's go. We're just wasting time here watering this cheap carpet."

We began our way to her car and she updated me on everything.

"Gracie is still unconscious, but they expect her to wake up and fully recover. Kids heal fast, you know. And, she's on oxygen because of the smoke to get some clean air in her lungs. So don't be upset when you see that. And she's got an IV, but they always give you an IV. Now, they put a pin in her ankle because she really cracked the hell out of it, so she ain't gonna be dancing for a while."

"My poor child!"

"She's okay. It will heal beautifully they said because she didn't walk on it. Alex went in to get her and found her unconscious and carried her out. Something must've fallen and hit her on the head. They gave him a big oxygen mask last night and he's fine but he's been sitting by Gracie's bed with Brad and Mimi and he's awfully upset. They all are."

"I just want to put my arms around her," I said.

"Well, in about five minutes you can do just that. I called my church and we got the prayer circle going."

"Thanks, Louise. Seriously. Thank you."

I could see her smile and I knew we were both thinking that we hoped the prayer circle worked as fast as heaven could bring it about. We were quiet then, just remarking on Alex's bravery, the loss of the restaurant next door in addition to ours, the shock and surprise of it all and of course, how the sinister hand of the devil himself was all over the disaster.

"You think the devil ain't got himself all wrapped up in Jason Miller's mind? Honey, that's possession if I ever saw it!"

"You're right, sister."

"Yeah, but you know what? The scuttlebutt is that the other people he had with him didn't know he had brought gasoline in his car and they said that when they saw him pouring it all around the foundation, that they tried to stop him."

"He's a total lunatic."

"Well, that's what the *Post and Courier* said this morning."

"That's some pretty fast reporting, isn't it?"

"Yeah, but by coincidence, this reporter named Bill Thompson who usually covers other stuff was at a friend's house until late and on his way back to Charleston when he saw the flames and stopped. He was there and saw the whole thing."

"Well, that's pretty crazy."

"That's how life is though, 'eah?"

"Yep. That's how life is."

It seemed that an eternity had passed between the airport terminal and the moment when we pulled up in front of the East Cooper Community Hospital Emergency Room entrance.

I ran in the door and saw Brad in the hall outside of what I assumed was Gracie's room. He waved me over, as though it was necessary, and I hurried so that I don't even remember going from the door to Gracie's side, except that Brad's face was the first one I saw.

Mimi was there, washing Gracie's hands and face, removing the remains of soot and talking to her.

"Your momma's here, Gracie. Do you want to say hello to her?"

I was so startled by the sight of my beautiful daughter, unconscious and in a hospital gown, that I had to hold on to the foot of her bed to steady myself. My beautiful Gracie, damaged and battered and her mind only who knew where. What was she hearing? I think I may have pushed Mimi aside when I climbed on the bed and kissed Gracie on her forehead.

"I'm here, baby. It's Momma. Please open your eyes for me, okay? Please open your eyes! Tell me how you feel? Everything's okay. You're going to be fine. You *have* to be fine." My tears began to flow and then choking sobs. I just couldn't help it. I took her hand, IV and all, and kissed it all over the palm and held it to my cheek. I felt Brad's arm around my shoulder and when I looked up I could see that he was crying too. So was Alex and Mimi and of course, Louise.

"I should have stopped her, Ms. Breland," Alex said. "This is all my fault. I am so sorry. I don't even know what to say."

"Stop it, Alex," I said, "you saved Gracie's life! Do you understand that I wouldn't have my daughter if you had not been there?"

"I know, but I shouldn't have let her go in there in the first place."

"No, son," I said, "you did a very brave thing and we are all so proud of you, you don't know. And grateful."

"I don't know," he said, "it just shouldn't have happened, that's all."

"Alex?" Brad said. "There's a lot of wickedness in this whole episode, but none of it is laid at your feet. I don't want to hear you say again that this is your fault. You listen to Linda. That's her child lying in this bed and if she doesn't blame you then you most certainly should not blame yourself."

"Your daddy's right," Mimi said.

"Amen," said Louise.

There was a little knock on the door and Alex opened it. It was O'Malley with a small vase of Gerber daisies.

"Hey," he said, in a whisper. "How's she doing?"

"I just wish she would wake up," I said and started to cry again. Brad put his arm around me and I put my face into his chest and just sobbed. He rubbed the center of my back, around and around, and I could tell by the way his body shook that he was crying again too.

"Oh, God," O'Malley said. "She broke her leg?"

"Ankle," said Mimi.

"Listen, Linda," Brad said, and handed me a tissue, "as soon as we got here, I called a top neurologist from the Medical University, this guy Philip Ragone, and he examined her. He's the best in the entire southeast. He said she's absolutely fine. He assured me *and* Mimi *and* Louise that she would regain consciousness. We have to trust that he knows what he's talking about. Right? So, come on now."

"It's just terrifying, you know?"

"Of course it is. This is a damnable thing."

The door opened again and in came Duane with a tray of coffee and a box of Krispy Kremes.

"Well, we have to eat, don't we*!*" Duane said and put everything down. He came to my side, and gave me a kiss on the cheek. "The Breland ladies sure have had one hell of a time lately!" He reached in the box of doughnuts and took one. "Move over, and y'all help yourselves." He passed the doughnut under Gracie's nose and said, "Gracie, Gracie, Gracie, it's Doowayne bringing you a *dough-nut*. Glazed with chocolate? Come on, girlie-whirlie! Duane's gonna take you shopping! We're going to the new Arden B! You can have *anything* you want! There's a shoe sale at Bob Ellis!"

There was a distinct fluttering of her eyes.

"Look!" Duane said.

We all stared at Gracie and began calling her name.

"Gracie? Gracie?" I said and shook her arm. "Come on, baby, wake up!"

Duane went around to the end of the bed and tickled the bottom of her elevated foot. When there was no reaction, he reached under the sheets and pulled out her other leg and began tickling her other foot.

"Maybe she ain't ticklish," Louise said, pushing by him. She went up to Gracie's head on the other side of her bed and whispered in her ear,

"Gracie? It's Louise, baby. It's time to wake up now. Come on. Let's wake up like a good girl."

"What?" Gracie said. "Lemme sleep."

A cry of relief went up in the room, prayers of thanksgiving and even a little applause. Gracie was awake and I was grateful to God. We couldn't know what had brought her back to us—prayer, our voices, the promise of a shopping trip or a Krispy Kreme doughnut. If I had been in Gracie's position, it probably would have been the smell of sugar and chocolate.

Later on, after all of us took Gracie home and she hobbled up the steps on Alex's arm, after we had settled her on the couch and elevated her ankle to reduce swelling, after we gave her a Diet Coke with a straw, the channel changer and the latest issue of *InStyle*, bought on the way out of the hospital at the last minute, only then did we begin to talk about the restaurant. Of course, the plan was to rebuild as soon as possible. They were discussing possible contractors and Duane and Louise were arguing about the dimensions and layout of the new kitchen. Mimi, who knew nothing about construction or anything remotely connected to running a business, was correcting them left and right. Even Gracie was a part of it, saying they should set the new restaurant back from the water a little and provide drainage on both sides of the building. Considering that she had nearly lost her life, I knew her input would be taken seriously.

I took my bag into my bedroom and tossed it on the bed to unpack later. Brad was right behind me.

"Want to go see the mess?"

"I don't know if I should leave. . . ."

"Don't worry, Lupe's on her way over here and she said she wants to take care of Gracie."

"Lupe's coming? I'm going!"

"Nice," he said.

"I'm just kidding! Jeesch!"

"Hey! Did you see the garage?"

"No! Did the guy come?"

"Yep, come on, I'll show you!"

I told Mimi, Louise, Duane and O'Malley I would be back and bring sandwiches, if anybody wanted anything.

"Wait a minute! Let me get a pencil!"

You would think that all we ever did was eat but then, our world did revolve around food.

I wrote down what everyone wanted and then because their orders were so varied and complicated I finally told them, "Look, I'm going to Bessinger's. You'll get what I bring back. End of story."

"Oh, barbecue!" Louise said. "I haven't had barbecue in ages!"

"No onion rings!" Mimi said.

"Yes! Onion rings!" Duane said.

"I'll go out and get beer," O'Malley said.

"Bud Light!" Duane said.

"Corona Light!" Mimi said.

"Make that two," Louise said and patted Mimi on the arm.

"Heineken," Gracie said. When the whole room stopped and stared at her she said, "God, can't anybody take a joke around here?"

Brad pulled me out the door. On the way out I hollered back, "Somebody call Lindsey, okay? She's probably worried half sick to death."

"Isn't she in class?" Mimi said.

"I don't know. Just dial your cell number. I left your phone in New Jersey."

"Oh! Well! Oh! Well? There went my cell phone! I'll just let her keep it!"

I closed the door and followed Brad down the steps. When he pulled open the big doors, I couldn't believe my eyes. It was empty, except for one box, but it had been swept clean. It seemed enormous.

"What do you think?" he said, smiling.

"I think you are incredible. How can I thank you?"

"I'll think of something," he said, with the most mysterious expression on his face.

"Brad Jackson? Is that a wicked grin I see?" Was I dreaming?

"Yes. It is a wicked grin, Linda Breland."

"What brought this on?" I started to back away from him, unsure if what I was thinking was the same thing he was thinking.

"What's the difference?" He took a step toward me.

"I want to know what your intentions are!"

"I cleaned your garage. My intentions are honorable."

"What's in that box?"

"Stuff for Lowell. Don't change the subject. Stop moving around. I'm not going to hurt you!"

"No, you don't understand! You're not going to do *anything* to me, Brad Jackson! I saw how you treated Amy." I knelt down and opened the box. I closed it and picked it up, attempting to avoid the very person I had been dreaming about since we had met.

"And, I saw how she treated you. She drove me crazy; you drive me wild."

"Yeah, sure. You're an ass."

"No, I am not an ass. Do you have any idea how long it takes to rebuild a restaurant? Put the box down."

The box landed with a thud on the floor.

"Six months? A year?" I took a deep breath.

"A long time. Do you have other plans?"

"What do you mean?" He backed me up against the wall and put his arm over me, blocking my escape.

"I mean, just what are we supposed to do with ourselves until then?"

"Are you saying we should pass the time by having an affair?"

"No, I'm saying we should be planning our wedding. Come on, Linda. Everyone knows we're in love except you."

Oh. My. God. I was going to drop dead.

"They do?" The tiny bit of moisture that I felt under my arms had now grown to a trickle. And, I refuse to even acknowledge what the other parts of my body were up to, twitching and pulsing like independent little idiots.

"Yeah."

"You don't understand, Brad. I don't fall in love. I raise children. I worry . . . that's what I seem to do best. Worry."

"What are you worried about?"

"I don't know. I mean, I'll admit that I have had the casual, intermittent, innocent thought . . ."

He roared with laughter and said, "Intermittent? Innocent? What are you? Dead?"

"No! I mean, Jesus, Mary and Joseph, you're asking me to marry you? Marry you? You've never even brought me flowers, taken me anywhere or even kissed me one time! Isn't this a little insane?"

"In my mind, we've been living together for months. In my mind, I have kissed you thousands of times. In my mind I have brought you so many dozens of roses . . ."

"Oh bull!"

"Not bull!"

"Well, maybe we should start with some kind of flowers?"

He laughed and shook his head and said, "Linda Breland, I am hell-bent and determined that I am going to laugh my way into old age with you and that is that."

"May I just ask what brought you to this conclusion?"

"Okay, that's fair. I'm assuming that you mean why I never even said something like *Nice haircut, Linda,* and now I'm proposing marriage?"

"Yeah. That's the little detail that has me going."

"Okay, well, it started with Loretta dying so suddenly. What happened were two very interesting things. One, I saw firsthand how fragile life really is, the same way that Alex did. I mean, you bury old people, but not people your age, right? You hear about it, but you don't believe it until it happens to you. And two, I didn't feel one ounce of remorse and for a long time I asked myself why."

"And the answer to that is?"

"That I knew I didn't love her and probably never did and that I would have stayed in that marriage forever, loveless and pathetic as it was, because I lacked the courage to do anything about it. But then fate stepped in and made me react anyway.

"Remember when we had that dinner for Lindsey? I watched you and how emotional you were and I wondered when the last time was that any-one ever cared for me that way—my mother, thank you—and I knew that the love you had for Lindsey was greater than the love you had for your-self. Then you got gumboed and said that thing about *Gee, it's a good thing she didn't hit my temple,* and I knew you were right. Another couple of inches and hearts would have been shattered and lives ripped apart. And then the fire and the whole drill with Gracie scared me out of my mind. I realized that I really loved Gracie and the world without her would be un-bearable for you and therefore, for me. And I thought about your love for Gracie and Lindsey and your sister and how your family cared for each other and I remembered that your family operates like mine used to—not with Loretta but with my folks and how I grew up. And, I saw that it all came from you. It all came from you. You were willing to pull the Jersey plug and flush almost twenty years there just to improve the quality of your relationship with your daughters. I wanted in. It's not just you I love because I want to get in your shorts—which by the way, have I told you that I want to get in your shorts? Anyway, it's the way you are that has me over the cliff—the stuff of your soul. That's all. I think."

"Oh," I said. "Well, then . . ."

And that was when he lifted my chin, looked in my eyes and laid one on my lips. Honey? That man could kiss like no other. It was also when I discovered that kissing was like riding a bicycle—it all comes back and you do just fine.

"Come on," he said, "I want to show you the remains of Jackson Hole."

"Okay," I said. I was a little disoriented.

We left the garage holding hands. Lupe was pulling into the yard and Louise was at the top of the steps. Lupe pointed to us and covered her mouth with her hand. When we looked back at Louise she was smiling wide.

"I like what I see now," she said, and wagged her finger at us. "I like what I see."

He opened the car door for me and I got in. He closed it, walked around the front of the car and I watched him like a hawk. He was so good-looking I thought his face should be on a coin. Better yet, the pent-up harlot in me thought, that face belongs on my pillow.

When he got in his side of the car, he turned to me. "Well?" he said.

"Well what?"

"Will you marry me or what?" His eyes twinkled with excitement.

"Yeah, sure. Why not?"

"Not much else going on?"

"Yeah. Something like that."

"Okay. Done."

As he backed the car up to turn it around, we started to laugh. We laughed and laughed and laughed. We told each other we were crazy and brilliant. Out of control and too conservative. Then he placed his hand over mine again and gave it that lovely squeeze. As ridiculous as the situation was, it made perfect sense.

"Did you really love Fred?"

"At the time I married him, I thought I did. Didn't you love Loretta on some level?"

"I think I felt she was a good choice. But I never felt like this."

"Me either."

Brad's cell phone rang and he answered it, mouthing *Robert* to me.

"Yeah, sure, I'm going there now."

It took all of four minutes to reach Shem Creek and I could hardly believe my eyes. If I was reeling from Gracie's accident and reeling again from Brad's proposal, I was reeling once again when I got out of the car. The stench of it was horrible and I knew we had to start removing the rubble immediately or it would hurt the business of the other restaurants. Part of the building was still standing, but a stiff wind would collapse the whole thing. It was mind-boggling that the politics of one nut could cause such a disaster in just a few hours.

"Brad, this is unbelievable."

He was kicking his way through it, but he could only go so far.

"What are you trying to do?"

"I'm thinking that there might be as much as ten thousand dollars in the safe and if I can get to it . . ."

"Oh, no you don't! We can call a company, somebody who does this, and they can come and do it. Don't you think we've had enough excitement for a while? I can see it all now! Headline! Brad Jackson, owner of Jackson Hole, Dies Stupidly Over Ten Thousand Dollars! Nah nah nah. Not happening."

"You're right. Of course, you're right. What was I thinking?"

"Really, Brad, sometimes you're scary."

"Just wait until dark."

"Excuse me; I thought we were going to start with flowers."

"Right! I'll call Belva's!"

Robert's car pulled up and he got out. He took off his sunglasses and squinted toward the restaurant.

"It was a dump anyway," he said. "Hey, Linda, glad you got back safely. Terrible about Gracie, she's okay?"

"Besides her broken ankle and concussion and some minor scrapes and burns," I said, "but at least she's conscious now."

"Yeah, Brad called to tell me and I was there for a while last night."

"Yes, I know. Thank you for that. She's home, resting."

Robert shook his head back and forth with the enormity of all that had happened. "Well, like my grandfather used to always say, it could've been a lot worse, right? Isn't that right? Thank God it wasn't. Susan sent some flowers. Let me know if they get there okay."

"Thanks," I said, "I don't think Gracie has ever been sent flowers before."

"Don't worry! She'll get tons of them!" Brad said. "And, hey, Robert, there's money in the safe but we can't get to it."

"How much?"

"Linda says it's chump change next to the risk involved trying to retrieve it now."

"Linda? I've been telling Brad for weeks that he should figure out a way to keep you around! You're the smartest woman I have met in years!"

"Well, I figured that out, Robert. I just asked Linda to marry me!"

"What? What? Married? You're shitting me! That's fabulous! Hold on, I gotta call Susan! You old dog." He slapped Brad on the back and then shook his hand. *"Come here, Linda! Let me kiss your cheek! Man, this is great!"* He pulled his cell phone from his pocket and called his wife. "Hi, it's Robert. Is Susan in the office? Sure, I'll hold." He put his hand over the speaker and said, "Don't you love this? I'm on hold. Don't they know what I bill an hour?"

I giggled and looked at Brad, dressed in sunlight, smiling for all the world.

"I didn't even know y'all were dating!"

"Well, now we are," Brad said.

"Yeah, *starting* now!" I said.

"Why not?" Robert said and then turned his attention to the phone. "Call Cypress or the Peninsula Grill! Get a table for four for tonight! Brad and Linda are getting married! Yes, married! What? Oh, hell, call his secretary. We can have dinner with Joe Riley anytime! Okay. Call me back." He flipped his cell closed and looked at us. "Unbelievable. Well, let me tell you something. The happiest years of my life have been the ones I've shared with Susan. I wish y'all the same."

"Thanks, Robert," Brad said and they shook hands.

I extended my hand to shake Robert's and he jumped back. "No, no! That's okay! How about a hug instead?"

"Oh, God, I will never live my handshake down, will I?"

We hugged in the most platonic way and Robert said, "It's important to have one flaw, Miss Linda, otherwise nobody will think you're human."

"Miss Linda?" I said.

"Well, now that you and Bradford are betrothed, which actually needs no explaining, and I have no objection, you have gone from the status of an available girl and I, and I, oh hell, never mind. I guess I just like the sound of Miss Linda."

"Tell you what," Brad said, "let's go pick up lunch, take it back to the house, feed the troops and start making phone calls. We gotta clean up this mess on the double or our neighbors will be very unhappy."

"Sounds good," Robert said, "I'll follow you."

"No, ride with us," Brad said.

"Oh, shit!" Robert said. "I *knew* there was something else I had to tell you! But between the news of your engagement and this horrible sight . . ."

"What?" Brad said.

"Loretta's estate lawyer called me on the way over here. Seems that old Theo signed the house over to Loretta on her thirtieth birthday."

"She never told me that," Brad said.

"She had no will. Now it's yours, all the contents and whatever she had that was worth anything."

"God, no kidding," Brad said as the color drained from his face. "Any idea what the house is worth?"

"Yep. I called my cousin who's a broker there. She just sold a house in the neighborhood, similar to yours. Three-point-two."

"Three-point-two what?" Brad said.

"Million, my boy! Three-point-two million dollars!" Robert started laughing at the shocked look on Brad's face. "Now after lunch, go buy Linda a diamond. Am I right, Linda? Am I right or what? This calls for a Cohiba! Later though. After lunch. Where are we going?"

"Bessinger's," I said.

"Bessinger's? You must be kidding! Well, I'll get a chicken sandwich."

"Robert! Since when are you kosher?"

"Since I got on the scales this morning! A ha ha ha! Right? Right?"

We started toward the car together. Brad was as white as a sheet.

"You okay?" I said.

"Three-point-two?"

"Oh, cheer up. Maybe you'll get three-point-three."

There was a lot of celebrating in my future and had I not been so exhausted I would have been euphoric to be able to say that. When we came to our senses we decided that we would say we were engaged for a while and see how it went. When the restaurant was rebuilt, if we hadn't fallen out of whatever the enchantment was that seemed to have swallowed us alive, we would be the first private party there.

I knew though that it was all for real. I knew also that there was a higher hand at work. The one whose mighty dreams breathed us into existence in the first place. How else could I explain the hits and the misses of my life? Everything about Brad was right. Everything about this place was right. All it had taken to get my show on the road was that first step and then events unfolded with such a ferocious velocity that I knew they had to be almost preordained.

After a fabulous dinner at the Peninsula Grill and after another bottle of champagne with Mimi and Louise, who had stayed together to watch over Gracie, I helped Gracie to bed that night and covered her up, kissing her forehead over and over. Then I sat down beside her.

"You gave me the scare of my life, you know."

"I know. I'm sorry, Mom. I'll never do anything crazy like that again."

"No, I don't expect that you will."

"Mom? Are you really gonna marry Mr. Jackson?"

I sighed with all the force of every woman who ever put her faith in a man and said, "Gracie? To tell you the truth, I don't know. I don't know if he asked me because he was so relieved that you survived the fire and that Alex got himself and you out alive. Or maybe he asked me because he was so traumatized by losing the restaurant and he thought I could be his rock. I don't know. Time will tell. If he shows up with a diamond, then we can say it's official."

"Or maybe he just loves you, Mom. Did you ever think about that?"

"Yeah, I think about that a lot."

"Do you love him? I mean, are you like *in love?* Wiggly knees and all that?"

"Yeah, maybe I am. We'll see. You get some sleep now, okay? I'll leave my door cracked so if you need anything, just shout."

"Okay. Love you."

"Love you too, baby. I'm just gonna get something from the garage and I'll be right back."

I went outside to retrieve the box, deciding that for some reason I had to know what was inside. Besides, it would remind me to call the Epsteins and tell them about it. I opened the door and saw it sitting where I had dropped it earlier. I lifted the box to my hip, closed the door behind me and then I stopped. It was so quiet and the air smelled so beautiful. I left the box to rest on the steps and walked around to the front of the yard, facing the harbor, and just stood there for a few minutes, taking in the view over the water of Charleston in the distance. There were thousands of stars above me and the world had grown quiet with the late hour. I was as tired as if I had run a marathon and then I realized I had not slept but a few hours, that my day had begun in the middle of the night. Still, I stood there, listening to the lapping water against the pilings and wishing for a dock. Maybe if I stayed in the place, I would put one up eventually. The moonlight was a siren's call and half drunk on its beauty I pulled myself away from swirling dreams to find well-deserved rest.

I climbed the steps and went inside, locking the door behind me, and put the box on the counter. I pulled the top flaps open and saw it was filled with photograph albums. I opened one, just out of curiosity, and could not believe what I saw before me. Picture after picture. They were all images of the old man from my dreams at various moments of his life. If I had any tears left in me or if I had still possessed the smallest amount of energy to call them forth, I would have cried a river. This old man had reached out from across the divide of life and death to let me know he was there, watching, doing what he could to protect us, caring about us.

I went to bed because it was too late to call Mimi and tell her about my discovery. She would believe it. So would Louise. They had been hearing stories like this one for all of their lives.

I wondered if things like this ever happened in New Jersey and could not recall ever having heard of something similar. But I knew for sure that they happened here all the time. But that was the magic of the Lowcountry. Heaven was always nearby.

EPILOGUE

W E all know it's vulgar to discuss money, but to fully bring you up to date we are going to have to wade in those waters for a few minutes. Remember Mimi? That biscuit-making Queen of the Pound Cakes from the Old Village of Mount Pleasant? That swirl of a girl with the frosted blonde hair, who was never seen without the perfect shade of a rosy-colored lipstick? That little sneak! She had been taking ten percent of her alimony every month and buying Microsoft for almost twelve years. Well, it had split and split and split, as the world knows. Mimi could now well afford to buy her Donna Karan control-top pantyhose at full price. Not that she really had to pinch pennies anyway, but who knew she had a nest egg?

"I have just been tithing for my old age," she said. "However, I'm thinking I would like to have a bakery. Do you think it would be possible for me to squeeze out three hundred square feet from the new restaurant? Even two hundred, if Duane would let me share the ovens. And, actually, it could be a good site for takeout and catering from the restaurant too?"

It was a brilliant idea. More and more, people didn't want to wait for tables and we had never successfully run a takeout business. If the public was unaware that you were in the takeout business, they would rarely ask for takeout and then they felt like it was an imposition if they did ask.

"You want to invest?" Brad said. "Is that what you're saying?"

"I guess so," Mimi said. "If you would have me. And, I was thinking too that if we had a little staircase next to my entrance, I could send folks up to the sunset deck to wait. Have a drink? We could get beepers, like they have at some of the other restaurants. Then they wouldn't have to stand around in my little space."

"Mimi? I think it's an outstanding idea and yes, I will gladly take your money! I'll call Robert and have him help me figure it all out. Has anyone heard from O'Malley?"

Duane said that O'Malley was at his girlfriend's house for the day and that he had spoken to the Zone Man and some of the others about coming back for the reopening on the first of February.

I said, "Listen, y'all, rehire the Zone Man for sure but the rest of them? It's like trying to herd cats!"

"Right!" Louise said. "Herd cats? I like that."

This was the conversation over Thanksgiving dinner, which we had at Mimi's house with almost the entire core gang. It had been a gorgeous day, the kind where the air is cool but the sky is brilliant blue and everything in the world is drenched in sunlight and good spirits.

I don't need to tell you that Duane cooked, but you would have been amused to hear not only Louise but now Mimi as well giving him a lot of coaching in the fine art of producing the quintessential Thanksgiving bird, one worthy of the cover of *Gourmet* magazine. *Cover the tips of those wings with aluminum foil! Turn that bird! Baste that bird!* Mimi had made the cakes, pies and biscuits. Louise had made the stuffing and the oyster stew. And poor Duane just suffered.

Gracie and Alex, sworn friends for life, were involved with other people. Gracie was dating a friend of Alex's and Alex had not only hooked up (in the parlance of the day *hooked up* meant they were dating, and if it meant more, I didn't want to know) with another sophomore, but he and Gracie had become friends with her friends. Gracie had achieved what six months ago seemed to be like finding the Holy Grail—a normal teenage existence, replete with bunches of giggly girlfriends and a driver's license. She found her niche dancing hip-hop because she felt she would never again meet the rigors of modern dance. Even though her ankle had healed, she continued her physical therapy to strengthen it.

"I just want to dance," she said, "it doesn't matter. Anyway, hip-hop's more fun."

If the number of times she professed that sentiment demonstrated her honesty, then she was surely telling the truth.

The framing of the restaurant was under way and a variety of ecological considerations were included in its design. It would still resemble a dump—hey, we have our traditions here in the south, you know—but now it was going to include a bakeshop for Mimi and probably a stairwell to the sunset deck.

That same day, Gracie lobbied for a rack to hold informational flyers about what was going on with the waters of Shem Creek and what the average citizen could do about protecting the environment. Gracie had promised to design them and write the text and by the time we got to pecan pie, Brad had agreed to pay for them. If we couldn't do anything ourselves to stop the developers, at least we could try to reach out to the public. Needless to say, the news that Jason Miller was scheduled to be sentenced the second week of January made its way around the table a few times.

Lindsey, who was home for the holidays, regaled us with colorful stories of living in Greenwich Village, so much so that we all promised to make a trip there to visit her. I thought it would be a thrill to take Brad to Rockefeller Center to see the tree and then to look at all the store windows. Maybe we would see a play or attend something traditional like the Christmas Show Spectacular at Radio City Music Hall. I knew Brad and Alex would love the Rockettes. All those legs! They were like a human centipede.

The day after Thanksgiving, I made reservations for all of us—that is me, Brad, Gracie and Alex—to stay at the Grand Hyatt and found reasonable airline fares through Winston-Salem. The day the kids got out of school for the holidays, we were on a plane to New York.

Gracie and I planned to stay in one room and Alex and Brad were supposed to be in the room next door. Oh fine, I can hear you saying that I'm an old frump and that no one would've cared if I had stayed with Brad, but in my mind there were certain details standing in the way, like a trip down the aisle, impressionable teenagers in tow, and then what would that have meant? That Alex and Gracie would stay in the same room? Over my dead body! I mean, I knew the odds were that nothing would have happened, but in my opinion, we had tested the boundaries of luck enough to last at least another decade.

Well, don't you know that Brad called ahead to the Hyatt and had us upgraded to a suite—two bedrooms and a living room in between them? It seemed like an unnecessary extravagance to me, but he had other ideas.

"Well, sweetheart? I thought Lindsey might want to sleep over and I wanted to be sure we had plenty of room," he said.

"Well, it's awfully generous of you, darling," I said, and gave him a kiss.

Yes, we called each other the old traditional names like sweetheart and darling. Every time we used the terms, Alex and Gracie rolled their eyes and said *ew!* I didn't blame them but for my part, I fell in love a little deeper with each endearing term. How peculiar that for the first time in my life I was someone's sweetheart and darling?

I was still ring-less and slightly uncertain, which of course was ridiculous because Brad did a million things to assure me that his love was forever. Still, I have to say that the whole idea of commitment to one person for the rest of your life was rather breathtaking. But insecure or not, I loved Brad with a passion I had never felt for any man. In fact, I didn't even know I could love that much.

So, when we checked into the Hyatt, I was slightly unraveled, thinking of all these things. We went up to our rooms and they were magnificent. The center room had a huge sectional sofa that converted to a queen-size bed, four armchairs, a dining table with eight chairs, a wet bar, a powder room, and a complete entertainment system. Naturally, the first thing the kids wanted to do was order video games. The adults prevailed. We had no intention of bringing them the whole way to New York for them to vegetate in front of a screen that rearranged their brain waves resulting in their favored techno stupor of fast-frame catatonia. Nope. *Don't even take your coats off!*

I was the designated tour guide, as I was the one most familiar with the city. My plan was to take them in a taxi to FAO Schwarz, walk the few blocks to see the tree and look at the windows along the way. We would stop at St. Patrick's Cathedral, light a candle and buy a bag of chocolate-covered orange rinds from Teuscher in Rockefeller Center. Next, I planned to give them a wild ride on the subway, pick up Lindsey at her dorm, and we would all have dinner in the Village.

Things did not go according to plan.

We got out in front of Bergdorf Goodman and Brad said, "Listen, why don't you ladies go look at what Bergdorf Goodman has and Alex and I will meet you right here in an hour?"

I looked at him and thought that this was perfect. We could slip over to the Bergdorf Goodman Men's Store and I could find something un-usual for Brad for Christmas. I had already bought him a gorgeous sweater from Berlin's in Charleston, and some cologne from Saks, but I wanted there to be something special under the tree for him. Something I couldn't find in Charleston.

Gracie and I made our way across the streets through the unbelievably enormous crowd of holiday shoppers.

"I forgot how many people live in this city! You can hardly stay on the sidewalk!"

"These people aren't New Yorkers!" I said. "They're all from Iowa or something. No one with good sense comes to the city after Thanksgiving until January!"

"Then, what the heck are we doing here?"

I laughed and said, "Because sometimes your momma ain't got good sense. Now, come on!"

We roamed the aisles, looking at ties and shirts, and after about thirty minutes I knew there wasn't anything here that Brad really needed or couldn't live without. If he worked on Wall Street, I could have bought him a Hermes tie. But our lives were so casual that I decided to look around again when we got home. Maybe I would buy him a kayak.

"Let's get out of here," I said.

"Thank God!" Gracie said. "It's so hot in this store and so crowded I was about to kick somebody!"

"Then, let's definitely get out of here."

We bought a hot pretzel on the corner of Fifty-seventh and Fifth and stood there waiting for the boys. It was getting dark and it was freezing cold. By five o'clock you would have sworn it was the middle of the night.

Brad and Alex popped out of the crowd. We had not even seen them coming. Their noses were red and I imagined ours were too.

"Let's grab a cab," Brad said.

"I thought we were gonna go see the tree and St. Pat's first," I said.

"Nah, I just called Lindsey and she wants to see it with us. So let's pick her up, come back to the tree and eat over on Third Avenue. There's a great Italian restaurant I want to check out. I got us a table for six o'clock."

I must have looked annoyed because Brad said, "What?"

My plan had been mashed like corn into grits, but I didn't say anything about that.

"You called Lindsey?" That was all I said. It just seemed a little peculiar for him to call her.

"Yeah, why not? I mean, shouldn't we do all this stuff together?"

"You're right, of course."

We raced downtown at the breakneck speed of thirty-five miles per hour in a dilapidated cab with no shock absorbers and a driver who had a name on his badge I could not have pronounced for love or money. Since there would be five of us going back uptown, the driver refused to take us all. After hailing another cab we were back at Rockefeller Center in what seemed like a flash.

It had begun to snow a little and we stood before the long row of lighted angels on the promenade leading to the huge tree with its thousands of lights. It was exactly how I knew it would be. Brad had his arm around my waist and the kids went on before us. We met up with them at the railing above the ice skaters.

"Mom? Can we go get skates?" Gracie said.

"I can't ice skate," Alex said.

"We'll show you how, bubba! Come on!" Gracie said. "Lindsey?"

"Let's go for it!" she said and they were off.

For the next thirty minutes we watched Gracie and Lindsey on either side of Alex as they took him around the rink. At one point Gracie broke away and did some spins and flying camels that Lindsey and Alex applauded. Then we watched Lindsey take the center of the ice and do her routine of skating backward and then a little jump and spins. Alex was very impressed, waving to us to make sure we didn't miss anything.

"Aren't they beautiful?" I said.

The snow continued to fall. Pure white flakes gathered in our hair and sprinkled our shoulders. Brad tightened his grip around my waist. "Yes, they are. We are going to be a beautiful family."

That was when the small but highly coveted blue box from Tiffany appeared.

"This is for you, Linda. Merry Christmas. I love you."

He put it in my gloved hand.

"Brad?"

"I bought you something else too, but I wanted to give you this now."

"Brad?"

"What?"

"Is this . . ."

"Open it! I can't do the next part until you open it!"

"Oh! Sorry!"

"Yeah, hurry up! You're holding back the wheels of progress here, missy!"

"Okay, okay!"

Well, it's not like I wrote the protocol for this, you know. And it's not like Fred Breland ever gave me a diamond either.

I saw our children heading our way and decided to wait until they were all there.

"Whatcha got, Mom?" Gracie said, knowing exactly what it was.

"Open it!" Lindsey said.

"Alex? No comment from you?" I said.

"I've already seen it," he said, "I'm pretty sure you'll like it."

My hands were shaking as I pulled the end of the red satin ribbon. As it fell away, Lindsey caught it and put it in her pocket. Inside was a velvet box and in that box was a beautiful round diamond set in platinum.

"Take off your gloves," Brad said, and took the ring from my hand as he dropped to one knee. "Okay, Linda, this is it. Will you be my wife?"

"And will you be my mom?" Alex said, dropping on one knee as well.

That was it for the waterworks in all of us. Brad slipped the ring on my finger. I grabbed Alex and said, Oh, it would be an honor, Alex! I am honored. Yes! I promise not to be a bossy boots mom! As I looked across their teary-eyed faces I said yes again and again, hugging and kissing them all. It was the most spectacular moment of my life and the last moment that I ever thought about our lives as separate.

From the moment we returned to Charleston until today, which is Valentine's Day, our lives have been moving forward in a kind of happy delirium. We had said that when the restaurant reopened the first private party would be our wedding reception. It was a very impractical thing to have said. First of all, Lindsey didn't finish classes until June and I wasn't getting married without her. Oh, I suppose I could have brought her home for the weekend and just thrown something together, but I didn't want our wedding to be like that. The other truth was that reopening the restaurant took a lot more energy than we thought it would.

Anyway, once you say that you are going to join your families together and if everyone wants it to happen, it will happen on its own timetable.

I knew that Brad was talking to Lowell about buying the big house from him for us to live in. They were in Pawleys Island almost all the time now. The big house had five bedrooms, two fireplaces, a new kitchen and it really was a fabulous piece of property. Brad suggested that we keep Lupe and thought it might be nice for her to live in the boathouse. Then we could all have some privacy. Maybe Lowell's father would come to her in her dreams and tell her to talk less and listen more. He knew I had reservations about her being around all the time, but Brad had hired Miguel the dishwasher to do his landscaping and the Epsteins had taken him on as well. Don't you know he was from Costa Rica and that he and Lupe had become very tight friends? And honestly? Lupe was a great housekeeper, which everyone knows is a rarity in the extreme. My hope was that if all this came to pass that Lupe would speak Spanish to Miguel and that I wouldn't have to be involved. Ah well, every blessing came with a cross.

Jackson Hole was back in business and the restaurant next door was scheduled to reopen in a few weeks. The constant hammers were driving us all to drink, but I was just as sure that our combined hammers gave migraines to all our other neighboring restaurateurs.

O'Malley was behind the bar serving drinks. The Zone Man had taken over the position of cat herder and this time he had all new cats. Duane and Louise were in their new kitchen cooking up a storm and arguing over sauces just like in the old days. And, my darling sister Mimi was as happy as a clam in her little bakery, which seemed to be doing a brisk business in baked goods and takeout, especially to single men.

I walked through the restaurant, which was jammed to capacity with Valentine's Day couples. There was a small group waiting outside. Some were reading Mimi's menus or Gracie's flyers and others were just talking. I climbed the steps to the sunset deck to have a look around for Brad. He wasn't there. In fact, it was so chilly that no one was. But old habits die hard and I thought he might have slipped up there for the sunset.

The sky was raging red and cut with jagged edges of gold and purple. It had to be the most outrageous sunset I had ever seen. I could follow the path of the creek and see the exact point where it spilled out into the glistening teal waters of Charleston's harbor. It was an awesome sight and one that I knew I would never abandon again.

I had become a serious woman since returning to the Lowcountry, one who came to treasure every heartbeat as a priceless gift. I had learned that for me to be alive, I had to have warm sun on my face and salt air in my lungs. Once I had it again, I wondered why I had denied myself something so splendid for so long. Maybe I had forgotten how splendid it was. Yes, and almost forgotten who I was along the way too.

I still mourned the years I had wasted in a soulless existence of merely making ends meet and not celebrating the love of my daughters over something as simple as a bowl of breakfast cereal. I could not regain those years. They were gone, marked off the calendar of my days forever.

But I had another chance at a family and this time with a son. He may have been Loretta's boy and I knew he would never be mine but, I would love him for her sake as she would have if she had been alive and able. I would love him for my own sake as well. And I had a wonderful man for my girls to admire and from whom they would see and learn what it was to love family.

A second chance, and this time I baptized my future with the waters of Shem Creek, knowing it was a sacred pact. I had been an amateur at living my life and I recognized that it was in the Lowcountry that I found my strength to try again. Really try. Living where you don't belong can be the saddest mistake you can make. But maybe I had needed the suffering and the loneliness to appreciate being home again.

I was going to relearn every square inch of the islands and rivers and of the city of Charleston herself and become a worthy citizen. I was going to share it with Gracie and Alex, like the long-promised trip to Bull's Island. As soon as it was a little warmer, we would go—Brad too. I would bring the binoculars he had given me for Christmas and try to name all the birds.

Much like lovers saw themselves in each other's eyes, we would gather the edges of the Lowcountry into our focus, see ourselves in its landscape and each other and hang on to that too.

I filled my lungs with the air and decided to go in search of Brad. It was Valentine's Day, after all. I looked down at the water once more and could not help but think of the ideas and plans friends and families shared here along this creek, over frozen drinks or a basket of fried seafood. I hoped the waters worked their magic on them the way they had on me.

I was struck by the fact that what I used to fear most, I now embraced—Lindsey and Gracie becoming women and my ability to give them what they needed to succeed in life. A year ago, I could not see a future for myself beyond endless struggle. And now there were Brad and Alex and so many others. I was surrounded with people who loved us and each other. I was so glad, yes, glad and grateful that I had not settled for less.

AUTHOR'S NOTE

THIS section will seem a little peculiar to some, hopefully useful to others and hilarious to my friend Nathalie Dupree of Charleston, South Carolina, who tells me that in my books I write way too much about food not to be a food writer and what is the matter with me anyway? Am I just hungry?

Well, Nathalie, here's the truth. I am hungry. And I love to cook.

I get a lot of e-mail from folks who tell me they made something I described and by golly, it was pretty good. I hope those folks will try these few recipes and tell me how they worked out. I am also completely emotionally prepared for all my other southern friends who bake and cook to tell me I don't know diddly squat. Like Gracie would say, *Wha'evah!*

My sister, Lynn—who is the pound cake queen of the world—was kind enough to give me her secret recipes for pound cake and biscuits, so I don't claim them to be mine. Besides, I ate so many of her biscuits this year that now I'm counting carbs. Anyway, the important thing is to follow her method.

Maybe someday I will compile a whole cookbook. I would love to do that, but not without the help of my sister and Nathalie, and so this section is dedicated to Nathalie Dupree, a *real* food writer, author of *Comfortable*

Entertaining: At Home with Ease and Grace, a monster talent in the kitchen and just a great gal. And, of course to my sister, Lynn Benton Bagnal of Edisto Beach, South Carolina, the finest woman I have ever known.

Like Brad Jackson would say, *Buon Appetito!*

THE DEEP DARK SECRETS
OF SOUTHERN BISCUIT BAKERS

———◆◆◆———

THE following recipes for biscuits each serve a different purpose. The first one is a basic biscuit recipe that's just about no-fail. The second one is more difficult and messier to make but produces a biscuit that melts in your mouth. The last is one to use for parties.

My grandmother, Olivia Kent Benton, always said that biscuits like to *start out cold and get hot quick.* Therefore, preheat the oven well. Keep your shortening and milk refrigerated and remember this—handle your biscuits as little as possible. If you abuse them they won't rise, and don't try to make the batter the night before, because it settles and gets gummy. Always roll gently with a floured pin and cut with a floured cutter.

———◆◆◆———

Mimi's Biscuits

> 2 cups all-purpose flour
> 1 tablespoon baking powder
> ½ tsp salt
> ⅓ cup vegetable shortening
> ¾ cup milk

Preheat oven to 450 degrees. Sift flour, baking powder and salt together. Cut in shortening. Stir in milk. Lightly flour a large cutting board or countertop. Place dough in center. Knead lightly, 15–20 times. Lightly roll out to ½-inch thickness. Cut with floured metal cutter. Bake 10–12 minutes. Serve hot. Yield: 12–15 biscuits.

Mimi's Short Biscuits

> 2 cups self-rising flour
> ⅔ cup shortening
> ⅔ cup milk

Preheat oven to 450 degrees. On a floured surface put down 2 cups self-rising flour. Take ⅔ cup vegetable shortening and cut in with fingertips until it looks like BBs. Make a well in the center and add ⅔ cup milk slowly, mixing with floured fingertips until it gets sticky. Then flap the whole mess onto a floured surface, knead it until it's smooth, roll to ½-inch thickness and cut with a floured cutter, placing them on an ungreased pan. Bake 10–12 minutes. Yield: 12–15 biscuits.

Mimi's Company Biscuits

2 cups self-rising flour
1 cup of heavy cream or sour cream

Preheat over to 425 degrees. Combine, roll out and pat dough on a lightly floured surface until ½-inch thick. Cut with small floured cutter and place on a lightly greased baking sheet. Bake 10–12 minutes. Yield: 12–15 biscuits.

Mimi's Pound Cake

3 cups plain flour—not self-rising
3 sticks salted butter
3 cups sugar
1 cup heavy whipping cream
6 large eggs
2 tablespoons vanilla

Preheat oven to 325 degrees. Generously grease and lightly flour a tube pan. Sift flour three times. Cream butter with sugar until light and fluffy. Add eggs, one at a time. Beat only until each disappears. Blend in 1 cup flour followed by ½ cup whipping cream. Repeat with 1 cup flour and ½ cup whipping cream. Add remaining flour. Fold in vanilla.

Add batter to pan, level it and drop it flat on the counter to knock out the air bubbles. Place in center of the oven and bake for an hour and fifteen minutes, or until it's browned on top and *begins to pull away from the sides of the pan.** Remove from oven. Wait ten minutes and invert on a cake plate. Do not cover until cool to touch.

---

*Important!

Lemon Glaze

  2 tablespoons cornstarch
  ⅛ teaspoon salt
  ¾ cup sugar
  ⅔ cup water
  3 tablespoons lemon juice
  1 egg yolk
  the rind of the lemon, finely grated
  1 tablespoon butter

Stir cornstarch and salt into sugar. In heavy pot or double boiler, add water, lemon juice and egg yolk. Put over high heat and stir in dry ingredients. Cook until you see a bubble or it thickens. Remove from heat, stir in finely grated lemon rind and butter. Cool and pour over cake.

Caramel Icing

  One box light brown sugar
  ¾ cup whipping cream
  1 stick butter

Mix it all in a saucepan and cook over low heat until boiling. Stir occasionally. Boil slowly for 5 minutes or until a drop of icing reaches soft ball stage when added to cold water. Remove from heat and beat until spreading consistency, which will be when it begins to lose its gloss and will coat a spoon. If icing becomes too hard, add a small amount of hot water. Ice sides and then top of cake.